# Praise for *The Penny Mansions*

"In *The Penny Mansions*, Steven Mayfield gives the history of the American West a good, hard shake and what falls out is an antic tale of small-town intrigue featuring, among other things, a homicidal dwarf, a rope-twirling child genius, a troupe of double-crossing thespians, and a town full of lovable eccentrics. Move over Mark Twain, Steven Mayfield is gaining on you."

—Michael Bourne, author of *Blithedale Canyon*, contributing editor to *Poet & Writers*

"Mayfield is a yarn-spinner extraordinaire, a literary hypnotist, your maître d' of immeasurable reading pleasures. Just crack these pages and see!"

—M. Allen Cunningham, author of *Q&A*

"Steven Mayfield has done it again! Like his 2020 novel, *Treasure of the Blue Whale*, *The Penny Mansions* magically evokes an entire town replete with characters as delightfully quirky and vivid as those we find in the best tradition of tongue-in-cheek American literature. With empathy and humor, a keen eye for detail, and a beautifully tuned ear, Mayfield's narrative grabs the reader from the start and doesn't let go."

—Barbara Quick, award-winning poet and author of *Vivaldi's Virgins* and *What Disappears*

"A Dickensian romp set in the early twentieth-century American West, Steven Mayfield's *The Penny Mansions* breathes life into a colorful gallery of rogues and dreamers, of scoundrels and heroes. Echoes of modern-day corruption and skullduggery are balanced against a satisfyingly old-fashioned storytelling voice. Reminiscent of the big-hearted novels of John Irving, you'll find yourself rooting for the lovable and plucky residents of Paradise, Idaho who go to extraordinary lengths to save their town…and each other."

—Phillip Hurst, author of *Regent's of Paris*, *Whiskey Boys*, and *The Land of Ale and Gloom*

"Steven Mayfield is a natural, old-school storyteller and *The Penny Mansions* is a yarn spun by a writer at the top of his craft. Replete with a villain named Dredd, a protagonist named Bountiful, and a 'vole-like' attorney named Mole, Mayfield's Twain-in-cheek mix of history, humor, mayhem, and romance satisfies all the appetites. Paradise, Idaho, may not precisely live up to its name, but there's definitely gold in them thar pages."

—David R. Roth, award-winning author of *The Femme Fatale Hypothesis*

"Heartbreaking, heartwarming and hilarious. Set in the early 20th century, *The Penny Mansions* is brimming with evocative characters, rich historical detail, and gothic chills. Enter the village of Paradise, Idaho, and hold onto your hat (with the hand that's not eagerly turning pages). This wild and wonderful community is about to battle catastrophe, villainy, and intrigue with all the competing heroics, conflicted loyalties, and quirky mischief it can muster. With surprises at every turn, this smart and funny novel hits all the high notes."

—Shirley Reva Vernick, award-winning author of *Ripped Away* and *The Sky We Shared*

Also by Steven Mayfield

*Howling at the Moon*
*Treasure of the Blue Whale*
*Delphic Oracle, U.S.A.*

# THE PENNY MANSIONS

Steven Mayfield

Regal House Publishing

Published by
Regal House Publishing, LLC
Raleigh, NC 27605
All rights reserved

ISBN -13 (paperback): 9781646034000
ISBN -13 (epub): 9781646034017
Library of Congress Control Number: 2022949416

All efforts were made to determine the copyright holders and obtain their
permissions in any circumstance where copyrighted material was used.
The publisher apologizes if any errors were made during this process, or
if any omissions occurred. If noted, please contact the publisher and all
efforts will be made to incorporate permissions in future editions.

Cover images and design by © C. B. Royal
Author photo by Hunnicutt Photography

Regal House Publishing, LLC
https://regalhousepublishing.com

The following is a work of fiction created by the author. All names,
individuals, characters, places, items, brands, events, etc. were either the
product of the author or were used fictitiously. Any name, place, event,
person, brand, or item, current or past, is entirely coincidental.

Printed in the United States of America

This book is dedicated to physician, teacher, and scientist, William Oh, M.D., whose fatherly lessons of focus, perseverance, and selflessness are goals I continue to pursue all these years later. Thanks, Bill.

# PROLOGUE

Goldstrike crouched at the edge of the stream for a dip, afterward giving the ice-cold, murky water in his pan a good swirl before picking out the larger rocks the way Old Butch taught him when Goldstrike was a pup and just starting out.

*Don't shake it. That gold be heavy, boy. It'll settle if you be patient. Don't shake it back into the creek.*

The stream lapped at the toes of his boots as the old prospector gently swirled, muddy water sloshing over the lip of the pan to reveal more and more sediment at the bottom.

*Ya don't wanna take an hour. I seen tenderfoots pan an hour to come away with a couple o' flakes. A man's time is worth somethin'.*

Shortly after arriving in Paradise, Idaho, in 1865, fresh from his time with the Maine 11th in the War Between the States, seventeen-year-old Goldstrike had partnered up with Old Butch, a veteran of both the California and Pike's Peak gold rushes. Old Butch's knees and back were shot and he offered young Goldstrike an equal share of his claim on Mores Creek in exchange for all the work and a third of the yield. Butch was a cranky old fart but had a soft heart and taught his protégé how to pan and dredge, how to snare game to keep them fed, and when to shut up and listen if an old man had a story to tell.

Goldstrike continued to swirl, allowing water to spill over the sloped edge of his tin. A few grains of gold gleamed in the mud and sand. He touched them, the tiny flakes sticking to his finger.

"Crissakes," he muttered, emptying his sample into the stream and then repeating the process once, twice, a third time. "Fer crissakes," he repeated, dropping the pan. He sat on the bank, oblivious to the cold water that seeped through the seat of his faded dungarees. Mores Creek was in its spring phase, wider and faster than it would be in less than two weeks. Diffident rapids ran at the center and the pan bobbed along gently at first, edging farther and farther into the stream. Suddenly, the gurgling current swept it up, knocking it into a smooth boulder, careening it into another. Then it was gone, swallowed by the bubbling water. Goldstrike stood and walked away.

"She's dried up," he said to no one, because no one had been his only partner since Old Butch died. It was 1890, twenty years since the peak days of the Bogus Basin gold rush and nearly thirty years before Paradise, Idaho, would have to fight for its life or become just another ghost town.

# 1

## Paradise for a Penny

Paradise, Idaho, had once been the largest city in the Pacific Northwest—bigger than Portland and Seattle and Boise—with more than 8,000 souls mostly crammed into shacks and tents. Gold created the town in 1860, primarily placer gold, the kind gleaned by panning or dredging. A few prospectors like Goldstrike attempted to blast shafts into the dense igneous granite, but dredging or panning was easier and safer. Erosion filled the streams with plenty of flakes and nuggets, and at the peak of the Bogus Basin gold rush, it wasn't unusual to sift out as much as eighty dollars per day. The cost of living in a boomtown like Paradise was as volatile as the dynamite Goldstrike tried once or twice before going back to panning. A fellow might leave the bed he'd leased for two bits a day only to return twelve hours later and find his rent increased to a dollar. The same was true of bread and beans and salt pork and whiskey. A gold rush town was the epitome of capitalism, and like most capitalist propositions, those producing the least amount of sweat very often amassed the greatest number of greenbacks.

Horace Goodlow was a reiver who came to Paradise at the beginning of the rush, sporting a top hat and pair of bushy sideburns that wove their way into a thick hedgerow of a moustache. He opened a bar, hotel, and general store, then imported sixty horse-drawn wagons full of building materials from Salt Lake City. Workers, mostly made up of Chinese immigrants who'd come to Paradise for gold only to learn that claims required the signature of a white majority partner, constructed the first of what would become five mansions in Paradise. The huge Victorian boasted two full stories topped by a lookout balcony designed to resemble the multi-windowed lantern room of a lighthouse. Following completion of the home Goodlow christened "Elysium," the town boss was a familiar sight, looking down from behind the low, ornately forged iron balustrade that surrounded the outdoor gallery of his crow's nest, a cigar and snifter of brandy proclaiming his dominion over the fortune-seekers scurrying about like ants on a then-busy street below.

Other opportunists followed Goodlow, only four as success-ful: Ned Rimple, a pharmacist and purveyor of opium from St. Louis; Irwin Feldstein, a doctor of medicine and dentistry; Rhode Island's John Stiveley, assayer, gold broker, and finan-cier; and Maude Dollarhyde, proprietor of the Busty Rose, a house of excellent repute among Paradise's morally challenged, mostly male populace. The Big Five, as they were known in those days, provided services that made them rich without ever wetting a knee in an Idaho stream, and at the peak of the rush, they built opulent mansions considered huge even by Boise or Portland standards.

Like all gold rushes, the Bogus Basin boom eventually pe-tered out, and by 1890 the town's census had shrunk to 500. In the 1900 census it was 246, then 129 in 1910. By 1918, three of the Big Five mansions had been abandoned for years with only Maude Dollarhyde and Ned Rimple's widow, Irene, re-maining in Paradise. In the autumn of that year—The War to End All Wars still raging in Europe and the Spanish flu now a full-fledged pandemic—Irene Rimple went to the Beyond and Maude Dollarhyde received a letter.

> 5 October 1918
> Paradise Town Council
> Maude Dollarhyde, President
> 1 Goodlow Road
> Paradise, Idaho
>
> Dear Mrs. Dollarhyde:
> Given that ten of your young men have been called to

serve with the Idaho 41st Division in the current European conflict, and your population of 129 in the 1910 census, Paradise may fail to reach the minimum town incorporation threshold of 125 persons in the upcoming 1920 census (Idaho Code § 50-101). In that event, your community will be subject to federal laws and regulations pertaining to eminent domain as the General Land Office of the United States moves forward with the national parks and forests plan.

Sincerely,
Gerald Dredd, Sr.
Lt. Governor, State of Idaho
Regional Director, U.S. General Land Office
State Director, Region III Selective Service System
Boise, Idaho

Maude well knew Gerald Dredd. In the old days, before she closed the Busty Rose, both Dredd and his father, Friederich, had been clients. It was a time when the politics of her trade were easily managed with small bribes and an occasional bit of reclining hospitality. But now, with Gerald Dredd's state and federal credentials, Maude could no longer afford to buy his good will, and she was almost eighty—both she and the Busty Rose closed for purposes of horizontal negotiation since around 1889.

"What do you make of this?" Maude asked her granddaughter, handing over the letter. The whip-smart and beautiful Bountiful Dollarhyde had returned to Paradise a few months earlier after thirteen years in Washington, DC, where she'd received a degree from Howard University and then remained to teach high school students.

"This is serious, Grandma," Bountiful said after reading the letter. "You need to inform Mister Nilsen. He'll want to call a town council meeting right away."

The letter had reached Maude by mistake. Weary after decades as council president—presiding over meetings with slim agendas, refereeing arguments, and then dealing cards for the poker game that followed—the long-time head of the municipal body had recently passed over the gavel to Oskar Nilsen. The general store proprietor was initially reluctant to abandon his traditional role as a bottleneck to resolution. "I ain't doin' it, doggonit, Maude," he'd protested, relenting after she pointed out that the council president could use the gavel to make everyone else shut up. "I'm gonna use this doggone hammer," Oskar threatened after ascending to the modest throne. "Don't think I won't. First time Goldstrike shoots his darn mouth off, I'll gavel the heck outta him!"

Maude and Bountiful dropped into Nilsen's general store to show him the letter from Gerald Dredd. The next day Oskar, Maude, and fellow councilmen Goldstrike and saloon owner Arnold Chang gathered at the former assay office, now the city government building. Ed Riggins was there to cover the proceedings for the *Idaho World* and Maude had invited Bountiful. After a review of the minutes from their September meeting, Oskar proceeded to a reading of the letter. This was followed by some head-scratching. Since the 1910 census a few more folks had packed up and left town. Moreover, four of the dreaded War Department telegrams had been received with accounts of the bloody overseas conflict making it more and more likely the remaining six Paradise boys still in uniform would be buried in Europe. Without them, the population of the little mountain village would settle at 109, sixteen souls below the incorporation threshold.

"We oughta offer up them abandoned places on Only Real Street," Goldstrike suggested. "Give 'em away fer a penny if the buyers fix 'em up and live there till we get counted." He'd meant it as a joke, but Maude didn't laugh.

"That's a wonderful idea," she said. She looked to Nilsen for his reaction and was met with a snort. Up late the night before to conduct an inventory that stalled in the whiskey department, Oskar had nodded off. Maude banged a hand on the table and the storekeeper jerked awake, then sat up straight, blinking.

"I vote no!"

"There weren't no motion," Goldstrike muttered.

Oskar grinned sheepishly. "I thought I heard a motion."

"Well, there weren't none, ya dumb Norsky."

The exchange was a familiar one. The two old men were friends most of the time, but Goldstrike had a musket ball in his rear end, put there in 1865 by an Oslo native in his own Maine 11th during the ironically named Battle of Deep Bottom. Both the ball and Nilsen—the firstborn son of Norwegian immigrants—were occasional pains in his butt.

Oskar banged his gavel on the table. "Shut the heck up, Goldstrike. I'm the president o' this here town council and you ain't got the doggone floor."

"We could post an ad in the *Idaho Statesman*," Bountiful interceded before the two seasoned combatants could advance from skirmish to all-out war.

"Yes," Maude agreed. "I can see it now. 'A home in Paradise can be yours for only one penny,' or something like that." She looked at Bountiful. "You can write it, dear... Make it sound smart and legitimate. We'll screen the applicants, pick the ones with the biggest families, and then tell that son-of-a-bitch Gerald Dredd to kiss our rosy red asses."

Oskar Nilsen was now fully awake with a hankering to obstruct, chairman's gavel be damned. "Why not put the ad in the *Idaho World?*" he countered. He nodded at *World* publisher, Ed Riggins. "It would be a lot cheaper."

Goldstrike snorted. "Good idea, Oskar. An ad in the *World* oughta reach... What's yer circulation, Ed...a hunnert? A hunnert ten?"

"We deliver to about a thousand," Ed told the group. "But the *Statesman* has a circulation of better than twenty thousand. And a story like this one has a good chance of getting on the national wire. That's thousands more."

"You hear that, Oskar?" Maude enthused. "The national wire... We'll be on the national wire!" She turned to Riggins. "What's the national wire, Ed?" Riggins explained how the

Associated Press and United Press International purchased interesting stories they sold to newspapers all over the world. "How about that, Oskar?" Maude gushed. "The big city papers will pick up on it and we'll have offers from everywhere."

Nilsen shook his head, lips flattened. "I don't know, Maude," he said. "I hear that doggone Spaniard's flu Ed writes about in the paper is killin' folks left and right all over the country. Do we really want outsiders movin' in? They say we're gonna see the flu in Idaho soon enough as it is."

"The soldiers are bringing it back from Europe," Riggins confirmed. "We're already in what the doctors call a second wave. They expect it to get worse…spread around the country."

"Besides, is there time to get people here before the government count begins?" Nilsen added. "We'll be weathered in soon and by the time the snow melts next spring, whoever buys our houses'll only have eight or nine months to get them places livable."

"We'll probably have more time, Mister Nilsen," Bountiful offered. "I doubt a census-taker will get to a remote place like Paradise until summer at the earliest… Maybe later if the flu outbreak is as serious as some think. Our buyers will probably have at least a year."

Nilsen remained skeptical. "I don't know—"

"Oh, shut up, Oskar," Goldstrike interrupted. "What the hell else we gonna do? Ya got a better idea?"

Nilsen reached into a pocket to retrieve a dog-eared copy of *Robert's Rules of Order*. He slammed it onto the table, the impact making a sound like a gunshot. "First of all, watch your darned language, Goldstrike," he barked. "This here's a public meetin' with records and such and I don't want your foul mouth in the official minutes. What's more, you ain't to talk till recognized by the chair." He touched his book. "It's in here. You hafta ask the chair to be recognized before you shoot your mouth off."

"Okay, I'm askin'," Goldstrike said. "Recognize me."

"Forget it," Nilsen responded. "Consider yourself unrecognized permanent-like."

"We need to require a financial commitment to make sure an applicant is serious," Bountiful intervened, her voice one that had settled an unruly classroom or two. It cowed the two old men and they lowered their eyes to the table like a pair of schoolboys caught passing notes. "It will be harder to give up and leave if there's money at stake," she added.

"How much money?" Maude asked.

"I don't know, Grandma. What do you think, Mister Chang?"

Arnold Chang was the fourth member of the council and owner of the Gold Rush Saloon. Born Chang Zhiqiang, he'd settled on "Arnold" for his American neighbors, reclaiming "Zhiqiang" when under his own roof. His birth name meant "strong-willed and resourceful" and Chang Zhiqiang was. Seventy years old, he was a stocky fellow with a high forehead and a long pigtail. After half a century in America, he still spoke in broken English, he and Mrs. Chang sticking to their native language at home. In China, he'd been an architect.

"Dem houses not bad on outsides," he said. "Paint, fix roof holes, make all betta. Insides...don' know. Dey wan' fancy, be many dolla. Dey want reg'lar, be less." He paused, face wrinkled in concentration as he mentally ciphered. "Maybe t'ousand dolla," he said. Paradise was lit by candles and oil lamps, but Boise's newly formed Idaho Power Company had run a line to town and Arnold factored it in. "More, dey want 'lectric," he surmised.

"A thousand-dollar stake oughta do it," Goldstrike opined. "Not many'll walk away from a number like that."

"And the buyer loses the deposit and the house if not in town to be counted by January 1920," Bountiful proposed. A motion to sell the homes—with the proposed investment and residency requirements—was made, seconded, and unanimously approved. The council then adjourned to inspect the houses.

It was mid-afternoon and the October sky was clear save pillowy clouds that hovered to the north as if snagged on the jagged peaks of the Sawtooths. Mores Creek paralleled Goodlow Road to the south, and although hidden behind aspen and dogwood trees, its rippling voice was audible as the members of the town council traversed the short distance to Only Real Street. In the old days, Paradise had consisted of a main drag—Goodlow Road—from which a spider's web of footpaths, rutted wagonways, and horse trails spun off. When the Big Five decided to build their mansions, a wide graveled street was carved north from the east end of Goodlow. Inaugurated as First Street with hope that an abundance of numbered and respectable avenues would follow, it rapidly became known to the mansionless of Paradise as Only Real Street. The five penny mansions were located there.

None of the residences was officially a mansion, such palaces defined by at least eight thousand square feet of living space. Horace Goodlow's Elysium incorporated six thousand square feet, but the other four were no more than four thousand each. As gold dwindled and the town emptied, all of the Big Five had remained for a time, encouraged by Rhode Islander John Stiveley's contention that Paradise could become a western version of Newport, the Atlantic coast enclave where Cornelius Vanderbilt and other New York City notables were constructing large and elaborate summer homes. Paradise and the surrounding area were lushly forested, crisscrossed by clear streams, and bisected by the dramatic Middle Fork of the Salmon River. With the craggy, snow-capped Sawtooth mountains to the north, the Danskins to the south, and the Boise range to the west, it was a serene and majestic setting Stiveley believed would eventually attract Gilded Age robber barons looking for a quiet retreat. It didn't happen. Newport, Rhode Island, was easily reachable by boat or carriage whereas the trek to Paradise required a tedious, multi-stop train ride to Boise followed by a jolting twenty-mile excursion across a deeply rutted, muddy road too often impassable due to snow or rockslides.

Eventually, Goodlow accumulated a mountain of debts comparable to the peaks surrounding Paradise. He absconded, and by 1900, was dead, as were Feldstein and Stiveley, their heirs uninterested in the upkeep and property tax obligations for a trio of backwoods residences in Idaho. Seized by the city, their homes lapsed into disrepair and neglect. The Rimples stayed in Paradise, but increasingly modest circumstances winnowed their housestaff until only Ned and Irene were left to manage their home and its two acres. Ned died with a rake in his hand and Irene replaced him with a herd of cats. She survived her husband by ten years, and upon her death, the home and property were bequeathed to the felines, none of whom had a plug nickel to offset household expenses or municipal levies.

The town council reached the first of the five mansions at the corner of Goodlow & Only Real. Horace Goodlow's once grand Elysium was desperately in need of paint, shingles, and tidied-up landscaping. Maude's well-kept place was next, repurposed to serve as both a private residence and home to the Paradise School. Farther along the same side of the road was the former Feldstein property, its flagstone sidewalk crackled by time and weather into gravel. The Rimple home was down the block and across the street—a Queen Anne with streaks of green mildew on the siding, moss speckling the tiled roof, and high weeds hiding the once-decorative latticework beneath the porch. The last home—assayer John Stiveley's former residence—was centered on the cul-de-sac that capped the north end of Only Real Street, an open meadow to the foothills behind it.

The council members hastily inspected each property and found that except for the Rimple home, which was odoriferously reminiscent of Irene's cats, the rest of the places were merely musty and dated. Better yet, despite a couple of sagging porches, some broken windows, and a few holes in their roofs, all were structurally solid. "So it's settled, right?" Maude posited after the council had completed their inspections and reconvened in the parlor of the home she shared with Bountiful and their ward. "Let's have a motion to authorize funding for the ad."

"I move fer that," Goldstrike offered.

"You gotta be specific," Nilsen chided.

"Fine, ya dumb bastard… I *specific-like* move fer what Maude just said."

"That ain't how you—"

"Goldstrike has put a motion on the table to use money from our general fund to place an ad in the *Idaho Statesman*," Maude refereed. "I second the motion." There was no further discussion and the vote went three-to-zero, in favor, with Goldstrike vindictively abstaining on his own motion. Bountiful was then enlisted to write the copy.

### PURCHASE A HOME IN PARADISE
### FOR ONLY ONE PENNY!

The town of Paradise, Idaho, is now accepting applications to purchase any one of four historic mansions built during the legendary Gold Rush days, each for the unbelievable price of one cent! Live the good life with sunny summers, crisp autumns, invigorating springs, and bracing winters in one of the most beautiful spots on Earth! If interested, send name, address, proof of indemnity, and personal essay (250-500 words) to:

A Home in Paradise
PO Box 257
Boise, Idaho

Married couples with children only
Buyer to invest $1000 toward renovation
Must be in residence by December 31, 1919
$100 deposit upon acceptance of application

The town council next appropriated $159 from the general fund, the cost of a full-page ad in the Sunday edition of the *Idaho Statesman*. "We won't need to run it more than once," Maude predicted. "Once their editor sees it, we'll have a reporter up here in no time."

The next morning Nilsen drove his truck to Boise to place the ad. Word of the unusual offer promptly swept through the

*Statesman's* offices and Oskar returned with a reporter tailing him on a motorcycle. Forced to accept the assignment, the fellow had little curiosity about a human-interest story from a backwater place like Paradise. However, his own human interest was piqued when he was met by the town council in front of the *Idaho World* office. With them was beautiful Bountiful Dollarhyde. Twenty-nine years old and the product of a union between a very bad white man and a very good Black woman, she expressed the best physical features of both—her ebony skin flawless, her startling blue eyes large and expressive, her bearing as regal as an African princess.

"A tour of the homes would be helpful, Miss Dollarhyde," the reporter suggested. "Perhaps, you could show me around?"

"Bountiful would love to show you our penny mansions, wouldn't you, dear?" Maude answered for her granddaughter. "But Goldstrike and Mister Chang and I will go along too. Mister Chang knows all about architecture and can answer any questions you might have about the properties." The reporter balked at the addition of chaperones, but when Goldstrike and Arnold Chang made clear that a hand anywhere near Bountiful Dollarhyde was likely to leave town with broken fingers, the fellow gave up. He pulled out his notebook and followed his hosts to Only Real Street, anticipating mansions that leaned heavily into the "so-called" category. The guided tour changed his mind. His expertise was in constructing sentences, rather than domiciles, but anyone could see that the four houses for sale were solidly and elaborately built with an attention to detail rivaling anything found on prestigious Harrison Boulevard or Warm Springs Avenue in Boise. The Rimple home reeked of cats but had polished mahogany baseboards and moldings; the Feldstein kitchen compared well to the finest restaurants in the world; and the Stiveley residence boasted marble floors, ceiling frescos bordered by gilded surrounds, and so many crystal chandeliers it seemed possible the illuminated windows might well be visible from the clouds. However, the most decadently ostentatious of the mansions was Horace Goodlow's Elysium, a place with wall panels depicting Greek and Roman gods framed in 22-carat gold leaf; floors of mosaic Italian tiles; a gigantic veranda with stunning views of the Sawtooth Mountains to the north; a carriage house in the back twice the size of the average home in Boise; and of course, the crow's nest observation deck where Horace Goodlow had strutted about at the end of every day, his power and wealth filling the air as much as the thick smoke of his cigar.

"Even run-down, they're impressive," the reporter observed after the tour ended. "Especially at a penny apiece. But what's a person to do once you're here? The sort of folks you're recruiting aren't likely to make a living as loggers or trail guides."

Maude dismissed his remark with a sniff. "We're after the life-of-leisure crowd," she revealed. "The road to Paradise won't always be dirt and gravel. Someday, it'll be paved and folks will come up here to escape the hustle and bustle of city life. We'll be like Switzerland. Once rich folks have made their nut, they always want to live in Switzerland. It's all the fresh air, the peace and quiet. You can't buy that in a city. Why, someday we'll have train tracks up here, and folks will come from as far away as San Francisco and Chicago just to get a week's worth of what we have all year long."

# 2

## Robber Barons and Sharecroppers

The reporter returned to Boise and wrote his story. The following Sunday, Lieutenant Governor Gerald Dredd was at his breakfast table when he opened the paper and read the banner headline. It chronicled the ominous flu outbreak in Spain—now a world-wide pandemic that threatened to insert a tentacle into Idaho. Dredd made it through the first paragraph of the story before losing interest and had just stuffed a huge bite of Belgian waffle into his mouth when he saw the lead at the bottom of the front page:

Paradise Lures Newcomers with Penny Mansions

The Boise politician and real estate developer angrily spat a half-chewed wad of waffle onto his breakfast plate, whipped cream oozing from the corners of his mouth like froth from a rabid dog.

"What is it this time?" The Fourth Mrs. Dredd asked her husband, without looking up from the garden section of the paper. Dredd answered by firing the housekeeper who had served their breakfasts.

"Get out and don't come back!" he bellowed at the girl, tossing half a grapefruit at her. She neatly ducked the projectile and then calmly retrieved it, afterward setting it on a sideboard tray before picking up a silver carafe. The young Russian girl, less than a year off the boat, wasn't worried. After three months on the job, she'd already been fired twice. There were four other house-servants, including a cook and a butler, all discharged at least a dozen times. The Fourth Mrs. Dredd always hired them back before they could gather their things.

"More coffee, Mister Dredd?" the maid asked. She winked

at Gerald Jr., eliciting a grin that made the twenty-one-year-old eerily identical to his father—the same thick, pouty lips, the same generous jowls inevitably destined to sag with age and weight gain, the same lifeless blue eyes scorning all they surveyed. Dredd Sr. scowled at the Russian girl, holding up his cup to be refilled.

"Remember your place," he snarled.

After the maid escaped to the kitchen, Dredd held up the front page for his wife to see. "Take a look at this," he said.

In need of spectacles she refused to wear, The Fourth Mrs. Dredd squinted until her eyes were mere slits. "What's a pandemic?" she asked.

"Not that, goddammit!" Her husband put his finger on a photograph. In the shot, Bountiful Dollarhyde stood in front of a large house.

"She's quite pretty," The Fourth Mrs. Dredd observed. "Do you know her?"

"It's not about her! Jesus Christ, can't you ever—"

"Language, Gerald," his wife quietly chided, glancing at their son, eight-year-old Freddie. The boy eyed his mother like a baby chick about to have a worm dropped into its beak, then resumed chewing a hole into the middle of a piece of toast, afterward peering at his father through the aperture as if studying a bug under a microscope. Along with Junior, Freddie had two other stepsiblings at the table. Nineteen-year-old Carl noisily slurped milk while glacially beautiful seventeen-year-old Geraldine seemed oblivious to them all. The elder trio were from Dredd's first marriage. He had three more daughters who lived with Mrs. Dredds Two and Three, mothers they injudiciously resembled—circumstances limiting their father's interest in them and the size of their inheritances. It brought to seven the total number of children waiting for Dredd to die and make them rich.

"Goddamned sharecroppers!" the real estate baron and Idaho politician muttered.

Carl chortled convulsively, issuing a shower of milk droplets.

"Cover your mouth, you goddamned idiot!" his father barked.

"Sorry, Dad," Carl said. He grinned sheepishly and then used the collar of his shirt to wipe his lips.

"What sharecroppers?" Geraldine asked.

Dredd Sr. responded to his daughter with an expression both paternal and predatory, something not lost on The Fourth Mrs. Dredd. Nine years earlier, when she was a file clerk in her early twenties and The Third Mrs. Dredd had inadvisably breached thirty-five, her husband had appraised her with similar hunger.

"Yes, dear," she posed, enough acid in her voice to recapture her husband's attention. "What sharecroppers?"

Dredd blinked as if trying to recall which position The Fourth Mrs. Dredd occupied on his roster of spouses. "It's about the land over in Paradise," he eventually went on. "It's an old gold rush camp… Practically a ghost town now. Nobody left there that matters. Bunch of old prospectors and whores is what they are. Too stupid to know what could be done with land like that."

The Russian maid returned and Dredd cupped his coffee mug as if he might throw it at her. The Fourth Mrs. Dredd reached out and put a hand on his wrist, less concerned for the girl than mindful that a broken cup would leave her with an uneven number in her china cabinet.

"What could be done if the people in Paradise were as smart as you?" she asked.

Dredd ignored her question. "I'm gonna talk to Wilbur Tarkel about this ad," he ranted. "He had no right to run it without checking with me first. I'll ruin the little son of a bitch." Wilbur Tarkel, diminutive editor-in-chief of the *Idaho Statesman*, was terrified of Gerald Dredd and his powerful friends, a group representing eighty percent of his publication's advertising revenue. He'd viewed the Paradise story as a human-interest piece and was surprised the next morning when the real estate developer turned up at the *Statesman*'s offices.

"I had no idea this would be a problem for you, Gerald," Tarkel whimpered.

"Well, it is. Take it down."

"I can't. But don't worry. They only paid for one edition. We won't renew it."

This assuaged Dredd until he learned that the story had gone out on the national and international wires and would run in newspapers all over the world. It prompted another enraged assault on the *Stateman*'s press room, where Dredd was told that Tarkel was away on a story, even though the editor was hiding under his desk. With his chambers loaded and no one to shoot, the real estate mogul next went home where he fired the butler and two of the maids, afterward retiring to his study with a bottle of Jack Daniels. The next day he drove his British Vauxhall D-Type automobile to Paradise with Junior, Carl, and Geraldine along. Freddie, a pale boy more interested in his indoor stamp collection than an outdoor excursion with his father, stayed in Boise where he philatelized while ignoring the odd sounds his mother and the rehired butler were making in the master bedroom.

Dredd's Vauxhall was the only automobile of its kind in North America. Luxurious and rugged, it had been designed to transport English generals between and across European battlefields. Officially authorized by the British War Office for sole use by their own military, Dredd had cobbled together a series of bribes to get one delivered to the States. He liked tooling about on-and-off Idaho mountain roads in the car. It was a beast on a climb, allowing Dredd to reach places where he could park the sturdy vehicle and then glide through pristine snow on fastidiously waxed cross-country skis inherited from his Austrian-born father. Better yet, every time he took the wheel of the machine, he was pleasantly reminded of the satisfyingly shady deals that brought it to him.

The start of the trip was on flat ground between the Boise River and the foothills of the Bogus Basin range to the north, but the car soon began to climb and entered the Boise National

Forest—over 2.5 million acres thickly blanketed with heavily needled subalpine fir and towering ponderosa and lodgepole pine. Several small villages like Paradise were within the expansive region, most slowly dying, save those necessary to keep the mail routes open north to Missoula and east to the Wood River Valley. Dredd wanted to acquire the settlements as part of his plan to create vacation resorts—luxurious places where descendants of America's entrepreneurial elite could enjoy their inheritances on a ski run or with a round of golf played in a former mountain meadow.

The top was down on the Vauxhall as they motored east, Mores Creek on one side and steep rockface on the other. Geraldine occupied the front seat with her father. Junior and Carl were in the rear passenger compartment, holding on for dear life as their father swerved back and forth to avoid boulders that had tumbled onto the old wagon trail.

"Smell that?" Dredd shouted to his daughter after inhaling a huge draught of mountain air, fragrant with wet pine needles and late morning rain. "That's money."

"Pull over, Dad," Junior yelled from the back seat. "I gotta take a leak."

"You can hold it," his father shouted back.

"I can't!"

"Just hold it, goddammit!"

A moment later the car bounced as it hit a pothole and Junior felt a short stream of urine moisten his underwear. He grimaced, eliciting a grin from Carl.

"Yahoo!" the younger brother yelped. "Go faster, Dad!"

Dredd eyed his sons in the rearview mirror. Junior's full bladder had pinched his face, making him look like a rodent.

*He's no prize bull like me.*

"Yahoo... Go faster, Dad!" Carl whooped. "Yahoo!"

*...but at least he's not a moron.*

Dredd glanced at Geraldine. A once cheerful child, her emotional inventory had begun to contract at thirteen, leaving her with two aspects: the impassive one she now displayed and an

icy stare of homicidal dismissiveness reserved for her brothers
and stepmother. No matter how reckless her father's driving
she was imperturbable, and not for the first time he appreciated
that, among his seven children, only Geraldine had grit.

*Too bad she's a girl,* he mused.

Around five miles outside Paradise the Vauxhall skidded on
a sharp curve, its rear tires dangerously close to a drop-off of
at least fifty feet.

"Holy shit, Dad!" Carl cried out, craning his neck to look
over the precipice. "You're hittin' on all sixes! Holy shit... I
mean holy shit!" Another sharp curve was ahead and Dredd's
foot depressed the gas pedal very slightly. The car sped up.

"Yahoo, Dad...yahoo!" Carl howled, as the Vauxhall accel-
erated.

Geraldine reached over and rested a hand on her father's
knee. He looked at her. Her eyes were forward, her lips forming
words he understood even though the sounds were drowned
out by the wind and the Vauxhall's motor.

"Slow down."

Dredd immediately backed off the throttle. "Sorry, darling,"
he shouted over the whine of the engine.

"Watch the road," she mouthed, removing her hand from
his knee.

The remaining miles to Paradise were invigorating but
not life-threatening, and upon reaching the mountain village,
they cruised past John Stiveley's former assay office, the first
building on the edge of the main drag and now home to the
modest city government. The rest of the town's business es-
tablishments were situated in wood-frame buildings along the
same side of the street: Nilsen's General Store, the Gold Rush
Saloon, Paradise Bait and Tackle, the office and print room
of the *Idaho World,* and a handful of antique, repair, and curio
shops. Several buildings were abandoned—one now serving
as a fire station, housing buckets, picks, shovels, Pulaski tools,
and a horse-drawn 500-gallon fire wagon. Next door, in the
old Busty Rose, a small clinic was staffed by mostly retired Dr.

Stanley June, a second-floor salon and one of the bedrooms converted to a waiting room and examination area. Ironically, the large parlor on the main level of the former cathouse was now a meeting place for non-denominational Sunday services overseen by a traveling Methodist from Boise, his congregation praying their faith might be strong enough to exorcise whatever amoral demons persisted from the place's original incarnation.

Dredd parked in front of the weathered gray building that housed the *Idaho World*. Once the most widely circulated publication in the state, the *World* was now devoted to local happenings and Ed Riggins's often fiery editorials. "Watch the car," Dredd instructed Carl, motioning for Junior and Geraldine to accompany him. Inside, the place smelled of ink and newsprint paper. Riggins was alone, setting type for his publication's next edition. Although small like Wilbur Tarkel, the comparison ended there, the white-haired newspaperman leathery and firm-jawed, his wolverine's eyes narrow and unafraid. Dredd handed him a note with ad copy.

"Run this in every edition until I tell you to stop," he demanded. Riggins's glasses were atop his head and he moved them to the tip of his nose to read the note.

To Whom It May Concern:

Due to a significant earthquake fault-line running beneath the town of Paradise, Idaho, the General Land Office of the United States is considering condemnation of all community properties under the auspices of eminent domain. Fair prices will be assessed by the federal government at no more than 50% of tax-appraised value. Those wishing to sell their property at market value in advance of the anticipated government action should contact:

Dredd Enterprises
PO Box 1
Boise, Idaho

"No," Riggins said after reading the copy. He handed it back to Dredd, then repositioned his eyeglasses atop his head.

Dredd's face reddened. "Whattaya mean, 'No'?"

"Just what I said… I'm not running it."

"What's wrong with it? Everything's spelled right. What's the problem?"

"It's a lie. Paradise is not sitting on a fault."

"I think I know quite a bit more about faults and earthquakes than some shithole newspaper editor," Dredd fumed. "And I'm telling you that every building in this town will collapse if a big one hits!"

"Then why do *you* want the properties?" Riggins countered. He let Dredd sputter about in search of a plausible lie, then put an end to the dispute. "I won't run this," he reiterated. "You'd best be on your way, Gerald."

Dredd spent a few minutes, cajoling and threatening the veteran journalist, but when it became clear that Ed Riggins would rather burn down Idaho's oldest newspaper than help Gerald Dredd hornswoggle the publication's readership, the real estate baron gave up.

"But this isn't over," he muttered, motioning to his children as he turned to go.

They trooped outside where Carl had abandoned the Vauxhall in favor of the boardwalk fronting Paradise's modest businesses, a better vantage point from which to watch fast-approaching Bountiful Dollarhyde. He and his brother were disciples of their father's philosophy that women—especially beautiful ones—were fruit to be plucked whenever they liked. Junior joined him and they barricaded the pine walkway, standing shoulder to shoulder as Bountiful neared.

"Hey, doll, where're ya headed?" Junior wisecracked.

Bountiful stepped into the street to go around, carefully picking her way through the mud. The Dredd boys kept pace on the boardwalk, and eventually, the young schoolteacher stopped and lifted her chin, imperiously piercing them with blue eyes that shone like sapphires. The poisonous stare paralyzed them and she veered back onto the boardwalk, then continued down the street. Dredd's sons watched, seemingly transfixed, and once she'd gone into Nilsen's General Store, Junior looked at his father.

"Jee-*zus*!" he exclaimed, his voice reflecting equal parts wonder and lust. "That nigger had blue eyes."

&

Goldstrike was inside the mercantile when Bountiful entered, he and Oskar arguing about the type of people they wanted for the penny mansions. Goldstrike favored the sort that mostly kept to themselves and were terrible poker players. Nilsen favored totals over temperament. "We need big families, doggonit!" the storekeeper insisted. Both men could tell from the set of Bountiful's jaw and the whitened knuckles of her clenched fists that she was angry.

"Everything all right, Miss Bountiful?" Goldstrike called out.

Her eyes flickered in his direction, for a moment chilling and lethal. Then her face softened.

"I'm fine, Goldstrike. Thank you for inquiring."

"You don't look fine," Oskar suggested. "I saw them Dredds drive into town. You have a run-in?"

Bountiful didn't answer, instead crossing to a display table where she picked up a bolt of fabric, feigning interest even though she was clearly more inclined to rip the material into ribbons than sew it into ruffles. Goldstrike scowled.

"I'll get some dynamite and blow them sons o' bitches to kingdom come, if'n ya want," he offered. "I'll blow up every goddamned one of them Dredd bastards. Hell, I doubt there's a court in these parts that'd hang me fer it."

"I'll help 'im, doggonit," Nilsen volunteered.

Bountiful fingered the edge of the fabric, the whisper of a smile slowly forming as promises to variously crush, dismember, or combust Dredds were offered by the two old men. Finally, she put down the bolt of fabric and joined them at the front counter, bussing Nilsen on the cheek and then rising on tiptoes to kiss the long scar a Reb sword had carved into Goldstrike's face.

"I appreciate the thought, gentlemen, but let's not blow up anyone today," she said.

With detonation of the Dredds off the table, Goldstrike and Oskar regaled Bountiful with gold rush stories she'd heard many times over. Eventually, the Vauxhall scrolled past the broad front windows of the store on its way out of town, and once the rumble of the car's engine was no longer audible, she said her goodbyes and stepped back onto the boardwalk. Early morning rain had been replaced by noonday sunshine as she headed down Goodlow Road, passing Elysium and then turning onto Only Real Street. Two hundred feet up the road, a huge house with a deep wrap-around porch was set back fifty feet from the street with a large carriage house behind it. Three dormers marked upstairs bedrooms with a pair of tall, wide windows centered above them ventilating an attic dormitory. Commissioned by Maude Dollarhyde and sitting on two acres, the mansion had been repurposed to function as both a residence and the Paradise School.

As Bountiful approached the house, fourteen-year-old genius Roscoe "Lariat" Comfort twirled a lasso on the pebbled front walk, the rope's loop parallel to the ground. The youngster hopped in and out of the circle as it spun, but upon spotting her, expertly rotated the spiral into a vertical twirl that gradually widened until he could step through it, going back and forth as if it were a gateway between two worlds. Bountiful reached him and he let the lasso settle to the ground.

"Hello, Miss Bountiful," he said, flashing a grin as he gathered his rope into coils.

They went inside where the young schoolteacher grilled him on the philosophical teachings of Cicero, Socrates, Aristotle, and Epictetus. Lariat adroitly constructed his arguments with logical premises, reaching conclusions with some and offering hypotheses for the others. His command of reason and logic was dizzying and Bountiful found her head spinning as she struggled to engage with him. Afterward she gave him a copy of *A Tale of Two Cities*. "This is a book by Charles Dickens," she told him. "When you're done, I'll give you another. I want you to read his complete works. I think you'll love his writing."

Maude had discovered Lariat eight years earlier, scavenging scraps from her compost pile. When asked about his mother and father Roscoe had remained silent, his eyes darting about like a fawn who has caught the scent of a wolf. Maude brought him into her kitchen for a plate of fish and biscuits he wolfed down, afterward nearly drowning himself in a glass of milk. There were other strays back then. In her comfortable attic dormitory, Maude housed two Shoshone orphan boys and a mixed-race girl whose Chinese mother had been beaten to death by her white father. She put Roscoe, the wild boy, in the attic with the other orphans, but despite a warm bed and a full belly, he slipped out a window on the first night and scrambled down a drainpipe. A couple of days later he turned up at the back door. "Got any more o' them biscuits?" he asked Maude.

The youngster couldn't read; indeed, he had never been in a classroom and so Maude put a picture book on his bed in the attic. It was a primer on the alphabet, each page showing a letter and a drawing. The next morning she found Roscoe in a dormer alcove, reading *The Wizard of Oz*, a book one of the other children had left out.

"You *can* read!" Maude exclaimed.

"I can now," the boy answered. He held up the primer. "I figured it out pretty quick. It ain't hard."

"It *isn't* hard."

"That's right… It ain't."

Eight years elapsed. The other boarders graduated and moved on, leaving Lariat as the sole inhabitant of the attic dormitory. By then Maude had taught him everything she knew with others around town helping. Goldstrike showed him how to hook fish and snare game, Oskar Nilsen the basics of accounting, and Arnold Chang the Chinese language as well as the finer points of architecture and bar-keeping. Maude helped him get started on the piano, then sat back as he surpassed her limited repertoire in less than a month. Nilsen's wife, Sonia, let him use her paints and brushes, and Ed Riggins paid him to help publish and deliver the *Idaho World*. Willie Barkley, an excellent trick roper before he went off to war, dubbed him with the nickname "Lariat" after teaching the boy the basics only to see him quickly best his teacher with astonishing mastery of the flat loop, the wedding rings, the spoke hops, and the butterfly.

Lariat grew into a forthright and curious boy. "Why don't you ever look right at me?" he'd once asked Goldstrike, wondering why the old prospector always angled his head to the right rather than look directly at someone.

"Don't wanna inflict my abominations on others," Goldstrike had responded, referring to the long scar on his cheek and a chopped ear, both the result of wounds made by a Reb officer's sword at Arrowfield Church during the War Between the States. "Besides, I don't hafta look at ya all that often," the Civil War veteran had added. "I know whacha look like."

"But I'm growing. I change."

"It's about evolution, Lariat. I don't need to know what the human species looked like as it went from fish to creepy-crawly thing to walkin' upright monkey. I just need to know what a full-fledged adult human bein' looks like. Same goes fer you. What ya look like now ain't all that important. Once yer growed up, I'll memorize what ya look like then. It's an appearance more likely to hold fast."

"But you won't have any memories. Mrs. Maude told me that memories are sometimes all a person has."

"Point well taken," Goldstrike had conceded, afterward carefully appraising the boy from head to toe. "There... I looked at ya. Memory banked. Check back with me up the road a bit. I'll look at ya again and make me another deposit."

Once Lariat had outstripped her own education and those of her fellow townsfolk, Maude had begged Bountiful to come home, certain her granddaughter's college degree and years of experience as a teacher in Washington, DC, would carry the boy along for a while. They underestimated him.

"He's learned everything I know," Bountiful told Maude just a few months after her return to Paradise. "He needs a better teacher, more books, a real school. He needs to go to a university."

"University!" Maude protested. "He's still a child, Bountiful."

"I know, Grandma, but he's ready. He's as smart as anyone I knew in college and more mature than most grown men."

It was true. Fourteen years old, as nearly as they could tell, Lariat Comfort was tall for his age with inquisitive eyes, an athletic frame, and a natural, unaffected charm. He could set a proper table and an effective rabbit trap, understand the musings of Thomas Aquinas as well as the trail signs of a bear, and imitate the hoot of an owl through clasped hands, then command the piano at the Gold Rush Saloon to play a nocturne by Chopin that moved his rustic audience to tears. He was a joy to be around and everyone loved him. But in the fall of 1918, the good townspeople of Paradise, Idaho, understood that he had exhausted the reserves of their own experiences and Bountiful's education. It was time for him to move on to an uncertain and dangerous world, a place where too many were exactly like Gerald Dredd and his sons, clinging to the notion that folks like Bountiful Dollarhyde and Lariat Comfort possessed an insurmountable disadvantage. They weren't white.

# 3

## THE COOLERS

As predicted, the story about the Paradise, Idaho, penny mansions was picked up by the Associated Press and United Press International wires and PO Box 257 in Boise was soon crammed to overflowing. Postal workers stuffed hundreds more letters into gunny sacks that Oskar Nilsen picked up during one of his weekly excursions to Boise. Two weeks after the ad ran in the Sunday edition of the *Idaho Statesman*, the council began their review of the applicants in earnest. Many of the communications were from real estate agents, wishing to broker the properties. Others wanted to circumvent the deposit of one hundred dollars, the subsequent $1000 investment for renovation, or both. A few sent telegrams:

> Dear Penny House Sellers: Wish to buy. No deposit but can offer Chink girl. Cooks good, keeps house okay. Jesse Marbright, San Francisco.

> Dear Paradise: Wife and I buy house, make good neighbors. Have $79. Will work off rest. Antoni & Lena Nowak, Chicago.

> To Whom It May Concern: Interested in your proposition. Deposit and living requirement are acceptable. Renovation unnecessary. Can live in anything. Joseph and Mary Targee, St. Louis.

> Paradise House Sellers: Ready to buy, penny in hand. Question: How long before we can resell? Donald and Jane Sabata, Omaha.

Among the first of the posted letters was from the Coolers of 225 Madison Avenue, New York City:

Dear Esteemed Citizens of Paradise, Idaho:

Rarely have I been as excited to take on a role I see as the feather on a cap of considerable theatrical renown (if I may be so bold). Indeed, to paraphrase the gloomy Dane, "I have been but now wish to be." Yes, dear friends, I have trod the boards these many years to applause and adulation, but as my own night draws near, I yearn for serenity rather than approbation, for tranquility rather than celebrity—to leave the bustle of the city and go to the woods, as our friend Thoreau has advised, to "…live deliberately."

As I put these humble words to paper, how eager am I to breathe air from mountain heights closer to God; how anxious to gather fish from crystalline rivers as did our Lord, Jesus Christ; how galvanized to match wits with the Almighty's creatures of the forest; how thrilled to bring my wife and seven children to a place so aptly named "Paradise."

Yes, esteemed Citizens of Paradise, I have seven strapping children, among them my dear daughter, Charlotte, who has achieved the age of consent, and thus, brings an eighth—her husband, Joshua Purdue of the vaunted Massachusetts Purdues. Moreover, I am pleased to report that Charlotte is with child; hence, will add a ninth member to your splendid community.

Regarding the sum of $100.00 to indemnify my application, I am most happy to comply, but given the complicated nature of my financial affairs, all of which are entangled here in New York City, I would ask for a temporary waiver until our arrival in Paradise. By then my affairs will have been put in order and all obligations can be satisfied.

Yours sincerely with utmost respect and esteem,
Thaddeus Maximillian Cooler, Esq.

Despite the flowery rhetoric, Goldstrike was unimpressed. "This fella sounds like he's all shirt and no trousers," he grumbled. "I knowed me a few like that. Most come without a pot to pee in and take yers on their way out."

"Oh, don't be like that, Goldstrike," Maude objected. "Mister Cooler writes so beautifully. He's obviously a gentleman. And he's an actor!" Maude was partial to actors. Before acting like the men in her bed were good lovers and didn't smell like an excess of creek mud and a dearth of bath water, she'd attempted a legitimate career on the stage in San Francisco. Low-paying parts ensued that too often required additional services for the plays' producers, and eventually, Maude decided it was more sensible to act in her bedroom while selling tickets to get under her blankets. Nevertheless, the proverbial "smell of the greasepaint and roar of the crowd" had never completely gone away and she was susceptible to a ham, even one with a suspiciously grandiose name, an unverifiable history, and entangled financial affairs. It prompted the usually shrewd former madam to toss aside nearly eight decades of common sense and intuition.

"I say we waive the deposit," she proposed. "I'm sure he's good for it...a prominent actor and all."

"I vote no," Goldstrike countered. "But if he makes the grade with the rest o' ya, I say make 'im pay up front. Otherwise, I 'spect our temporary waiver'll turn permanent in a big damned hurry."

Bountiful agreed. "We really don't know anything about him other than what he says, Grandma," she cautioned. Maude was undeterred.

"...a man who writes so beautifully."

"Words ain't dollars," Goldstrike muttered.

"...with seven children. *Seven*! And a son-in-law from the vaunted Purdue family of Massachusetts! And a baby on the way! Why, they take care of more than half our problem by themselves!"

There was further discussion, but Maude had been working the town council into her way of thinking for years and eventually convinced the others to postpone collection of the deposit and accept Mr. Thaddeus Maximillian Cooler, Esquire,

and his family as Paradise's first penny mansioneers. She made
the motion, which was seconded by Nilsen. It carried, three to
one, with Goldstrike dissenting. Given the size of the Cooler
family, Maude suggested they be assigned Elysium. "Maybe
Mister Thaddeus Cooler will spout some Shakespeare from the
crow's nest," she speculated. "Wouldn't that be something? Our
own little theater in the sky!" Another motion to offer Elysium
to the Coolers was made and seconded, the vote to carry again
three to one.

With approval of the Coolers, Bountiful suggested they
might be more circumspect. "Half the road to one hundred
twenty-five has been paved," she argued. "And the houses are
in much better shape than we figured. Our buyers can live in
them while they renovate. There's really no rush to choose."
It was solid logic the council rewarded with an invitation for
Maude's granddaughter to join their number. Oskar Nilsen
promptly resigned as president of the body and Bountiful was
installed as his successor. Her first duty was to draft a response
to the Coolers, which Oskar carried down to the post office in
Boise the next day. Snow followed him home, falling steadily
for a week. More snow came soon thereafter, closing the pass
between Paradise and the Idaho capital city. It would be spring
before it reopened and the council spent the winter reviewing
applications, winnowing them to twenty-five finalists—five per
council member. After considerable debate, and overriding
Goldstrike's vociferous objection, it was agreed that each list
would include at least one lawyer.

"Dredd has an army of them," Maude contended, her good
sense reacquired when non-thespians were in the mix. "And
you can be sure he'll put those bloodhounds on the scent, even
if we make our census."

"But only one, goddammit!" the old prospector insisted.
"Otherwise, afore we know it, we'll have so many laws, the
name o' this town'll get changed to Hades."

❧

In early April 1919—with the 1920 census count just eight months off—the Coolers arrived in Paradise. They came in two parties, separated by a day. Mr. and Mrs. Cooler were in the first group with three sons and a daughter, all crammed into a Whiting Model C that wheezed and rattled into town, then parked in front of three-story Elysium on the corner of Goodlow Road and Only Real Street. A considerable crowd was there to greet them, backfires from the Whiting's faulty muffler heralding the family's arrival. Thaddeus Cooler, the family patriarch, was pleased to have an audience assembled. He stepped from the Whiting and struck a pose—shoulders back, chin up, feathered Homburg tipped jauntily, a hand over his heart. Tall and slender with a prominent Van Dyke goatee and waxed moustache, he was at least seventy years old, but carried himself with the vigor of a man half his age.

"How elegant," Maude whispered to Bountiful, although closer inspection and a knowledge of current men's fashions would have judged his suit as more 1890's Victorian than 1918 Edwardian—the coat sporting a frock-cut, his vest's lapels outdated, his shirt collar too high.

"Good citizens of Paradise," Cooler began, "please accept our bottomless gratitude for a greeting, that in my humble estimation, rivals the very best of welcomes I have experienced on the Great White Way of Broadway."

It was an opening barrage of language that briefly flummoxed the townspeople, but with a tip of his head and a whimsical smile, he cued most of them to burst into applause. Cooler bowed deeply. "'I can no other answer make but thanks and thanks and ever thanks,'" he recited from Shakespeare's *Twelfth Night*. He flung an arm outward, eyes angled upward as if imaginary dignitaries watched from the crow's nest of the mansion he'd purchased for a penny. "'What's to do? Shall we go see the relics of this town?'"

While most folks chewed on his words, Goldstrike and Bountiful appraised the Cooler children, who were not children at all, one of them a balding and grizzled fellow named Gus who looked nearer in age to his father than his brothers. Two other sons—Vic and Nat—sat with him in the back seat of the Whiting, both at least forty years old, their stony eyes rimmed in darkness, bowl-cut hair making their lumpy noses and cauliflower ears more prominent.

"They look more like boxers than actors," Goldstrike observed.

Wanda Cooler, the matriarch of the family, and her daughter, Trixie, were in the front seat—a pair of mannequins with a small amount of face getting into the way of their makeup, their lips painted bright red, their eyebrows arched with grease-pencils, rouge smeared so thick it seemed possible the women intended for a single application to last a year. Both had ample breasts making a valiant effort to spill over their tight bodices, their expressions so predatory when appraising the men of Paradise the air practically rang with the sound of a cash register.

After working through the requisite "How do you do's," and "It's a pleasure's," the Coolers were led on a tour of their new home. Horace Goodlow had raided castles from all over the world to obtain fireplace surrounds, statuary, fountains, ornately painted tiles, and elegant furniture. But with the items haphazardly thrown together, the home had no identifiable décor, resulting in a chaotic museum without genre-specific salons, one where a sixteenth century Henri II walnut buffet from France was shoved against a wall tiled in thirteenth century Italian ceramics, the shelves of the cabinet displaying a cluster of disparate artifacts: pre-Columbian masks, intricately painted Russian Madonna icons, a selection of American Indian arrowheads, and an eleventh century pop-eyed jade bust from the Chinese Sanxingdui discovery. The place stank of decadence, an homage to tasteless pretentiousness. Thaddeus loved it.

"Marvelous…just marvelous!" he extolled.

As they moved through the house, Maude insinuated herself between Mr. and Mrs. Cooler. The former madam was typically sensible and occasionally gruff, but she'd come undone with the premiere performance of Thaddeus Cooler, Esquire, and as they strolled from room to room, she reacted to his frequent bon mots with inexplicable eruptions of high-pitched laughter. They ended the tour in the ballroom where the actor whispered something in her ear that provoked another shriek of faux amusement. The screeching echoed off the vaulted ceiling and then out a broken window. Moments later it was answered by a trio of barking dogs who had dropped by to see what all the howling was about.

"Oh me," Maude quacked girlishly, linking her arm in Cooler's as the dogs barked and yapped. "I'm such a silly duck."

Goldstrike was a bit hard of hearing, but Maude's caterwauling was loud enough to painfully vibrate the oldest of eardrums and he took advantage of the brief intermission to resurrect the Coolers' unpaid deposit.

"Of course," Thaddeus responded. He retrieved a worn leather wallet from inside his coat, wrote a check for one hundred dollars, and handed it to Goldstrike. The old prospector inspected the logo and then scowled.

"Bank o' New Venice? Where the hell is *that*? And whatta we gonna do with a goddamned check, anyway? Ain't ya got no cash?"

Maude took the check from the old prospector, using a finger to trace Cooler's signature. The actor had exquisite penmanship, its flourishes as sweeping and flamboyant as his personality. "It looks fine to me," she said.

Goldstrike sniffed skeptically. "I still say we don't turn over the keys till we know this here check's good."

"If I may, Mister Goldstrike—" Cooler interjected.

"Jes' Goldstrike."

"Just Goldstrike... Of course. I beg your pardon. And I perfectly understand your concern. I, too, would hesitate to accept a bank instrument." Cooler retrieved a watch from his vest pocket and handed it over. The gold finish was dull but not tarnished. "This timepiece was presented to me by Queen Victoria in 1886 upon successful completion of my run as *Hamlet* at the Royal Theatre in London," he claimed. "Open it... Read the inscription." Goldstrike hefted the timepiece in one hand to assay its weight, then read the engraving. Afterward the watch was passed around, and when it reached Maude, she read the etched words aloud.

"'To my dear husband on his birthday—*A.*'" She looked at Cooler, puzzled.

"Yes, indeed, my dear Mrs. Dollarhyde," Cooler explained. "It is exactly as you surmise. The watch was a gift from her Royal Highness, Queen Victoria, to her husband, Prince Albert. The *A* is for Alexandrina, the queen's christened name." He sighed theatrically. "This watch was a beloved remembrance of their time together…the prince tragically cut down too early. It remained in Her Majesty's possession until gifted to me, so moved was she by my performance." He lifted his chin and gazed dreamily into an imaginary distance. "Alexandrina and I shared many congenial afternoons together. I reminded her of the prince, don't you know."

Maude was impressed by the hue of royalty, however faint, and fluttered her eyelashes to show it. But Goldstrike remained unconvinced.

"How much is this watch worth?" he asked, taking it from Maude and holding it to his ear.

"I would say priceless, my dear Goldstrike. However, when I had it appraised…for insurance purposes, don't you know, as I would never part with such a cherished memento…it was valued by Lloyds of London at ten thousand pounds."

"How much is that American?"

"More than fifty thousand dollars, I'd wager, given the current rate of exchange."

"There…you see, Goldstrike," Maude said. "Mister Cooler's lovely watch will more than offset the deposit." Goldstrike remained skeptical but offered no further objection and a motion to accept the watch as collateral was made, seconded, and passed three to zero with the old prospector and Bountiful abstaining. The next day the final two members of the Cooler clan arrived, driving a Ford roadster. Once again, most of the town was there to greet them when they rolled to a stop in front of Elysium, an audible gasp arising when Charlotte Cooler Purdue—a beauty about twenty years old and obviously pregnant—leapt into Thaddeus Cooler's arms and wrapped her legs around him.

"Thaddie!" she exclaimed, eagerly planting a kiss on the actor's mouth that was about as daughterly as a nickelodeon peep show. Meanwhile, her husband, Joshua Purdue of the vaunted Massachusetts Purdues, lurched from the roadster, swaying unsteadily as he sized up his new neighbors. Appearing more debauched than vaunted, his thick, curled moustache and chin patch were joined to several days' growth of cheek whiskers. He wore a suit of garish plaid, its trouser knees shiny with wear, the vest adorned by a tarnished jeweler's chain that disappeared into a watch pocket notably absent the bulge of a watch. Only his hat—a broad-brimmed, straw Toyo with a wide black ribbon—befitted the florid greeting he offered his new neighbors.

"Halloo, good citizens of Paradise, halloo! Joshua Purdue bids you halloo!" He then fell onto his face in the dust of the street and it was immediately apparent that Joshua Purdue of the vaunted Massachusetts Purdues was drunk. It was an inauspicious debut, but the Cooler son-in-law had sufficiently recovered by that evening to stop by the Gold Rush Saloon with his sister-in-law, Trixie. A handful of fellows were there, including Goldstrike, three men who logged for the sawmill in Horseshoe Bend, and a couple of diehard prospectors who still panned Mores Creek for gold. Purdue took up residence on a barstool to enjoy the companionship of a bottle of whiskey while Trixie produced a deck of cards and cleaned out the rest of the bar patrons, departing with $9.67 in pennies and nickels, along with a little gold dust, an 1896 William McKinley campaign button, a Colt .45 that lacked a firing pin, and Goldstrike's St. Christopher's medal, an icon he was happy to be rid of after getting fleeced, as it had proven far less protective *against* lost causes than attractive *to* them.

# 4

## This Cockamamie Plan

Everyone on the council went to church at the Busty Rose on the following Sunday morning. The traveling pastor—weary of preaching with the ghosts-of-harlots-past leering at him—then delivered less a sermon than a thinly veiled pitch for one of the penny mansions to be donated to his Methodists. His plea fell on deaf ears. Nilsen was a Lutheran who attended Methodist services because it was the only game in town, whereas Goldstrike was an agnostic and Chang a Buddhist, the latter pair devoted to the potluck that followed the worship rather than a Christian deity. As for Maude, the former madam had seen enough clergyman in their underwear to make her cynical about them and Bountiful had long ago learned that white pastors spoke only for the white Almighty.

After the potluck, the council convened at the old assay office—their first order of business to award one of the remaining three mansions to a lawyer. Despite prior agreement, Oskar Nilsen's candidate lacked a law degree. Goldstrike's pick—Charles Dunworthy from Council Bluffs, Iowa—leaned toward the preparation of wills, something the old prospector figured would prove valuable, given the mounting threat of Spanish flu. "Half the folks in Yellow Pine are in the ground," he reminded everyone. "And that flu is comin' our way." Dunworthy boasted a large family—a wife, a mother-in-law, a maiden aunt, and seven children—while Arnold Chang's recommendation, Michael Summerville of Philadelphia, had an even bigger family with a wife and ten children. Summerville's personal statement was filled with flowery accounts of the various bank robbers, forgers, and murderers he'd kept on the streets of Philadelphia.

"That's all we need," Oskar groused. "A bunch of doggone

crooks comin' here to rob us blind, 'cuz this fella can get 'em off." Maude and Bountiful had combined their choices to support a single candidate:

Dear Citizens of Paradise:

By way of introduction, we are the Peycomsons, Meriwether and Evangeline, of Portland, Oregon. We have one child, our son Felix, who will be five years old on the sixth of June. Our interest in your community is not monetary, but pastoral. We long to exchange the burdensome clamor and pace of city life for the idyllic existence promised in your charming advertisement. Moreover, I am aware of your situation regarding the upcoming census and the possible actions of the U. S. General Land Office. I am an attorney, specializing in mining and real estate law, having argued against the assignment of eminent domain for many of my clients whose properties were in danger of being acquired by the government. Accordingly, should our application be approved, I would be happy to provide legal services free of charge as part of my civic responsibility.

I have enclosed a certificate of demand, which you may present to the Boise City National Bank where I have deposited $1000 to indemnify our application.

Yours sincerely and with all good will,
Meriwether Peycomson
Attorney-at-Law

Oskar quickly put his support behind Peycomson. Arnold Chang then withdrew his candidate—the criminal defense attorney Summerville—in favor of the larger Dunworthy clan. Goldstrike didn't trust Peycomson. "I never knowed a lawyer willin' to part with his money afore somebody signed away their own goddamned life in return," he opined.

"Whatta we got to lose?" Oskar countered. "The man put his cash on the line. If he don't come through, we're that much richer."

"We ain't cash poor, Oskar," Goldstrike retorted. "We're

butts in the barn poor. We need at least one hunnert twenty-five people in this town by 1920. There's twelve o' them Dunworthys against three Peycomsons. Don't take a genius like Lariat to add them numbers up."

"With the Coolers, we're already at one hundred seventeen, Goldstrike," Nilsen rebutted. "And that girl, Charlotte, is gonna pop another out by the fall."

"Even if I trusted 'em…which I *don't*…them Coolers ain't been through a Paradise winter yet," Goldstrike pointed out. "We'll see how many o' them dandies is still around next spring."

Oskar shrugged off the old prospector's concerns, moving to approve Meriwether Peycomson's application. Maude seconded, but the vote that followed evened at two apiece with Goldstrike and Arnold Chang still in the Dunworthy caucus. It was left to Bountiful to break the tie.

"Sorry, Grandma," the young schoolteacher began, aiming an apologetic smile at her grandmother. "I realize Mister Peycomson is our candidate, but Goldstrike isn't wrong. I'm not sure we can count on the Coolers one hundred percent…and there are a lot of Dunworthys." She paused, her eyes on the table, lightly tapping her fingers on the varnished oak. "Mister Peycomson has a small family," she murmured as if debating herself. "But he'll provide legal services for free." She was quiet for a few moments more, then looked up. "Okay…if we can only have one lawyer, then I vote yes on the Peycomsons. There will be other big families and Mister Peycomson has legal experience with cases involving eminent domain."

With the Peycomsons approved, Oskar Nilsen quickly made another nomination. "This one ain't a got a big family either," the storekeeper said. "But he may have somethin' even better." He began to read aloud from a letter:

"'Dear Paradise, Idaho.

Upon learning of your offer, my wife and I were filled with hope and excitement. We currently reside in Missoula where I am on the faculty at the University of Montana in the Department of Electrical Engineering. We have two children, ages three and five, and with God's blessing, would like to add to our family.'"

Goldstrike sniffed. "An egghead… What's he gonna do up in these mountains?"

"Just listen," Oskar rebutted. "It gets better."

"'I have expertise and skills in the area of electrical science and would be most happy to apply both, without charge, in order to facilitate the town's conversion to electrical power.'"

Oskar set the letter on the table. "Howdaya like them apples, Goldstrike? He can help us go electrical in Paradise!"

Maude picked up the letter and perused it, then abruptly gasped. "Oh my God… He's a *Goodlow!* Listen to this!" She revealed the author's name, John Goodlow, then read the post-script aloud.

"'P.S. I am the late Horace Goodlow's nephew, although I make no past or present claim on property nor can I assume prior debt.'"

Maude well remembered the long-ago occupant of the crow's nest atop Elysium. Horace Goodlow had relished the wide-open gold rush town he first encountered, a place short of inconvenient laws limiting how much he could acquire or how he acquired it. He'd taken more than one run at the Busty Rose and Maude hadn't forgotten.

"A goddamned *Goodlow!*" she spat. "I vote no."

"Grandma, there's no motion for a vote," Bountiful pointed out.

"I don't care. He may promise not to make claims, but he's still a Goodlow. Horace made a lot of promises too. Motion on the table or not, I vote no."

Considerable discussion followed with Oskar lobbying hard for his candidate, the idea of a general store with electric lights outweighing the stain Horace Goodlow had left on the community. Eventually, the storekeeper abandoned persuasion and moved to approve John Goodlow's application.

"I've said it twice and I'll say it again!" Maude insisted. "I vote no."

"Well, I vote yes, doggonit," Oskar countered.

Arnold Chang weighed in next. Shortly after the then-young Chinese immigrant arrived in Paradise, Goodlow's enforcers had pinned him down and gleefully cut off his pigtail. Afterward Horace and assayer Stiveley blocked any attempt by the fledgling prospector to pan richer sections of the area's streams. Getting by on odd jobs while mining abandoned claims at night, Arnold outlasted both men, putting together enough nickels and dimes to buy Goodlow's saloon and hotel at foreclosure in 1890. He'd defiantly regrown his pigtail, but like Maude, hadn't forgotten his former tormenter.

"No!" the bar owner emphatically asserted. "My vote...a goddamned no!"

Goldstrike voted next. "It's the twentieth century and the whole world's goin' electrical," he said, backing off his earlier objection to eggheads. "These new folks ain't stayin' if we won't let electrical and the twentieth century come with 'em. So...I guess I'm a yes."

With Bountiful holding the deciding vote, she made a suggestion. "We can ask Mister Goodlow to come for a personal interview," she proposed. She looked at her grandmother and then Arnold Chang. "If you're both still opposed after we meet him, I'll vote to reject his application. That's a promise."

A motion was made and seconded to invite Mr. John Goodlow of Missoula, Montana, for a personal interview. The motion carried, and afterward, the council moved on to the next application, a review unexpectedly interrupted when freshly excommunicated Amon DeMille drove into town with his wife, Sarah, and their four children.

☙

The DeMilles were from Ogden, Utah, where Amon had been a carpenter—a true craftsman skilled enough to frame a house and then fashion artisan's furniture to populate it. He and Sarah were devout Mormons, and following their marriage, faithfully attended Temple, tithed the church, and added three sons and a daughter to the flock of the Latter-Day Saints: sixteen-year-old Benjamin, fifteen-year-old Gideon, thirteen-year-old Jeanette, and twelve-year-old Oliver. It was Jeanette who prompted their exodus from Ogden after she caught the attention of a powerful fundamentalist bishop who viewed the modern Mormon church's repudiation of polygamy as merely a suggestion. "I am most happy, Brother DeMille, that your daughter is of a suitable age for marriage," observed the corpulent fifty-five-year-old paragon of lust and flatulence, further implying that Jeanette would be an excellent addition to his stable of wives.

"Jeanette is a child," Sarah fumed when her husband apprised her of the bishop's intentions. "I'll not see her marry an old man with more hemorrhoids than hair. He'd probably give her idiots for children." Amon agreed and the bishop was rebuffed. The church official then used his influence to engineer an official indictment for apostasy and the DeMilles were threatened with excommunication. Not long thereafter, the bishop cornered Jeanette in a private room at the Temple where he offered to withdraw his indictment of her family if the teenager agreed to provide marital duties absent the inconvenience of actual marriage. When she declined, the bishop pressed his two hundred seventy pounds of fat and entitlement against her, pinning her to a wall until her knee found his groin.

Amon respected his church's precepts, but there was no canon in the Book of Mormon stronger than his love for his daughter. After Jeanette told her parents what had happened, Amon went after the bishop and apostated the living daylights out of him. Subsequently anticipating both excommunication and jail for assault and battery, he loaded his wife, four children, and life savings into a panel truck and drove, pulling a trailer full of furniture and other possessions. They drove and drove until there were no more roads to drive on, a spot coinciding with the mountain hamlet of Paradise, Idaho.

Lariat Comfort was on the bench fronting Nilsen's General Store when Amon parked the DeMilles' truck in front of the mercantile. The teenager was deep into *David Copperfield*, his latest Dickens novel, but put the book aside with the family's arrival and took up his rope. Idly twirling a modest, horizontal loop that spun just above the rough, unfinished planks of the boardwalk, he watched the DeMille sons spill out the rear door of the vehicle. Amon and Sarah were next, emerging from the front seat. Lariat flicked his wrist. The small horizontal loop went waist-high and vertical, progressively enlarging until big enough to step through. That's when pretty Jeanette climbed out of the panel truck and Lariat's eyes went silver-dollar wide. He immediately began to jump back and forth through the huge loop as if dancing on hot coals, all the while whistling "Greensleeves." Jeanette had never encountered a person of color before—much less one of the exotic, handsome, whis-tling, rope-twirling variety—and she was immediately smitten, indicating her interest in Lariat by completely ignoring him. The young man was undaunted, transitioning his rope to a smaller loop he twirled about his head a couple of times before cast-ing it out. It settled around Jeanette's shoulders and he gently tugged it tighter. She giggled.

Like his daughter, Amon had never encountered a person of African descent, much less a calf-roping one, but he preferred his daughter not be lassoed, skin color notwithstanding. He fashioned an expression to reflect that opinion, then relaxed when Lariat released the tension on his rope, allowing the loop to slip off Jeanette. It fell to the ground and she stepped out of it, shyly watching as the boy gathered his lasso into coils and then approached her father with a hand extended.

"Welcome to Paradise. I'm Roscoe Comfort. Folks call me Lariat."

"Amon DeMille," the Mormon carpenter replied, impressed by the young man's firm grip and steady eye. "Thank you for your welcome, Mister Comfort…and thank you for releasing my daughter. Perhaps, you might stick to cows in the future?"

Like most teenagers, Lariat could turn literal at the drop of a coin and did. "We don't have cows in Paradise," he responded.

"Yes…and my daughter is a person, not a calf to be roped, okay?"

Lariat grinned. "Sorry, Mister DeMille. He eyed Jeanette, head tipped. "Sorry…?"

"Jeanette."

Lariat's grin widened. "Jeanette," he repeated. The two young people then went googly-eyed over each other, until Amon broke it up with a question.

"Could you direct us to a hotel?" he asked.

Lariat pulled his eyes off Jeanette. "Don't have any. Are you folks here to buy one of the penny mansions?"

"Penny mansions?"

"We have four mansions for sale… Actually, three now. You can buy one for a penny if you promise to fix it up and live here."

"A house for a penny?" Sarah DeMille exclaimed. "That's real? It's not a joke?"

Lariat shook his head. "It's no joke, ma'am… And they're not shacks. They're big houses built during the gold rush. The town council is meeting right now to decide who gets them. They're down to the final bunch of applications." He gestured toward the old assay office. "They're meeting over there…right now."

Tears formed in Sarah's eyes. "So it's too late?"

Lariat shook his head. "It's not too late, Mrs. DeMille. C'mon…I'll take you folks over there." He winked at Jeanette. "You should all come. They want big families. You folks'll impress them."

Amon and Sarah looked at each other. Two days had passed since they'd abandoned everything for the unknown of the road. It had been terrifying, and they'd assiduously avoided discussing a future without the blanket of their church to warm them.

But now—standing on a dirt road in a majestic and beautiful place at the end of the world, talking to their first person of color about daughter-roping and penny mansions—it seemed their flight from Utah and the spiteful bishop might have been as providential as the Israelites' escape across the parted Red Sea. Sarah swiped at her tears.

"Come on," she said, taking her husband's hand. "Let's go get our home."

Lariat led them to the former assay office. Inside, the town council was gathered around a large circular table. Ed Riggins was there to cover the proceedings for the *Idaho World*, providing the sixth of six faces that turned to the door when Lariat and the DeMille family trooped in.

"This is Mister and Mrs. Amon DeMille and their family," Lariat announced. "You should sell them one of the houses."

The DeMilles lined up for inspection, tallest to shortest. They were a stark contrast to the flamboyant Coolers—their clothes simple and modest, their mannerisms unassuming, their eyes level and sincere. Amon was six feet, five inches tall and square-jawed. Unlike the painted and shellacked Cooler women, Sarah was unaffected and lovely. The fresh-scrubbed boys looked like their father and dewy Jeanette like her mother.

"We understand if we're too late," Amon began.

"But we'll be good neighbors," Sarah broke in. "*Really* good neighbors."

The search committee was delighted to learn that Amon was a carpenter and Sarah an expert seamstress who had sewn all her family's clothing, much of it from her own designs. The family shared the rest of their story, hiding nothing.

"So I might be a fugitive," Amon finished up. "Although I doubt anyone will come looking."

"Maybe Mister DeMille oughta have a look-see at one of our places," Goldstrike suggested, impressed by both the number of DeMilles and their unpretentious ways. "A proper carpenter might fix it up for less than a thousand." He offered a motion to suspend the council's deliberations long enough for the DeMilles to tour the mansions. It was seconded and passed, and the group trekked over to Only Real Street, by-passing Cooler-occupied Elysium and the Paradise School. Down the road and across the street was the former Rimple home.

"Oh my goodness, Amon, look at that house," Sarah exclaimed, her eyes tearing. "Just look at it. It's so beautiful!"

The original residence of Ned and Irene Rimple had been built in the Queen Anne style. Asymmetric and eclectic with a variety of surface textures, the place had two full stories topped by a single, centrally placed attic dormer. An expansive front porch ran the full width of the house, its roof supported by five sets of sturdy double pillars. A large second-story gable was on one side of the home's upper level with a turret on the opposite side, a bell-roofed gazebo atop it. Despite its regal heritage, the residence's brick walls needed fresh whitewash, its copper roof was tarnished green, the front path stones were crumbled, and several windowpanes were cracked or broken.

"But nothing sags," Amon observed. "She's still got her pride."

They went inside and were met by an overpowering stench. The Rimples had employed maids in their salad days, but after Ned's death, circumstances forced Irene to let them go, one-by-one, until only she was left to tend things. Ill-suited to housekeeping, the widow had made matters worse in her final years by joining an excess of cats to a deficiency of kitty litter. The resultant odor drove Goldstrike, Maude, and Oskar Nilsen back onto the porch. Arnold Chang had always wanted to get a look inside the place and stayed, pinching his nose. Bountiful pinched her own, apologizing to the DeMilles for the messy and malodorous state of the home, afterward suggesting they move on to one of the other mansions.

"Nonsense," Sarah said. "Stink is not a permanent thing. We'll paint the walls and refinish the floors and moldings and stair rails, right, Amon? Give this lovely old lady the smell of fresh paint and floor wax. We'll clean and scour and dust...

make everything spick and span in no time. Soap and hard work... That's all it will take...soap and hard work to make this wonderful house a home again. Children, help me while your father speaks with Mister Chang. We'll open all the windows. It will air things out in no time."

The DeMille children scattered to open the windows with Lariat trailing Jeanette. Sarah and Bountiful went off on their own, Mrs. DeMille excitedly pointing out the features she most loved, her list comprised, more or less, of everything. Her enthusiasm was infectious and Bountiful was making plans to help her sew new curtains by the time they reached the final upstairs bedroom—a master suite that incorporated the exterior gable, giving the room a rounded sitting area lined with large windows. Meanwhile, Arnold Chang and Amon walked about, knocking on walls with their knuckles, pressing on the hardwood floors in search of creaks, and opening and closing fireplace flues. As men do, they pointed out sensible decisions the original builder made and criticized what might have been done better had they built the house. Mostly, they talked about the cost to make the place livable.

Eventually, everyone—Maude, Goldstrike, and Oskar Nilsen included—regathered in the first-floor parlor, the cat smell having gone from asphyxiating to mildly acrid as fresh air flowed through the house.

"I think we could fix this place up for a lot less than a thousand dollars," Amon concluded.

"How much less?" Goldstrike asked.

Amon shrugged. "At least three hundred, probably more. There aren't any structural defects. The roof is sound and the foundation is solid. The walls don't have cracks in the plaster so there's no settling. This place has great bones and Mrs. DeMille is right about the smell...some paint and varnish, a little lye and elbow grease... That'll take care of most of it." During his inspection, Amon had made notes on a small pad. He held it up. "I'd be happy to itemize the job. You could check out my figures with someone you trust." He smiled and then took

Sarah's hand. "Of course, we've put the cart before the horse. You've not made a decision about us."

Bountiful promptly offered a motion to reconvene the council meeting on-site. Arnold Chang seconded and the motion passed unanimously. This was followed by a second motion to invite Amon and Sarah DeMille and their family to purchase the Rimple home. It, too, passed, and afterward, Amon produced a penny.

"Not yet, Mister DeMille," Bountiful told him. "We'll go back to the city building and sign the papers. Then you can pay us and we'll give you a receipt. Everything proper and legal."

"You forgot about the deposit," Amon offered. The five council members studied one another for a moment or two.

"I don't think a deposit will be necessary, Amon," Goldstrike said.

They returned to the city building and completed the paperwork, the council then adjourning to the Gold Rush Saloon to celebrate their progress. Winter had stalled the hoped-for population explosion, but with almost eight months remaining before the start of the 1920 census, the former boomtown had added eight Coolers and six DeMilles. Three Peycomsons were on the way and Willie Barkley had survived the war and was home from Europe. Paradise now claimed 127 residents with Charlotte Cooler Purdue set to add a 128th. Best of all, one penny mansion was still vacant, awaiting a new family to further pad the town's population.

"I'll be goddamned go to hell," Goldstrike observed to his fellow council members as he lifted a glass of beer for a toast. "It looks like this cockamamie plan is gonna work!"

# 5

## "'Vengeance, plague, death, confusion!'"

As predicted in Gerald Dredd's letter to the town council, most of the boys who left Paradise to fight in The War To End All Wars didn't return. John Winston died in the Battle of Château-Thierry, Walter Pease at Belleau Wood, and the Marcus brothers during the Meuse-Argonne offensive. Five survived the conflict but fell victim to the Spanish flu. Oskar Nilsen's son, Anders, was among them, dying in a quarantine tent outside Paris with best friend Willie Barkley at his side, masked and gowned. The gear cost Willie three dollars and the German field knife he'd taken off a dead Hun. "But at least Andy didn't pass on with strangers," he told Oskar. Healthy on a Saturday and dead on the following Tuesday, Andy babbled incoherently for most of his final hours, abruptly opening his eyes at the end.

"Confusion," he said to Willie.

Within days, Willie almost joined him in the hereafter. Despite his mask and gown, he contracted the virulent disease, languishing in the same field hospital where Andy had succumbed, plagued by nightmares of the trenches and the shelling and the futile charges into No Man's Land. Willie's fever eventually broke, but the nightmares persisted, joined to hallucinations that visited without warning even after he returned home—the only Paradise boy who'd shipped out with the Idaho 41st to make it back.

He returned in early March of 1919, no longer the chipper young fellow who'd marched off to France, all full of pepper and brag. He was now a man, although not one most in Paradise, other than Goldstrike, could fathom. None of those good folks had seen an artillery shell take off someone's head or heard a buddy scream as a bayonet ran him through. They still had a long view of things whereas The War To End All Wars had taught Willie Barkley that life was momentary. To make matters worse, war and Spanish flu had rendered him intermittently crazy. The military doctors called it "shell shock," even though Willie had been sane, albeit haunted, prior to battling the high fevers and cold sweats of the deadly virus. Regardless, the poor fellow was no longer right in the head about half the time. Asleep most days, he was too often awake all night, wandering around Paradise and shouting at the trees as if they were reincarnations of his fallen comrades. "'Vengeance, plague…!'" he called out to the towering pines. "'Vengeance, plague, death, confusion!'"

Not long after Willie returned to Paradise, Goldstrike was awakened at three o'clock in the morning by a voice outside his shack. "Goddamned mule thief," he muttered, grabbing his shotgun. He climbed into boots and then burst onto his ramshackle porch in long underwear, the double barrels of his Winchester pointed at the darkness. Spring snow was falling, popcorn-sized flakes piled four inches deep on the ground and decorating the tree branches like white Christmas flocking. The voice sounded again.

"'Vengeance!'"

Goldstrike lowered his gun.

"'Vengeance, plague, death, confusion!'"

Shoeless, Willie Barkley emerged from the storm, wearing merely a thin chambray shirt and dungarees. Goldstrike brought him into his shack, sat him by the fire, and further warmed him with blankets and whiskey. He gave the boy the cot he'd slept on after Old Butch took him in and Willie stayed, abandoning the log home where he'd been raised.

Willie's parents had died when he was sixteen and he'd worked as a hunting and fishing guide, occasionally rowing a group of thrill seekers through the tumultuous rapids on the Middle Fork of the Salmon River. Although he'd not finished high school, the young man was an avid reader who often regaled his clients over campfires—performing Shakespearean soliloquies, telling scary stories by Edgar Allen Poe, and reciting poems by Walt Whitman and Carl Sandburg. Upon his return, folks worried he might abruptly lose his marbles and strand a hunter out in the woods or capsize a boat filled with helpless city people. But with May and the appearance of hunters and adventurer seekers, Willie came back from an excursion or two with his clients intact, encouraging the townsfolk to relax even though they kept a collective ear pointed should a voice call out from the night in bad weather.

Every so often Oskar Nilsen sought Willie out, hoping his son's best pal might be clear-headed enough to recount Anders's final moments.

"His last words, Willie… Were there any last words?" Oskar repeatedly asked.

Willie always lied. "There were, Mister Nilsen," he'd tell the old man. "Andy said, 'Paradise.'"

"Paradise?"

"Yes."

"Which one, Willie? Which one?"

"I suspect both of 'em, Mister Nilsen."

"Yeah…both of 'em. That sounds like Anders, doggonit. He woulda meant, 'Both of 'em.'"

Two of the four penny mansions in Paradise remained unoccupied. The Peycomsons had yet to arrive and John Goodlow's interview was pending. However, work was well under way on the other two homes. Amon DeMille's construction crew included his boys, an eager Lariat Comfort, and an occasional Goldstrike, the place resounding from dawn to dusk with the sounds of sawing, hammering, singing, and Goldstrike's opinions. Meanwhile at Elysium, large trucks from the valley arrived almost daily, their loads hidden behind canvas siding. The rigs—driven by hulking fellows wearing pork pie hats or newsboy caps pulled low enough to shade their intentions—came one by one, backing up the long driveway to the rear of the house. The drivers remained in their cabs, smoking to the accompaniment of non-stop banging and cursing from inside the house. After a couple of hours, they left and the next truck arrived. Near evening, the last of them pulled out and all was quiet again at the Cooler residence, save the occasional sounds of raucous laughter or an argument often centered around Joshua Purdue of the vaunted Massachusetts Purdues.

"We oughta do an inspection," Goldstrike suggested to the town council a few weeks into this routine. "I don't trust them Coolers." Maude vociferously defended Thaddeus, but eventually a motion was made and carried to dispatch Goldstrike and Arnold Chang on a fact-finding mission. On their way to Elysium, Willie Barkley joined them.

"Where're you headed?" he asked.

"Elysium," Goldstrike answered.

"That near Ypres?"

"It's just up the street, Willie. We're in Idaho."

"Not Belgium?"

"No, Willie. We're in Idaho. We're headin' to the Coolers to make an inspection."

Willie snapped to attention. "Private Barkley, ready for inspection, sir!"

Arnold put a hand on the young man's shoulder. "You go to Gold Rush, Willie, okay? Mrs. Chang make you dinner."

Willie took a deep breath, released it in a rush, and was suddenly lucid. "I'm okay, Mister Chang," he said. "Let me go with you."

It was nearly six p.m. when the three men arrived at the most impressive of the penny mansions, the last truck of the day pulling out of the Cooler driveway. Goldstrike motioned for the driver to pull over.

"Yer tires need some air," he told him. "They look low."

"Mind your own goddamned business," the man shouted through the window, an unlit cigar clamped between his teeth. The bad-tempered fellow shoved the truck back into gear and it rumbled and swayed off as Thaddeus Cooler emerged from the house.

"Hail, good fellows, hail," the actor called out from the front porch as his pregnant daughter, Charlotte, joined him, her baby belly sizeable even though her due date was purportedly three months off. Length of gestation aside, she fixed Willie with the sort of look that had likely gotten her gestating the first time.

"Well, hello handsome," she called out.

Willie looked at the ground.

"Didn't you hear me?" Charlotte continued. "I said, 'Hello, handsome.'"

The tall ex-doughboy responded by more diligently contemplating the white pebbles on the freshly landscaped front walk rather than Charlotte Purdue's pouty lips and suggestively tilted hip. "Confusion," he murmured.

"To what do we owe this pleasure, gentlemen?" Thaddeus intervened, moving to the porch railing. "What tidings dost thou bring?"

"We ain't got no tidin's," Goldstrike said. "We come to make sure everything is goin' okay."

"It's going quite well… Just bully," the Cooler patriarch exhorted. "Thank you so much for asking. I would, of course, invite you in, but we were just about to take our supper. Perhaps, another time?"

"We're real glad it's bully fer you," Goldstrike said. "But we need to have our own look-see… Make sure it's bully fer us too."

Panic flickered across Cooler's face, so quickly gone it passed as imaginary.

"We got the right to make an inspection," Goldstrike pressured him.

"Quite so, my dear Goldstrike, quite so."

"It was in yer contract."

Cooler hesitated as if sorting through masks that might send his visitors packing. He found one that rendered him crestfallen, added drooped shoulders, and then offered the character he'd contrived to Goldstrike and Chang. Charlotte had joined him at the porch railing and he next looked at her as if they shared a devastating secret.

"Perhaps, we should tell them, my dear," he said.

"Tell them..." Charlotte echoed, interrupting a head-to-toe inspection of Willie Barkley to look at her father.

"Yes, of course you're right," Thaddeus added.

Charlotte tipped her head. "I'm right... What am I right about?"

"Indeed...these fine people are friends, my dear. We cannot keep the secret to ourselves any longer." Cooler turned back to the Paradise councilmen. "Gentlemen, forgive us," he continued. "For we have not been completely honest...not wishing to alarm the community, don't you know? Because our concern and regard for our new and good neighbors here in Paradise is boundless. Simply boundless."

He paused as if fighting back tears.

"First of all," he went on, "I must assure you, that despite the terrifying reputation of Mrs. Cooler's affliction, the general citizenry is not in danger." He then revealed that his wife had contracted the Spanish flu, presumably infected by one of the truck drivers. "She suffers abed, gentlemen...delirious with fever; indeed, at times, so close to angels the flutter of their wings is in her ears."

As a boy, Arnold Chang had lived through a bubonic plague pandemic in his native China. Afraid of no man, infectious diseases spooked him and he used his shirttail to cover his nose and mouth. "Wômen xià cì zài lái," he spluttered, tugging on Goldstrike's sleeve. "We come back 'notha time... 'Notha time, Goldstrike, 'kay? We go. Wômen qù xhidào. We go now!"

Goldstrike shrugged off the anxious saloonkeeper. "Why ain't *you two* sick?" he demanded, squinting at Cooler and his daughter. "Why ain't Purdue and that other girl o' yers sick? They're both down at the Gold Rush every goddamned night. Ya got flu in this house, shouldn't yer whole bunch be quarantined?"

"Quarantined? Yes...quarantined. Quite right, my dear Goldstrike...quite right. You are obviously well-versed in the microbiological sciences. Your question is on the money. Absolutely on the—"

"I ain't well-versed in bullshit if that's what you're sayin'," Goldstrike interrupted. "It don't take no genius to know this Spaniard's flu gets around damned fast if it ain't corralled. So I ask again, why ain't the rest o' ya sick? Why just yer missus?"

Cooler slowly fashioned a reassuring smile. "Ah, forgive me," he said. "I should have told you immediately. You see, my dear Goldstrike, all in our household, save Mrs. Cooler, contracted the Iberian malady while still in New York. We are no longer contagious."

Charlotte Cooler Purdue had resumed eyeballing Willie Barkley and suddenly spoke to him. "What's wrong with you, anyway… Are you touched?"

Willie lowered his gaze to the ground. "Confusion," he murmured.

"What?"

"Nothing… I beg your pardon, Miss Cooler."

"It's Missus Purdue."

"Missus…I beg your pardon, *Missus* Purdue."

"You wanna come in for drink?" Charlotte countered.

"Charlotte, my dear," Thaddeus cooed, squeezing his daughter's elbow. "Remember now…we are, as our good friend, Goldstrike, has suggested…in quarantine. Until your mother has recovered, we are unable to entertain guests." He smiled at their visitors. "Of course, we look forward to many evenings of merrymaking and fellowship once Mrs. Cooler has recovered and no longer represents a danger to others."

"I could bring a bottle out here to the—"

"Was that your mother's voice?" Cooler posed, head tipped. "I believe she's calling out. Perhaps you should see to her, my darling?"

"I didn't hear anything."

"There it is again… Yes, I'm quite certain I heard your mother call."

Charlotte sniffed, making clear that whatever call she'd

heard had landed below her waist rather than on her eardrums. "I didn't hear a damned thing," she said. A brief stand-off between father and daughter ensued, but Charlotte eventually gave in, flinging a look of unadulterated carnality at Willie before tossing her long hair prettily and then sweeping off, her skirt flying.

"Young women," Thaddeus chuckled after she was gone. "So dramatic, are they not? That one, especially. Destined for the stage like her father, I'll wager." The actor bade them farewell, and afterward, Willie trailed Goldstrike and Arnold as they renegotiated the front pathway, their boots crunching on the loose stones. They reached Only Real Street and headed toward the main drag of Paradise with Willie descending back into madness with each step.

"'Vengeance,'" he repeated when they reached Goodlow Road, "'plague, death… Confusion!'"

# 6

## Showdown at the Idanha

It was nearly June, but patches of dingy snow still dotted the road when Bountiful left Paradise in her grandmother's Model T Ford. She was to meet John Goodlow in the tearoom of Boise's Idanha Hotel at ten-thirty. "No point in everybody goin', Miss Bountiful," Goldstrike reasoned. "We ain't changin' our votes. It'll come down to you, anyway." She drove the open-air car, wearing gloves and a scarf to ward off the chill. The road was remarkably clear and level. Even this late in the spring it was typically scarred by mudslides or rocks, but since the arrival of the Coolers, crews from the Idaho highway department had kept the pass open. "The outfit what delivers buildin' supplies to the Coolers probably knows someone at the road department," Oskar Nilsen speculated. "As many trips as them truckers make, there's gotta be a lot of money flowin'. I'll betcha a bribe or two changed hands."

Bountiful often had a passenger for her excursions to Boise but was alone this time, something she appreciated. An opinionated college beau had taught her to drive, and after putting up with his incessant nagging, she'd come to enjoy the luxury of motoring without the burden of a man, particularly a white man, telling her what she should or should not do. It had been thirteen years since Maude sent her granddaughter to Howard University in Washington, DC, seeing her off at the train station in Boise with Goldstrike. Bountiful had been sixteen years old at the time. "When ya had yerself enough of them goddamned crooks back there, come on home. We'll keep a light on," the old prospector promised before she boarded. More than a decade would pass before she took his advice.

Bountiful excelled in her studies at Howard and thrived in

the collegiate community. Off-campus, however, the nation's capital was less obliging—Washington, DC, restaurants, public rest rooms, and moving picture theaters all strictly segregated. It was enough to send a less stalwart person running back to Paradise, but Bountiful stayed after graduation. Inspired by the writings of W.E.B. Du Bois and Ida Bell Wells, she taught in Black schools and worked with the fledgling NAACP. She became a suffragette. She grew up.

The political movements were, at times, disheartening. Her lighter skin and startling blue eyes rendered her as suspect in the Black world as she was in the white one. Eventually, loneliness became nearly as great a burden as prejudice and she was relieved when her grandmother wrote, asking her to come home for Lariat's sake. "I'm going back," Bountiful told her beau, an earnest Justice Department lawyer she'd agreed to marry, yet considered a trifle.

"To Idaho? Are you out of your mind?"

"Not Idaho…Paradise."

"Whatever for?"

The conversation had taken place in Washington's Meridian Hill Park, the couple sitting on a bench in the shade of a linden tree near the public rest rooms. Between the entrances to the facilities were two drinking fountains, one for WHITES ONLY, the other marked COLORED.

"Labels," Bountiful had replied as she removed her engagement ring and handed it to him. "In Paradise, the only label they put on me is 'Maude Dollarhyde's granddaughter.'"

Bountiful's foot spent more time on the brake than the gas pedal of the Model T as she cruised from mountains to foothills to the flat plain paralleling the Boise River, descending three thousand feet by the time she reached the elegant homes Boise's elite had built on East Warm Springs Avenue. The temperature there was twenty degrees higher than in Paradise and she removed her scarf and gloves. A few blocks farther along, she was at the center of the downtown and found a parking place near the Idanha Hotel—a grand, six-story structure with towering turrets on three corners. Second in stature only to the state capitol a few blocks away, its registry was perhaps more prominent, boasting such notables as Theodore Roosevelt, William Howard Taft, and famed Scopes "Monkey Trial" opponents William Jennings Bryan and Clarence Darrow. A tall, slender doorman greeted Bountiful when she walked up the short flight of steps to the main entrance of the hotel. His hair was white, his manner gentlemanly, his skin black.

"Good morning, Lester," she greeted him.

"Mornin', Miss Dollarhyde," he said softly, pulling open the door. "Welcome to the Idanha Hotel."

Inside, a modest lobby led to a front desk where a thick-browed clerk in a stiff collar penned entries into a ledger. Opposite him was a wide staircase with a small bar tucked beneath it. The Volstead Act would not be in force until January 1920 and the glass shelves behind the bar still boasted bottles of whiskey and gin. The rest of the lobby had a modest collection of padded furniture, a few round tables, and a grand piano.

The desk clerk looked up when Bountiful entered. His name was Hershfield. She knew him and he knew her. Even though the exorbitantly priced ten-dollars-per-night rooms were reserved for white guests only, Bountiful had visited the lobby-level tearoom many times, the quaint salon accessible to anyone who could afford ten cents for a cup of tea with another twelve cents for a rum-soaked almond croissant or piece of cranberry cake. Hershfield offered a frown in place of a greeting.

"I'm here on business," Bountiful told him. "I'm to meet Mister John Goodlow in the tearoom. He's a guest of this hotel."

"What sort of business?"

"I'm to interview him. I'm representing the town council of Paradise."

The clerk sniffed. "Really? Since when did colored women start doing a white man's job?"

"Since I became president of the town council."

Hershfield put down his fountain pen and reached for his desk telephone. "Room 5F, Nancy," he said to the hotel operator. He looked at Bountiful, eyes poisonous. "I'll notify Mister Goodlow that you're waiting... And you'd best watch your damned tone, girl."

Inside the tearoom Bountiful took a seat near a bank of tall windows overlooking Main Street. A server in an immaculate short-coat and carefully knotted tie took her order, then scurried off. He returned with a pot of tea, a small pitcher of milk, and a blueberry scone. Bountiful sat and waited, sipping tea and nibbling on the scone as she looked out the window. The mid-morning sun was still behind the hotel, and as it rose, the tall spires of the Idanha cast shadows that extended down west-bound Main and south-bound Ninth. It was an evocative conflation of light and dark, but Bountiful was oblivious.

*Every time*, she fumed... *Every goddamned time!*

Hershfield's attitude was not unusual. She'd endured similar treatment in Washington, DC. On the few occasions when her lighter skin and blue eyes had evoked enough uncertainty to allow service at a whites-only establishment she'd never relaxed, knowing the pinch-nosed maître d' would evict her the moment he realized she wasn't pale enough to meet his restaurant's standards. Bountiful glanced at the clock on the wall, an elegant Victorian piece with a frame boasting intricate leaf and flourish carvings on the top and bottom. It was twenty minutes past ten o'clock in the morning. She was early, her meeting with John Goodlow still a few minutes off. The wait, combined with the acidic looks Hershfield tossed her way from his lobby station, made her nervous and she finished her tea quickly, afterward pouring another cup as a horse-drawn wagon rumbled past on the street outside, the loud clip-clop of the horses' hooves on the brick-paved thoroughfare muffling the sound of approaching footsteps.

"Well, well, well... What brings you down to the big city, Miss Bountiful Dollarhyde?"

Bountiful looked to the voice. Gerald Dredd stood in the

tearoom entry. He crossed to her table, then stood closer than a gentleman should. It was his way. A large man, both in both height and girth, he used his stature to intimidate—his face too close, his handshake held far too long, his general presentation calculated to overwhelm with size rather than character.

"Mister Dredd, I'm afraid that—"

"Another cup here, boy," the real estate mogul called out to the server as he took a seat at Bountiful's table. His dyed hair was swept into a cartoonish comb-over, his face caked with makeup. His suit was expensive but oversized and the too-long tail of his red necktie draped over a substantial belly. He eyed her scone. "I'll have one of these blueberry things too," he told the waiter. He watched the fellow hurry off, then reposed his question. "So…what convinced you to grace we humble Boise-ans with your presence, Miss Dollarhyde?"

"I'm here to represent the town council," Bountiful told him. "I'm meeting someone. He'll be here shortly, so you might want to—"

"Represent them for what?"

Bountiful glanced at the ornate wall clock. Her appointment with Goodlow was still five minutes off.

"It's about the houses we're offering."

Dredd nodded. "Clever move…putting those places up for sale. I didn't see it coming. Your idea, right?"

"No."

"You're being modest. You're the smartest person in that shithole. I get it. I'm a very smart person myself. The smartest, really. I have a very large…."

Dredd hesitated, as if searching for a word to impress her.

"Buh-rain," he finally managed, tapping the side of his head with a finger. "I have a very large brain."

"How nice for you," Bountiful replied.

The waiter returned with Dredd's scone, along with an emp-ty cup and saucer. "I'll have another pot ready in a moment, sir," he said.

"No need," Dredd replied, reaching for Bountiful's teapot.

He served himself, then leaned back in his chair and slurped noisily.

"What's this we have here?" he mused, setting his cup down as he looked out the window. Bountiful followed his gaze. Up the street, a policeman hurried toward the hotel, the sides of his head shaved, patches of straw-colored hair poking out from beneath his short-billed cap. His wide belt held a holstered service revolver with an empty loop for the nightstick he gripped in one hand, ominously tapping its blunt end against his thigh. He reached the hotel and took the front steps two at a time. Moments later he appeared in the tearoom doorway, his eyes settling on Bountiful.

"Get up, girl!" he barked. "You ain't supposed to be in here." He approached the table, his face twisted into a scowl, his knuckles scarred. "Didja hear me? You ain't got no right to be here."

Bountiful placed her cup back on its saucer. *Count to five before responding to an angry white man,* Professor Beale, her faculty advisor at Howard, had always recommended. *And don't look them in the eye. They hate it when a colored person looks them in the eye.* It was sage counsel, although she preferred the attitude of a female cohort at the NAACP office. *Fuck those white bastards,* the large, unapologetic woman often advised. *Look 'em in the eye. This is the nation's capital. We ain't in the land o' fuckin' cotton.*

"I'm here to meet someone," Bountiful told the officer, her gaze directed at the pressed, white tablecloth. "The clerk at the front desk...Mister Hershfield...he knows me. I've been here before...many times."

The cop snorted. "Who do you think called the precinct, girl?"

Bountiful looked through the open doorway. Hershfield stood in front of his tall desk, arms crossed over his chest. He looked pleased.

"Now, get up!" the cop demanded. "Let's go!"

Bountiful felt her heart rate quicken. Hershfield was not her first snotty hotel clerk nor the brute of an officer towering above the table the only racist policeman she'd ever encountered. Such men were usually satisfied to merely humiliate her. But this cop was different. His rage wasn't on the surface; rather, it was rubbed into him like a thick hair pomade. The policeman's upper lip curled into a sneer.

"I ain't gonna tell you again—"

Perhaps, I can be of assistance, officer," Dredd unexpectedly intervened. Bountiful eyed him. He had once fancied her; indeed, the lascivious, old scoundrel's lurid attention was one of the reasons Grandma Maude had sent her away. *But people sometimes change,* she considered. Then Dredd fashioned a perverse smile and she realized he was the same man who'd unfailingly lived down to his reputation before she went away.

"We have laws here," the real estate baron began. "Lots of beautiful laws, very important laws, truly the best laws. More important, we have customs. Surely, you knew *that* Miss High-and-Mighty Dollarhyde. Surely, you knew niggers and white folks can't be in here together?" He nodded at the policeman. "Do your duty, officer," he said.

The cop grinned malevolently. "Didja hear that, girl? Get your black butt outta that chair."

In Washington, DC, Bountiful had once been slapped by a white woman who didn't want to share an elevator. She'd slapped her back and was subsequently arrested, afterward spending a night in jail with a few prostitutes. The women told her dirty jokes that were very funny and convinced her to take a puff from the only cigarette she'd smoked before or since. Professor Beale bailed her out the next morning and the charges were later dropped.

*Jail wasn't so bad,* she mused as she pointed her blue eyes at the cop.

"As I told you, I'm here to meet someone. I have a right to be here."

The cop's lips parted with surprise. Then his face slowly turned radish red, his ropy neck veins enlarging. "You ain't got no goddamned rights but the ones I give you!" he roared. He grabbed her arm and would have jerked her from the chair had a new voice not stopped him.

"What on earth are you doing?"

The straw-haired policeman stopped pulling and half-turned, maintaining his grip on Bountiful's arm. Framed in the tearoom entry was a handsome fellow in a perfectly tailored suit. He appeared youthful although silver peppered his hair at the temples.

"This young lady has every right to be here," the man said. "I insist you unhand her…immediately!"

*Goodlow?* Bountiful wondered. She'd pictured him as a white version of Professor Beale: small, vaguely absent-minded, horn-rimmed glasses, a tweed jacket with leather patches on the elbows. This fellow, however, was more than six feet tall and quite dashing—more a John Barrymore than a Professor John Goodlow. The well-dressed stranger approached the table. Close up, he was even taller and better-looking.

"Did you hear me, officer? Let her go and stand down." The confident, urbane fellow fixed steady eyes on the policeman, fashioning an aspect ironically both respectful and relentless. Slowly, the big cop's expression faded from snorting bull to dairy cow getting milked, and after a few moments, he released Bountiful's arm. "There's a good fellow," the stranger said.

As Bountiful reclaimed her chair, the cop retreated a few paces, nearly bumping into another hotel guest as the man entered the tearoom. Two or three finger-widths shorter than the cop, this one wore spectacles and a tweed coat, absent elbow patches. He carried a leather portfolio.

"I beg your pardon," he said to the officer, afterward leaning sideways to look around the mountainous fellow. His expression brightened when he saw Bountiful. "Miss Dollarhyde, I presume? Thank you for meeting me." He brushed past the cop and approached her with a hand extended.

"Who are you?" the policeman demanded.

The tweed-jacketed man stopped and turned. "You mean me?"

"Yeah, I mean you. Who are you?"

My name is Goodlow...John Goodlow."

The officer's head swiveled back to the handsome stranger. "And *you*... Who the hell are *you*?"

"Peycomson," the elegantly dressed man answered. "Meriwether Peycomson... Attorney at law."

Goodlow joined Bountiful at her table while Peycomson invited the cop and Dredd to join him in the lobby. There, the police officer offered up a good bit of fist shaking and finger pointing, but Peycomson remained unflappable, and eventually, the cop threw in the towel and left. Afterward Dredd and the dashing lawyer shared a few words and shook hands. Peycomson, alone, rejoined Bountiful and John Goodlow in the tearoom. "You already know my name, but let's make our acquaintances official," the attorney said when he reached their table. "I am Meriwether Peycomson." He nodded at Bountiful, a gesture made gallant by the way he accomplished it. He turned to Goodlow, offering a hand.

"A pleasure," Goodlow said, taking it. The two men then had a friendly hand grip contest that ended in a draw. Afterward Peycomson appraised Bountiful. "I heard the name Dollarhyde. Are you Miss Bountiful Dollarhyde...from Paradise, Idaho?"

"I am."

"What a wonderful coincidence...despite our inauspicious beginning. May I join you?" Bountiful nodded and he took a seat.

"Mister Peycomson is buying one of our homes in Paradise," she told Goodlow. She shifted her attention back to the lawyer. "Although, I didn't know you were in the area."

"I'm actually in Boise on another matter," Peycomson replied. "A quick bit of business as it turns out. I leave tomorrow." He looked at Goodlow. "Another penny mansion purchaser, I presume. We're to be neighbors?"

"Perhaps," Goodlow said. "I hope so, anyway. I'm here for the interview."

Peycomson's eyes flickered. "I'm intruding," he said. "Forgive me. I'll leave you both to it."

He rose, then paused.

"I'm free this evening. Perhaps, we could all dine together? I'm told the restaurant in this hotel is excellent."

"Good of you to ask," Goodlow responded. "I would very much enjoy that."

"Miss Dollarhyde?" Peycomson urged Bountiful. The handsome lawyer stroked the side of his nose. There was a wedding band on his ring finger.

"Thank you, Mister Peycomson," Bountiful quickly declined. "But I must return to Paradise this afternoon."

"A pity," he replied, adding the smile of a man who understands the effect he has on women. "Another time, perhaps?" He looked at Goodlow. "Until this evening, sir... Shall we say seven o'clock?"

The men agreed on the time. Peycomson then made his way back to the lobby and out the front door of the hotel. Bountiful watched through the window as he walked up the street, his strides long and confident. She'd not been with a man since her brief engagement to the Justice Department lawyer was kiboshed by her own reluctance and her fiancé's white family. It had been months, but she could still recall the touch of his hand, the weight of his body on hers. He had been a decent enough fellow and was very good-looking. The tall Portland lawyer was terribly good-looking, too, although his Mrs. Peycomson-deficient demeanor made her wary.

"You're frowning," Goodlow said.

"Am I? I wasn't aware. Forgive me."

"If you need a moment—"

"I'm fine, thank you."

Bountiful dabbed at her lips with a cloth napkin, rearranged it in her lap, and then let her gaze again settle on Goodlow.

"I must be honest," she began. "Some in Paradise have memories of your uncle that are less than favorable."

Goodlow grinned. "So...we've begun the interview?"

"Yes."

"May I first ask a question?"

"Of course."

"From Mister Peycomson's reaction, it would seem I am the only applicant for whom an interview was scheduled?"

Bountiful nodded. "Yes... Please don't be offended."

"And your reservations are because of my uncle?"

"The others on the council all knew him. I did not. They thought it most fair if you made your case solely with me."

"Judge and jury?"

Bountiful smiled. "More like employer and job-seeker. I'm not that severe."

Goodlow chuckled. "Thank goodness. So...a job interview. I completely understand, particularly since Uncle Horace apparently left a bad impression. I'm not surprised. That was his *modus operendi.*"

"You were close?"

"Not really. He was my great-uncle...my paternal grandfather's brother. They inherited a wholesale grocery and dry goods business in Chicago. Grandfather Dodsworth was younger but a much better businessman. When my great-grandfather died, Grandpa Dodsworth was named overall head of the company while Horace merely got a seat on the board."

Goodlow removed a sheaf of papers from his portfolio and tapped them on the flat surface of the table to straighten their edges. "My grandfather was very astute. He fostered expansions into finance and real estate, then started a brokerage that held one of the first seats on the Chicago Stock Exchange. Eventually, the original wholesale business became a relatively insignificant part of the portfolio and Uncle Horace was allowed to run it."

He smiled. "Forgive me, Miss Dollarhyde. I'm giving you a history lecture. It's a bad habit. Name a topic and I'll take an hour to reach a conclusion that's only two minutes away."

"Not at all," Bountiful answered. "Please go on."

Goodlow laid his papers flat on the table. The server was

nearby and he motioned to him. "May I have a cup of coffee, please?" he requested when the fellow approached. He looked at Bountiful. "Anything more for you?" She shook her head and the server withdrew to his coffee station as Goodlow went on. "Long story short...Uncle Horace embezzled a good bit of money and then absconded. He reappeared in Chicago years later. He'd supposedly made and lost a bundle here in Idaho during the gold rush."

The server returned with Goodlow's coffee before he could continue. He blew the steam from it and tentatively sipped, afterward returning the cup to its saucer.

"Is your uncle still alive?" Bountiful asked.

"No... He's been gone a long time. An unfortunate end, I'm afraid. He fell in with Diamond Jim Colosimo's gang...numbers, off-track betting, shylocking, and so forth. He embezzled from Diamond Jim too. Not a good idea." He issued a low whistle, drawing a finger across his throat.

Bountiful caught her breath. "They *killed* him?"

"That's the story. I was only twelve at the time. My mother hid the newspaper when it happened, but I dug it out of the trash. There was a picture on the front page of Uncle Horace lying in a pool of blood."

"I'm so sorry," Bountiful said.

Goodlow shrugged. "I was twelve, remember? Gory pictures were fascinating. Besides, I hardly knew him. He was loud and wore flashy clothes. My mother hated him and so I did too."

"Were you and your mother close?"

"We were. I'm much more like her than my father."

"Tell me about her."

"She's gone now. A lovely woman...gracious, warm, and very musical. An excellent pianist. She loved books."

"And your father?"

Goodlow hesitated. "Good provider... He worked a lot when I was growing up. Still does, I'm told. Not the type to get on the floor and play with children. I have two brothers. They joined Dad at the firm, but I wasn't interested in the family business." He laughed humorlessly. "In Dad's eyes, I'm the black sheep of the Goodlows."

"Even though you're a college professor?"

"Even though."

Bountiful liked him. John Goodlow seemed to understand the context of his life. He'd come from money, but money didn't drive him. "Tell me about your wife and children," she pressed on.

Goodlow's face lit up. "My wife, Annie, is the dearest person one could imagine… A wonderful mother, a wonderful partner in life. I am so fortunate. We have a boy, George, and a girl, Francine…little Frannie. She just turned three and is so much like her mother."

"And is George like you?"

"George, I fear, will not follow in my footsteps. We both like climbing trees, but I'm the only one interested in photosynthesis." Goodlow laughed at his own joke. "Maybe that will change," he continued. "But it doesn't matter. He's a happy boy and very affectionate…very sweet. He likes to climb up next to Annie or me and find a hollow in us he can curl into."

The steam was off Goodlow's coffee and he took another drink. "What else can I tell you? Do you need to see my financials? I brought them." He reached for his sheaf of papers.

"That won't be necessary, Mister Goodlow," Bountiful said. "I vote yes."

By one o'clock, she was on her way back to Paradise. That evening John Goodlow and Meriwether Peycomson dined at Morrison's, the elegant restaurant attached to the Idanha Hotel. Goodlow enjoyed lamb chops with scalloped potatoes while Peycomson had Idaho trout and rice. After dinner they retired to the lobby bar where Gerald Dredd joined them for scotch and cigars.

# 7

## July and the Bolshevik Revolution

Gerald Dredd was in a foul mood. Firing two of the maids didn't help, particularly when The Fourth Mrs. Dredd rehired them while he was still within earshot. He then accused Freddie of deficient manliness and Carl of freeloading and general dim-wittedness, afterward storming out and climbing into his Vauxhall for the trip to the downtown headquarters of Dredd Enterprises. He insisted that Geraldine come along. His eldest, Junior, was already at the office.

Dredd's private executive suite at Dredd Enterprises was a workplace lacking evidence of much work—no filing cabinets, no open ledgers, no correspondence in either his incoming or outgoing boxes. His desk was similarly virginal with only a leather-wrapped inkpad, an unsullied fountain pen inside its holder, and a framed eight-by-ten photograph of his current family—the stunning Fourth Mrs. Dredd glamorously assessing the camera lens with then-infant Freddie in her lap, her toothy, grinning husband offering an inexplicable thumbs-up. Standing behind them, Junior smirked, Carl sulked, and Geraldine looked miserable.

"Everything's in place now, right, Dad?" Junior inquired after joining his father and sister from his own office down the hall.

"I don't know what you mean," Dredd, Sr. said, glancing uneasily at Geraldine. She'd taken a wing chair in the corner near the office's only window. Deer Point, a peak north of the city, was framed in the opening and Geraldine seemed lost in the distant clouds that hovered above it.

"How much is it gonna cost us?" Junior asked.

Dredd glowered at his son. "Are you not listening? I don't know what the hell you mean."

"I was just wondering—"

"Walls have ears, goddammit!"

Junior wilted, and not for the first time, Dredd lamented the feudal mandate that demanded he bequeath the family business to an inept eldest son. His objection was ironic since Dredd was inept as well—a terrible businessman who'd inherited his fortune from a canny and ruthless father. Friederich Dreffke had run away from a noose in Austria, arriving at Ellis Island in 1856 where a sardonic immigration official rechristened him Friederich "Dredd." After a few years in Virginia as a bounty hunter of runaway slaves, he'd joined the Confederate Army in 1861, deserted it in 1863, and then ventured west to Millers Camp, Idaho, a gold rush town on the Secesh River. There, he discovered that panning for gold was hard work and moved again, this time south to Paradise where Horace Goodlow made him the town sheriff. Paid per arrest with supplemental bribery and extortion income, he was rich by the time his only son, Gerald, was born in 1868.

"May I leave?" Geraldine suddenly asked her father. They were the first words she'd uttered all day. Dredd Sr. appraised his daughter. Tall with ample breasts and shapely legs, Geraldine's long hair was the color of threshed wheat, her complexion flawless, her lips full. Her father's face was partly hers, as well, but she more resembled her mother, and on those occasions when the sway of her hips or a soft line of cleavage recalled his first wife, Dredd Sr. was at a loss to remember why he'd replaced The First Mrs. Dredd with The Second, Third, and Fourth models.

Dredd angled a look at Junior, lifting his chin toward the door. "I need to go over something with your sister. Head down to Morrison's. We'll join you for lunch in half an hour."

Geraldine's typically impassive expression faded, her face turning ashen. "No, Daddy," she protested. "Let's all go together."

"It will only be a few minutes."

"But I'm really hungry. Can't we all go now?"

"What I have to show you is very important, darling."

Dredd took Junior by the elbow and led him toward the reception area outside his office. "We'll be along," he said, pushing him out and then closing the door. Junior waited until he heard the click of the lock, then looked at Dredd's assistant. Forty-three years old, Iris Campbell had been with her employer since young enough to get a couch's-eye view of the ceiling on the other side of the same heavy, closed door.

"Bye, Iris," Junior said.

"So long, Junior," she replied.

Twenty minutes later Geraldine and her father emerged from his office. Geraldine hurried into the outer corridor and kept going, but Dredd stopped at Iris's desk. "Call Bertram Mole," he told his assistant. "Have him meet me here at one-thirty."

Dredd had a regiment of lawyers to cover a wide range of legal problems, including simple real estate transactions, tax-avoidance schemes, and more than occasional payoffs to women who'd had the effrontery to protest unwanted advances or become pregnant. Bertram Mole was a member of the Idaho attorney general's office, but the AG looked the other way when Dredd used a state employee to leverage political opponents and campaign donors. Mole—a conniving and ambitious little attack chihuahua—had jumped at the opportunity to tie his own possibilities to the lieutenant governor, later adding Dredd's business and family matters to his legal responsibilities after the real estate magnate discovered that The Fourth Mrs. Dredd had hedged against possible disinheritance by sleeping with his other lawyers. Mole was impregnable to such forays, his prodigious ambition obscuring a pusillanimous libido.

The vole-like attorney showed up at exactly one-thirty but had to wait, sitting on the edge of a reception area chair for half an hour, one knee nervously quivering, his eyes flitting about the room as if searching for cast-off scraps of food. He half rose when Dredd returned alone from his luncheon at Morrison's, but the big man swept past without acknowledging him, issuing a loud fart on the way to his private office. A moment later Dredd called out through the open door.

"Get in here, goddammit!"

Mole went in and closed the door, and for the next few minutes, the only sound leaking through the thick, darkly stained walnut was the rumble of Dredd's voice. Eventually, the little attorney poked his head out, squinting as if suddenly exposed to bright light.

"Boss wants a copy of his will," he told Iris.

She retrieved a file for him from a corner safe and Mole again retired to Dredd's private chamber. Fifteen minutes later he reemerged. Dredd followed him out.

"I'll write up the changes you've proposed and get back to you by Friday," Mole said.

"By tomorrow."

"I'll need more—"

"By tomorrow."

Mole flinched, then nodded. "Fine...by tomorrow." Dredd returned to his office and Mole made for the door leading to the outer corridor, pausing to look back when he reached it.

"Good day, Miss Campbell," he said with a perfunctory nod.

"See ya, Bertram," Iris replied without looking up.

❧

By July 1919, the new families were all in town. John and Annie Goodlow were in the old Feldstein place while Meriwether Peycomson, his wife, Evangeline, and their son, Felix, had moved into assayer John Stiveley's former mansion at the top of the cul-de-sac marking the end of Only Real Street. The Portland attorney and his wife arrived with a nanny they introduced to their new neighbors as Frau Gerta. "She don't look like no nanny I ever seen," Goldstrike opined. It was true. The tall German woman's figure was not stout but svelte, her legs clad in silk stockings rather than support hose, the hair falling to her shoulders not dishwater gray but the color of hay at harvest. Indeed, with her imperious demeanor and classical beauty she seemed a better match for the debonair lawyer than Evangeline Peycomson, a pale woman with shadows beneath her deep eyes, her hair mousy brown, her expression vaguely fearful.

Evangeline immediately established herself as nothing more than an occasional face in a window. "My wife has suffered from the blues since our son was born," Peycomson explained. "That's why I hired Frau Gerta…to help with little Felix while his poor mother recuperates." Evangeline never ventured out, instead dispatching Frau Gerta to shop for groceries and other household items. Oskar Nilsen spoke German, and because his son, Anders, had succumbed to the Spanish flu rather than a Hun bullet, he felt no ill will toward the Peycomson governess.

"Guten morgen, Frau Gerta," he cheerfully greeted her when she visited his store. "Und wie geht es dir an diesem schönen tag?" *And how are you this fine day?*

"Bitte erfüllen sie diese liste," she'd respond in a flat voice. *Please fulfill this list.*

As odd as Mrs. Peycomson was, her son Felix was even odder—a freakish, disproportionate little fellow whose head was too large for his body. Usually carried about by Frau Gerta, the boy didn't skip or run; rather, he waddled with his elbows held high, or swayed like a sailor trying to stay upright on a pitching deck. He was as shy as his mother, and even after several weeks in town, he'd been seen only from a distance.

"The kid's five years old," Maude remarked at the first town council meeting after the Peycomsons' arrival. "And his mama is still down in the dumps? Pretty long time for baby blues if you ask me."

"They're four more warm bodies added to the population," Goldstrike pointed out. "I suspect we oughta count their goddamned heads rather than shrink 'em."

Peycomson had engaged a contractor during his previous visit to Boise and a renovation crew was on-site shortly after the family's arrival, repairing the roof, rebuilding the rear veranda, and cleaning up the overgrown landscaping. The lawyer renewed his promise to review the town's legal status free of charge. "There's no need to hire another attorney," he reassured the council. "Paradise is my home now. It's my civic duty."

Up the street from the Peycomsons, the daily truck deliveries to the Coolers had slowed along with the bangs and thuds of work. With the slowdown, Cooler's sons—the somewhat venerable Gus and his simianesque brothers, Vic and Nat—camped out almost every night at the Gold Rush Saloon along with sister, Trixie, and brother-in-law, Joshua Purdue of the vaunted Massachusetts Purdues. Like Charlotte and her father, Trixie and her brothers were more familiar than familial with each other and the boys joined the regular gaggle of millhands, loggers, and trail guides who enjoyed watching Trixie bend over a pool table in a way that offered an enticing view of cleavage from the north and another of her wide bottom to any backside connoisseurs stationed to the south.

Joshua Purdue was less enthusiastic about the addition of his brothers-in-law to the Gold Rush's regulars. He was fussy and effeminate and Gus, Vic, and Nat delighted in flicking his ears or reaching under his coat to pull down his trousers, howling with laughter as the de-pantsed fellow struggled to cover himself. In mid-July, around two o'clock in the morning, Lariat Comfort was awakened by the sounds of a violent argument coming from the Cooler mansion next door. He scrambled from bed, climbed onto the roof from a window, and watched as Joshua Purdue spilled out of the house in a way unlikely to have been voluntary, landing on his face in the grass of the backyard.

"I didn't sign up for this, goddammit!" the only in-law in the Cooler brood shouted after regaining his feet. Vic Cooler—a lantern-jawed knuckle-dragger with wide-spaced teeth—then lurched out the door and chased Purdue to the front of the house. The next morning Joshua's roadster was no longer parked on Only Real Street.

"Joshua has been called away on business," Thaddeus reassured Goldstrike and Oskar when they were dispatched to press him for an explanation. "Prominent family, don't you know?

Complicated affairs and all that. Do not despair. He shall return."

That evening, Goldstrike, Oskar Nilsen, and newspaperman Ed Riggins gathered on the boardwalk fronting the mercantile, passing around a jug while discussing the contraction of Coolers from eight to seven. "From what Lariat told me, I don't 'spect we'll see that Purdue fella back," Goldstrike observed. "And we ain't seen hide nor hair o' the missus since she took sick. Next thing we know, they'll tell us she's kicked the damned bucket. Good thing that gal o' theirs is gonna have a baby, the way them folks is whittlin' away at themselves."

Up the street from the Peycomsons, the DeMille renovation was finished with Amon and Sarah happy to give tours. Bountiful and Sarah had become fast friends and the young schoolteacher reported to the town council that the cat odor was gone, replaced by the smell of paint, varnish, and clean sheets. Sarah and Amon were a good team, proud of one another's efforts. "Look how Amon rebuilt the railing to these stairs," Sarah proudly pointed out when snoopy Oskar and Sonia Nilsen stopped by to check things out. "The boys helped," Amon quickly added. "And Sarah and Jeanette made those curtains."

"Well, look at that," Nilsen exclaimed, fingering the perfect stitching on the drapes. "Gosh all Sunday, Sarah, I'll betcha these could be store-bought in Boise or Salt Lake City. Heck, I could sell curtains o' this quality in my store if you've a mind."

The only laggard among the newcomers was Goodlow. His wife, Annie, was as delightful as he'd described and his children, George and Frannie, were adorable. However, in planning the renovation of their mansion, both John and Annie were a pair of thumbs searching for fingers that might get a proper grip on the project. "We're still trying to decide on contractors," Annie reported to Bountiful. "John is researching each of the candidates very carefully. He's methodical and thorough. It may take him some time to decide, but it's always the right decision."

"It would be good to get started," Bountiful cautiously encouraged the former college professor's wife. "It's already July. You won't be able to get supplies up here in the winter. We get weathered in early, sometimes by October."

"Weathered in?"

"Snow… We're sometime snowed in by the end of October. Didn't Missoula get shut in sometimes? They're at a higher elevation than Boise."

"Oh yes, snow… We got a lot of snow…in Missoula. It's very pretty. I love the snow."

Eventually, the council asked Amon to perform a walkthrough with the Goodlows. "I did my place for about six hundred dollars," he told John after completing his tour. "Yours is in better shape. If you like, my boys and I could fix it up for five hundred…maybe five-fifty."

"Five-fifty," Goodlow repeated, brow furrowed. "Does that include your profit?"

"We're neighbors, John. I'll do it at cost. If you get electricity up and running, you can return the favor…help us power up." The men shook hands, and soon, the former Feldstein residence rang with the hammer-and-saw clamor of remodeling.

Relieved of the obligation to vet contractors, Goodlow immediately turned his attention to Paradise's electrical grid, his foot-dragging replaced by confidence as he took the reins of a horse he understood how to ride at a gallop. The fledgling Idaho Power Company had run a cable to the west edge of town with the power stepped down to 400 volts at the terminal end. "That's much too high for residential use," the electrical engineer told the council at a special meeting. "I can build a transformer to bring the voltage down to a useable level, but we'll have to pay for it on our own, along with the line that runs through town. I've spoken with Idaho Power. They won't cover those." Questions followed, all aimed at determining the cost. "The basic transformer will be cheap," Goodlow revealed. "It's just copper coils around an iron core. I can build it for about fifteen dollars. The bigger cost is in the cover. It must be fabricated according to IPC specs…weatherproofing and so forth…another twenty-five or thirty dollars. As for our power line, if we place our transformer near the terminal point of the IPC pole, Meriwether Peycomson's home would be the most distant at about one thousand feet away. The posts we'd set can't be farther apart than one hundred feet, so that's ten of them installed at about seventy dollars each. The connecting wire, insulators, fasteners, and labor will round it up to about one hundred dollars per pole. Then there's the Idaho Power charges to connect each household to our common line and add a meter…fifty dollars…plus the cost to rough-in and finish-wire the homes."

Bountiful had scribbled figures on a tablet as Goodlow spoke. "That's almost eleven hundred dollars to get power to one house," she remarked when he was finished. "We don't have enough in the town treasury. We'd have to impose a special assessment."

"Eleven hunnert goddamned dollars!" Goldstrike complained, his ascetic Maine roots resurrected. "When I threw in with this electrical bullshit, I didn't think it was gonna bankrupt me. Hell, I been gettin' along with oil lamps my whole life. Don't see what use I'd have fer electrical now."

Goodlow's face fell. "It's possible my numbers are wrong," he said. "They're just estimates." He suddenly brightened. "I'm willing to cover the cost of the transformer on my own, Goldstrike. That would save some money."

"Thanks, John," Goldstrike said. "But that don't cover much. Most o' the cost is in them poles. Sorry, but I make a motion we shit-can the whole goddamned thing." A murmur of assent arose, but Bountiful gaveled it down by lightly tapping her finger on the table.

"There's another option," she said. "We could form a cooperative."

"Cooperative?" Oskar Nilsen echoed squinting suspiciously. "That's a Bolshevik thing, ain't it? I've read about them doggone Reds what took over Russia. They steal a man's profit and give it to folks that ain't willin' to break a sweat. It ain't American, doggonit. Heck, it's treason. That's what it is…treason! I want one of them new-fangled neon signs for my store, mind you, but I ain't willin' to betray my darned country to get it."

Bountiful smiled. "It isn't treason, Mister Nilsen. The cooperative wouldn't be a government enterprise. It would be both jointly and privately owned. The common property would include the power poles, the main cable running through Paradise from the IPC line, and John's transformer. The founding members of the cooperative will bear the initial cost and they'll be the owners. Materials and labor to connect the cooperative's common line to an individual home will be private property with its installation and upkeep the responsibility of the homeowner. After the cooperative is established, new members will pay a pro-rated fee to join. That way, once the entire town has electrical power, everyone will have contributed equally over time."

Ed Riggins had voted for socialist Eugene Debs in the 1912 presidential election. He loved Bountiful's proposal. "That's an excellent idea, Madame President," he said. "Well done."

"It's a perfect solution," John Goodlow agreed. "In fact, when everyone is on board, I'm sure IPC will pick up the cost to repair and maintain the common line. They'll probably buy out the cooperative. That's what's happened back in Pennsylvania."

"Pennsylvania?" Goldstrike posed. "I thought you was from Montana."

"I read about it, Goldstrike. It's common knowledge among electrical engineers."

"Regardless," Bountiful interceded, "it appears we can form a cooperative without risking a Bolshevik revolution." She smiled at Oskar. "Would you agree, Mister Nilsen?"

A brief discussion ensued, mostly listening to Oskar complain about the one Russian he'd encountered in his life, a fellow who took off his shoes and put his smelly feet on the seat next to Sonia Nilsen during a train trip the storekeeper and his wife once made to Seattle. After he ran out of steam, the council authorized John Goodlow to determine how many citizens wanted to be part of the inaugural Paradise Electrical Cooperative. A week later another special session was held where the engineer reported that the founding membership would number eight: the owners of the five mansions on Only Real Street plus Nilsen's General Store, Arnold Chang's Gold Rush Saloon, and Ed Riggins' *Idaho World* office. All prospective members were in attendance and were pleased to learn that the estimated cost had been reduced after Amon DeMille offered to cut and set the poles at half the Idaho Power Company charge.

"Amon can do the rough-in and finish work to wire participating homes and businesses too. He estimates the cost at around eleven cents per square foot," John Goodlow further reported. "That's a bargain. I've seen it cost two or three times that much."

A motion to create the PEC was passed and Oskar Nilsen was the first to invest, the Red Scare paling in comparison to the novelty of a neon sign above the door of his mercantile. "It'll be worth every penny to see 'Nilsen's General Store' blinkin' on and off at night," he offered while putting his signature on an official pledge.

"Waste o' money, if ya ask me," Goldstrike cautioned. "Ain't nobody wanderin' around this town at night 'cept'n coyotes. None o' them critters can read, so yer goddamned sign'll be blinkin' on and off fer nuthin'."

The other founding members of the PEC signed, as well, including Thaddeus Cooler who provided an Egyptian ruby ring as collateral. "This ring once belonged to Cleopatra," he claimed. "Pasha Abbas Helmi the Second gave it to me in 1900 following my performance in Cairo as King Lear." He assured his new partners that his financial affairs would at last be disentangled within a few weeks, allowing him to provide actual money in place of Queen Victoria's pocket watch, the Pasha's ring, and the tab his children had run up at the Gold Rush Saloon. "There will be cash aplenty at that time, dear friends... Cash aplenty."

After the meeting, Bountiful and Maude went home and

apprised Lariat of the council's decision. He immediately bolted for the old Feldstein mansion. "I'm your husband's new electrical apprentice," he announced after Annie Goodlow responded to the banging on the front door. She sent him to the stable in back where John had set up a shop. The former college professor hadn't anticipated an assistant, but following a brief discussion with the boy genius, was glad to have one; indeed, it wasn't long before the pair were happily discussing megawatts, direct versus alternating current, and Faraday's Law while making plans to build the PEC transformer.

Other than the boisterous sounds of construction that dominated days on Only Real Street and the late-night domestic disturbances at the Coolers—less frequent with the departure of Joshua Purdue of the vaunted Massachusetts Purdues— nothing much happened in Paradise for the rest of the month and the calendar turned the corner on August. Five months were left in 1919, the ominous 1920 census drawing nearer and nearer.

# 8

## OUR AMERICAN COUSIN

"Thaddeus is gonna stage a play," Maude excitedly informed the town council at their August meeting. "He plans to cast people from right here in Paradise. I've been promised an important role." Oskar Nilsen—the son of Norwegian immigrants—encouraged Cooler to pick a play from the canon of Henrik Ibsen. Told the actor/director planned to stage the once popular *Our American Cousin* by Tom Taylor, Oskar sulked until learning that he was in line for the role of Sir Edward Trenchard.

"Cooler says I got a regal look about me," he told Goldstrike.

The former prospector snorted. "About as regal as a mountain goat...*Sir* Oskar."

"Yeah, well, Cooler's an actor so he for darn tootin' knows more about it than you do, I betcha," Oskar retorted. "He says I'm perfect for this Sir Edward fella... Called me a 'fine representative of the bourgeoisie' here in Paradise."

"Booze-waujee?" Goldstrike observed. "Sounds like soup to me."

As more details emerged, it was revealed that Thaddeus and Maude would play Lord Dundreary and Mrs. Mountchessington, respectively, with still pregnant Charlotte Cooler Purdue as Mary Meredith, a humble milk maid. The remaining roles would be cast after open auditions. Cooler further reported that his wife, Wanda, had recovered and would provide piano accompaniment, his sons serving as stagehands. The play was to be performed at the Gold Rush Saloon, which had an actual stage and piano. The auditions would take place there, as well, and when the day arrived it was apparent that more people wanted to be on the stage than in the audience. With hopefuls coming from as far away as Horseshoe Bend, Glenns Ferry, and Placerville, the line extended down Goodlow Road to Only Real Street.

Maude, whom Cooler had named co-producer, joined him for the auditions, the pair of them side by side in chairs facing the stage. Thaddeus had a clipboard with a worksheet listing the play's characters, a blank line after each of the yet-to-be cast parts. Oskar Nilsen was the first to try out, and as promised, he was rewarded with the role of Sir Edward Trenchard. Meriwether Peycomson was next. Following an exciting rendition of "Charge of the Light Brigade," he was tapped to play the dashing Lieutenant Harry Vernon of the Royal Navy. After Bountiful's audition, Thaddeus asked her to play Georgina Mountchessington—love interest for his character in the production and daughter to Maude's. "You and Mrs. Dollarhyde as mother and daughter will bring verisimilitude to the roles," he rationalized. Bountiful declined, worried the director's romantic attention might not be confined to the stage. Cooler then offered her the part of Florence Trenchard, fiancée to Lieutenant Harry Vernon. Bountiful accepted and the auditions proceeded.

As the day went on it was apparent that most of the would-be actors were quite terrible, their expositions bellowed at the rafters or whispered to the stage floor. The more enthusiastic evoked despair by histrionically wringing their hands or joy by clasping them to their breasts, falling to their knees, and gazing heaven-ward with religious zeal. Thaddeus capped each audition with the same encouragement. "Wonderful! Absolutely convincing! We'll be in touch!" After a break for lunch, the casting session stretched into the afternoon with two critical parts yet to be assigned: Asa Trenchard and Richard Coyle. While Cooler's Lord Dundreary was a comic turn with the most lines in the play and myriad opportunities for laugh-inducing improvisations, Asa and Coyle were the official leading man and chief villain. Cooler had tentatively penciled in a millhand from Horseshoe Bend for Asa, but still considered him a last resort. The fellow was decent-looking and had Asa Trenchard's rough-edged qualities, but he couldn't act—his audition an imitation of the manic grinning and leaping about he'd seen Douglas Fairbanks accomplish in his derring-do moving pictures. As for the role of Richard Coyle, no realistic candidate had emerged as the day grew longer and the line shorter.

Around three o'clock Willie Barkley moved to the front of the queue. He had combed his hair and wore his army uniform. A sword, made from a three-foot-long lath, was tucked into his belt. Wrapped with adhesive tape on one end to make a haft, the other end was whittled to a point.

"And what fine-looking fellow do we have we here?" Thaddeus boomed.

Willie pushed an unruly lock of hair off his forehead. "Private William Barkley, sir."

Maude leaned toward Cooler. "Willie's crazy sometimes," she whispered. "Maybe it would help if we gave him a small part to play."

The old actor studied the ex-soldier. Three inches above six feet tall with wavy, chestnut hair and a rugged build, Willie was quite handsome, his nose Roman, his chin manly.

"He may be crazy," Cooler softly observed. "But he *looks* like a star." He smiled at Willie, holding up a hand. "Proceed, my boy... Fill the room with your talent."

Willie unsheathed his makeshift sword and faced the rear of the stage. For a few moments he was motionless. Then he whirled about, his eyes blazing, his face heroically alit.

"'Once more unto the breach, dear friends, once more,'" he cried out, thrusting his sword at the ceiling. "'Or close the wall up with our English dead! In peace there's nothing so becomes a man as modest stillness and humility. But when the blast of war blows in our ears, then imitate the action of the tiger: stiffen the sinews, conjure up the blood, disguise fair nature with hard-favored rage. Then lend the eye a terrible aspect; let it pry through the portage of the head like the brass cannon; let the brow o'erwhelm it as fearfully as doth a galled rock o'erhang and jutty his confounded base, swilled with the wild and wasteful ocean.'"

"My God," Thaddeus murmured. "He's Henry the Fifth!"

Willie went on, pacing about the stage as if truly encouraging troops to enter, "once more unto the breach."

"'On, on, you noblest English, whose blood is fet from fathers of war-proof!" Willie continued, his voice pure and resounding. "'Fathers that, like so many Alexanders, have in these parts from morn till e'en fought and sheathed their swords for lack of argument.'"

It was a soaring performance. Willie was in full command of the role, offering more than the words of Shakespeare in the mouth of a character named Henry V. War had partially robbed him of sanity, but the insanity of that same war suffused his performance with the blood and sweat and flesh of an actual warrior king, elevating it into something larger and more profound than just art. It was life; indeed, Willie was not merely an actor playing Henry V. For those few magical minutes on the small stage of the Gold Rush Saloon in Paradise, Idaho, he *was* Henry V.

"'For there is none of you so mean and base that hath not noble luster in your eyes,'" he finished up. "'I see you stand like greyhounds in the slips, straining upon the start. The game's afoot. Follow your spirit, and upon this charge, cry God for Harry, England, and Saint George!'"

His performance completed, Willie held his pose—legs wide-spread, a fist on one hip, sword held high and triumphant. No one spoke for a few moments. Then Cooler stood and approached, kneeling when he reached the edge of the stage.

"Sire."

Willie blinked, staring at the old actor as if perplexed to see one of his knights assembled without his armor. He slowly lowered his arm and the lath with the carved tip slipped from his hand, clattering against the bare wooden planks.

"You must return to the castle and rest, your majesty," Thaddeus said, rising. He stepped onto the stage and picked up the sword, then took Willie's arm and led him off. "When you are refreshed, there's someone I want you to meet... His name is Asa Trenchard." He walked with Willie outside to the wide, uneven boardwalk fronting the Gold Rush Saloon. "Now away, my liege," Cooler proclaimed. "We shall meet anon."

"Which day is anon?"

Thaddeus chuckled. "It's not a day, dear boy. It's means *soon*. We shall meet *soon* to discuss your future. Your future arrives anon, and it's a very bright future… A very bright future, indeed."

Strung along the boardwalk outside the saloon, the line of aspirants yet to audition had diminished to a final dozen and Willie looked them over. As he did, the mask of Henry V dissolved, his face slowly twisting into a fevered grin.

"'Vengeance, boys!'" he abruptly shouted. "'Vengeance, plague, death, confusion!'"

Goldstrike was with the remaining auditioners. He had no desire to be in the play; rather, he'd shown up to see Willie's audition, sharing the opinion, while they'd waited, that Cooler's play, and theater in general, were both a lot of hooey. He approached and took Willie's arm.

"He'll be like this awhile," he told Cooler. "I'll look after 'im."

"Confusion," Willie muttered.

Goldstrike nodded. "It's okay, Willie… We're all confused."

The old prospector and the ex-doughboy headed up the street, Cooler watching until they'd stepped off the boardwalk and headed in the direction of the shack the two men shared on Mores Creek. Then he rejoined Maude inside the saloon and wrote Willie's name next to Asa Trenchard on his worksheet. "That young man may have been a private in the army," he told his co-producer, "but he's definitely a leading man in Paradise, Idaho."

The auditions resumed with a very nervous Jeanette DeMille next in line. Lariat Comfort—who had already won the part of Abel Murcott, a clerk—offered last-second encouragement.

"Talk loud and look at Mister Cooler," he told her. Jeanette nodded, then mounted the stage and assiduously avoided eye contact while breathily attempting something by Emily Dickinson inaudible to anyone beyond the tip of her nose. Halfway through, she was interrupted.

"WE'RE HERE!"

Jeanette stopped speaking, her eyes wide as she stared at the saloon's entry. Framed in the doorway were Gerald Dredd and his daughter.

"GERALDINE'S READY TO AUDITION!" Dredd bellowed. The real estate baron took his daughter's arm and pulled her toward the stage. Thaddeus rose as they approached him, lifting his chin.

"See here, sir…Miss DeMille was in the middle of her—"

"She's done," Dredd announced. He shot a look at Jeanette that spooked the teenager off the platform. She bolted for the door, neatly ducking under Cooler's raised hand without breaking stride, and then dashing past the Dredds, a trailing rush of air very slightly lifting the real estate baron's combover to reveal the bald, uncombable head beneath it.

"Very nice, Miss DeMille!" Thaddeus called out as she reached the door and then spilled onto the boardwalk. "Absolutely convincing! We'll be in touch!"

With the saloon's batwing doors still swinging and Gerald Dredd eyeing him expectantly, Cooler took a few moments to reestablish his authority as the play's director, giving his back to the real estate mogul and Geraldine, as he scribbled Jeanette's name onto his clipboard. "We'll find a minor part for Miss DeMille," he said to Maude. "The servant, Miss Sharpe, will be just the thing. I shall work with her…teach her how to project to the balcony."

"Jesus Christ! Are you gonna audition my daughter or do I have to—"

Cooler turned with pronounced deliberation and imperiously considered Dredd—his head tipped back, his expression one of contrived ennui.

"Thaddeus Cooler, Esquire," he sniffed.

Dredd's eyes narrowed to slits. "Lieutenant Governor Gerald Dredd," he responded, his title carefully enunciated.

"Mister Dredd, your daughter—"

"Lieutenant Governor Dredd...or *Mister* Lieutenant Governor. And it's Geraldine's turn. The other girl was terrible. Only an idiot would give her a part."

Cooler hesitated, sizing up the Boise politician. They were eye to eye in height, but Dredd had at least sixty pounds on the erstwhile Broadway luminary. It took the sniff out of him.

"Very well...*Mister* Lieutenant Governor," the actor said. "Your daughter may audition out of turn."

Dredd went to the bar and claimed a high, backless stool while Geraldine moved to the stage and Cooler remained standing. Once there, the young heiress adopted a finishing school pose—back arched, one foot forward, fingers clasped just below her breasts. She lifted her chin and began.

"'La Belle Dame Sans Merci,'" she recited. "By John Keats."

Her voice echoed with shocking malevolence that reverberated about the room, silencing the murmurs of the waiting auditioners and letting the air out of Thaddeus Cooler's knees. "My word," he whispered to Maude, sinking back onto his chair as Geraldine forged ahead, her pitch rising and falling with natural theatricality, her grasp of Keats's grim portent impeccable.

"'O what can ail thee, knight-at-arms,
Alone and palely loitering?
The sedge has withered from the lake,
And no birds sing.

'O what can ail thee, knight-at-arms,
So haggard and so woebegone?
The squirrel's granary is full,
And the harvest's done.'"

It was the second transformative performance of the day. Standing atop a low stage of unvarnished planks, and lacking backdrop and costume, Geraldine Dredd utterly personified the poet's Lady Without Mercy, a woman bereft of charity or kindness, a creature who encouraged the fiercest of fairy tale monsters to shrink in terror.

"'She took me to her Elfin grot,
And there she wept and sighed full sore,
And there I shut her wild eyes
With kisses four.

'And there she lulled me asleep,
And there I dreamed—Ah! woe betide!
The latest dream I ever dreamt
On the cold hill side.'"

In the front windows of the saloon, faces of those yet to try-out were pressed against the glass, the braver souls poking their heads into the door opening as Geraldine raised her arms, her fingers curled into claws, her voice growing louder and more ominous.

"'I saw pale kings and princes too,
Pale warriors, death-pale were they all;
They cried—'La Belle Dame sans Merci
Thee hath in thrall!

'I saw their starved lips in the gloam,
With horrid warning gaped wide,
And I awoke and found me here,
On the cold hill's side.'"

The descriptions of starved lips and anything both "horrid" and "gaped wide" provoked a collective gasp, save from Thaddeus Cooler who had become progressively more contemplative as Geraldine's performance unfolded. He leaned back in his chair, thoughtfully stroking his goatee. "What fun," he murmured, considering an improvisation for his play as the young woman's voice crescendoed to a finale, her eyes piercing Thaddeus and Maude as if she might transmogrify them into stone.

"'And this is why I sojourn here,
Alone and palely loitering,
Though the sedge is withered from the lake,
And...NO...BIRDS...SING.'"

Geraldine's recitation had pulled in the waiting auditioners from the boardwalk like ships drawn onto the rocks by a siren's call. Now, they clustered at the rear of the saloon, the room filled with the silence of their collectively held breath. Geraldine was silent too, her pose maintained, her gaze directed over their heads as if the jagged fangs of death hovered above them. Suddenly, her father erupted.

"BRAVA!" he cheered. "BRAVA!"

Sporadic applause followed, coalescing into an ovation as Dredd spurred them on.

"BRAVA!" he shouted over and over. "BRAVA!"

Cooler left his chair and approached Geraldine, lightly clapping his hands.

"Marvelous, my dear! Just marvelous!"

He reached the edge of the stage and offered his hand. She took it and stepped down. "You have inspired me; indeed, blessed me with an epiphany," Thaddeus told her. "An absolute epiphany! I have just the role for you, one that guarantees your performance shall be the most talked about of our play. It shall be a very unique performance in a very unique role for a very unique actress!" He escorted her to the bar and her father. "A rare talent, Mister Lieutenant Governor…a rare talent, indeed! I shall post the cast list within the hour." He smiled at Geraldine. "I am certain you shall be pleased, my dear."

After the Dredds left, Thaddeus wrote Geraldine's name next to the character of Richard Coyle. "She's our villain," he revealed to Maude. "Our Richard Coyle."

The former madam frowned. "I don't know, Thaddeus. It's a man's part. Her father…"

Cooler shrugged off her concern. "Nonsense, my dear Maude. Why can't a woman play a man? In Shakespeare's time, men played all the women's parts. It's time to turn the tables."

Only two remained of the eleven in line before Geraldine's audition, the rest so daunted by her performance they'd abandoned dreams of a career in the theater by the time the birds had stopped singing in Keats's poem. Thaddeus allowed the diehards to emote, the last one departing the stage at three-thirty. At four o'clock, he posted the cast list. Among the leading players were:

LORD DUNDREARY: THADDEUS COOLER

ASA TRENCHARD: WILLIAM BARKLEY

SIR EDWARD TRENCHARD: OSKAR NILSEN

FLORENCE TRENCHARD: BOUNTIFUL DOLLARHYDE

LT. HARRY VERNON: MERIWETHER PEYCOMSON

RICHARD COYLE: GERALDINE DREDD

MRS. MOUNTCHESSINGTON: MAUDE DOLLARHYDE

MARY MEREDITH, A HUMBLE MILK MAID: CHARLOTTE COOLER PURDUE

ABEL MURCOTT, A CLERK: ROSCOE COMFORT

GEORGINA MOUNTCHESSINGTON: TRIXIE COOLER

MISS SHARPE, A SERVANT: JEANETTE DEMILLE

That evening, Charlotte questioned her father's decision. "This isn't Memphis or New Orleans, Thaddie," she pointed out. "Hell, it's not even Omaha. These bumpkins might decide to tar and feather a director who puts pants on a girl. Give *that* some thought."

"As an artist, my dear girl, I must be true to my art," Thaddeus countered. Nevertheless, he penciled in County Sheriff Henry Wilcoxon of Horseshoe Bend as Geraldine's understudy. The fellow had a booming voice and the properly curled moustache of a villain. "In case our female Richard Coyle encourages the audience to storm the production with torches and pitchforks," he reassured Charlotte.

"From the looks of her father..." she replied. "It's not the audience you should worry about."

# 9

## THE BATTLE OF ENTER STAGE RIGHT, EXIT STAGE LEFT

Two days after the auditions, the cast of *Our American Cousin* assembled at the Gold Rush Saloon for a table reading. Gerald Dredd drove his daughter to Paradise and stayed to watch. Even though it was nine o'clock in the morning he had Arnold Chang draw up a beer, half the draught sloshing over the rim of the mug when Dredd slammed it onto the bar. Geraldine's character of Richard Coyle had just delivered his first line.

"What the hell... What's going on here? Why are you talking like that?"

His daughter looked up from her script. "It's a man's voice, Daddy. I'm playing a man. He has a low voice."

"A *man*! You're playing a man?" Dredd clambered off the barstool and tore across the room like a junkyard dog off its chain. He thrust a finger at Cooler's nose. "You've got my daughter playing a *man*? What the hell is wrong with you?" The two men retired to Arnold's office, the thin walls and Dredd's enraged voice making every word audible to the cast. "You will not put my daughter in a suit and tie, goddammit!" the furious real estate baron shouted. The tongue-lashing turned more profane as it progressed, and eventually, Thaddeus emerged from the storeroom, his face ashen.

"I've decided on a change," he announced as Dredd reclaimed his post at the bar. "I believe Miss Dredd would be so perfect as Mary Meredith, it would be a travesty to have her play a man. Casting her as Coyle was a novel concept...a creative risk, I daresay. I still find it intriguing, but perhaps not at this particular time."

Charlotte Cooler Purdue, the original Mary Meredith, was unhappy about the change. The humble milk maid's love interest in the play—Asa Trenchard—was to be played by Willie Barkley, and even though he was occasionally insane, the pregnant woman had been sizing him up like a female praying mantis anxious to mate and then eat his head.

"I'm not giving up my part," she told her father, pouting mightily.

"My dear—"

"I'm not giving it up!"

Cooler was a man who weaponized charm, but just as he'd been no match for Dredd's anger, he couldn't measure up to his daughter's petulance. Maude rescued him, aiming an uncompromising look at Charlotte's belly.

"This milk maid, Thaddeus, isn't she supposed to be...untaken, I guess you'd say?"

"Quite so."

"That tummy of yours, Mrs. Purdue," Maude went on, "suggests you've been pretty darned well taken, doesn't it?"

Charlotte glanced at the bulge on her abdomen, instinctively using a hand to shift the load upward.

"Mrs. Dollarhyde has a point, my dear," Thaddeus agreed. "Those in the seats must suspend disbelief for all plays, but a chaste maiden with child is perhaps more suspension than an audience steeped in innocence and matrimony can muster."

He took Charlotte aside and a second meeting in Arnold's office ensued, this time with voices too low to allow eavesdropping. Upon their return, the younger of the Cooler daughters gestured at the cast with a haughty sweep of her arm. "I'm the stage manager," she declared. "From now on, you rubes gotta do what I say."

It was the last hiccup of the day and the table reading for the comedy, *Our American Cousin*, proceeded without further interruption. The following morning, official stage rehearsals began and immediately took a lead role in town gossip. Initially, the chinwagging came in the form of protests after locals

learned that *Our American Cousin* was the play Abraham Lincoln
attended when he was assassinated. "Think of our production
as a tribute to the revered Mister Lincoln," Thaddeus cajoled.
This seemed acceptable and folks quickly put aside their grief
over the loss of The Great Emancipator, cheerily asking about
the upcoming production whenever their paths crossed with its
director. "How's the play goin'? It gonna be any good?" they
asked. "It's going marvelously," Cooler reassured them. "Just
bully. It will be a triumph, I can assure you…an unequivocal
triumph. Reserve your seats now as I expect a sellout."

In reality, it was not going well; most of *Our American Cousin*'s actors struggled with the stilted language in the fifty-year-
old script. "Who the hell talks like this anymore?" several complained when Thaddeus gently urged them to learn their lines.
Trixie Cooler was another problem. She was more interested
in gin than her character of Georgina Mountchessington, and
eventually, Thaddeus had to sack her, consoling his daughter
with the position of assistant director. "With so many amateurs
in our production, my dear, we need an experienced hand in
the second chair," he told her. He needn't have worried. Trixie
was a pint into the day when informed of her demotion and
belched in response, relieved to have a job where she could get
drunk in peace. Jeanette DeMille, who had discovered her stage
voice with some coaching from Thaddeus, was promoted to
Georgina, although her parents insisted that scripted kisses between Cooler's Lord Dundreary and their daughter's character
be rewritten as handshakes.

A third problem for Thaddeus was the limited availabili-
ty of Sir Edward Trenchard. "I can't be prancin' around on
a stage durin' peak business hours, doggonit," Oskar Nilsen
complained, even though peak business hours at Nilsen's General Store rarely saw more than three or four customers at any
one time. In truth, Oskar wanted out. When cast, he'd figured
the part would mostly involve mucking about in formal attire,
drinking free brandy, and attempting a British accent no one

recognized as belonging to any country, much less England. However, once rehearsals began, the storekeeper discovered that his character's wardrobe was pedestrian, the brandy was tea, and he was expected to memorize pages of unfamiliar language and then figure out where he was supposed to stand when he delivered it. "I gotta go to one place on the darned stage and say somethin', then go somewhere else and say some other doggone thing," he griped to wife Sonia. "It don't make sense. Why can't I just stand in one darned spot and tell the audience direct-like? They're the ones that gotta hear my lines. Why the heck am I lookin' at some other actor? Everybody in the play already knows what this Sir Edward fella is gonna say, doggonnit. It's them folks in the seats what's gotta hear 'im."

Eventually, the shine of Sir Edward Trenchard's star so considerably dulled, Oskar withdrew from the production. His understudy was Dr. Stanley June, but the Spanish flu sweeping through rural Idaho had forced the semiretired physician to fully unretire or lose his license. He was now a circuit doctor, traveling among mountain settlements from New Meadows to Challis. Cooler's choice for his replacement was a surprise.

"I don't wanna be in yer goddamned play!" Goldstrike barked at the director when first approached.

"My dear Goldstrike, your charming Maine accent is merely a hairsbreadth away from a British one," Thaddeus encouraged him. "Moreover, you have an undeniable presence and a forceful voice. Both will lend themselves well to the stage."

"Drape some presence on somebody else, goddammit! I ain't doin' it!"

The negotiation went on without resolution, until Bountiful intervened. "Please take the part, Goldstrike," she pleaded. "Everyone is looking forward to our play and we need a Sir Edward."

"Get Riggins to do it," the old prospector argued. "He's a newspaperman. Learnin' all them words won't make him no never mind... Probably knows most of 'em already."

"Mister Riggins already has a part," Bountiful countered.

"He's Mister Buddicombe." She eyed Thaddeus. "You can re-write the script so there are less lines to memorize, right?"

Cooler nodded.

"There…you see?" Bountiful said, taking Goldstrike's hand. "Nothing to it. And we'll be father and daughter. That'll be fun, won't it?"

Goldstrike was unmoved by a decrease in lines he probably wouldn't learn anyway but had noted that Thaddeus Cooler was too fatherly with Bountiful—his encouragement too enthusiastic, his advice too sage, his appreciation of her performance as Florence Trenchard too prideful. "She don't need another father," the old prospector later explained to fellow surrogate dads Oskar Nilsen, Arnold Chang, and Ed Riggins. "So I took the goddamned part. I figger a turn as that there Sir Edward'll let me keep an eye on Cooler afore he sets his hooks in our girl."

As rehearsals progressed Willie Barkley's lapses into madness noticeably dwindled. Given a character and a script, he was either sane or simply acted like it, and once Thaddeus understood this, he provided the former doughboy with lines he could use off-stage, as well. Subsequently people might greet Willie on the street only to be answered by First Lord in *All's Well That Ends Well*.

"How's it goin', Willie?"

"'The web of my life is a mingled yarn, good and ill together.'"

"I don't understand what the hell he's sayin' about half the time," Goldstrike told people. "But Willie knows, so I guess it's better'n the way he was."

Willie's transformation wasn't the only surprise. After the casting change ordered by her father, the Lady Without Mercy—Geraldine Dredd—shed the skin of Richard Coyle and eagerly embraced Mary Meredith, a humble milk maid, as if the character's on-stage charm and sweetness gave her permission to evince off-stage charm and sweetness as well. She and Willie seemed well-matched as hero and heroine, but a problem remained in the final act when Willie, as Asa Trenchard, was expected to kiss her.

"Her first kiss shouldn't be from someone like me," Willie explained to Thaddeus, shyly glancing at his leading lady. "A first kiss should be from a beau...not a lunatic."

"Oh, dear boy, I'm quite sure Miss Dredd has been kissed by now," Thaddeus reassured him, looking to Geraldine for confirmation.

She nodded. "It's okay, Will... You may kiss me."

"It's Willie."

Geraldine considered him with half-lidded eyes. "*I* prefer *Will*...if that matters."

The ex-soldier bowed. "'Then tis hatched and shall be so.'"

Despite his promise, Willie remained hesitant to buss the play's humble milk maid during rehearsals. However, he vowed to perform his duty on opening night. "'Upon thy cheek, I shall lay a zealous kiss,'" he reassured his co-star.

❧

As rehearsals proceeded Gerald Dredd tired of the daily commute from Boise, and he leased the only multiroom suite in the Busty Rose to accommodate occasional stayovers for his daughter that quickly became permanent. Subsequently, the actress refused to return to Boise after moving into the four-room apartment—once Maude's during the cathouse's salad days—citing excuse after excuse to stay in Paradise. As their separation lengthened and the first of September approached, Dredd's moods grew darker.

"We need to light a fire under somebody," he barked at Junior from behind the big desk in his office. "Get one of those head counters into Paradise as soon as the clock strikes midnight on the New Year."

Junior didn't respond, instead nervously contemplating the recently manicured fingernails of one hand.

"Answer me, goddamit!"

The young man cringed. He occupied a precarious part of

the Dredd realm, a place where the slightest hint of failure poured blame on him like hot tar from a castle battlement. Geraldine's absence had exacerbated things, shortening his father's fuse and threatening to move the company's future president below his sister in the corporate hierarchy.

"Right, Dad," he replied. "I agree one hundred percent. We should get one of those Census Bureau men out here on New Year's Day."

Dredd's scowl deepened.

"You want *me* to do it. Is that it?" Junior amended. "You want *me* to light a fire under someone. Okay. I can do that… Absolutely, Dad. I'll do it."

Dredd exhaled hard through his nose, the sound filling the room with his frustration.

*Why can't he be more like me?*

As provided for him by his own father, Gerald Dredd had bought Junior a degree at a decent university and then installed him as assistant to the company's chief operating officer. "He'll show you the ropes and then you can take over," he'd told his eldest. But, thus far, the twenty-one-year-old had demonstrated an excess of braggadocio and a dearth of both backbone and brainpower. *He's not smart or ruthless enough to be boss,* his father worried. The real estate baron glanced at his desk drawer. The revised will Bertram Mole had prepared was still inside, unsigned. He appraised his son through slitted eyes, making Junior fidget uncomfortably. Typically thickheaded about most things, the scion to the Dredd fortune was a seismologist insofar as his father's eruptions were concerned and sensed that lava was about to flow.

"I wish I were more like you, Dad."

"That's the first goddamned useful thing you've said today."

Less than an hour later Dredd was alone in his Vauxhall, headed for Paradise. Skidding on the turns, he raced up the road and arrived in record time, afterward slipping into the Gold Rush Saloon where he quietly took a seat at the bar and watched as three members of the cast rehearsed a scene from

Act II. The players were Bountiful Dollarhyde, Willie Barkley, and Geraldine Dredd.

"Florence, Asa, you enter from stage right," Thaddeus instructed his actors. "Mary is waiting in the garden." He narrowed his focus to Willie and Geraldine. "Remember, Asa and Mary, you are meeting for the first time. You are both smitten but must not overplay it. No slackened jaws, no cow eyes. Let your gazes linger for the briefest moment before averting them. Let your handshake linger, also for the briefest moment. And, Will, this time allow Geraldine to take your hand. Don't pull away. Our play is a comedy but not farce. We are not vaudevillians, yes?" His actors nodded and Thaddeus took a chair near the front of the stage. He lightly clapped his hands. "And begin," he said. Bountiful as Florence Trenchard and Willie Barkley as her cousin, Asa, stepped onto the stage where Geraldine's Mary Meredith waited.

> FLORENCE TRENCHARD: Come along, come along. I want to introduce you to my little cousin. (She crosses to Mary and kisses her on the cheek.) I've brought you a visitor. Miss Mary Meredith...Mr. Asa Trenchard, our American cousin. This young gentleman has carried off the prize by three successive shots in the bull's eye.

> MARY MEREDITH: I congratulate you, sir, and am happy to see you.

Geraldine's character reached for Willie's hand, and for the first time since rehearsals began, he allowed her to take it. The ensuing electricity was palpable, the "briefest moment" becoming several and then several more as the young couple rushed past "lingering" and went straight to "mooning over."

"Stop there," Thaddeus called out, standing. "Asa...you are smitten, not bewitched. And, Mary, you are intrigued, not enraptured. It's lovely acting, both of you, but too much, too soon. Your characters' love will blossom, but at this place in our story it is merely a seed in the wind, looking for a fertile patch of ground." Geraldine and Willie nodded and Thaddeus returned to his seat. "All right," he said. "From stage right… let's begin again."

Bountiful and Willie once more entered to a waiting Geraldine and the scene progressed, this time with the "briefest moment" carried off as instructed. Eventually, the actors reached Mary Meredith's exit, stage left.

> MARY MEREDITH: Well, I must look to my dairy or all my last week's milk will be spoiled. Goodbye, Florence, dear. Goodbye, Mr. Trenchard. Good morning, sir. (Mary moves stage left to exit. Asa follows her.)

> ASA TRENCHARD: Good morning, miss. I'll call again.

"Very nice," Thaddeus congratulated his actors, rising from his chair. "Very, very nice…all of you. Let's break for ten minutes."

Gerald Dredd motioned to the director, who joined him at the bar, the scene partners drifting to the piano area where the rest of the company had claimed a few tables and chairs. Geraldine took a seat on the piano bench next to Bountiful. Willie sat on the floor beside her with Goldstrike dragging over a chair to sit nearby.

"Why is my daughter still paired up with that madman?" Dredd demanded when Cooler reached him.

"Young Mister Barkley is, uh…peculiar. I'll grant you," the director replied. "But our Asa Trenchard is quite talented. A natural actor…inhabits the role, don't you know?"

"Get rid of him."

"My dear Mister Dredd, I must point out that it's not your decision—"

"I said get rid of him."

Dredd slipped off the barstool, giving Cooler his back as he moved toward the lounging actors. By the time he reached his daughter, his scowl had been replaced by a syrupy smile.

"Hello, darling," he cooed. "I thought I'd surprise you. I've missed you so much." He leaned down and attempted to kiss Geraldine on the lips, an effort she managed to redirect to her cheek. "Darling, aren't you happy to see me? We've been apart for ages."

Geraldine hesitated, eyelids fluttering, her lips slightly parted. "Yes...of course. I'm happy to see you, Daddy," she said, her voice a note higher than its normal pitch. "Of course, I am. It's just that..."

"It's just what?"

"I wasn't expecting... I have—"

"I've put things aside in Boise and can spend the night, darling."

The color rushed from Geraldine's face. "Daddy, tonight isn't a good..."

Dredd's features darkened. "A good *what?*" he responded. "Don't you *want* me to spend the night?"

"It's just that..."

"It's just *what?*"

Dredd eased onto the piano bench opposite Bountiful, sandwiching his daughter between them.

"Daddy!" Geraldine protested. She wriggled free and rose. Bountiful stood, too, but Geraldine's father remained on the piano bench, appraising his daughter like a cobra lifting its head from a snake charmer's basket. When he spoke, his voice was silken.

"What about tonight isn't good...*darling?*"

Geraldine didn't answer, her eyes darting about. Cooler had left the bar to join his troupe, and when the young actress's search for help landed on him, the actor/director promptly discovered something fascinating about the ceiling, at the same time fussing with his necktie, straightening his pocket square, and in general, making clear that he had been a principal in many domestic disputes over the years and had no desire to be in this one.

"Why isn't tonight good, darling?" Dredd kept on, rising from the piano bench. "What about it is not good?"

"Nothing, Daddy. It's just..."

"It's just *what?*"

Geraldine again looked to her director. As a leading man, Thaddeus Cooler had fictitiously rescued many leading ladies, and despite his reluctance, his actor's instincts suddenly kicked in. "A girl's night," he blurted, his words less uttered than burped. The sound of his own voice seemed to lend him courage and he went on, speaking more forcefully. "Our young women have scheduled a girl's night."

Dredd's head slowly swiveled until he faced the old actor, his upper lip curled into the hint of a sneer. "A *girl's* night? What the hell is *that?*"

The real estate magnate's razored aspect evaporated Cooler's manufactured gallantry as quickly as it had formed. "To… bond," the Broadway veteran stammered, his demeanor now less the confident actor/director and more like a material witness desperately searching for a way to become immaterial. "Our actresses must bond *off-stage* so that what takes place *on-stage* is authentic," he added. Thaddeus scoured the faces of the women in the company to see if there was a scene partner among the bevy of bewildered expressions, his relief conspicuous when Bountiful volunteered.

"It's tonight, Mister Dredd," she improvised, indicating the other women in the cast with a lift of her chin. "Our girl's night… It's tonight, isn't it, ladies? We've been planning—"

"Cancel it," Dredd demanded.

Bountiful's features momentarily narrowed. Then her face relaxed and she pressed on. "I'm afraid that's not possible. We've had it planned for some time. It's a shame you didn't tell us you were coming."

"I said cancel it."

"My dear Mister Dredd, the ladies must have their night," Cooler insisted, reentering the fray after sifting through the many characters he'd played over the years to reclaim one with a stiffer spine. He smiled wearily. "I'm afraid the theater is a demanding mistress…indeed, an exceedingly demanding mistress."

"I don't give a good two shits what the theater is," Dredd snarled.

Willie Barkley and Goldstrike were on their feet now, and when the angry politician clenched his fists, they moved together, stepping into the space that separated him from the director. Dredd bared his teeth, and for a moment, it seemed the fleshy politician might throw a punch.

"'I'll fight till from my bones the flesh be hacked,'" Willie murmured. At the same time, Goldstrike peered at Geraldine's father as if aiming down the long barrel of the Springfield rifle he'd carried in the War Between the States.

"These here women got bondin' and other such bullshit to work on tonight...Miss Geraldine, included," the old prospector rasped. "Ya'd best be on yer way, Gerald."

It was the final shot of what became known to the company of *Our American Cousin* as the Battle of Enter Stage Right, Exit Stage Left. Facing a brace of oxen without a whip to tame them, Dredd unclenched his fists and then angrily fled the battlefield, storming out of the Gold Rush Saloon. Less than a minute later, the sound of the Vauxhall's engine broke the silence, at first loud and demanding, then slowly fading. When it was no longer audible, Thaddeus spoke.

"So...let's go again," he said. "Florence and Asa enter from stage right."

# 10

## SPARKS, SMOKE, AND THE COMMON LINE

Wanda Cooler was not the only chronically indisposed woman in Paradise. "It's about goddamned time Mrs. Peycomson got herself disposed if'n ya ask me," Goldstrike groused after Evangeline's husband rebuffed a fourth attempt to inspect work done on the former Stiveley mansion. The renovation was nearing completion if a decrease in the sounds of hammering and sawing were any indication.

"Inspection or not, we need an update on our legal situation," Bountiful submitted at a town council meeting. This was greeted by a chorus of head nods and the council adjourned, reassembling on the Peycomson front porch. The lawyer did not invite them in.

"At present, I cannot accommodate a meeting inside," he told them. "But we could gather on the rear veranda if you like."

"Why not inside?" Goldstrike asked.

Peycomson smiled wearily. "I'm afraid my wife is again indisposed. Lady problems... I'm sure you understand."

"Ya got workers in there all goddamned day," Goldstrike argued. "The stir them fellas is makin' don't seem to indispose her none."

Peycomson blinked nervously. "It's a bit more complicated, I'm afraid... Evangeline is..."

"We understand, Meriwether," Bountiful rescued him. "Your veranda will suffice, thank you."

Peycomson covered a sigh of relief with a grin and then led them around the side of the house to the back, where they found a wide, newly built covered porch with a swing, a round, clear-finished pine table with six seats, and a pair of green Adirondack chairs adorned by khaki-colored pads. "Settle in," he said. "I'll arrange for refreshments." Peycomson went inside and returned a few minutes later with a pitcher of cold tea. Frau Gerta followed with six glasses and a plate of store-bought oatmeal cookies on a wooden tray. The statuesque, fashionable German house-servant set the tray on the table for the guests to serve themselves and then gracefully reclined on one of the cushioned Adirondack chairs, her long legs crossed to reveal shapely ankles, her eyes systematically surveying the members of the Paradise town council like a spider trying to decide which insect might be tastiest.

"I'm an Oregon lawyer but have familiarized myself with relevant Idaho statutes," Peycomson began. "However, if you prefer a local attorney, I won't be offended." He paused for objections, then forged ahead when none were offered. "So… eminent domain. Essentially, the government may encroach upon personal property for public use. In other words, they can take your land if they go about it in the proper way."

"That ain't right," Oskar Nilsen blurted, cookie crumbs exiting his mouth to join the hand he slammed against the table. "How can they steal a man's property, doggonit?"

"The government doesn't steal it, Oskar," Peycomson said. "They buy it. The property owner must be given just compensation. Moreover, eminent domain doesn't abrogate your right to due process. Rules vary from state to state, but in all cases the government can't condemn and take your home without further adjudication. You have the right to appeal."

"What about Idaho law?" Bountiful asked. "How likely are we to be condemned and taken if we don't make our census threshold?"

"That depends on the condemnor," Peycomson responded, going on when the unfamiliar word was met by puzzled expressions. "A condemnor is a person appointed by the government to oversee the process of eminent domain. In Idaho, the condemnor is given broad discretionary power. His decision, in most cases, is rubber-stamped; hence, it's effectively final."

"So one person decides our fate," Bountiful said.

Peycomson nodded. "More or less... You can appeal, but it's an uphill battle. The law requires the condemnor to exercise his power in good faith and it's the *good faith* part that becomes the legal issue. You see, the condemnor must only justify his decision as contributing to the public need, but the so-called *public*, as defined by law, isn't necessarily a large group of people and the *need* is broadly interpreted. That makes his decision difficult to legally challenge. On the other hand, there's no public other than us for twenty miles in any direction; hence the *public* becomes the state, at large, and its voters. That works in our favor because taking private property, particularly an entire town, is never popular. It will make voters nervous about their own towns and the governor and state legislators know it. Elected judges too. Taking Paradise will be easier to justify if the town isn't incorporated."

"So it's back to the census," Bountiful concluded.

"Yes."

"Which leaves us all right for now."

"For now... We could still have a fight on our hands if the condemnor holds a lot of political capital. In that regard, I've a contact with statehouse connections who believes there's a backup plan to move forward even if we make the incorporation threshold."

"And what about that *condemn*-whatever?" Goldstrike growled. "They already pick that bastard too?"

"While it's only a rumor," the lawyer said, "I'm told the condemnor will be—"

"Gerald Dredd," Bountiful finished for him.

"Yes," Peycomson answered, his face grim. "I'm afraid so."

Goldstrike rose and went to the porch railing where he spat a wad of chewing tobacco into Peycomson's back yard. "Sonuva-goddamned-bitch," he muttered.

After the meeting adjourned Frau Gerta went inside and the others headed out. Peycomson asked Bountiful to remain behind. "I feel we should meet more often," he told her once they were alone. "To discuss our legal strategy…in our roles as council president and town lawyer, of course."

"What more is there to discuss?" Bountiful said. "We've reached our population goal, so that avenue is closed to Dredd. If we're incorporated, he must arbitrarily declare that acquisition of Paradise serves the public need, as you put it, and then take us regardless of its popularity. If you're right, such a decision will create a lot of political backlash across the state. Pushing through against it could have consequences. It could take down someone even as powerful as Gerald Dredd. He likes his power. I question whether he's willing to wager it just to get our little town."

"How clever you are, Miss Trenchard," Peycomson replied, using the British accent of Lieutenant Harry Vernon.

"Don't, Meriwether. This isn't funny."

The lawyer walked Bountiful back to the Paradise School, bowing to kiss her hand after they climbed the porch steps, a pale impression still on his skin from the wedding ring he'd removed at the start of rehearsals for *Our American Cousin.* Bountiful gently pulled her hand away.

"Perhaps your wife would appreciate a visit," she said. 'Sarah, Annie, and I could call on her."

"How wonderful of you to think of Mrs. Peycomson," the lawyer responded. "But I'm afraid she's not ready for visitors. Our move from Portland continues to weigh on both she and little Felix. They have fragile dispositions."

When Bountiful later shared this remark with her grandmother, Maude sniffed. "If they're all that fragile, why did he move them here in the first place? Far as that goes, their boy doesn't seem so much fragile as feral. Maybe they oughta let wolves have a go at raising him." It was true. Even from the considerable distance Frau Gerta cautiously maintained between her charge and the rest of the town, it was apparent that Felix Peycomson was Doctor Caligari's somnambulist, his eyes darkly receding, his manly expression both ominous and cryptic. He did not play outside and had no friends in Paradise;

indeed, he continued to be as much an apparition as his mother, save those rare occasions when he accompanied his father and Frau Gerta on a trip to Boise in their green Liberty Cadillac. He sat on his nanny's lap for such outings with his moppet's hair curling out from under a cap pulled so low it was impossible to know if he were happy or sad.

A larger concern for Maude was Peycomson's obvious interest in transplanting scenes between Lieutenant Harry Vernon and Bountiful's Miss Florence Trenchard from a fictional drawing room to an actual bedroom. "I know a man who's twisting away from marriage," she confided to Thaddeus Cooler. "And in that regard, Meriwether Peycomson is a damned pretzel."

"Oh, don't be alarmed, my dear Maude," the actor reassured her. "It's the nature of the theater. Leading men and ladies fall in love during a production and fall out again as soon as the curtain descends on closing night. Such things are not true romances but flirtations; indeed, sparks abound in our little play. Have you not noticed the longing glances between young Lariat and his sweet Jeanette…or Geraldine, of course, and our gallant Asa Trenchard?"

Maude had noticed. Neither couple worried her. Lariat and Jeanette were just children testing out their hormones while Willie and Geraldine were caught in the river current of first love past the age of consent. But Bountiful and Peycomson had passed both milestones. Moreover, everyone in Paradise could see that Maude's beautiful granddaughter was a better match for the handsome lawyer than his gaunt, spectral wife. *Perhaps Evangeline doesn't care*, Maude worried, the Peycomson union merely a titular thing. She understood. The former brothel proprietor had bestowed a "Mrs." upon herself when she opened the Busty Rose, figuring a proper madam ought to forward a working knowledge of what many of her establishment's customers were trying to get away from. In truth, she'd never wanted a husband, although that had somewhat changed since Thaddeus Cooler's arrival. He was a second-hand proposition, for sure, but Maude sometimes wondered if she should stake a claim, given that Wanda Cooler seemed to have abandoned hers. Bountiful was a different matter. "She deserves a first plate, not a warmed-up leftover," she suggested to Thaddeus. "Flirtation or not, Lieutenant Harry of the Royal Navy had best keep his trousers buttoned around my girl or I'll take my old buggy whip to his pecker."

*❧*

Because *Our American Cousin* dominated talk around town, the status of the Paradise Electrical Cooperative had moved to the back seat by the time John Goodlow and Lariat finished building their transformer. While the device's metal shell was being fabricated, the Idaho Power Company sent out a lineman. An electrical engineer, Walter Jewell, came with him, a talkative fellow excessively proud of his education at Purdue University. As Jewell watched from the ground, searching for a place to ram in a mention of his alma mater, the lineman—wearing spiked boots and a logger's belt—nimbly climbed the terminal IPC pole in a half-dozen stutter steps, then began work to install a breaker.

"Where'd you go to school, Mister Goodlow?" Jewell queried. "I'm a Purdue man myself...Purdue University. You've heard of it, of course."

"Everyone has heard of it. It's a great place."

"Top notch...cutting edge, that's for sure. Where'd you say you went?"

The lineman interrupted them, shouting from his perch atop the pole. "All done up here, Walt. You want me to hook up their transformer?"

"No! We didn't build it." Jewell shot a pointed look at Goodlow. "No offense, but Idaho Power is liable if your transformer blows up and starts a forest fire. You'll have to tie in on your own."

"It's not gonna blow up," Lariat said, an opinion the Purdue alumnus did not appreciate, a shadow crossing his features.

"Best button that lip o' yours, boy," he said.

After the lineman used his climbing belt to rappel down the pole in a pair of long, acrobatic swoops, John Goodlow borrowed the belt, then pulled detachable cleats over his boots and scampered up the post as adroitly as the IPC man. He attached a cable from the transformer he and Lariat had built.

"Ready?" he called out, his hand on the breaker.

Lariat was at the transformer, a voltmeter in his hands. He nodded and Goodlow flipped the lever, closing the circuit. The quiet mountain air remained undisturbed by an electrical pop or puff of smoke. "What are you reading?" he shouted at Lariat.

The teenager peered at the dial of the voltmeter.

"Two-forty."

"Aces!"

Goodlow flipped the breaker switch to OFF, climbed back down, and unhooked the cable from his transformer. "We'll tie in for good when the cover gets here," he told the IPC men.

Before they headed back to Boise, Walter Jewell and the lineman made a stop at the Gold Rush Saloon. The IPC engineer invited Goodlow to join them. Lariat came along, too, and once there, Arnold Chang drew up beers for the men and mixed up a glass of soda water with chocolate syrup for Lariat. Play rehearsal was over for the day, and while the lineman schmoozed up a tipsy Trixie Cooler at the bar, Lariat listened to Goodlow and Jewell discuss the famous AC-DC war between George Westinghouse and Thomas Edison, the infant field of electronics, and the relative efficacy of hydroelectric versus coal-powered generating stations. Eventually, the IPC engineer maneuvered the discussion back to his former university.

"Where'd you say you went to school?" the Purdue alumnus pressed Goodlow.

"I didn't say."

"Stanford? Cal?"

"Neither of those...nothing that elite."

"Really? Don't tell me...Idaho Tech?"

Goodlow took a drink of his beer. "Missoula," he said, after setting the glass mug back on the table.

"University of Montana? That surprises me. I didn't know they had an electrical engineering program."

"It's fairly new."

"Must be. I thought I knew all the electrical engineering programs around the country. I keep up, you know…industry journals and all that. Being an academic type you've probably been published in some of those journals, haven't you?"

Goodlow shifted in his seat, tapping his fingers on the table. "There have been a few publications," he said.

"Which journal? Maybe I've read one of your articles."

"What do you know about neon signs, Mister Jewell?" Lariat broke in. "Mister Nilsen wants one for his store."

Jewel's features darkened. "Keep to your own business, boy," he sniffed. "You wouldn't understand the science, anyway."

"Try me."

Jewell lips parted in surprise. "Are you gonna let this goddamned little nigger sass me?" he growled, eyeing Goodlow.

Goodlow's eyes narrowed.

"Well…are you?"

Goodlow stood. "We have to go now, Walt," he said. "Have a safe trip back to Boise." He nodded at Lariat. The teenager rose and they headed for the saloon's exit. After a few steps, Goodlow turned back. "For the record," he said, "I'm quite certain Lariat knows more than you about the science of neon signs."

"Now just a damned—"

"He knows more than you or me about the science of pretty much everything."

"I ain't gonna sit here and—"

"He only asked you to make conversation. He was being polite, something you might give a try."

"I hardly think—" Jewell sputtered.

Goodlow stopped him with a raised hand. "Finally something we agree on," he said.

They left the Gold Rush and made their way to Only Real

Street, walking in silence until reaching the Paradise School. Finally, Goodlow spoke.

"Don't let men like that get to you, Lariat."

"They don't, Mister Goodlow."

"John."

"They don't, John." Lariat shrugged, then added, "I'm used to it. It happens every time I go to Boise. The town's full of people like him."

They said their goodbyes and Lariat went inside, heading straight for the kitchen where Maude was chopping an onion, her eyes watery. "You've worry on your face. Are you all right," she asked after he picked up an apple from a bowl on the counter and then returned it without taking a bite. She set aside her knife, used a dish towel to dry her eyes, and then approached him to put a hand on his forehead. "Do you have a fever?"

Lariat wriggled away from her touch.

"I'm fine."

"Are you sure, honey? Is there something you want to tell me?"

There was, but Lariat didn't. With his fifteenth birthday nearing, he was a measured fellow and understood that suspicion was too often smoke with no fire. However, the architect of Paradise's electrical grid and owner of the former Feldstein mansion had put off a lot of smoke when Walter Jewell pushed him into a diploma contest. Lariat had tossed water on the blaze with his question about neon signs, but enough embers still glowed to make him suspect that the pretentious Purdue graduate might be right about the engineering department at the University of Montana...making Lariat's friend and mentor, John Goodlow, a liar.

After dinner, Lariat retired to his bedroom and his latest Dickens novel—*Nicholas Nickleby*—following the book's namesake as the impetuous protagonist struggled to tread water in a prodigious sea of connivers and villains. Near midnight the young genius set it aside and doused the oil lamp on his bedside table. He lay awake in the darkness, wondering what conniver or villain had forced a good man like John Goodlow to concoct the history of a life he'd not led. The next day he learned that the Paradise Electrical Cooperative had a bigger problem than the credentials of its chief engineer. The planned route for their common line was dominated by granite.

❧

"I told you I could set the poles without dynamite, but it was my sinful pride talking. I'm very sorry," Amon DeMille told the town council. They were in the meeting room of the old assay office after a special session had been convened. "The footings have to be deep," he added. "We'll need explosives." He suggested they contract an expert to blast holes in the dense rock but couldn't recommend anyone. "I knew a few demolition men in Utah but no one here in Idaho."

Maude chuckled. "It's okay, Amon… We know someone."

And they did. Goldstrike had been the best landmine sweeper in his regiment during the War Between the States, needing less than five minutes to dig up and disable one of the "torpedoes" the Rebs packed with gunpowder, afterward reenabling it for use as a grenade. When the conflict ended in 1865, he'd confiscated a box of captured torpedoes and made his way west to the gold rush in Paradise, confident he could easily blast tunnels into the mountainside. "I'll stroll in and pluck nuggets off the ground like pickin' mushrooms," he told the skeptical panners and dredgers on Mores Creek. Instead, the novice prospector learned that rudimentary black powder explosives were no match for Idaho granite and he was soon back with Old Butch, wetting a knee with a pan in his hands. Around 1871, he'd come across some recently innovated dynamite. More powerful than black powder and far more stable than nitroglycerin, Goldstrike used it to produce a single tunnel—a seven-foot-high, seven-foot-wide wormhole with its adit about a quarter mile past the rear of Meriwether Peycomson's mansion. The tunnel cut twenty yards into the side of the mountain, a point where Goldstrike realized that hauling out the rock and reinforcing his mine with timber was brutal work when compared to panning and dredging.

"I still got me some dynamite from the old days," he told the council. "But them sticks likely wept out a long time ago. Be unstable at best. I left 'em in the mine. They're still there, far as I know, but we probably oughta get ourselves new material."

"You need a license to buy dynamite in Utah," Amon observed.

"Same here," Goldstrike told him.

"Do you still have your license?"

Goldstrike snorted. "Didn't have no license to begin with, Amon. Back in them days, folks weren't so persnickety as they are now. But don't worry. There's a fella I know at the Belshazzar mine up north…Mike Cavanaugh. He's got dynamite. I worked with his uncle Butch fer years. Mike'll spare me a few sticks."

"What about a license?"

"What about it?"

Amon hesitated, tracing the grain of the wood on the conference table with a finger.

"Perhaps we should contract the work," Bountiful suggested. She smiled at Goldstrike. "I know you'd probably do a better job than anyone, but—"

"It's okay," Amon intervened. "Pardon me for interrupting, Bountiful, but it's really all right. It has to be. Who knows how long it would take to get a license…or if we could even *get* one, given Gerald Dredd's connections?"

He shrugged, issuing a humorless laugh.

"There's law and there's sin. They're not always the same. I've already broken one law and been excommunicated. A couple more transgressions shouldn't matter." He then offered to drive Goldstrike to the Belshazzar mine.

"There ain't no direct roads between here and there," the old prospector told him. "Ain't nuthin' but backcountry. If'n we was to drive it, we'd hafta go past Boise and come in from the west. It'd be a couple hunnert miles by car. It's only fourteen fer me and my mule, so thanks, Amon, but we'll go it alone.

You and yer boys can figger out where to put the posts and drill holes fer the dynamite while we're gone."

After stocking up on water and hardtack, Goldstrike headed out, and despite 1,500 feet of rugged elevation and a stubborn mule, took just fifteen hours to negotiate the round trip. He returned with blasting caps, a manual detonator, and twelve sticks of dynamite. Meanwhile, Amon DeMille and his boys had drilled ten holes along the route of the new cooperative's common line, each about four feet deep with a diameter of just over an inch. The next morning Goldstrike, Amon and his sons, John Goodlow, and Lariat met at the first of the drill sites. DeMille was nervous around the dynamite.

"Don't fret, Amon," Goldstrike reassured him. "This ain't nitroglycerin. That stuff is like wakin' snakes. Dynamite is stable till ya put a blastin' cap in it." Nevertheless, DeMille kept his boys well clear when Goldstrike lowered a stick of dynamite into the first drill hole. Lariat and John Goodlow were at his side.

"I wanna do the next one," the teenager told Goldstrike.

"I figgered ya'd do *this* one," the old prospector answered.

And Lariat did. With the dynamite set, the teenager ran the attached wire to a detonator twenty yards from the blast site. Goldstrike showed him how to connect it and the boy knelt.

"Should I count to three or something?" he asked, gripping the detonator handle.

Goldstrike shrugged. "If'n ya want... With or without the arithmetic, that goddamned dynamite is gonna go off."

Lariat fashioned a serious expression, lips folded inward, forehead rutted, jaw hardened.

"On the count of three..." he said.

He gave the handle a twist.

"One...two..."

He pushed it down.

"Three!"

A split second later the quiet morning was interrupted by a

dull explosion and a shower of small rocks erupted from the drill hole.

"Crackerjack!" Lariat yelled. He ran to inspect the blast site, discovering a shallow basin, three feet in diameter, gravel and small rocks on its surface. "It's not deep enough," he called back to Goldstrike. The former minesweeper with the Maine 11th grabbed a pickaxe, and along with the others, joined Lariat.

"Stand back," he said, afterward giving the heavy tool a swing that buried the full length of its point in the center of the basin. "It's gonna be loose like that all the way to the bottom," he promised. "The dynamite blows the rock into crumbles and stones. They fall into the hole and ya gotta shovel 'em out."

Amon and John Goodlow retrieved tools and began to dig while Goldstrike, Lariat, and the DeMille sons went to the next place on their route. "Do this one by yerself," Goldstrike told Lariat, handing him a stick of dynamite and a blasting cap. He looked at the DeMille boys. "Watch how Lariat does it, and after this one, you fellas can each have a go if yer pap allows." Less than a minute later Lariat had armed the thin cylinder of dynamite, inserted it into the drill hole, and run the wire back to the detonator. Another explosion and shower of pebbles ensued.

The remaining eight footings were similarly excavated. Lariat and the DeMille boys—Benjamin, Gideon, and Oliver—rigged and detonated the dynamite. Goldstrike, Amon, and John Goodlow then shoveled out the gravel and rocks, the former prospector and the engineer from Missoula holding their own with the muscular Mormon carpenter. Thaddeus Cooler showed up shortly after the end of morning rehearsal for *Our American Cousin*. Goldstrike had been absent for several days, and with opening night fast approaching, the play's director wanted to see if a third Sir Edward would have to be recruited. He was delighted when Goldstrike grumpily agreed to continue in exchange for even less lines.

"Bully!" the actor exclaimed, afterward remaining to take a turn with a shovel, on one occasion dropping it to hoist and then toss aside a small boulder the size of a snare drum. Gold-strike issued a low whistle of approval.

"That had to weigh fifty goddamned pounds, Cooler. Ya got a catapult hid under yer shirt?"

Thaddeus laughed. "Two hundred push-ups every day for the last fifty years, my dear Goldstrike... An actor must be fit!"

Once the footings were excavated, the crew found each to be roughly conical, three feet wide at the mouth, four feet deep, and twelve inches in diameter at the bottom. While Amon mixed concrete in a barrow, Goldstrike harnessed his mule to one of the pine posts the Mormon carpenter and his sons had cut and hand-lathed. The animal dragged it to the first site and four staking lines were attached to points about three feet from the top, the mule pulling on one to raise the post while the rest of the crew used the other three to keep it straight as it rose. Once the pole was vertical, the lines were secured using stake-holds drilled into the rock. Afterward the footing was filled with concrete and the crew moved on to the next site. It was hard, methodical work, dusk threatening to become night by the time they finished. The next day, with Benjamin DeMille and Lariat climbing to the top of the poles on railroad spikes hammered in at two-foot intervals, they ran the cable for the common line and connected it to the Paradise Electrical Cooperative transformer. Afterward they ran one last voltage test—the crew positioned along the town's new power line with John Goodlow perched on the IPC pole at the west edge of town and Lariat a quarter mile away atop the last pole, a roost putting him at eye level with the second floor of the Peycomson mansion.

"Ready," Goodlow shouted. Word traveled up the route until it reached Lariat. He attached the voltmeter and gave a thumbs-up that journeyed back down the line to the former college professor. Goodlow flipped a lever to close the circuit, and one thousand feet away, the needle of Lariat's voltmeter jumped.

"Two-forty," he called out with a grin and the Paradise Electrical Cooperative was officially open for business.

# 11

## SECRETS

As the summer of 1919 meandered to a close, Gerald Dredd discovered that neither he nor Junior could speed up the American bureaucracy. An official headcounter was not scheduled to visit Paradise until June of 1920, and according to the Bureau of the Census, neither God nor the devil could make it happen any sooner. "Pin-headed bastards!" Dredd griped when a letter reached his desk informing him of the Bureau's decision. "What's the point of a *goddamned* government if they can't *goddamned* govern the way I want!" Dredd tore the letter in half—incurring a paper cut that further infuriated him—then ripped the document into smaller and smaller pieces that he flung into the air, the scraps of paper drifting to the floor of his office at Dredd Enterprises like huge snowflakes.

"Why do we have to wait until the official census, anyway?" Junior proposed after his father fired off a chain of fiery epithets that sent a shower of spittle in the eldest son's direction. "We already have an official count, of sorts."

"What the hell are you talking about?"

"They had one hundred twenty-nine in the 1910 census, right? That's official. And nine died in the war. It was documented by the Selective Service board you're on, correct? So that's also official. Put those figures together and you have an *official* population of less than one hundred twenty-five. Why not move on them now?"

Dredd picked up a paperweight from his desk, a replica of an Idaho potato made from solid brass. He hefted it, eyeing Junior's head, then put it down and crossed to the window of his office. From there he could see the foothills lying in great lumps on the north edge of the city. The long dry summer had turned them yellow-brown, a stark contrast against the more distant blue-green silhouette of Deer Point, a 7000-foot elevation prosecuting the sky as a backdrop. Suddenly, Dredd whirled about to face his son. He was grinning.

"By God, boy, for once I think you might have something," he said. He called out to Iris through the open door of his office. "Get Bertram Mole on the telephone."

Mole responded quickly to the lieutenant governor and a petition to exercise eminent domain was filed by the afternoon. Gerald Dredd was listed as the provisional condemnor in the matter of *The State of Idaho v. Paradise*. The next morning Dredd met privately with an associate—a fellow known in his shadowy world as "Le Lutin."

"Why am I here?" Le Lutin demanded after Iris showed he and his tall bodyguard into Dredd's office. His voice was tinged with the French accent of his native Montreal. "I've told you before, Gerald. I don't give progress reports. We take the job. We do the job. We get paid. We leave. You know that."

"There's been a change in plans," Dredd said, afterward apprising Le Lutin of the lawsuit to immediately acquire Paradise. "So I may not need you much longer. I won't know for sure until we get a ruling on our petition. If it's denied, we go back to the original plan." Dredd crossed to a small sideboard and poured a finger of scotch into a glass. He threw it back in a swallow, then poured himself another. "Where do we stand with Goodlow?" he asked.

"It's being handled. Why did I need to come down here for this?"

Dredd gestured with the bottle. "You?"

"I don't fucking drink. I've told you that!" Le Lutin moved toward the door, hurling words over his shoulder. "Don't whistle me down here again, Gerald. I'm not your goddamned bird dog! That bloody goat path practically bounced my balls into my cheeks!"

Dredd bristled. "Don't forget who you work for, goddammit!"

Le Lutin turned back, eyes slitted like a rattler about to strike. "I don't forget anything, Gerald," he hissed. "I suggest you remember *that*."

Once Le Lutin and his bodyguard were gone, Dredd phoned Bertram Mole. "How long before we get a ruling?" he demanded.

"We just filed the petition yesterday," Mole replied. "It will take time."

"How much time?"

"Difficult to say…weeks, at least."

"If I wanted a *goddamned* lawyer who couldn't answer a simple *goddamned* question because it's too *goddamned* difficult, then I wouldn't ask *you*. How long?"

"Depends on the judge. They haven't assigned one yet."

This sent Dredd into another rage and he spent several minutes castigating judges and lawyers, the town of Paradise; the doctor who advised him to eat more vegetables and cut back on sweets; the governor who insisted his lieutenant governor occasionally preside over the senate as required by the state constitution; the chef who removed honeyed cornbread from the menu at Morrison's; the nineteenth amendment to the U.S. Constitution that forced him to campaign for women's votes in the upcoming election; his various ex-wives; The Fourth Mrs. Dredd who refused to be discreet when cheating on him; Geraldine who was too absent; Junior who was too present; Carl who simply existed; and Freddie whom he thought weird and annoying. Eventually, he tired.

"For the record, Mister Lieutenant Governor, let me reiterate," Mole advised as his boss caught his breath. "Our petition will likely be denied. Your appointments with the General Land Office and the Selective Service System give you no standing with the Bureau of Census. The population figure from 1910 will stand until there's a new count. That's how a judge will see it. Frankly, when your son proposed this approach, I presumed he was trying to scare the people in Paradise…see if you could convince them to sell now."

"I don't give a good goddamn what you presumed, Bertram. I just want... Wait a minute. What did you just say?"

"I assumed this was a tactic rather than a serious lawsuit," Mole reiterated. "I figured you thought they'd panic and sell to you directly. That would obviate the need to exercise eminent domain at all...save you the trouble of negotiating land use contracts with the government once the property is taken."

Dredd considered Mole's observation for a few moments. "Some might sell," he decided. "But there's a diehard group up there that'll have to be dragged off that mountain." He took a deep breath and noisily released it. "No...it'll have to be the eminent domain thing. Either now or later. I prefer now. Make the lawsuit work...today."

"It can't be done today or probably ever," Mole calmly replied.

Dredd picked up his brass potato paperweight, eyeing the large window that looked out to the northern mountains.

"Rotary Club, Gerald," Iris suddenly called out.

Dredd looked to her voice. She stood in the open doorway of his office.

"And put the paperweight down," she added.

Dredd loved Rotary Club meetings where he could shove his way around, bullying small business owners who dared not incur his disfavor. Although a mediocre intellect, Dredd was a genius at revenge and more than one shop owner had disputed him or made an unflattering comment that provoked doubled rents, cancelled leases, or pulled ads in the *Idaho Statesman*.

"If you leave now, you'll have enough time to rub shoulders before the luncheon," Iris reminded him.

Dredd nodded and then spoke into the phone. "Either make the lawsuit work, Bertram, or figure out a way to get someone from the Bureau of Census in there before June."

❧

The girl's night Thaddeus Cooler had contrived during the Battle of Enter Stage Right, Exit Stage Left went from improvisation to impromptu after Bountiful suggested that the female members in the company of *Our American Cousin* might actually spend a night together in the parlor of the Paradise School. After several postponements, and with the play's premiere just more than a week off, it finally happened with August and three weeks of September behind them. All the women and girls in the company came, shoving furniture against the walls and tossing about pillows and blankets for sleep that didn't arrive until the wee hours. Wanda Cooler and Maude joined the slumber party for a time, eventually retiring to the kitchen and a bottle of cognac. Three glasses in, Wanda confirmed Maude's suspicion that the pair of them shared a history as members of the world's oldest profession. Mrs. Cooler further revealed that she and Thaddeus were not formally wed. "We have an understanding," she told Maude. "If you know what I mean."

Without the inconvenience of men in the way, tongues in the parlor were loosened, secrets shared. Trixie Cooler peeled off her makeup to reveal deep acne scars. Charlotte confessed that the still absent Joshua Purdue of the vaunted Massachusetts Purdues was not a candidate on her unborn infant's large slate of prospective fathers. "I love Joshua," Charlotte told her new pals. "He's really very sweet, but he's not…uh, boudoir-inclined, you might say."

"*Your* boudoir, anyway," Trixie guffawed.

This earned a frown from Charlotte and the sisters might have had an argument had Bountiful not intervened, suggesting they play a game called "The Minister's Cat."

"I'll start," she said, rhythmically clapping her hands. "The minister's cat is an *awful* cat…" She nodded at Sarah DeMille who began to clap along.

"The minister's cat is an *angry* cat," Sarah sing-songed. It carried on from there, the women going through the alphabet a couple of times. By then Trixie had followed the scent of cognac to the kitchen where she joined Maude and her mother. The rest went on to share their thoughts about the male actors in *Our American Cousin*—initially cautious observations that grew bolder after midnight.

"Willie Barkley is so good-looking," one of the minor cast members offered. "And you've got him wrapped around your little finger, Geraldine." It was true. Following the Battle of Enter Stage Right, Exit Stage Left, Willie and Geraldine had become inseparable. When not on stage they huddled together, speaking in hushed tones. After rehearsals, they took long strolls, exploring the foothills to the north or gurgling Mores Creek to the south. The outings always ended outside Geraldine's apartment at the old Busty Rose where Willie bowed and murmured the same farewell. "'Parting is such sweet sorrow… that I shall say goodnight till it be morrow.'"

"Don't be silly," Geraldine countered to the girls. "Will's just acting. If anyone's wrapped him around a finger, it's Mary Meredith, the humble milk maid." This was met by a chorus of good-natured hooting. "It doesn't matter, anyway," the Boise heiress went on. "He's crazy. My father would never approve."

"He's not crazy around *you*," Bountiful said.

Once Willie had been properly dissected and catalogued, the girls put Lariat Comfort in their sights, gently teasing Jeanette. Eventually, they got around to Meriwether Peycomson, more than one inferring that Miss Florence Trenchard and Lieutenant Harry Vernon of the Royal Navy had something going on both on and offstage. "Stop it," Bountiful scoffed. "He's the town's attorney. He's working on our case. Our relationship is business. Besides, he's happily married." Her tone was convincing, even though Meriwether Peycomson was the least wedded of any married man she'd ever known, never mentioning Evangeline. Bountiful had been pursued by more than a few similarly rakish fellows in Washington, DC, both white and Black, all of them dangerous regardless of skin color. Still, attention from a charming and attractive man after a long time without it made her instinctively glad to see him when he appeared at the door of the Paradise School on the Monday after girl's night.

"I've something you must hear," he said, his expression

grim, the charming Lieutenant Harry Vernon supplanted by sober attorney-at-law, Meriwether Peycomson.

Bountiful led him into the parlor. "So…" she began after they were seated on opposite ends of a sofa. "What have you to tell me?"

"A couple of things," the lawyer responded. "First of all, a petition has been filed to immediately acquire Paradise. The state of Idaho is listed as the plaintiff, but Dredd is behind it. A hearing is set for early October." Bountiful visibly paled, prompting Peycomson to slide down the couch and take her hand. "Are you all right?" he asked. "Can I get you something?"

Bountiful shook her head, then gathered herself with a deep breath. "I'm fine," she said, withdrawing her hand from his. "Please go on."

Peycomson studied her face for a moment, then continued. "Dredd claims his roles as a federal agent with the General Land Office and the Selective Service Board allow him to unilaterally amend the census from 1910."

"One hundred twenty-nine."

"Right… According to the brief filed by the state's attorney, nine Paradise men were officially declared dead by the War Department and can be legally subtracted from the 1910 count. Without them, the so-called official count becomes one hundred twenty…five beneath the incorporation threshold."

"So-called…?"

Peycomson nodded. "The suit is frivolous. Dredd may have positions with the Selective Service System and the General Land Office, but neither appointment gives him standing with the Bureau of Census. Moreover, he's yet to be officially appointed as a condemnor. He gave himself the title. The suit is specious."

"So we're not worried?"

"Insofar as the lawsuit, no, I'm not worried."

Bountiful frowned. "You might have led with that, Meriwether."

"Sorry."

"So we're back to where we were… Waiting until the 1920 census has been completed, right?"

"Yes and no. Dredd's lawyer…a fellow named Bertram Mole…knows the lawsuit will go nowhere. I think the intent is to frighten people into selling their property now rather than wait for the count."

Bountiful chewed on her lip as she considered his information for a few moments. Then she shrugged. "I think we're all right. One or two might sell…folks who live alone…but it won't offset the newcomers in town. We'll still be over one hundred twenty-five."

Peycomson didn't respond, instead studying a reproduction on the wall that depicted the death of Crispus Attucks during the American Revolution. "Bountiful, how well did you research your buyers?" he finally resumed, speaking as if the words stung his lips. He shifted his eyes away from the painting to look at her. "Did you ask for personal references or contact prior employers?"

"You're worried about the Coolers, aren't you? I get it. They're colorful—"

"Too colorful. My goodness, Bountiful, everyone in three counties knows they aren't who they say they are. The question I have is, Are they working for Dredd? If so, are they the *only* ones? I'm quite sure Amon and Sarah are legitimate, but…"

He stopped, allowing his thought to finish itself. When it did, Bountiful's lips parted with surprise. She shook her head. "You're not saying that John and Annie Goodlow are…"

"I know how much you like them, Bountiful. I like them too, but…"

"You're wrong. I interviewed John. He was vetted."

Peycomson didn't respond, his mouth drawing a thin line, his gray eyes piercing her.

"You're wrong. You must be," Bountiful repeated.

Peycomson rose and crossed to a window. Two hundred feet away, the Goodlow's penny mansion sat, the tennis court commissioned by original owner Irwin Feldstein replaced by a luxurious back yard. George and Frannie Goodlow were on their hands and knees, peering into the thick grass as if hunting for lost gems. The lawyer watched them for a few moments before turning back to Bountiful.

"A fellow from Idaho Power reached out to me...because I'm the town's attorney," he revealed. "For some reason, he called the University of Montana. Apparently, there's a school of engineering, but they don't offer a degree in *electrical* engineering. John couldn't have received his training there. Moreover, no one named John Goodlow has ever been affiliated with the university...not as a professor, not even as a student."

Bountiful didn't respond. Instead, she rose from the couch and crossed to the fireplace, giving her back to Peycomson as she studied the photos on the mantel—she and Maude, Lariat and Maude, the three of them together.

"There must be some mistake," she said. "John is obviously an electrical engineer. He built a transformer. It works."

She turned to face him.

"Maybe the man from Idaho Power is not telling the truth. Lariat told me about him. He was very competitive with John. Maybe he's lying."

"I contacted the dean, Bountiful. He confirmed everything. It's all true."

Bountiful let her gaze drift down to the ornate carpet on the floor. It was Persian, a compilation of kaleidoscopic shapes and reddish hues that melted into a single color as she stared at it.

"Is that all?"

"I wish it were...but there's something else," Peycomson said. "The day of his interview with you in Boise, John and I had dinner, remember?"

"You invited me... I declined."

"Yes, but John and I did meet. Afterward we went to the bar in the lobby of the Idanha for drinks. While we were there, Dredd joined us. I got the feeling he and John already knew each other."

Bountiful's eyes began to well with tears and Peycomson

rose from the couch. He crossed the room and took her into his arms.

"Dear God, what have I done?" she wept, her face pressed against his chest. "I was the deciding vote. Why didn't I ask for credentials...for references...for something? Everyone depended on me...told me how smart I was. And I got caught up in it. My stupid pride!"

"You couldn't have known," Peycomson whispered.

"If we lose them...*and* the Coolers."

Bountiful looked up at him. Their faces were close together, then suddenly closer. He leaned in and their lips brushed. An instant later she shook free as if the kiss had burned.

"No!"

"Bountiful—"

"No!"

She began to move around the room, anxiously straightening a painting that wasn't crooked, plumping an adequately plumped pillow, pressing a key on the piano—the solitary note lost in the flood of words that next poured out. "There must be another explanation," she insisted. "Another reason he and Annie hid the truth. There just *must* be." She went on, less angry than unsure of whom she should be angry with. Eventually, she stopped, leveling her sapphire eyes on Peycomson. "I have to give them a chance to explain," she said. "That's only fair. I'll talk to John and Annie...hear their side of it. There are two sides to everything."

"Bountiful—"

"I've no reason to wait, right? I'll go now."

Peycomson hesitated, then nodded. "Okay...but as the town's lawyer, I must point out that folks might want to think about selling to Dredd before the government moves in. He wants the land and is willing to pay more now, rather than file for use permits after it's taken. It's not fair, I know, but frankly, if you don't make the census, you'll probably lose your homes. You might as well get the best price for them while you can."

"I want to hear John and Annie's side of this."

"Please just consider what I'm saying."

"I heard you...and I'm not selling anything until I've talked to the Goodlows."

Bountiful swept across the parlor, through the main hallway, and out the front door. Peycomson followed, catching up with her on the porch.

"Bountiful...wait!" he called out.

She turned at the top of the steps. "You don't have to go with me," she said.

"I want to go."

Bountiful hesitated, studying Peycomson's face.

"All right, you can come along," she said. "But I meant what I said in there, Meriwether. What just happened... It can't happen again. It won't." She descended the steps and headed up the walk without waiting for his response.

Bountiful wore a long-sleeved blouse tucked into an ankle-length skirt, and with the warm September sun and the distance from the Paradise School to the Goodlows, a thin layer of perspiration glazed her skin by the time they reached the former Feldstein mansion. Amon DeMille and his sons had masterfully restored the old place for the Goodlows. The broad front steps, once rotted and sagging, had been rebuilt. Warped planks on the porch had been replaced by truer ones, and a trellis for roses had been added along with a porch swing wide enough to hold three people. The window and entry trim were new, as well—perfectly mitered and lacking a single visible brush stroke in the forest green paint. The front door opened before they reached the top of the steps.

"Bountiful...Meriwether!" John Goodlow greeted them. "How wonderful to see you." He invited them into the parlor, a hexagon with a bay window occupying the center three facets. "Sorry about the mess," he said, picking up a couch pillow from the floor." He tossed it onto a deep easy chair, fronted by a wide ottoman. "Sit down. I'll get Annie."

While Goodlow retrieved his wife, Bountiful and Peycomson took the couch, sitting apart by the width of a pillow.

They didn't speak, the abbreviated kiss they'd shared rendering the lawyer's knees fascinating to him, while Bountiful inspected every part of the room without a Peycomson in it. *This place looks lived in*, she thought, a few of George and Frannie's toys scattered about, a knitted throw tossed onto the ottoman as if waiting for feet to cover. Two books were out, one small like a diary or book of poetry. It sat on the coffee table, closed with a bookmark in place, the print of the title too faded to make out. The other book was on a side table next to the easy chair. It was thick, its spine leather-bound, its title easily readable:

INTERNATIONAL LIBRARY OF TECHNOLOGY
ELECTRICAL ENGINEERING

When John returned with Annie, she carried a small tray on which she'd balanced a pitcher of iced tea, four glasses, and a plate of lemon squares. "You must try these," she insisted, placing the plate on the coffee table. "They're quite delicious, if I say so myself." Bountiful and Peycomson politely allowed themselves to be hosted, and once everyone was ice tea'ed and lemon-squared, Annie sat next to her husband on the wide ottoman.

"So what brings you by?" John asked.

"Something of concern has come up," Peycomson began.

"No, Meriwether," Bountiful said softly. "This is for me to do." She faced the Goodlows, her sober aspect slowly transforming Annie's sunny expression into something gray and fearful.

"John…" Annie whispered, linking her arm in her husband's.

Goodlow bowed his head to look into her eyes. "It's okay," he said. "It's going to be okay." He straightened to face his guests, then took a deep breath and released it. "So…" he continued, "you know about the University of Montana."

Bountiful nodded. "Help us understand, John."

Goodlow picked up a lemon square, then returned it to the plate without taking a bite. "We can explain… We *want* to explain."

"Just tell us the truth."

"The truth…"

Goodlow looked at his wife, then back at Bountiful.

"Okay…here's the truth," he said, going on to reveal that he and Annie had not come from Montana. "We've never been there. Annie and I came to Paradise from Pennsylvania. That's how I knew what might be done with our cooperative after we were fully established. I worked for the Westinghouse Corporation… Started on the factory line. I had an aptitude for engineering, but I couldn't afford to go to college."

"An aptitude!" Annie sniffed. "John is a genius."

Her husband shrugged. "I've always liked science and math, but I'd hardly call myself a genius. I studied on my own and one of the engineers at Westinghouse took me under his wing…got me off the line and into his department. He taught me things, and the more I learned, the more I was given to do."

"John is brilliant," Annie interrupted. "He was the smartest person in the company and everyone knew it."

"I doubt that, Annie," her husband said, smiling.

"I don't," she argued. Her expression suddenly soured. "'Under his wing!' He was the worst, that engineer. John would come up with something and that awful man would present it as *his* idea. *He* got the promotions. *He* got the bonuses. He said John had gone as far as he could without a college degree. But he wouldn't lift a finger to help him *get* a degree."

"It wasn't his responsibility, Annie."

She frowned. "Then whose *was* it? You asked him for a recommendation to the University of Pittsburgh, didn't you, John? He could have shown a little *responsibility* and given you one, but what did he do? 'You're bright, but not bright enough for college,' he told you."

"Annie—"

"No, John! Don't make excuses for him." Annie hushed her husband with a finger on his lips, then looked at Bountiful and Peycomson. "'Not bright enough.' That's what he had the gall to tell my husband. Can you believe it? John…not *bright* enough! That's absurd and that son of a... Well, he knew it! He knew you were bright enough, John. You always defend him, but he was *using* you and it wasn't fair."

"Annie—"

"Well, it wasn't, John! It wasn't fair!"

Tears trickled down her cheeks and Goodlow used a napkin to dab at them. "I love you," he said. Neither spoke for a few moments. Then John again faced their visitors. "We read your ad in the paper. It was a chance for us to have a real home, a better life for the kids. We'd put together some savings but not enough to buy a house. We just thought..."

"You could have been honest from the beginning, John," Bountiful said. "It was *you* I liked, not a diploma."

Goodlow nodded. "I wish I'd known that, Bountiful. But I didn't and we wanted to stand out. With no electricity up here, I figured an application from an electrical engineer would separate us from the pack."

"It's not as if he can't do the work," Annie said. "You know he can. He's proven himself."

"I just didn't have a piece of paper that said I could do it," John added.

"What about the postmark?" Bountiful asked. "Your letter was mailed from Missoula."

"I have a friend who actually does teach at the university," John explained. "He posted it for me and forwarded your response."

"And the rest...Horace Goodlow, your family in Chicago?"

"That's all true. I was born and raised in Chicago and Horace Goodlow was my great-uncle."

"But you couldn't afford to go to college? I don't understand. If your family is wealthy—"

"John's father disowned him," Annie said. "He disapproved of me because I'm Catholic."

Goodlow nodded. "It was just Father and my brothers. If Mother had been alive, she'd have loved Annie."

"And your father wouldn't pay for your education?" Peycomson posed.

"Or anything else. I wasn't lying about being the black sheep of the family."

"What about Gerald Dredd?" Bountiful asked. "You met with him in Boise after the interview."

Goodlow's face wrinkled with confusion. "Dredd? I don't understand."

"After dinner," Peycomson said. "Remember? He stopped by the bar?"

"I didn't invite him. I thought *you* did, Meriwether."

The lawyer shook his head. "I didn't invite him either. I guess it was just a coincidence."

Silence followed until Bountiful again spoke. "So your transformer and the power line...they'll work? We'll have electricity?"

"The transformer and the line already work," Goodlow reassured her. "It was always important that they would. A viable electrical system was a necessary part of our plan. Annie and I are getting by on savings right now, but eventually I'll have to make a living. We figured that once Paradise was powered up, other remote areas would want in. When that happens, IPC will need an engineer with experience as they expand into rural townships. I don't think they'll worry much about credentials... Other than their Purdue man, they sure haven't so far."

"So once we'd converted to electrical power, you planned to leave us?"

John shook his head. "No, of course not," he said. "Bountiful, we lied to *get* here, and I'm sorry about that, but Annie and I didn't lie about wanting to *be* here. It will take years to bring power to the nearby towns and a lifetime of work to maintain and update the systems. We'll live here and I'll commute to worksites. Paradise will continue to be our home." The Goodlows unlinked their arms and joined hands. "Bountiful, we made a promise to stay," John continued. "And if you can forgive us for not being entirely truthful, it's a promise we'd like to keep."

Bountiful studied the young couple. If they were evicted and their penny mansion repossessed, the population of Paradise would remain above 125 even if the house was not occupied by new owners. The town could afford to lose them.

*But for what? A secret that hurts no one?*

She glanced at Peycomson. She and the handsome attorney now shared a secret too…one that could cause a lot of hurt.

John and Annie had edged to the front of the ottoman and now perched there like unruly children awaiting a scolding. The room was mostly quiet, save George and Frannie's voices wafting into the parlor from a distant part of the house. The children had ended their search for jewels in the back yard and come inside. Something had delighted them and they were laughing. It was a comforting sound and Bountiful smiled. "You know, Annie, you're absolutely right," she said, picking up another lemon bar. "These are delicious."

They did not further discuss John's credentials, instead focusing on Annie's lemon squares, Frannie's impending fourth birthday, and the upcoming inauguration of the Paradise Electrical Cooperative—set to coincide with the premiere performance of *Our American Cousin* in just five days. Before Bountiful and Peycomson departed, the lawyer and Goodlow solemnly shook hands while Bountiful and Annie hugged. Back at the Paradise School, with Peycomson on his way to Nilsen's General Store, Bountiful swore Maude and Lariat to secrecy, then recounted the afternoon's events as they prepared dinner. She didn't tell them about the kiss in the parlor. Meanwhile, across town, Meriwether Peycomson entered the mercantile. The place was deserted except for Oskar.

"I need to make a phone call," Peycomson told him.

Nilsen collected a nickel and then retired to the bench out front to give the lawyer the privacy he always requested. Once certain the storekeeper wasn't listening, Peycomson rang up the operator and gave her a number. She made the connection and a voice came on the line.

"This is Richard," Peycomson said. "It didn't work. She forgave them."

"So they'll be staying?"

"They'll be staying," the lawyer echoed. "And nobody up here will be selling. I'm sure of that."

# 12

## Opening Night

By opening night of *Our American Cousin*, the eight homes and businesses in the PEC had been wired and fitted with lights and outlets—the work done for all, save the Cooler mansion, by Amon DeMille and his boys. "As experienced grips, my sons are more than able to wire Elysium," Thaddeus reassured Amon. It was the first time anyone other than out-of-town workers had been inside the Peycomson mansion and Amon reported that the renovation had tastefully modernized the interior. "Didn't meet Mrs. Peycomson or Felix, though," the carpenter reported. The boy was in Boise with his nanny and Mrs. Peycomson stayed out of sight."

The Gold Rush Saloon was scheduled to be powered up first, the rest of the PEC members keeping their master switches off until after the premiere. "We'll go live just before the curtain rises," John Goodlow promised. "It will be a big surprise for the audience." Thaddeus Cooler felt obliged to point out that plays were typically performed with the house lights lowered. "However, one cannot dispute that the novelty of Paradise's debut stage production, joined to our community's first electrified lights, will make it a night to remember," he eventually conceded.

Cooler had guided, flattered, cajoled, and challenged his cast into what promised to be a more-or-less adequate presentation of *Our American Cousin*, the amateur thespians mostly in command of their lines. Following Geraldine's recasting, Sheriff Henry Wilcoxon—a capable actor after years of perjury on the witness stand to obtain desired convictions—had assumed the role of Richard Coyle. Since everyone in Paradise was either in the play or a member of the audience, the sheriff brought along a deputy to patrol the otherwise deserted town while the actors were emoting on stage

"I'm more worried about yer deputy than a burglar, Henry," Goldstrike opined. "Them boys o' yers been dippin' their snouts in other people's troughs ever since ya took office." Sheriff Wilcoxon was a genial sort who limited his corruption to courtroom performances and an occasional jug for turning a blind eye to a still. He resented implications to the contrary and reached for his handcuffs. Bountiful intervened before the play had to cast a third Sir Edward.

"Your deputy is much appreciated, Sheriff Wilcoxon," she said. "Thank you very much."

Thaddeus worried that last-minute stage fright might prompt some desertions before the curtain rose, but as the cast donned their makeup, including a rubber ear Charlotte Cooler Purdue glued onto Goldstrike's mangled one, the company's only no-show was Trixie Cooler. Following her demotion from the role of Georgina Mountchessington to assistant director, she had mostly assistant-directed a bottle to her lips. "She's at home, resting," Thaddeus informed his cast in his pre-show remarks. "I'm afraid her production duties have quite exhausted her."

"Gin exhausted her more than any *production duties*," Charlotte remarked to Goldstrike as she worked to attach his fake ear and cover the scar on his cheek with makeup.

On the other side of the curtain audience members filed in as the actors prepared, and after the last of the ticketholders was seated, the Gold Rush's oil lamps were doused, pitching the place into darkness. Then John Goodlow flipped the saloon's master switch and the overhead electrical lights came on, followed by gasps of wonder and delight. Shortly thereafter, the curtain rose on Act I, Scene I of *Our American Cousin*, followed by an unscripted pause when the minor characters of Miss Sharpe, Mr. Buddicombe, and Mrs. Skillet froze, blinking at the packed audience like confused moles emerging from their burrows in broad daylight. Eventually, Miss Sharpe managed to whisper her opening speech to Mr. Buddicombe, and before long, the three actors were murmuring their lines into the floor like a trio of Tibetan monks.

"Project actors…project!" Thaddeus encouraged them from the wing, his whisper loud enough to be heard among those seated in the front rows. Mrs. Skillet then shrieked her next line, followed by an even noisier response from Mr. Buddi-combe, and soon, members of the audience were covering their ears as the actors bellowed at each another like competitors in a hog-calling contest. Mercifully, the cue for Bountiful and Peycomson was finally given and they entered as Miss Florence Trenchard and Lieutenant Harry Vernon of the Royal Navy. They were a charismatic couple and their first lines, delivered at a volume that didn't attract dogs, were interrupted by a smat-tering of instinctive applause, a few of the old army veterans in the audience rising to salute Lieutenant Harry's uniform. The crowd saved their greatest enthusiasm for Thaddeus Cooler when he made his initial appearance as Lord Dundreary.

"'Good morning, Missth Flo—'" the veteran actor managed before thunderous applause interrupted him. Cooler immedi-ately broke character, stepping to the center apron where he doffed Dundreary's deerstalker hat and grandly accomplished three theatrical bows—one for each third of the amassed theatergoers. Afterward he reclaimed his assigned place on the stage, visibly lapsed back into character with a slight shudder, and delivered his line, his voice filling every corner of the sa-loon.

LORD DUNDREARY (With exaggerated lisp): Good morning, Missth Florenth.

FLORENCE TRENCHARD: Good morning, my Lord Dundrea-ry. (Approaches Dundreary from stage right) And who do you suppose has been here? What does the postman bring?

LORD DUNDREARY: Well thometimes he bringth a bag with a lock on it, thometimes newthpaperth, and thometimes letterth, I thuppoth.

Cooler's affected lisp elicited howls of laughter and the play

lurched forward with bossy stage manager Charlotte Cooler
Purdue rushing about to make sure actors entered on their cues
and made the correct costume changes. "You're gonna go into
labor if you don't slow down," Maude advised her during Act
II as Charlotte helped her pull on a dress the character of Mrs.
Mountchessington wore in the next scene. Meanwhile, Wanda
Cooler had shown up only one sheet to the wind, rather than
her usual three, the missed notes of her accompaniment at-
tributable to deadened keys on the Gold Rush Saloon's ancient
piano. Her sons—Gus, Vic, and Nat—were mostly sober as
well, raising and lowering the curtain at the right times and
successfully getting props in place until Act III, Scene III when
Sheriff Wilcoxon, as villainous Richard Coyle, blindly sat where
a chair was supposed to be, landing on his backside to a roar of
laughter from the audience.

"What the heck...?" he exclaimed when his butt thumped
onto the splintered boards of the stage. The sheriff quickly
scrambled to his feet, scowling at the hyenas in the audience before slipping back into his role. "'A glass of wine, Mister Binny,
and a capital place to drink it,'" he recited.

"Seems like ya already had one glass too many, Sheriff,"
someone yelled from the audience. This was followed by an ad
libbed exchange between Sheriff Wilcoxon and the comedian,
after which *Our American Cousin* got back on track.

As they approached Act III, Scene VII—the climactic attempted suicide of Sir Edward Trenchard—Goldstrike had
assayed the part of the play's country squire capably, his lines
reduced by Cooler's editing to a few words here and there.
However, with the curtain lowered between scenes, he was
nervous. His only long speech of the play was upcoming and
he struggled to recall his lines as Charlotte worked to fix his
fake ear. The hot overhead electrical lights had softened the
glue, causing the rubber appendage to swivel clockwise until it
was upside down. Charlotte finished repositioning the ear and
Goldstrike immediately began to push and tap on it.

"Stop fiddling or it's gonna come off again," Charlotte

warned him, applying more glue as the Cooler boys scurried about, converting the set from *Richard Coyle's office* to *The library at Trenchard Manor*.

Goldstrike desperately searched her face. "I can't remember my lines," he whispered. "It's my big scene and I can't remember what I'm s'posed to say."

"'The clock is on the stroke of two...'" Charlotte cued him.

Goldstrike sighed with relief. "Right... 'The clock is on the stroke o' two and Coyle is awaitin' my decision.' I remember it now. Thanks."

"You're welcome," Charlotte replied. "Break a leg."

"What?"

"Good luck."

Scene VII opened with Goldstrike, as Sir Edward, seated at a table in his fictional library—alone and despondent, a prop gun to accomplish suicide on the table next to his chair. The curtain rose, the audience quieted, and thirty seconds of dead silence ensued as Goldstrike studied the floor as if searching for a crack wide enough to slip through. Finally, a hoarse whisper floated in from the wings.

"'The clock is on the stroke of two,'" Charlotte hissed.

The script called for Sir Edward to remain seated, but Goldstrike suddenly leapt from his chair as if something had bitten him on his rear end, the jolt causing his rubber ear to come loose.

"THE STROKE IS ON THE COCK!" he shouted, his fake ear now dangling from the side of his head like an oyster clinging to its shell. He tried to push it back into place. Instead, it came off in his hand, provoking a chorus of guffaws that rendered Goldstrike wide-eyed and panic-stricken. He spun around and delivered his next line to the backdrop.

"'AND COYLE WANTS...'"

He looked to the wing for help.

"'A decision... Coyle is awaiting my decision,'" Charlotte whispered, adding, "and turn around... Look at the audience."

Goldstrike surveyed the crowd, peeking over his shoulder

with the horrified expression of a dog caught defecating on the carpet. More laughter hurtled at him, and as if it were the cue for his next line, he whirled about and struck a proper Sir Edward pose—back ramrod straight, a thumb hooked in the watch pocket of his vest, his other arm dramatically flung outward.

"'THE STROKE IS ON THE COCK!'" he shouted, again flubbing the line. "'AND COYLE IS AWAITIN' MY DECISION.'"

He hesitated again, an open invitation for one of the millhands from Horseshoe Bend to join the cast. "Ya got two strokes on yer cock, Goldstrike. Ya better get one o' them gals backstage to come finish things off."

Goldstrike glared at the heckler. "SHUT THE FUCK UP!" he shouted as the audience howled. He searched the wing, found Charlotte. "Line!" he pleaded.

"'I'll be embittering my life…'" Charlotte called out in a stage whisper.

"'I'LL BE EMBITTERIN' MY LIFE…'"

"'…to save my fortune.'"

"'TO SAVE MY GODDAMNED FORTUNE.'"

The laughter crescendoed and a few of the rowdier fellows began to throw handfuls of popcorn as Sir Edward valiantly forged ahead without Charlotte's prompts.

"'I WILL NOT SURVIVE,'" he went on, "'THE DIP… THE DIPDOWN?'"

"*Downfall*, you idiot," an exasperated Charlotte Cooler Purdue yelled, tossing her script at him.

The millhand, Toby Briggs, suddenly threw a peanut that struck Goldstrike in the nose, neatly plugging one nostril. The reluctant actor recoiled as if it were a pinch of snuff, shook his head like a horse, and then issued an explosive sneeze that shot the peanut from his nose like a tiny cannonball. It hit and bounced off the forehead of a woman in the front row, prompting another explosion of laughter that encouraged a new batch of theater critics to hurl popcorn and peanuts at poor Sir Edward. Finally, Goldstrike had had enough.

"AW FUCK!" he roared, "I DIDN'T WANNA BE IN THIS FUCKIN' PLAY ANYWAY!"

He threw his rubber ear at Briggs, then snatched up the prop gun from the table, pointed it, and pulled the trigger. The sharp report of a gunshot elicited a shocked gasp from the audience and an expression of utter terror from the millhand.

"AIN'T SO GODDAMNED FUNNY NOW, IS IT, TOBY?"

Goldstrike brandished the fake weapon—a starter's pistol with a plugged barrel—as a panicked Briggs lurched to his feet and pushed his way through the packed row, stomping on toes until finally reaching the open aisle with a leap over an elderly woman. "Most erotic experience of my life," she later confessed to her friends after Toby's crotch brushed against her tightly wound hair bun.

"THAT'S RIGHT...RUN, TOBY BRIGGS, YA LOUD-MOUTH SONUVABITCH!" Goldstrike thundered.

Briggs raced for the exit in a half crouch, slanting anxious looks over his shoulder. He'd nearly reached the saloon's double front doors when they flew inward and Henry Wilcoxon's deputy spilled into the bar. For a moment or two the deputy gasped for air, trying to regain his breath. Then he delivered what would be the final line of that evening's performance.

"FIRE!" he shouted.

❧

No flames were visible—just thick brown-gray smoke pouring from every window of Elysium and crawling up the sides of the house to form a single plume that stood against the night sky as if embossed upon it. Sheriff Wilcoxon assumed command, shouting to be heard.

"Get a bucket line goin'," he yelled as the sky to the north flashed with lightning, followed by a rumble of thunder. The actors and theatergoers had stopped at the fire station long enough to grab buckets, picks, shovels, and Pulaski tools, and they quickly formed two queues, transporting buckets of water hand-to-hand from wells behind Elysium and the Paradise School next door. Meanwhile, the town's horse-drawn fire-wagon arrived, its five-hundred-gallon tank full. The hose was unrolled and Willie Barkley manned the nozzle, dragging it dangerously close to the burning house while a couple of loggers volunteered to take the first shift on the see-saw pump. The loggers were a hefty pair, but their best efforts only produced enough pressure to send a modest stream of water into the bottom level of the home.

Suddenly, the wire running from the house to the power line of the PEC snapped loose. It hit the ground, igniting a nearby patch of dry grass. "Stay back!" John Goodlow shouted. "It's live! The wire is live!" He made a dash for the post as others doused the grassfire, leaping over the quivering electrical cable and then climbing the tall pole as adroitly as a lumberjack. He reached the top, pried open a breaker box, and cut power to the line.

On the ground below, Bountiful, Maude, Thaddeus Cooler, and Lariat had joined the line to the well behind the Paradise School. Meriwether Peycomson was with them, while Goldstrike, Oskar Nilsen, Arnold Chang, the entire DeMille family, and Annie Goodlow were in the other queue. The makeshift crews labored valiantly, the acrid smoke burning their eyes as buckets were passed from one person to the next—each pail of water tossed at the burning house like a splash in the ocean, the columns of smoke merely thickening as the volunteers began to tire, the oldest of them panting ominously. Maude was among the latter, coughing as she struggled to keep up. Eventually, Bountiful and Lariat, with Peycomson trailing them, half-carried her to a safe place on Goodlow Road about 400 feet from the fiery center of the battle zone. A small collection of other seniors had gathered there, wheezing and coughing as they struggled to breathe.

"Stay here, Grandma," Bountiful insisted, eyeing the sky

where jagged bolts of lightning raged across the firmament, explosions of thunder less than a second behind them. The storm was close, perhaps a mile away. It was moving in their direction, the lightning capable of a strike that could ignite the forest and burn down the rest of Paradise.

"I want to help," Maude protested.

"No," Bountiful said, as a few raindrops began to fall. "You have to stay here."

Suddenly, there was a low roar as flames broke through the roof of Elysium. The tongues of smoke pouring out the broken windows were abruptly sucked back into the house—revealing an interior blaze that glowed red-yellow against the night-darkened exterior sandstone—and a moment later, the third-level crow's nest collapsed with a stupendous crash into the second floor as the fire chimneyed out the top of the house and began to color orange the clouds of dirty smoke billowing overhead.

Willie Barkley had dragged the fire hose closer to the house and Wilcoxon called out to him. "She's vented, Willie! Get back!" An instant later the top of the house seemed to erupt, shooting an explosion of embers into the sky like a Roman candle. Popping and sizzling as they cascaded downward, a few landed on Willie and the loggers manning the fire wagon with others sparking new fires in the dry grass and weeds. "Get back, Willie!" Wilcoxon repeated as a second eruption sent another shower of embers into the night, several landing on Bountiful and the rest of the small group gathered on Goodlow Road. From a few feet away, Peycomson pointed at her feet.

"You're on fire," he said, his voice eerily disembodied.

Bountiful followed his finger. An ember had landed on the bottom of her long skirt and flames now licked at the hem, their heat palpable. Motionless—as if it were happening to someone else—she looked up at the lawyer, her face expressionless.

"I'm on fire," she said.

"Oh my God, Miss Bountiful!" Lariat suddenly shouted. He fell to his knees and began to beat at the flames with his hands.

Bountiful still didn't move. She seemed detached, as if she were not kindling but a bored teacher proctoring an examination. When the last of the flames were extinguished, the teenager stood, his face lined with worry.

"What's wrong with you? Why are you acting like this?"

Bountiful took his hands and examined them front and back. "You're okay," she said. "They aren't burned."

"What's wrong with you?"

Bountiful probed Lariat's face for a few moments, then abruptly shuddered. "I'm fine," she said. "I'm okay now." She next looked at Peycomson, her eyes widening as if seeing him for the first time. Minutes earlier on the stage of the Gold Rush Saloon, he'd artfully portrayed the dashing Lieutenant Harry Vernon as a brave and stalwart hero. But now, with flames overwhelming Elysium and the lawyer at a safe distance from the center of the battlefield, he seemed more craven than courageous. A frown creased her features. "Why are you here, Meriwether?" she demanded. "Why aren't you helping fight the fire?"

"I...must evacuate Evangeline and Felix," he replied, his voice lacking its usual resonance. "I want to stay and help. I really do, Bountiful. But Evangeline...she and little Felix...and Frau Gerta. I must rescue them." He studied the ground. "You understand, don't you? Of course, you—"

"It's okay, Meriwether," Bountiful cut him off. "You don't have to explain. Just go... Get your family to safety. But take the rest of these folks too." She indicated the seniors sprawled about them with a sweep of her arm.

Peycomson blinked nervously. "I'm not sure—"

"About a mile west of town there's a clearing," Bountiful continued. "Mores Creek is wider there. It's far enough from the treeline to be safe if the whole forest goes up. Take your family and Grandma. Then get the rest of these folks to the clearing. Make as many trips as needed. Afterward stay put. You don't have to come back."

"Bountiful, I'm—"

"You'll be safe there."

"But—"

"Just *do* it, Meriwether." She looked at Lariat, adding, "Let's go."

Bountiful and Lariat headed back to rejoin the firefight, leaving Peycomson behind. They found the bucket lines still running, but Elysium was nevertheless wrapped in flames with dozens of small satellite blazes scattered about the dying mansion, a line of them headed for the Paradise School. Suddenly, the 500-gallon water tank on the fire-wagon went dry, the hose drooping as the last of the water dribbled from the nozzle.

"Forget the house!" Wilcoxon yelled. "It's gone! Let it go! Contain the fire! Keep it from spreading! That's all we can do now!"

Three crews formed to dig firelines and a pentagonal perimeter around Elysium was established with Goodlow Road and Only Real Street comprising two of its sides. Goldstrike led a group to the open ground between the Cooler mansion and the Paradise School; Amon DeMille organized a second crew to the north between Elysium and the forest; and John Goodlow took a small platoon to protect the area between the burning house and the buildings that made up the tiny business district of Paradise. Most of the fireline workers had no idea what to do and began by clearing shallow paths little more than a foot wide.

"Like this!" Goldstrike shouted at his crew, digging out combustible duff across a three-foot span and then scraping the ground down to mineral soil. "Tell them others how to do it!" he told Lariat and the teenager dashed off, going first to De-Mille's group and then Goodlow's. When he returned, half of Goldstrike's team had stopped working and sat on the ground or leaned over their shovels and picks, gulping great draughts of smoke-laden air. The teenager grabbed a shovel and began to dig and scrape alongside Bountiful and the old prospector, moving at twice the pace of the others. "Slow and steady, son," Goldstrike told him, sweat dripping from his chin. "This ain't a horse race. We're plowin' a field."

Elysium was now in its death throes, the creaks and crashes of falling rafters and joists joined to the pop and crackle of the blaze as Goldstrike, Bountiful, and Lariat toiled silently with their friends and neighbors, the heat of their labors and the fire soaking them in sweat. Their lungs ached, their eyes burned, and their muscles cried out, but they kept working as orange flames licked at the sky and more embers burst like popcorn from the top of the house. The storm had moved closer with scattered raindrops offering hope of providential assistance, but as if the devil, rather than God, had decided their fate, a bolt of lightning suddenly struck a solitary pine near the forest's edge. It ignited the oily needles and the tree exploded, producing its own shower of embers. A few landed on the roof of the Paradise School, others falling within the thick blanket of pine trees to the north or on the high, dry grass that separated Elysium from the rest of the town.

Bountiful looked toward the Paradise School. The dim light from a single oil lamp on the porch revealed a figure climbing the steps.

"It's Maude," Goldstrike shouted. He grabbed Bountiful's arm. "Get her outta there!"

Bountiful ran for the house with Lariat on her heels, the pair of them bolting up the porch steps and through the front door. They found Maude in the parlor, kneeling by a low sideboard, one of its cabinet doors pulled open.

"The photo albums, your baby things," the former madam sobbed. "They're all in here! We'll lose them!" Lariat retrieved a pillowcase and they filled it with mementos. He and Bountiful then dragged Maude back outside in time to see the taillights of Peycomson's automobile as it headed west on Goodlow Road, the last of the elderly refugees, save Maude, in his car. Bountiful turned to Lariat.

"It's up to you now," she said. "Get Grandma to the clearing on Mores Creek." She hoisted up her long skirt, reached under to pull off her petticoat, and handed it to the teenager. "Once you're at the creek, rip this into bandanas. Soak them in the creek and pass them around. Have people cover their faces. Get everyone into the water when the fire gets close."

Lariat took the petticoat, then hesitated.

"Get going!"

"Miss Bountiful—"

"Lariat, I don't have time to argue. Please do as I ask!"

"But what about you?"

"I'll be fine. Get going!"

Lariat reluctantly took Maude's arm, but they'd taken only a few steps when the boy turned, grinning. The rain had begun in earnest, fat droplets loudly spattering onto the flagstone walk of the Paradise School.

"Hear that?" he said. "Look up."

Bountiful did. Overhead, the clouds were high, unlike the low nimbi that dropped soft, late afternoon rain on Paradise nearly every day. Lariat pointed at the clouds, a grin on his face. "We're gonna be fine," he shouted. "Don't you remember, Miss Bountiful? You taught me this. Raindrops from high clouds have farther to fall. They get bigger. It's gonna come down heavy. It'll put out the fires. We're gonna be all right."

He continued to speak, but his words were muted as the storm abruptly roared in—not a timid shower, but just as Lariat predicted, an intense, torrential rain that cascaded onto Elysium, beating down the flames that spiraled from the top of the mansion, drenching the forest to the north, and soaking the exhausted volunteers. The great curtains of rain made quick work of the flames on the roof of the Paradise School and transformed the satellite fires on the ground into hiss and steam. It turned the excavated firelines into mud and Only Real Street into a running stream—the deluge saturating the earth and everything on it as Bountiful, Lariat, and Maude laughed and cried, huddling together to form a canopy over the pillowcase that contained the history of their lives.

Within minutes it was over. The clouds moved on, uncovering a full moon, and everyone gathered in front of the smoking, charred rubble that was once the grandest of the penny mansions. With ghostly light silhouetting the blackened husk of Elysium against the night sky, the exhausted firefighters shook hands and exchanged hugs, congratulating one another for saving the town—indeed, for saving each other. Eventually, someone noticed that Thaddeus Cooler was missing.

"He was on a bucket line at the start of things," Oskar Nilsen remembered. "I saw 'im."

"Far as that goes, where were the rest o' them goddamned Coolers?" Goldstrike pointed out and for the first time the townspeople realized, that other than Thaddeus's brief tour of duty, nary a Cooler had joined in the fight.

"Maybe they're in the carriage house," someone suggested. The large edifice behind Elysium was still intact and Wilcoxon dispatched his deputy to search it. The fellow returned a few minutes later.

"Deserted," he said. "Car's gone too."

Sheriff Wilcoxon scanned the faces in the crowd. "Did anyone see the Coolers leave the Gold Rush?" No one had and the sheriff put his deputy in charge, then headed back to the saloon. Goldstrike came along. When they reached the establishment it was still brightly illuminated, the deserted stage inside awaiting the completion of *Our American Cousin.* The table where Sir Edward had contemplated suicide was there, as was the prop pistol Goldstrike fired at Toby Briggs and the rubber ear he'd thrown at the millhand. However, Lord Dundreary was nowhere to be found—the same true of Assistant Director Trixie Cooler, Stage Manager Charlotte Cooler Purdue, Musical Director Mrs. Wanda Cooler, and the play's stagehands, Gus, Vic, and Nat. Indeed, the backdrop on the theatrical production the Cooler family had staged for the community of Paradise over the last several months had at last been lifted, revealing what many in town had always suspected was behind it… Nothing.

Goldstrike pointed at the stage floor. Lying on the apron was the only remaining member of the Cooler clan—a two pound-eight ounce, bouncing baby couch pillow, the ribbons Charlotte used to secure it to her abdomen still attached like umbilical cords. "Them sons o' bitches!" the old prospector cursed, his words hurled into the air where they smoldered only briefly before evaporating under the heat of the saloon's brand-spanking-new electrical lights. "Them goddamned sons o' bitches!" he repeated when the sheriff didn't respond.

# 13

## A Rumor in the Family Tree

The next morning the town council inspected the damage along with Sheriff Wilcoxon, Ed Riggins, and the remaining penny mansioneers: Meriwether Peycomson, John Goodlow, and Amon DeMille. Although the crow's nest had collapsed into the second floor, the stone walls of Elysium's lower two levels were still standing, save places at the top where fallen rafters had dislodged blocks of sandstone, leaving spaces that looked like missing teeth. Goodlow went to the breaker box on the side of the house. He returned a minute later. "The master switch was on," he reported. "It shouldn't have been flipped until after the play." With Wilcoxon leading the way, the team cautiously climbed the blackened steps and went inside. Ed Riggins snapped photographs for the next edition of the *Idaho World*, issuing a low whistle after the first of several shots. "They gutted it," he murmured.

It was true. As the inspectors cautiously negotiated the rubble it was apparent that the Coolers had picked the place clean. Gone were the gold leaf frames surrounding the wall murals. Gone, too, were the Italian tiles, the ornate marble fireplace surrounds, the magnificent chandeliers, the crafted metal railings, the heavy porcelain-coated bathtub in the master suite, and the huge teak dining room table and matching side buffet; indeed, any furniture once belonging to Horace Goodlow was gone, replaced by the twisted metal legs of a folding table in the kitchen, the ashen remains of wood-and-canvas camp chairs, and the twisted wires and shattered tubes of what had been a countertop radio. Even the mahogany floors on the main level had been pirated, leaving only the raw subfloors.

"Them goddamned trucks wasn't haulin' stuff in," Goldstrike observed. "They was takin' it out."

The sweeping stairs to the second level had collapsed and a gaping hole in the center of the expansive foyer revealed the wreckage of the crow's nest. Its metal balustrade had been torn loose and dangled through the opening. Goldstrike gripped the bottom of the suspended ironwork and tested it with a tug.

"Best not go up there, Goldstrike," Wilcoxon warned, but the old prospector ignored him, scrambling up the makeshift ladder and then disappearing into the second level. He reappeared after less than a minute.

"It's gutted up here too," he reported, looking down at the others. "Nuthin' but what's left o' cots in the bedrooms…and these." He held up a five-gallon metal bucket in one hand and a length of wire in the other. The bucket was warped from the heat. "One end o' this wire was in the bucket and the other was hooked up to one o' them goddamned electrical outlets," Goldstrike added. He dropped the bucket through the opening. Wilcoxon caught it and sniffed tentatively.

"Kerosene," he reported. "This wasn't no accident… Them Coolers stripped the place clean, then tried to cover their tracks with the fire." He looked up through the opening. "Get back down here, Goldstrike. We need to clear out before this place falls in on us."

The inspection team reassembled outside, where Goldstrike offered several opinions, all centered around the different types of bastards or sonuvabitches the Coolers represented, what ought to be done with them once they were caught, and why he was best suited to do it. Eventually, Sheriff Wilcoxon maneuvered him back to the problem at hand: the Coolers were missing.

"They're up in them mountains, I betcha," Oskar Nilsen speculated, gesturing at the foothills to the north.

Wilcoxon shook his head. "They ain't the campin' types, Oskar. They'll try to flee the jurisdiction. I already contacted Sheriff Killeen down in Boise. He promised to put a man at the train depot and get word out to his patrol officers. He was gonna call the sheriffs over in Canyon, Elmore, and Owyhee Counties too. Those are the directions them Coolers'll most likely head."

"What do you suppose they did to Thaddeus?" Maude wondered. She pulled a lacy handkerchief from inside the neckline of her dress. "I know they were grifters, but my Thaddeus…my dear, sweet Thaddeus. He didn't do this!"

During the production of *Our American Cousin*, Bountiful's grandmother had taken to heart Wanda's inference that the Cooler marriage was more contractual than connubial. Lord Dundreary and Mrs. Mountchessington's daily co-producing had subsequently spilled into occasional nights in Maude's bedroom. It was a girlish crush that puzzled folks in Paradise. The former madam was a tough old bird—skilled at keeping her heart out of a man's reach, lest someone like Thaddeus Cooler try to break it. Nevertheless, the self-decreed "legend of the stage" seemed to have broken it after all.

"Thaddeus didn't do this," Maude reiterated, her tears freely flowing. "He wasn't entirely on the up-and-up. I know that. But he would never have started a fire. He knows a fire up here could take the entire town!"

Sheriff Wilcoxon narrowed an eye. "Do you know where he is, Maude? You two been in contact?"

"What's that supposed to mean?"

"It's a simple question," the sheriff replied. "You two been peanut butter and jelly since he got here. Do ya know where he is?"

Maude swiped at her tears. "Fuck you, Henry! I don't have to answer your—"

"Now, Maude, don't get yer knickers in a twist."

"No, Henry, I mean it! Fuck you! I don't have to explain myself to some tin star from Horseshoe Bend!"

Maude stomped off, and because he'd learned not to lie on the tracks when a woman with a head of steam was barreling down them, Wilcoxon did not follow. Later that morning another meeting was held, this one in the parlor of the Paradise School. The town council was there along with Meriwether Peycomson, the DeMilles, the Goodlows, Willie Barkley, and Geraldine Dredd. Goldstrike wasn't happy about the unscheduled gathering. After a long night battling the fire and then standing guard with a few others to make certain an ember didn't burst back to life, he'd been sound asleep when Willie roused him.

"Who called this damned thing, anyway?" he griped once everyone was there.

"I did," Geraldine said. Seated close to Willie on one of the sofas, the young heiress had bandages on her hands after fighting the fire alongside the rest, carrying buckets of water and then digging and clearing on one of the firelines until her hands were covered in blisters. "This was my father's doing," she tearfully told the group in the parlor. "I'm sure it was and I wanted you all to know that I'm terribly sorry."

"Geraldine, this was not your fault," Bountiful said. "And we don't know that your father had anything to do with it." A chorus of reassurances followed, but the young heiress was unconvinced.

"Perhaps if I'd not auditioned for the play…"

"Nonsense, dear," Maude said. "This would have happened anyway. You couldn't have stopped it."

Goldstrike agreed. "Even if yer pap was involved, Miss Geraldine, you ain't to blame fer what he does."

"That's right, dear," Maude added. "The father bears the child's sins… Not the other way around. That's in the Bible."

Oskar Nilsen, who read from the Holy Book every night, shook his head. "That ain't exactly what the Bible says, Maude."

"Then fuck the Bible," the former madam countered.

Her remark provoked laughter, and once it had subsided, Bountiful took advantage of the gathering, asking Peycomson to apprise the assembly of his plan for the upcoming hearing in the matter of *The State of Idaho v. Paradise*. After chauffeuring the last of the seniors back to town from their downstream sanctuary on Mores Creek earlier in the day, he was now bathed and shaved; indeed, he looked ready for his court appearance even though it was a few days off. He filled the next few minutes with *ergo's* and *ex facie's* and *fumus boni iurum* until Goldstrike became impatient.

"I ain't got that many years to live, Peycomson... Get to the goddamned point."

The lawyer chuckled. "Quite right, Goldstrike... So here's the point. I expect the lawsuit to be dismissed, whether next week or at a future hearing. It will force Mole and Dredd to wait for the official census...give us time to get above the incorporation threshold again." He paused for questions, then added, "As we all know, without the Coolers, we're at one-twenty-four. We need one more person."

"Then you've got her," Geraldine said, taking Willie's hand.

☙

Two days later, on the first Monday of October, Bountiful drove Peycomson to Boise for the court appearance. Geraldine and Willie came along. "I want to show Will the tearoom at the Idanha," Dredd's daughter justified to Bountiful. "He's never been there." After reaching the capital city, Bountiful dropped off Peycomson at the courthouse, then drove to the Idanha Hotel and parked on the street.

"I'll meet you back here in an hour," she told Geraldine and Willie. The young couple went inside the hotel and Bountiful walked the two blocks separating the Idanha from the offices of Dredd Enterprises.

"Is he in?" Bountiful asked Iris Campbell upon entering the reception area.

Iris nodded. "I'll let him know you're here."

Dredd's assistant went into her boss's inner office. Bountiful next heard muffled voices, and when Iris reappeared, Dredd was with her.

"Miss Dollarhyde, to what do I owe this pleasure?" he

boomed. He held open the door and Bountiful went in. Junior was there, tucked into an upholstered chair by a wall of bookshelves. He didn't get up.

"We need to speak privately," Bountiful said to Dredd, glancing at Junior.

"Oh now, whatever you have to say, I'm sure my son won't faint."

"I'd prefer to keep this between you and me."

Junior wriggled more deeply into the chair cushions. "We don't really care what you'd prefer," he said, smirking. "Do we, Dad?"

Bountiful leveled her sapphire eyes on Junior's father, and for a moment, the senior Dredd's face flickered with fear.

"Get out," he abruptly barked at his son, his eyes still on Bountiful.

"But, Dad—"

"Get out!"

Junior disentangled himself from the chair and went to the door. He put his hand on the knob and then paused, eyeing Bountiful. "Blue eyes or not..." he sneered. "You're still a nigger."

After he was gone, Dredd eased into the high-backed, padded swivel chair behind his desk. Its seat was slightly elevated, allowing him to look down at visitors seated opposite him. "Make yourself comfortable," he said, gesturing at a pair of chairs on the other side of his big desk.

"I'll stand," Bountiful said. "This won't take long."

Dredd chuckled. "Dispensing with niceties, are we? Perhaps, I should prepare myself." He rose, went to the sideboard where he kept his liquor, poured two fingers of scotch into a glass, and then looked at her, holding the bottle aloft. "May I offer you a drink, Miss Dollarhyde?"

"No."

Dredd reclaimed the padded swivel chair and held up his glass to the light, peering at it as if evaluating the facets of a gemstone.

"So…I heard you had a fire up there? Not one of your penny mansions I hope."

"Don't be coy, Gerald. I know the Coolers were on your payroll."

Dredd smiled. "Were they? That's news to me, but I suppose it's possible. I do most of the firing around here, but others do the majority of the hiring." He sampled his scotch. "Regardless, they're gone, aren't they? Where does that put your census? Around one-twenty-four?"

"One hundred twenty-five when Doctor June returns," Bountiful replied, resisting the urge to throw Geraldine's defection into her father's face.

"Quite a thing, the board of medicine did," Dredd observed. "Forcing Stan to ride the circuit. Unprecedented, really. I wonder how that came about?" He finished off his scotch and set the glass on his desk. "I heard he's laid up in Yellow Pine. Got infected, himself. Be a shame if he dies. That'd leave you folks a man short in the census. Bad disease, that Spanish flu."

"I'm not here to talk about Doctor June or the census," Bountiful said.

"Really?" Dredd smiled, a reptilian thing that made her involuntarily shiver. "Then it's a purely social call? I confess that I'm flattered… Surprised, mind you, but flattered."

Bountiful shook her head. "It's not a social call. It's about Friederich."

The mention of Dredd's father was a surprise to the real estate baron and he showed it, his serpentine smile slowly melting.

"Friederich? My father, Friederich? What business is he of yours?"

"I'm sure you know."

"I'm sure I don't," Dredd managed, even though he *did* know, recalling his father's words from thirty years past. *You have a nigger sister*, Friederich had revealed to his son, age and alcohol fueling the late-night confession. The girl's mother—a fifteen-year-old runaway slave the bounty hunter kidnapped before fleeing the Confederacy—had escaped after Friederich reached Idaho, turning up at the Busty Rose. Maude took her in and eventually adopted the girl, encouraging her to pick a new name. "Lily, I think," the runaway had decided. "Lily Dollarhyde." Subsequently Maude kept Friederich at bay—first with a shotgun, and later after he'd moved on to Boise, with a secret room beneath the Paradise School where Lily hid whenever Friederich showed up in search of transactional companionship. The former Paradise town sheriff eventually discovered the subterranean chamber and had his way with Lily. She was in her forties by then, the resultant pregnancy complicated. She died in childbirth, naming her daughter Bountiful before she passed. Not long thereafter, Friederich Dredd was shot and killed on his way home from a Boise saloon. His murderer was never caught.

Friederich had never revealed the identity of Gerald's half-sister, and after his father's death, the real estate baron forgot about her, save occasional concerns that another heir to the Dredd fortune might turn up. Such anxieties were always short-lived. His father had scattered a number of his only namesake's half-siblings around Idaho. None had ever come forward with the proof or the nerve to stake a claim, and as the years passed, Dredd's Black baby sister gradually dissipated into nothing more than a rumor to him. Unfortunately, as he looked into blue eyes uncomfortably identical to the ones in his bathroom mirror each morning, it seemed the rumor had climbed back into his family tree.

"You've no proof... No proof whatsoever," he said. "No one will believe you."

Bountiful laughed, a humorless thing. "Won't they? Will your white friends really care about proof? Will your private clubs? Will voters? Seems to me a rumor is as good as the truth to most people...especially your kind."

Dredd clenched his teeth. He knew she was right. He'd spent years floating paper boats into the little puddles of Boise society and Idaho politics. A muddied family history would sink memberships in clubs that insisted on unsullied bloodlines, as well as the political career he'd industriously exploited to line his pockets.

"So what do you want…money?" he snapped. "That's not a problem. Name your figure."

"I don't want money. I want you to withdraw your petition."

Dredd's face flashed with anger. Then he took a deep breath and released it like steam from a locomotive. Slowly, a smile formed—the same one he trotted out at back-slapping fund-raisers or when baby-kissing on the campaign trail.

"Bountiful, let's slow down for a minute," he cooed.

"And no more petitions to force us out," the young school-teacher continued. "You leave Paradise alone and I'll leave you alone."

"Let's talk this over," Dredd said, the warmth in his voice believable if one didn't know him. "Perhaps if you understood why I need your properties? I apologize if I seemed rude be-fore. But to be fair, you took me by surprise, didn't you?" He chuckled. "It's a bit of a shock to discover that I have a sister." He then articulated his plan to seed the Rockies with vacation destinations catering to America's version of landed gentry—a class of people whose parents and grandparents had worked hard to build fortunes their heirs would work just as hard to deplete. Paradise was to be the first of many such spots. "Now, I know your grandmother is quite the businesswoman," Dredd went on, "and she'll understand when I say there are millions to be made in this, Bountiful…literally millions. Of course, now that I know you're family, I'd want you to profit from it as well. As a shadow partner, of course…times being what they are." He fashioned a smile, a disingenuous thing more suited to a scorpion than a sibling. "Don't get me wrong, Bountiful. I've no problem with you colored folks, but you know how people are. I'm afraid my investors might be skittish if they thought a…uh, mixed-blood person…was on my side of the bargaining table. I don't agree with them, mind you, but—"

"I already told you. I don't care about money," Bountiful interrupted. "And you don't need Paradise. There are many places where you can put your resorts. One less shouldn't matter."

"Oh, but you're wrong, dear sister," Dredd purred. "The process by which I obtain the land in Paradise will provide legal precedent for other acquisitions. My lawyers tell me it's critical to the entire plan. Indeed, without Paradise, there is no plan."

"Then it would appear you have no plan," Bountiful said. She turned to go.

Dredd raised both arms as if she were robbing him at gunpoint. "Now, just wait a minute, Bountiful," he said. She turned back and Dredd lowered his arms. "Okay, you've got me… I give up." He shook his head, again chuckling. "You're right, sister," he conceded. "I don't absolutely need Paradise. But I had to give it a try. You understand, right? I wouldn't be doing my job if I didn't try."

"You're making this more complicated than it needs to be, Gerald. We're not really family. I don't want to be your sister any more than you want to be my brother."

Dredd quickly sobered. "Right… It's business. I get it. You're selling your silence and I appreciate that, Bountiful. I do. No offense, but the circles I run in… It's like you said. They're… uh, exclusive. I won't argue the right or wrong of it. It's just the world we both live in, am I right? We must lead our lives with that in mind, yes?"

"All I want is for you to leave Paradise alone," Bountiful repeated. "You back away and I'll make sure my Black face doesn't turn up at one of your white clubs."

Dredd stroked his chin for a few moments, then reached for his pen.

"And no one will know about our father?" he said, scribbling on a blank sheet of paper.

"Grandma has always known, but she'll comply with any agreement you and I reach."

Dredd continued to write, creating a contract he replicated on a second sheet of paper. Afterward he signed both and placed the two handwritten documents on Bountiful's side of the desk. He set his pen down between them. "I'll need you to sign off on this."

"Is that really necessary?"

"I's dotted, t's crossed…always best."

Dredd had a well-established history of ignored signatures and broken promises. It rendered any contract suspect, signed or not. Nevertheless, Bountiful picked up the documents, perused both and then compared them. The terms were elusive. In his proposal she agreed to non-disclosure of "mutually agreed upon information" in return for Dredd's promise to "permanently cease and desist in the pursuit of mutually agreed upon actions." Both parties waived the rights to future claims on their respective estates.

"I'm no lawyer," Bountiful said as she placed the tip of the pen beneath the body of the first note. "But even I know that this won't hold up in court. It's too vague."

"Perhaps," Dredd said. "My lawyers have won judgments with less."

Bountiful began to sign, then hesitated. "In that case," she posed, "there is one more thing.

From behind his big desk, Dredd stiffened.

"Geraldine wants to remain in Paradise," Bountiful went on. "You must agree to respect her wishes."

For a moment, Dredd's face registered disbelief. Then, he abruptly exploded, his swivel chair sent spinning as he leapt from it and headed around his desk. "She's my goddamned daughter," he barked, his fists clenched. "And I won't have some darkie bitch—"

Bountiful didn't move, her gaze unwavering. "Careful… *brother*," she said.

Dredd jolted to a halt, his momentum leaving him slightly bent at the waist, arms dangling in front of his body like an ape. For several seconds he wobbled in place, issuing a low vibratory growl, his eyes tracking back and forth between a sharp letter opener on his desk and the soft hollow in Bountiful's neck.

"So we're agreed?" she said.

Dredd remained silent, glaring at her.

"Gerald?"

The real estate baron held up under her unyielding gaze a bit longer. Then his shoulders slumped and he nodded. No more words were exchanged. Bountiful signed both contracts, tucked one into her purse, and left without saying goodbye.

# 14

## SHEEP'S CLOTHING

A second car followed Bountiful, Geraldine, Willie, and Peycomson after they left Paradise for Boise that morning, maintaining a discreet distance to avoid detection as they traversed the winding road to the capital city. A woman drove with a single passenger close beside her, his head barely clearing the dashboard. They parked in a small lot behind the brick-and-mortar edifice that housed Dredd Enterprises but stayed in the vehicle, watching as Bountiful made her way up the street and entered the building. Less than twenty minutes later the Paradise schoolteacher exited and headed toward the Idanha Hotel. The tall woman and her short companion then went in and were soon joined in Dredd's office by Richard Bright, the man known in Paradise as Meriwether Peycomson. Bright claimed a padded chair by the bookshelves, but Frau Gerta Frobe remained standing with Felix "Le Lutin" Ombre in her arms. Although dressed in the short pants of a small boy and sporting bowl-cut hair like a moppet, Le Lutin was not a child but a grown man in his mid-thirties with the broad forehead, short fingers, and slightly curved spine typical of achondroplasia—a disorder of bone growth resulting in adult dwarfism. His child-like appearance, augmented by clothing and makeup, was merely a bizarre and sinister calling card, one well-known in the underworld he inhabited. "Don't call attention to it," Dredd warned Bright before the lawyer's first encounter with Le Lutin and Frau Gerta months earlier. "He's a touchy little bastard. Say the wrong thing, he'll slice your neck open."

The three ersatz Peycomsons listened as Dredd reviewed the details of his meeting with Bountiful Dollarhyde. "We need to manage the situation," he finished up.

"Not part of our contract, Gerald," Le Lutin said. He wriggled impatiently until Frau Gerta set him down on one of the chairs in front of Dredd's desk. From there he scrambled onto the broad, flat surface, took a fountain pen from its holder, and began to scribble on the inkpad like a toddler. Frau Gerta took the pen away and picked him up.

"No, no," she said as Le Lutin whimpered plaintively, struggling to grab the pen from her outstretched hand. "No, no... be a good boy."

"Stop acting like that and pay attention, goddammit!" Dredd growled from his high-backed desk chair. "Did you hear what I said? She needs to be managed...both she and her grandmother."

The little man bared his teeth, freakishly morphing from impudent toddler to Le Lutin. "I already told you, Gerald!" he hissed. "It's not in our contract. Kill them yourself."

"*Kill* them?" Bright protested, rising from his seat in the corner. "What are you talking about?"

Dredd frowned. "Keep your voice down!"

"You can't *kill* them!" Bright said, this time in a whisper.

Dredd glanced at the door as if an ear were pressed against the other side. "I didn't say anything about *killing* anyone, understand?" he said. "I want the situation *managed*. Get it? Just managed." He picked up the pen Le Lutin had used to doodle and began to tap it on the edge of his desk. "Besides, what's it to you, Richard? You dipping your wick in that nigger girl? It's not a bad idea, mind you. Maybe you can put some different ideas in her head. Get her to see reason."

"I can't hear any more of this," Bright said, moving toward the door. "This isn't protected by attorney-client privilege and I want no part of—"

"Now just hold on, Richard," Dredd cajoled.

The lawyer stopped and turned, bravely exhibiting the same expression he'd used to de-fang the straw-haired cop in the tearoom of the Idanha Hotel. In an instant, Le Lutin produced a knife and was out of Frau Gerta's arms, the point of his switchblade touching the surprised attorney's crotch. "Sit down and shut the fuck up," the little man snarled.

Bright didn't move, his face suddenly colorless.

"I'd do what he says if I were you," Dredd advised, chuckling.

Bright slowly backed up and then lowered himself into the corner chair. Le Lutin followed, his knife kept poised at Bright's groin. Once the lawyer was again seated, the little man closed his blade, slipped the weapon into a pocket, and returned to Frau Gerta. She picked him up, and Le Lutin and Dredd took a few minutes to discuss Bountiful's fate. Bright listened from the chair by the bookshelf, still astounded that everyone in Paradise had been so easily fooled by the diminutive cutthroat. Even from the distance Frau Gerta had carefully maintained between her husband and their Paradise neighbors, Le Lutin seemed more a gnome than a nipper. Yet even so shrewd a pair as Goldstrike and Maude Dollarhyde had accepted that Felix Peycomson was five years old rather than thirty-five.

Dredd and Le Lutin concluded their discussion by deferring immediate action. "We'll deal with Miss Dollarhyde when the census is closer," Dredd decided.

Still in Frau Gerta's arms, Le Lutin shrugged. "If that's how you want it." He tugged on the lapel of his wife's fashionable hip-length jacket. "Zoo," he said in a child's voice. "And I want to go *now*."

After the little man and his wife were gone, Bright spoke freely. "I can't do any more of this, Gerald. If Louise and I have to spend one more night cooped up with Rumpelstiltskin and that ghoul of his, I believe we'll go stark, raving mad. The little bastard is terrifying. Sometimes we wake up in the middle of the night and he's standing at the foot of our bed, just staring at us."

"Oh now, it can't be that bad, Richard."

"It's worse than bad. Louise and I want out...now."

Dredd frowned. "You want out? Really? How will that work? If you go before the New Year, the house title transfers back to the town. They'd only need a family of five to make their census and I'm sure there's a long waiting list of candidates."

"I'll find a loophole in the contract," Bright argued. "Then I'll sell the house to you as we originally planned…just earlier. That's all."

Dredd began to inspect Le Lutin's doodle on his inkpad, tracing its margin with a finger. Suddenly, he looked up.

"By the way, where the hell did you get that name? Why not Smith or Jones?"

"My name? What are you talking about?"

"That stupid, fucking name…Peycomson. Where did it come from?"

"Don't put me off, Gerald. I'm serious."

"I'm serious too. How the hell did you come up with *Peycomson?*

Bright sighed with frustration. "It's an anagram, Gerald," he finally replied. "From *Great Expectations*…just something clever I—"

Dredd held up a hand. "Oh, shut up, Richard," he said. "Sometimes you're just too goddamned clever for your own good. Frankly, I don't give a shit where you got the name. And you can't leave Paradise yet. That's the end of it."

"Please, Gerald—"

"I want you to hang on for a couple more months… And stay close to the nigger girl. She's the brains up there. She's got me over a bit of a barrel and I need to know what she's thinking until I figure out a way to get off it."

"I've tried, Gerald. She's—"

"Try harder. I need you to keep a leash on her."

Bright sighed. "Fine," he conceded. "But Louise and I will need more money. Our end has to be bigger."

Dredd laughed. "Why would I give you more money?"

The Portland lawyer squared his shoulders. "After this is over, Gerald, I don't want to work for you again. Louise and I will need enough to tide us over in Portland until we can get a proper start elsewhere."

"Elsewhere! And do what? You've been disbarred. You can't practice law. Without me, what's left for you?"

Bright shrugged. "I don't know. Maybe I can get my law license back...or go someplace where they don't care about licenses. A small town like Paradise."

Dredd bellowed with laughter. "Go to some podunk hole-in-the-wall and be a country lawyer? I don't see that happening, Richard. You're not equipped to be a law-abiding citizen."

Bright looked out the office's only window, studying the distant mountains. "Maybe I wasn't before," he said. "But people change."

Dredd sniffed. "People don't change... They give up, but they don't change."

"Just the same, I want more money."

"Forget it!"

"I mean it, Gerald."

"Or what?"

Bright rose and crossed to the door before answering. "I think you know," he said. "You may control the newspaper and the law here in Boise, but the *Portland Oregonian* and the feds are another matter." Anger flickered across Dredd's face, quickly replaced by the genial affect used to bamboozle voters into believing he was down-to-earth and honest.

"C'mon now, Richard," he said. "We've been friends a long time. Let's not go there. Besides, our communications are protected, right...attorney-client privilege and all that?" He left his chair, joined Bright at the door, and put a hand on the lawyer's shoulder. "I can get you more money, my boy. There's no need for ugliness. But I need you and Louise to stick it out until the first of the year, okay? After that, we can go our separate ways. In the meantime, I'll talk to Felix... Get him to behave."

Bright studied Dredd's face as if searching for the loophole in a contract. Finally, he nodded. "All right," he said, afterward exiting the real estate baron's office. As soon as the door swung shut behind him, Dredd's expression devolved from amiable political candidate to rapacious scoundrel.

"Ungrateful sonuvabitch!" he muttered.

Dredd waited until certain Bright was no longer in the building and then left his office and went to the parking lot. He climbed into his Vauxhall and drove to Julia Davis Park—a lush tract on the Boise River and home to the fledgling Boise Zoo. He parked and walked around the animal sanctuary until encountering Le Lutin and Frau Gerta. The couple stood before a wolf enclosure, the little man and one of the sharp-fanged creatures staring at each other like rivals for the same downed sheep. Dredd and Le Lutin had a brief conversation. Afterward Dredd went back to his Vauxhall while Le Lutin and Frau Gerta stayed to visit the reptile house.

❧

"Case dismissed," Peycomson told Bountiful, Geraldine, and Willie after joining them in the Idanha Hotel tearoom. Because it was nearly noon, they decided to delay their return to Paradise long enough to lunch at Morrison's, the elegant restaurant located just off the hotel lobby. At first haughty and indignant over Bountiful's black skin, the maître d' seated them once he recognized the daughter of Idaho's lieutenant governor in the party of four. They dined and headed back to Paradise, a nip in the air as the Model T negotiated the twisting mountain road. The chill was a reminder that the calendar had turned its page on the first of October. Summer and fall in the mountains were promises never entirely kept and the leaves were already changing, reds and yellows truer than the short-lived greens of July and August. A dusting of snow had come in the wee hours of the new month, already melted but still a harbinger of the great drifts that would close the pass within weeks. Paradise was already preparing for the long, cold winter ahead—cords of wood chopped and stacked against houses and cabins, vegetables and fruit canned and stored in root cellars, game meat smoked to preserve it. Arnold Chang had begun to stockpile whiskey for his Gold Rush Saloon while Oskar Nilsen would soon have trucks deliver enough dry goods and food to stock the shelves and ice locker of his general store until spring.

Winter in Paradise with its months of isolation was Bountiful Dollarhyde's favorite season. People of color were a rarity in the mountain West, but racism was not, and too many summer tourists packed fearful glances or unapologetically disdainful expressions alongside their underwear and toiletries. Only the hardiest folks visited Paradise in winter, mostly returning cold weather hunters or yurt campers who snow-shoed in. They understood Paradise and its people, embracing Bountiful as headmistress of the Paradise School and Maude Dollarhyde's granddaughter.

It had been four days since the single and final performance of *Our American Cousin* was curtailed by the fiery destruction of Elysium, and as Bountiful approached Paradise with Peycomson sharing the front seat and Geraldine and Willie in the rear, the stale, acrid smell of the extinguished fire still hung in the air. Peycomson asked to be dropped off in front of the Gold Rush Saloon, and after he'd exited the Model T, Bountiful drove on until they reached what was left of Elysium. Its loss filled her with sadness. She'd left Paradise as a teenager and been away for thirteen years; yet when she returned the town was virtually unchanged. Nilsen's, the Gold Rush Saloon, the *Idaho World* office, the Paradise School, and the mansions on Only Real Street were the same—artifacts time had preserved. Elysium had been one of the most important of those relics, a constant and reassuring presence at the corner of Goodlow Road and Only Real Street—a bit of forever in her bedroom window. Now it was gone, forcing her to accept that death was inevitable. Her grandmother would one day pass as would Goldstrike, Oskar Nilsen, Arnold Chang, and Ed Riggins. Like Elysium, they had always been something forever to her and the blackened and desolate remains of the grandest of the penny mansions were a bitter reminder that childhood had ended and the day approached when she might face life alone.

Bountiful allowed the car to glide to a stop in front of the

ruins, the engine still running. At the center of the house, a
giant insect had been contrived from the rubble, its legs formed
from fallen rafters, the collapsed crow's nest its head, reflected
sunlight off the glass shards of the lantern room windows providing eyes.

"Cantigny," Willie murmured from the back seat, his voice
filled with echoes of the madness he'd brought home from
the war. He caught Bountiful's eyes in the rearview mirror and
smiled, a melancholy thing that made him look old. "Cantigny
was a village in France," he told her. "By the time we moved in,
most of the buildings had been bombed into rubble."

He nodded at the Cooler mansion.

"Dead hulks…like this place." He stared at the blackened
wood of Elysium, the sooty sandstone blocks, and the broken
glass, then shook his head as if puzzled. "Even as we fought
our way through the town…at Cantigny…I couldn't stop
thinking about the people who'd lived there. I wondered what
happened to them…if they were still alive. I was in a kitchen at
one point, firing at the Germans with a baby's high-chair next
to me. The roof was gone. There was a doll on the floor and a
slice of bread on the table. I dusted off the bread and ate it. I
was hungry."

"You're home now, Will," Geraldine said, squeezing his
hand.

"I know," he said. "But this house… It reminded me. That's
all."

The two young people sat close together in the back seat.
Cast adrift from different shipwrecks, and utter strangers just
weeks earlier, they had found a way to keep each other afloat,
forming a bond that transcended their years. Bountiful had
never yearned for such a thing. Like her grandmother, she was
prepared to forge ahead on her own. Still, she couldn't help
envying them.

"What's going on with you two?" she asked.

Geraldine smiled, an enigmatic thing that defrosted the last
of the cold, imperious girl who'd come to Paradise just two

months earlier. She reached into her purse and Willie into his pocket, each retrieving a gold band. They slipped the rings onto their fingers.

"After you dropped us off, we found a justice of the peace," Geraldine revealed.

Bountiful stared at their wedding bands, her throat suddenly full as she weighed feelings of both delight and fear. When she'd left Paradise for Howard University, Willie Barkley had been a mischievous and bright-eyed youngster; the Willie who returned from The-War-to-End-All-Wars almost unrecognizable, his face gaunt, his eyes haunted. Thaddeus Cooler's play and Mary Meredith, the humble milk maid, had discovered a knight in shining armor beneath his soldier's fatigues—one who rescued a princess imprisoned in ice. *It's a fairy tale*, Bountiful mused, uncomfortably mindful that like many fairy tales, Geraldine and Willie's included a fire-breathing dragon—one in a three-piece suit.

"Does your father know?" she asked.

Geraldine shook her head.

"He'll find out," Bountiful cautioned. "It's inevitable."

The newlyweds smiled at each other. "It may be inevitable," Willie said. "But it isn't inevitable today."

They drove on to the Paradise School. Inside, the fall term had begun, and with the addition of four DeMille children, the student body had ballooned to seventeen, spread across five grades. Geraldine and Willie were enrolled, too, the ex-doughboy one term short of a diploma while Geraldine needed only to complete her independent study senior thesis before claiming a degree from Boise High School. Plans for another new pupil—Felix Peycomson—had been scotched by the boy's father. "Frau Gerta is both nanny and tutor," Meriwether claimed.

The students assembled Monday through Friday in the library, and as Bountiful, Geraldine, and Willie approached the large room, they could hear Maude's voice. Bountiful hurried ahead. Her grandmother tended to replace classroom assignments with entertaining recollections, the line between actual and apocryphal swept aside.

"And so I told Abe," Maude held forth as her granddaughter approached, "'Mister President,' I said... Even though we were old friends I called him Mister President when other folks were around... Anyway, 'Mister President,' I said, 'the play isn't even all that funny. I wouldn't go if I were you.'" The former madam paused, looking at the doorway where Bountiful had stopped, arms crossed, face pinched. "Let's finish this story another time, class," Maude said.

With Bountiful back in charge, the pupils worked on a variety of subjects, Lariat helping the younger students. Geraldine worked on her thesis: "The Nineteenth Amendment and the Suffragette Movement in America." Willie still had a handful of courses to finish, but instead mooned over his new wife. Neither newlywed seemed to get much done, repeatedly grazing one another's hands or exchanging looks that made the other students giggle. Their intimacy reminded Bountiful of the kiss she'd shared with Meriwether Peycomson. It had changed things. "Secrets will do that," Grandma Maude once told her. "A kept secret can be more sensual than sex." Bountiful didn't agree. The secret she shared with Meriwether Peycomson had resulted in shame rather than yearning, his cowardice at the fire that destroyed Elysium sparking distrust. He had once been charming, but now smelled of chicanery, and she wished the town council had sold the Stiveley mansion at the end of Only Real Street to Charles Dunworthy of Council Bluffs, Iowa, or Philadelphia's Michael Summerville.

# 15

## Room 3D at the Idanha Hotel

The rest of October was uneventful. The town heard nothing from Dredd and unseasonably warm weather extended into November, although night-time temperatures in the upper twenties reminded townsfolk that heavy snow would soon come. Renovations on Paradise's remaining three penny mansions were finished and open houses scheduled for two of them. Amon and Sarah DeMille held the first housewarming party while John and Annie Goodlow followed with their own soirée a week later. The latter affair was an afternoon event and Meriwether Peycomson attended without his wife, trailing Bountiful around the house until they were alone. He wanted to talk about anything other than their legal issues, but his unwanted advances had become painfully desperate and she refused to talk of anything else.

"The petition was denied. Do you think that's the end of it?" she asked after he'd cornered her in the den.

"It appears so," he answered, touching her hand. Bountiful pulled away.

"Don't, Meriwether."

"Bountiful, ever since—"

"Lariat is reading *Great Expectations*," she said, cutting him off. "He's finished all six of the Dickens novels you gave him. By the way, those books were a lovely gift. Very thoughtful. Thank you."

Peycomson's eyes widened almost imperceptibly. "*Great Expectations?*"

"Yes. He just started it, but I suspect he's more than halfway through by now."

"Halfway?"

"Yes, he's a fast reader."

Peycomson didn't answer, instead tilting his head as if listening to a voice only he could hear. "Oh my gosh," he suddenly exclaimed, blinking nervously. "I completely forgot. There's a phone call I need to make."

"Now?"

"Yes, I'm afraid so. It's quite important… It's about our case. I need to call the judge. It slipped my mind."

"I thought our case was dismissed."

"It was, but there are necessary filings still to be accomplished. Nothing to worry about. However, I need to call the judge. You understand, I'm sure." He excused himself and hurried over to Nilsen's General Store. Oskar had hired Benjamin DeMille to mind the register during the Goodlows' party and Peycomson paid him the going rate of five cents to use the establishment's telephone, then made his call while the young Mormon waited on the bench outside. The lawyer left after hanging up. "So long, Ben," he said to the eldest DeMille son. They were the last words anyone from Paradise would hear from Meriwether Peycomson.

Well before dawn the next morning—November 19, 1919—the lawyer affixed a notice to the front door of his penny mansion:

Friends and Neighbors:

Evangeline's health took an unexpected downturn overnight and we are away to seek specialized medical attention. Given the dire nature of her condition, we may not be back until January. However, rest assured that we shall return in time to be counted in the census.

—Meriwether Peycomson and Family

All four members of the erstwhile Peycomson clan then surreptitiously left town. Richard and Louise Bright were in the rear seat of the family's green Liberty Cadillac. Frau Gerta was behind the wheel with Felix "Le Lutin" Ombre in her lap. She had curled his long locks, and as they crossed the town limit and departed Paradise, he lit a cigar.

The tall German woman sped dangerously down the mountain road and they reached Boise with pinks and purples shading the eastern sky. After breakfasting at an all-night diner, they lingered over second and then third cups of coffee. Around eight a.m. they drove to the offices of Dredd Enterprises where Le Lutin, Frau Gerta, and Bright were ushered into the inner sanctum of the CEO. Louise waited in the car.

"That stupid fucking name," Dredd spat as he retrieved cash from a wall safe.

"I'm sorry, Gerald," Bright apologized. "I had no idea the boy would be assigned Dickens to read. Once I knew, I bought six other titles to keep him away from *Great Expectations*. I thought it would be enough to occupy him until January, but he's a fast reader. The kid's a genius."

"I needed you up there through the end of the year," Dredd groused. "This better not have wrecked things." He split the cash retrieved from his safe between two envelopes, then handed one each to Le Lutin and Bright. Le Lutin immediately gave his to Frau Gerta. She extracted the cash and began to count it, placing small stacks of bills on the front edge of Dredd's desk. Her husband watched, stogie still clamped between his teeth even though its flame had died.

"You don't need to count it," Dredd said. "It's all there."

"We'll make sure."

The real estate mogul eyed Bright. "I suppose you're gonna count yours too?"

The lawyer shook his head, then signed papers selling his mansion in Paradise to Dredd Enterprises. The price was one cent, the date of sale post-dated to January 1, 1920. Afterward the two couples went to the Idanha Hotel. Richard penned the Brights' real names onto the register. Le Lutin and Frau Gerta signed in as Mr. and Mrs. August Grobermann of Reno, Nevada.

"You folks traveling together?" the desk clerk asked.

"My wife and I are passing through," Richard Bright replied. "Our train leaves tomorrow."

"So you four aren't together?" the clerk persisted, eyeing Le Lutin and Frau Gerta.

"Mind your own goddamned business," the little man growled.

The clerk assigned them rooms on separate floors—the Brights in 3D, the Grobermanns in 4F—then recruited Lester, the doorman, to help with their luggage. Both couples put DO NOT DISTURB signs on their doorknobs and remained inside for the next several hours. As dinnertime neared, 3D called room service to request entrées along with strawberries and champagne. Half an hour later a waiter delivered the order, just as Le Lutin and Frau Gerta exited the elevator on the lobby level of the hotel. The little man had changed into a child's nineteenth-century sailor suit with a feathered cap and a wide middy collar. Dredd Enterprises was just two blocks away, but the sinister couple drove there in the Liberty Cadillac, parking behind the building and entering through a rear door. The staff, including Iris, was gone for the day and Dredd was alone to greet them when they entered his top floor office. He handed Le Lutin a thick envelope along with a single sheet of paper on which he'd written a short note. "I'll have the *Geraldream* waiting for you," he told them.

The shifty-eyed, vampiric Hershfield was on duty at the front desk when Le Lutin and Frau Gerta returned to the Idanha. "Evening folks," he called out, tracking them across the lobby as if they were a mother ogress and her hobgoblin rather than Mr. and Mrs. August Grobermann of Reno, Nevada. After the little man and his elegant wife stepped into the elevator and the door had closed, Hershfield looked at Old Pat, a permanent hotel resident who spent most days in a lobby chair.

"They're on the fourth floor," he informed the stoop-shouldered man.

"I don't give a shit," Old Pat responded.

Had either of the men shared the elevator with Le Lutin

and Frau Gerta, they would have seen them exit the car on the third floor, rather than the fourth. Frau Gerta noiselessly padded down the carpeted corridor with her husband in her arms. She stopped at Room 3D, put Le Lutin down, and knocked on the door. Richard Bright opened it. Behind him and across the room, Louise sat on the end of the bed in a long, frilly nightgown, a half-filled flute of champagne in her hand.

"Dredd needs one more thing from you," Le Lutin told the lawyer, brushing past him. There was a small writing desk in the corner and the little man waddled over to it. He climbed up on the chair, and after Bright joined him, handed him the note from Dredd. At the same time, Frau Gerta crossed the room, reaching into her deep handbag to extract the thick envelope. She put it on the desk and reached back into her purse to retrieve a pen and a small greeting card, its accompanying envelope orchid purple. She held out the pen for Bright to take.

"Copy the note onto that card and sign it. Put the nigger girl's name on the purple envelope," Le Lutin said.

Bright remained standing to read Dredd's note, and once finished, he looked down at Le Lutin, the little man still a foot shorter than the disbarred lawyer despite standing on the chair. "I won't do this," Bright said.

"Sure you will," Le Lutin replied. "There's two thousand in the fat envelope…for your trouble."

"I don't care about the money."

"Sure you do, Richard. Gerald said you wanted a bigger take." The little man pointed at the thick envelope. "So there it is…an extra two grand. Now, copy the note."

"I'm telling you, I can't—"

"Ne vous inquiétez pas…uh, don't worry. Gerald wants Gerta and I to have a talk with her. That's all…just talk. Make her see reason." The little man attempted a reassuring smile that came off as a sneer. "C'mon now, Richard. Personne ne sera blessé… No one will get hurt. Just write the note… And don't forget to put her name on the envelope."

Bright picked up the greeting card. A watercolor of delicate violets was on the face. The inside was blank. He looked at Le Lutin, the memory of the little man's knife in his crotch uncomfortably fresh in his memory.

"C'mon, Richard," Le Lutin repeated. He nodded at Frau Gerta and she again offered Bright the pen. This time the lawyer took it and bent to write on the card as the German woman moved toward the bathroom.

"I need to use your facility," she said.

With Gerta in the lavatory and Le Lutin watching from atop the desk chair, Bright transcribed Dredd's message with one change.

> Meet me in the carriage house behind my place at ten o'clock tonight. It's urgent. Come alone. I'm sorry for the drama, but I'll explain everything. Trust me. It's not what you think—*HV*

"*HV*... Ce qui donne?" Le Lutin objected after reading the signature. "Sign the damned thing, 'Meriwether.'"

"I don't want this tracking directly back to me," Bright responded. "Don't worry. She'll know who *HV* is." He penned Bountiful's name onto the orchid-colored envelope, tucked the card inside, and handed it to the little man. "No one gets hurt... Right?"

Before Le Lutin could answer, Frau Gerta emerged from the bathroom holding a towel. The tall German beauty smiled at Bright, an eerie thing that made him involuntarily shiver. At the same time, Le Lutin slipped the card into his coat pocket, then answered the former Meriwether Peycomson's question with a lightning flick of his wrist. A horrid gurgle abused the quiet of the room and the terrified lawyer dropped to his knees, struggling to breathe through the deep gash sliced across the full width of his throat. Frau Gerta quickly placed the towel on the floor to catch the blood, afterward removing her scarf. Approaching Bright's wife, she expertly twisted the neckwear— maroon silk with embroidered roses—into a rope-like length. Louise's face turned ashen and she dropped the champagne flute, scooting back on the bed as if the pillows against the headboard might provide refuge—her lips parting to herald a scream that never came, silence falling upon more silence as Frau Gerta noiselessly strangled her.

When it was over and two dead bodies lay on the floor of Room 3D at the Idanha Hotel, Le Lutin and Frau Gerta shared a cigarette while eating the strawberries and drinking the last of the champagne the Brights had ordered from room service. Afterward they wrapped the bodies and the bloody towel in extra bedsheets from the linen closet, binding them with heavy twine Frau Gerta retrieved from her seemingly bottomless purse. A brief search of the room turned up the money Dredd had given the Brights that morning. Frau Gerta added it to the additional two thousand and shoved the bills into her purse. Then she piled the room service dishes onto their tray, set them in the corridor, and straightened up the space as expertly as a hotel maid, working around the cocooned corpses as if they were merely lumps in the carpet. Last of all, she packed the Brights' suitcases with the dead couple's things. "Ready?" she asked her husband. He nodded and they left, taking the Brights' luggage with them.

Around eight o'clock that evening, the two assassins appeared in the lobby bar, buying a couple of rounds for a house that rapidly grew once the gossipy Hershfield got on the phone and spread word that a real live midget was doing handstands on the bar at the Idanha Hotel. And Le Lutin did. A former circus clown and acrobat, he entertained the crowd with stories, jokes, gravity-defying tumbles, and muscle-bound gymnastics. Around ten o'clock, with the floor show still in progress, Frau Gerta quietly slipped away. She retrieved the Liberty Cadillac, parked it in the alley behind the hotel, and then stealthily negotiated a back stairwell to the third floor. With all the hotel guests in the bar, the corridor was deserted and she toted the bodies down the stairs and stuffed them into the trunk of the car, one at a time. Afterward she rehung the DO NOT DISTURB sign on the outer doorknob of Room 3D and returned to the lobby bar.

Shortly after midnight, the couple bade Le Lutin's audience goodnight and took the elevator to the fourth floor. Rather than retire to their own Room 4F they climbed out a corridor window, scrambled down the fire escape to their waiting automobile, and headed for the Arrowrock Dam reservoir, twenty-eight miles away. They reached it shortly after two o'clock in the morning. A single powerboat—the *Geraldream*—was tied up at the lake's rudimentary dock, gently bobbing in the dark water. Frau Gerta lugged the bodies from the car to the boat, then retrieved her twine and a pair of small anvils taken from the carriage house behind their former home in Paradise. Afterward she fired up the boat engine and nosed the watercraft into open water with her husband in her lap and the Brights propped up on the rear passenger bench, their bedsheet wrappings making them look like giant larvae in love.

No one else was on the water when they reached a moonlit spot at the deepest part of the narrow canyon reservoir. Frau Gerta killed the inboard engine, giving up the night to the sound of waves gently slapping against the hull. With her sleepy husband watching, she tied the anvils to the cocoons' bindings. Then she unceremoniously dumped the bodies of Richard and Louise Bright into the water. By the time the dead couple reached the muddy bottom of Lake Arrowrock, the killers were well on their way back to shore.

"It's handled," the little man told Dredd later that same day after Iris showed the couple into her boss's office. It was just past noon. Le Lutin was once again in Frau Gerta's arms, this time wearing a cowboy outfit—his ten-gallon hat huge, his hand-tooled boots tiny, the gun-belt strapped around his waist holstering nothing more deadly than a cap pistol. Richard and Louise Bright had been dead for about eighteen hours. Dredd eyed the diminutive cutthroat.

"I don't want to deal with something later, so I hope you—"

"I told you it was handled, goddamit, Gerald! You want details?"

"No... No details if you please."

The little man produced the orchid-colored envelope with Bountiful's name printed on the outside "You want us to take care of her?" he asked.

Dredd took the envelope. "That won't be necessary. I'll handle it myself."

"That's it then," Le Lutin said. "We're off. You know how to reach us."

"I won't be needing you again, Felix," Dredd said. "Richard was a friend. This was not exactly… Well, this didn't go the way I'd hoped. Let's just leave it at that. I think it best we part ways."

The little man laughed, a sound frighteningly similar to the gurgle Richard Bright emitted when blood gushed into his windpipe.

"You won't need me again, Gerald?" he echoed. He grinned at his wife. "We've heard that one before, haven't we, baby?"

"Ja," she replied, her low, sandy voice passionless and spectral.

# 16

## GREAT EXPECTATIONS

When Lariat Comfort found the orchid-colored envelope pinned to the front door of the Paradise School on the afternoon of November 20, 1919, he recognized the handwriting. It matched lettering on a note Meriwether Peycomson had added to a gift of six Dickens novels given to the teenager weeks earlier. Lariat went looking for Bountiful and found her in a former guest accommodation once known as the "pink" room after Maude painted and furnished it in that delicate color. A large space, Bountiful had claimed it for her bedchamber after returning to Paradise, transforming it into a serene blend of taupe walls and tastefully patterned bedding. A reading area with a plump easy chair and a modern floor lamp, acquired after the PEC was formed, occupied one corner. Bountiful was tucked into the chair, her legs folded beneath her, the latest issue of *McClure's Magazine* in her hands.

"Found this tacked to the front door, Miss Bountiful," Lariat told her.

Bountiful took the card and quickly perused it. Afterward she climbed out of the chair, went to the window, and looked out. The conflagration that destroyed Elysium had made it to within thirty feet of the Paradise School, and in the meadow outside, a wavy line now separated high yellow autumn grass from low black ash. It had been almost seven weeks, but she still recalled the night of the fire, working together with her family and friends to save Paradise. *He was too quick to leave the battlefield,* she thought, recalling Peycomson's actions. And now the lawyer and his family were gone—forced by Mrs. Peycomson's condition to seek medical help elsewhere, the note left on their door promising a return in time to be counted in the census.

Bountiful reread the card with the delicate flowers on its face.

*It's not what you think.*

"Who's it from?" Lariat asked. "Looked like Mister Peycomson's writing on the envelope."

"It's nothing," Bountiful answered. "Let's go raid the pantry."

"But—"

"It's nothing, Lariat. I'm hungry. Let's go."

They went downstairs, found a box of cookies Maude had hidden behind a flour tin, and ate half. Lariat then went outside to practice rope tricks, while Bountiful helped Maude prep for dinner. "I don't know why I bother," the former madam griped as they peeled potatoes and chopped carrots for a pot roast. "You've both ruined your appetites." Bountiful did not mention the note to her grandmother nor did the subject come up at dinner nor later when all three sat together in the parlor, quietly discussing the day's events. They each retired to their rooms shortly after eight o'clock. Lariat read from *Great Expectations* and was near the end of chapter forty-one when he heard the front door open and then softly close around nine forty-five. He climbed out of bed and went to the attic dormer window. Below, Bountiful had reached the end of the front walk and was heading north toward the Peycomson mansion. She was alone. The moon was cloud-covered, but even in the soft light, he could see the orchid-colored envelope in her hand.

Lariat flopped back onto his bed and resumed reading. As Bountiful predicted, he loved the work of Dickens. Some thought the renowned British writer had too many characters in his books, but the young genius viewed them as signposts on a complicated roadmap used to navigate the story. He finished chapter forty-one and turned the page.

Chapter Forty-two

"'Dear boy and Pip's comrade, I am not a-going fur to tell you my life, like a song or a storybook...'"

The speaker was Abel Magwitch, a criminal sharing his past with the book's protagonist, Pip. As Lariat read on, Magwitch described an encounter with as dastardly a villain as Dickens had ever fashioned, a man not simply malevolent, but one who thrived on malevolence. According to Magwitch, this charming and handsome bounder had once ruined the life of a pitiful fellow named Arthur Havisham, using him to gain favor with Arthur's sister, Amelia, a woman the heartless cad left at the altar.

> "'He was a smooth one to talk and was a dab at the ways of gentlefolks. He was good-looking too. Meriwether Compeyson's business was the swindling, handwriting, forging, stolen bank note passing...'"

"Sonuvabitch!" Lariat cursed. He leapt from his bed, grabbed his lasso, and bolted out the door, frantically scrambling down the steep attic steps and the wide staircase leading to the ground floor. Oblivious to the chill of snow in the air, the teenager dashed from the Paradise School in pajamas and moccasins, racing up the front walk with a prayer on his lips that he could stop Bountiful before she reached the Peycomson mansion—praying he wouldn't be too late.

ॐ

As Bountiful neared the carriage house snow had begun to fall, a few flakes lazily drifting down through dull moonlight. Paradise would wake to an ocean of it—flocked tree boughs, meringue snowdrifts, fresh glaze capping the distant peaks of the Sawtooths. The former stable behind the Peycomson penny mansion was set back forty feet from the rear of the home, and as she approached, dim yellow light shone from its windows. Bountiful reached the double-door entry and paused. After receiving the card with the cryptic signature, she'd vacillated about coming. A sensible woman, she knew everything about this situation was wrong—the Peycomsons' pre-dawn departure, Evangeline's vague affliction, the mysterious note with violet flowers inside an orchid-colored envelope, this clandestine meeting on a dark night. All of it encouraged her to turn around and go home. But she didn't. Instead, Bountiful pulled open one of the tall stable doors and stepped inside.

Although original owner John Stiveley had commissioned the structure's shingled exterior to reflect his Cape Cod sensibilities, the interior was a typical Idaho barn with three ground-floor bays and a few horse stalls. A pair of lit kerosene lanterns dangled from nails on the wall opposite the entry. Tools hung between the lanterns, including a scythe with a splintered wood handle, a rusty pitchfork, an ancient post-hole digger, a broom, and a few newer implements left by the construction workers who'd recently worked on the property. Overhead, half the upper level was occupied by a haymow open to the center bay. A single wooden crossbrace, ten feet above the dirt floor, bisected the distance from the midpoint of the loft to the east wall, a narrow balance beam piercing the dusty air. The place smelled of nitrogen-based fertilizer, the odor originating from a half-open bag slumped against the wall with the hanging tools.

Bountiful retrieved the greeting card with the violet flowers and had just confirmed the appointed time of ten o'clock when a voice startled her.

"Well, well, well…if it isn't Miss Bountiful Dollarhyde."

Bountiful dropped the card and whirled around.

"Where's Meriwether?" she demanded, as Gerald Dredd moved from the shadows and into the flickering lamplight. "What are *you* doing here?"

Dredd moved toward her, then stopped to pick up the greeting card. "I thought it was time to renegotiate our agreement," he said. Bountiful retreated until her back was against the wall.

"Renegotiate? What are you talking about?"

Dredd moved closer.

"Meriwether should be here at any moment," Bountiful said, unable to keep the tremor from her voice. She pressed her back against the roughhewn planks of the barn wall, felt the head of an extruded nail poke her, then brandished the empty orchid-colored envelope. "He sent this invitation. He knows I'm here."

Dredd laughed, holding up the greeting card. "You mean *this* invitation?" He put the card in his pocket. "*Meriwether* won't be coming, Miss Dollarhyde. Don't you understand, yet? I thought you were smart…colored college and all. I guess not."

It had been thirteen years since Goldstrike taught Bountiful how to defend herself. "A gal venturin' into the wilds of Washington goddamned DC oughta know how to fight," he'd told her. She'd never had to use the skills he'd taught her or the advice he'd given.

*First of all, stay calm. Look fer a way out.*

She scanned the dimly lit interior of the carriage house. Dredd barred her way to the wide stable doors, but a single door was to her right on the far west wall, and she knew there was a hatch in the haymow if she could reach the ladder.

*If'n ya can't run. Look fer somethin' sharp.*

Bountiful glanced to either side. The flat-edged broom hanging on the wall was reachable. The sharp-tined pitchfork was not.

*A bully can smell fear. Don't let 'im know you're scared.*

"I'm leaving," Bountiful said. "Please get out of the way, Gerald." She stepped away from the wall, but Dredd blocked her way, cocking his head.

"You're a pretty little nigger, aren't you?" he said. "I've a taste for pretty little niggers. And, of course, you know how much our daddy had a taste for 'em too. 'Like wild animals,' he told me… 'African jungle beasts when their legs are spread.' Are you a jungle beast, Bountiful?"

Without warning, Dredd suddenly launched himself at her, the result almost comical. Out-of-shape with a belt-stretching belly and veiny legs more able to waddle than spring into action, he was too slow. Bountiful dropped the envelope, darted away, and grabbed the pitchfork, the orchid-colored sleeve fluttering toward the ground as Dredd's momentum sent him crashing into the wall. His impact dislodged the scythe. It fell, the wooden handle hitting his head, the entire implement then whipsawing with the point of the blade slicing his trousers dangerously close to his groin. He yowled and spun about, face purple, teeth bared.

*Keep on yer feet. Don't let 'im get ya on the ground.*

Bountiful moved into the center bay, gripping the pitchfork like a gladiator's battle staff, slowly rotating as the enraged real estate baron crouched like a wrestler and began to circle her.

"Did you really think this was over?" he taunted. "Did you really think you could blackmail Gerald Dredd?" He lunged at her, retreated in the face of the spiky pitchfork; then resumed circling, relentlessly shortening his arcs. He backed her into a corner and then threw himself at her again. Bountiful dodged and he smashed into a stack of empty paint cans, scattering them like bowling pins. A baling hook hung on the wall. Dredd scrambled to his feet and grabbed it. Bellowing with rage, he charged at Bountiful, wildly swinging the hook. She blocked it with the pitchfork, once, twice, a third time. On the fourth parry, it caught her weapon behind its base.

"Aha!" he shouted, jerking the pitchfork from her grasp. It hurtled through the air and speared the wall behind him as Bountiful ran for the door. Halfway there, she stumbled and Dredd caught up. He wrestled her to the ground, the fingers of one hand gripping her throat as he tore at her clothes with the other, twisting the waistband of her skirt, popping the top button from her blouse.

*If'n he gets ya down, go fer his eyes.*

Bountiful pounded on his head and shoulders with her fists, managing to stick a thumb into one of his eyes. He issued a great roar, slapped her hard across the face, and then straddled her, both hands around her neck, her arms pinned to her sides.

*Bite if ya hafta.*

She tossed her head about, sank her teeth into the meat of his hand.

"You goddamned nigger whore!" Dredd howled, striking her

again, this time with a closed fist. It missed her face, landing just above her ear, the blow filling her eyes with sparkles, the already muted light of the kerosene lanterns suddenly fainter. Now, his face was too close—his teeth yellow, his breath sour, the sweat on his chin dripping onto her lips. Both hands were around her neck, his thumbs pushing deeper as he closed off her windpipe. His grip tightened and Bountiful struggled harder to breathe, her ribs and breastbone collapsing with the effort, her mouth agape, her strength fading. An odd vibration began, coalescing deep inside and surging outward—a thing primordial and terrifying, a buzz both inexorable and pervasive. Dredd's fingers squeezed tighter and tighter and the buzz grew louder, her body tingling from it, her arms and legs morphing into hollow stems, her will to fight drifting away like smoke.

*Is this how I end?*

The light from the kerosene lamps seemed far away now, the overhead darkness turning darker, so black and forbidding she could no longer tell if her eyes were open or closed.

*Please God…don't let Grandma find me.*

Suddenly, a sound almost like a gunshot rang out as Dredd lurched upward as if jerked by the scruff of his neck. Simultaneously, his fingers released her throat, his eyes widened, and his head tipped at an impossible angle. Unblinking, he began to gently sway from side to side, arms dangling, his knuckles brushing the dirt of the barn floor. The knot of his necktie had been pulled off-center, and just above the collar of his shirt, the skin of his neck was creased by a rope. Stretched taut, it quivered as it tracked upward, crossed over the center crossbeam, and looped down to where Lariat Comfort held onto its free end, suspended a foot off the ground.

"Move, Miss Bountiful!" the boy cried out.

Bountiful remained motionless, staring at the teenager as if he were a mirage.

"Miss Bountiful…please move!"

*Move…please move.*

"Get out from under him, Miss Bountiful! He's too heavy!"

Dredd suddenly dropped a few inches, his wide-open, un-seeing blue eyes now just inches from hers.

*Stay calm. Look fer a way out.*

Beneath the real estate baron's suspended body Bountiful could see the west door of the carriage house and Lariat's feet, his moccasins now less than six inches above the dirt floor.

*Move...*

Trembling violently, she rolled onto her stomach and began to laboriously crawl out from under the dead man. Inch by inch, she pulled herself free, and when she was at last clear of the dangling corpse, Lariat released the rope. He dropped to the ground, landing softly while Dredd's body fell heavily, hitting the floor with a great whump. In an instant, the young genius was at Bountiful's side.

"C'mon," he pleaded, wrestling her onto her back and then shaking her by the shoulders. "You're okay. Please be okay."

Bountiful stared at him, lips slightly parted, her breathing uneven, her limbs still hollow. The buzz began to subside.

"Please..." he repeated, tears streaming down his face. "Please say something!"

Bountiful reached up and touched his face. "My throat hurts," she said.

Lariat collapsed onto her, tucking his face against her bosom. "I love you, Miss Bountiful," he sobbed. "I love you so much."

Bountiful put her arms around him. "I love you too, Lariat," she murmured, her voice raw.

"I love you so much!"

"I love you too."

They lay in each other's arms, the strength in Bountiful's limbs slowly returning, the buzz dissipating. After what seemed a very long time, she tapped him on the back.

"You're heavy, Lariat... Get off."

He lifted his head and looked at her, cheeks streaked with tears.

"You're okay?"

His nose was running and he involuntarily snorted, then exhaled noisily, the sound like the braying of a donkey. Bountiful laughed.

"Don't laugh at me! It's not funny!"

Then he did it again, and suddenly Lariat was laughing too, both of them laughing convulsively in the dirt of the barn floor, laughing so hard they couldn't catch their breath. They laughed with incredulity and relief, laughed at the irony of a murderer murdered, laughed at the surreal company of Gerald Dredd's dead body just inches away. They howled with laughter until their sides ached and they gasped for air, laughing until nothing came out but raspy wheezes and whimpers, until they were empty of it and spent—rendered grave and silent as they lay on their backs, hands joined, contemplating the distant high ceiling. Bountiful spoke first.

"How did you—?"

"*Great Expectations*," Lariat answered before she could finish. "Meriwether *Compeyson*...Meriwether *Peycomson?*"

"Dickens," Bountiful said. She sat up. "Meriwether loves Dickens...has his complete works. He talked about him all the time." She looked at Lariat. "I've only just started *Great Expectations* myself. I've never read it. I assigned it so I'd be forced to read it too...so we could discuss it. What chapter are you on?"

"Forty-two."

"That's where Peycomson appears?"

"Compeyson."

"Right...Compeyson. Meriwether's name was an anagram."

"And a dumb one... Too easy to figure out. I'd have gone with 'McSpooney.'"

The young genius recounted his movements after dashing out the front door of the Paradise School. "By the time I got here, you were already inside," he told Bountiful. "I looked through the window and saw you up against the wall." He'd used his rope to lasso the lift beam above the outer haymow door and scaled the side of the barn. After slipping through the hatch, he walked the crossbeam, calf-roped Dredd, and jumped off. The real estate mogul tipped the scales at just over 250, but the haymow was ten feet above the floor of the barn and the combination of Lariat's 130 pounds and gravity were enough to break the blackguard's neck when the rope snapped taut.

Bountiful looked at Dredd. Although prone, his head was twisted, forcing him to look at the ceiling. The odd angle of his neck and the open and fixed blue eyes made him resemble a lizard. The rope was still around his neck and she nudged him with her foot. There was no response.

"Dead," she murmured, surprised at her ambivalence. Her religious indoctrination at Howard had imprinted a vague fearfulness of spiritual retribution should she commit murder or even contemplate it. Yet Dredd's demise was unattended by fear, guilt, or remorse. Perhaps, a reckoning with the Almighty would come, she mused, but for now Dredd's death was merely a distasteful chore at last completed—a grease-trap cleaned, a spittoon cleared, a rat trap emptied.

Bountiful rose, brushed the dirt from her bottom, and then inspected her clothing. Her long skirt was twisted at the waist, but there were no rips. A button from her blouse was missing. She lent a hand to Lariat to help him up.

"Get your rope," she said and he did, unlooping the noose from Dredd's neck. Bountiful retrieved the pitchfork and scythe and rehung them on the wall, next surveying the dark interior of the carriage house as if searching for witnesses. Satisfied there were none, she took Lariat's hand. "Let's go," she said.

He eyed the body. "Shouldn't we…?"

"We need to tell Grandma…and Goldstrike. They'll help us."

Outside the carriage house, the world had been transformed into a real-life snow globe. Snowflakes like miniature doilies drifted through the air, the night so quiet one could hear the soft rushes as they brushed the pine needles of the trees. The snow was already accumulating and Bountiful and Lariat disturbed the otherwise pristine groundcover with their footprints as they made their way back to the Paradise School. Once there, they climbed the stairs to Maude's second-floor bedroom. Bountiful knocked on the door. They heard footsteps and then the door opened just a crack.

"What's wrong?" the former madam asked through the narrow opening.

"We've something to tell you," Bountiful said. "May we come in?"

Maude shook her head. "Let's go downstairs," she said. She closed her bedroom door, then reappeared seconds later, wearing a robe and slippers. Once they were all in the kitchen, Lariat filled a tea kettle with water and lit a stove burner while Bountiful told her grandmother what had happened. Maude listened without interruption. When the kettle whistled, she rose and retrieved a bottle of whiskey, adding generous pours to both her tea and Bountiful's.

"What about me?" Lariat asked.

"What about you?" Maude chided. She finished her tea, then went upstairs to dress.

ॐ

As Maude, Bountiful, and Lariat made for Goldstrike's shack on Mores Creek, a figure approached the carriage house behind Meriwether Peycomson's penny mansion, the fresh tracks carved in the accumulating snow filled nearly as quickly as he made them. It was nearing midnight on November 20, 1919. The man went inside and reappeared less than a minute later with Dredd's dead body slung over his shoulder, carrying it as if the deceased real estate baron weighed no more than a child. Dredd's Vauxhall was behind the stable and the mysterious figure put the body in the passenger seat, fired up the automobile's engine, and drove into the roadless darkness separating the estate from the foothills to the north. When Maude, Bountiful, and Lariat returned to the carriage house with Goldstrike and found it empty, the old prospector was peeved.

"This ain't funny," he complained. "I'm too old to be drug out in the middle of the goddamned night fer a joke."

"It's not a joke, Goldstrike," Lariat said. He pointed at the floor where signs of the life-and-death struggle remained. The baling hook Dredd had used to disarm Bountiful lay just outside the battle-zone and Goldstrike retrieved it.

"Are ya sure he was dead?"

"I'm sure," Bountiful confirmed. "We left him here."

Goldstrike lightly stroked his scarred cheek with the curled tip of the baling hook, scanning the dirt floor. "There's two fresh sets o' tracks in here what ain't Miss Bountiful's or Lariat's," he noted. "One set is Dredd's. The other…"

He hesitated as if mentally scrolling through a list of suspects.

"Willie," Goldstrike finally decided. "It had to be Willie. Ain't nobody else in this town strong enough to tote a fella that big by hisself." He went to the wall of hanging tools, grabbed the broom, and began to sweep the barn floor. "Who else knew about that there note, Miss Bountiful?" he asked.

"I don't know. It was Meriwether's handwriting, so he must know."

"Ya still got the note?"

Bountiful paled. "No…I dropped it. Gerald picked it up. Then, we fought and I don't remember what happened." All four scoured the dirt floor with their eyes, finding nothing.

"If'n he dropped it, Willie musta taken it," Goldstrike decided. He resumed sweeping, then stopped to appraise his effort. "Broom ain't workin'. Don't look natural." He went outside and returned with the branch from a pine tree, its needles still attached. "Get outta here," he told them. "Go on home and don't none o' ya tell nobody what happened here. I'll be along."

"What about Willie?" Maude asked.

"I'll talk to 'im…find out where he took the body," Goldstrike said.

After they were gone, the old prospector carefully swept the floor with the tree branch, creating irregular swirls. Then he returned to his shack on Mores Creek. Willie's cot was empty.

It snowed all night and into the following day, covering the earth in an unspoiled blanket of snow that hid the boulders and dark soil beneath, weighing down the sweeping branches of the pine trees, and piling up in great drifts on the porch steps of the penny mansions. It snowed again the next day and the one after; indeed, it snowed for ten consecutive days, record snowfall erasing all traces of the Vauxhall's tire tracks and the boot prints of the mysterious body snatcher. On the eleventh day, the sun appeared and a huge shelf of snow clinging to the mountainside on the road between Boise and Paradise let go of its rocky perch, provoking an avalanche that buried the road. The pass was closed for the rest of the winter, and it was March of 1920 before motor vehicles were again able to get through. By then the official United States Census had been under way for three months.

# 17

## ROBERT CAMPBELL

Ten years earlier, shortly after the current Mrs. Dredd became The Fourth, she'd had a reclining consultation with her new husband's then-attorney of record. He'd apprised her of the precarious position spouses typically occupied in Dredd's will and the newlywed wife immediately took out a policy with Mutual of Omaha, listing her husband as the named insured and herself as the beneficiary. The death benefit was one million dollars and in early December of 1919, with Gerald missing for about two weeks, it seemed to have been a prudent decision. The Fourth Mrs. Dredd dried her crocodile tears, eagerly bought a selection of black dresses, and made a claim. Informed her husband would remain alive in the eyes of Mutual of Omaha until he had been missing without a trace for seven years, she returned the funereal clothes and settled in for a long haul. After three months, she ran out of patience. "This is ridiculous," she told Iris Campbell. "If Gerald was alive, we'd have heard something from him by now."

Before Iris, the executive assistant's desk at Dredd Enterprises had been occupied by twenty-somethings—a roster including the Second and Third Mrs. Dredds, the Fourth promoted directly from file clerk to lady-of-the-house status—but by the time Iris turned thirty and her boss began to troll the secretarial pool for younger fish, she'd made herself invaluable, functionally running the legal side of his operation. It was an arrangement both Dredd and the board welcomed, and with her boss's disappearance, Iris was named temporary CEO, leapfrogging over Junior. The former executive assistant's desire to remove the "temporary" from her title matched The Fourth Mrs. Dredd's hunger for her million dollars, so when Mutual of

Omaha balked at declaring the missing man dead, Iris made a recommendation. "My brother is a private detective in Chicago," she told the aspiring widow.

"Get him," The Fourth Mrs. Dredd responded. "I'll pay whatever he wants."

Iris's brother, Robert Campbell, was a former Marine who had mustered out after fifteen years in the Corps, mostly serving as an investigator for the military police. Upon entering civilian life he'd briefly worked for the Baldwin-Felts detective agency, only to discover his duties required less investigating than strikebreaking. Preferring to crack cases rather than heads, he soon moved on, subsequently working as a contractor for life insurance companies wishing to make certain beneficiaries hadn't assisted a named insured into the Beyond. Campbell was happy to hear from his older sister. He'd not spent time in the Pacific Northwest nor seen Iris in several years. "I've got one case to finish up and I'll be on my way," he told her. Two weeks later, just after the first of March 1920, he arrived in Boise on the same day the pass to Paradise reopened.

The train trip from Chicago had taken several days, the country outside Campbell's railcar window transitioning from plains to foothills to mountains. When not gazing at the changing scenery he had mostly read from Mark Twain's *Roughing It*, a book the detective felt appropriate for his first trip to the American West. Somewhere around Rock Springs, Wyoming, he set it aside and retrieved a dossier his sister had prepared. It included a timeline and a list of the principals in the case. The Fourth Mrs. Dredd's numerous peccadillos were catalogued, and by the time the train reached Pocatello, Campbell concluded that his investigation might well implicate the missing man's wife.

"She's the one hiring you, Bobby," Iris argued after he'd disembarked in Boise and joined her in the CEO's office at Dredd Enterprises. Since moving into the executive suite from her former station outside the thick walnut door, the former assistant had populated her boss's typically unoccupied desktop with documents and ring binders while framed photos on the wall of the toothy lieutenant governor alongside various dignitaries had been replaced by bulletin boards peppered with graphs and lists. A bust of Dredd on a pedestal had been moved to a corner in favor of a round table where ledgers of various sizes competed for space.

"If she's covered her tracks well enough, it's a smart move," her brother countered. "It doesn't matter, anyway. I won't be working for her." He informed Iris that Mutual of Omaha had retained his services after the wannabe widow's persistent demands for a settlement aroused suspicion. Iris laughed, assuring him that The Fourth Mrs. Dredd possessed the inclination, but not the wherewithal, to murder her husband. "Brain's in her bodice," she remarked.

"What about the others…the oldest son and the rest?" her brother asked.

Iris shook her head. "Junior isn't a killer. That's why his father hates him. Freddie's nine…and Carl? Well, Carl makes Mrs. Dredd look like Albert Einstein."

"And the daughters?"

"Three of them live with their mothers. They've not seen their father in years." Iris hesitated before continuing, chewing on her lower lip. "As for Geraldine…I don't know. She's smart. And she has a motive."

"Which is?"

Iris told her brother about the rumors of Dredd's late-night visits to his daughter's bedroom. "There's always been talk," she reported.

"Maybe the talk got to him," Campbell said. "Or someone else was about to talk and he took off before the scandal reared its head in the papers."

Iris again shook her head. "Gerald might abandon his wife and children, but he'd never abandon his money." She revealed that no draws had been made on any of her employer's accounts since his disappearance. "Besides, he controls the press around here," she went on. "Wilbur Tarkel at the *Statesman* wouldn't dare print anything negative… No, Bobby, something has happened to him. I know it."

Campbell took a few moments to appraise his older sister. She looked comfortable behind her boss's big desk. "I'd be remiss if I didn't point out that you have a motive, too, sis," he said.

"For God's sake, Bobby…"

"Relax…I'm joking. Probably, anyway."

"I was at home with Margaret when he disappeared," Iris said, alluding to her live-in relationship with a local female artist. She then pointed him toward the penny mansioneers in Paradise. "Two of the four families that bought houses up there cleared out before the end of last year. One of them…the Coolers…probably worked for Gerald. I'm quite sure of that. They burned down the house they bought."

"What happened to them?"

"Beats me. I've left it up to the police… Now you, I guess."

"And the other family?"

"The Peycomsons. They left town around the same time Gerald disappeared."

"What can you tell me about them?"

"Nothing. I never met them. Supposedly, the husband was a bit of a wolf. Apparently, he was very interested in Bountiful Dollarhyde, the schoolteacher up there. That's understandable. She's quite beautiful."

"And the wife?"

Iris frowned at her brother. "I sent all this stuff to you. It was in the dossier…which you apparently didn't read."

"I read it. Go on about the wife."

"I'm told she was a bit cuckoo…never went out, never entertained company. There was a child and a nanny, too, but I don't know anything about them." Campbell next quizzed his sister about Dredd's movements prior to his disappearance and she apprised him of a meeting with the sinister Le Lutin. "It was the day before Gerald went missing," she told her brother. "Felix is a scary little bastard, Bobby. His wife, too, if that's what Gerta is. They both give me the creeps." She revealed that her boss had used the couple's services several times over the years. "Whatever their services are," Iris added. "Nothing legal, that's for sure. Gerald always kept me out of that side of his business."

"What were they doing for him this time?"

"I just told you, Bobby. I've never been involved in that part of Gerald's operation."

"But you must have seen contracts or a record of payments? You handle that stuff, right?"

Iris shook her head. "Gerald had a cash-only relationship with them. There were bank withdrawals whenever they showed up but nothing else."

She held up a finger.

"Wait a second… I remember hotel invoices from their last visit. Would that help?"

"It might."

Iris went out to the reception area, rummaged through a filing cabinet, and returned with two documents. "According to these, Gerald booked rooms at the Idanha Hotel on November nineteenth of last year," she divulged. "That was right before he disappeared." She looked at her brother. "He took care of the reservations himself. That was strange. Usually, he had me do it."

"Rooms, you said…for more than one party?"

Iris studied the invoices. "Two parties in separate rooms booked for one night each. Richard Bright and his wife were in one of them. He's a lawyer from Portland. He's worked with Gerald on various things over the years."

"What kinds of things?"

"I really don't know. I was never privy to their relationship, either, although if I had to guess, I'd bet Richard was facilitating a bribe or blackmailing someone. That's what got him disbarred in Oregon."

"And the other room? Who stayed there?"

Iris perused the second invoice. "Mister and Mrs. August Grobermann of Reno, Nevada."

"Who are *they*?"

"Felix and Gerta, I suspect," his sister surmised. "The meeting I told you about was on the same day the Grobermanns were in town. Richard Bright was at the meeting too. Did I already tell you that?"

"Bright...the lawyer."

"Disbarred lawyer."

"Right...disbarred. Was Bright's wife at the meeting?"

"No... I don't even know if she was the one with Richard in the hotel room. She'd never come with him on previous trips to Boise, so it could have been one of the working girls from Levy's Alley...or a mistress. Richard is a bit of a rake and he's very good-looking. A mistress or two wouldn't surprise me." She handed her brother the invoices and he reviewed them, tapping on one of them with his finger.

"According to this, the lawyer and his wife stayed an extra two days and left without checking out," Campbell noted.

Iris nodded. "There was a DO NOT DISTURB sign on their door for more than two days, so no one knows when they actually left. They stole a towel and two bedsheets. A few days later a police detective came here to ask about it. The company booked the room, so we were responsible for theft and damages."

"Anything come from the investigation?"

"Nothing as far as I know. It was just a towel and some sheets...a couple of extra days added to their stay. The company reimbursed the hotel and the police didn't pursue it any further."

"Did you contact Bright about it?"

"For crying out loud, Bobby, it was a towel and some sheets! Gerald was missing. The company was reeling. I had more important things to work on."

"And since?"

Iris shrugged. "Richard returned to Portland as far as I know," she said. "I've not heard from him."

That night Campbell had dinner with Iris and Margaret at their Franklin Street home near the statehouse. Afterward he slept in their comfortable guest room, a welcome change after three days of train travel. The next morning he began his investigation in earnest, starting with the usual suspects in a murder case: family and household servants. All, save Geraldine, were quickly excluded. The butler and four housekeepers welded enthusiastic desires to kill their boss to ironclad alibis. Likewise, Junior and Carl were able to account for their whereabouts with reliable witnesses. That left Geraldine, who was still in Paradise, and The Fourth Mrs. Dredd, a woman Campbell ruled out as a suspect following a brief interview. That might have been the end of it for the prospective widow had she not been so taken with the rangy ex-Marine, his shock of dark hair and strong chin resurrecting previously forgotten details about her husband's disappearance. "I suddenly remembered something that needs your urgent attention," she told him over the phone for two days running, subsequently greeting him at the door wearing a clingy silk robe and a come-hither look. On his second visit she lured him to her bedroom with the promise of new evidence, slipping out of her robe after closing the door to reveal the evidence she needed urgently attended. Campbell politely declined. "You're very attractive, Mrs. Dredd," he told her. "But it wouldn't be professional of me to become romantically involved with a suspect." The chill of the air on her naked skin and the demotion from budding widow to subject of interest promptly cooled her off, and The Fourth Mrs. Dredd had no more recollections.

In between return visits to the Dredd home, Campbell canvassed prestigious Warm Springs Avenue, going door to door. Every one of Gerald Dredd's neighbors had an opinion, but none had relevant information. On his fourth day in town the detective left Iris's guest room and checked into the Idanha Hotel. "I need to know more about the Brights and the Grobermanns," he explained to his sister. "The desk clerks and maids are more likely to talk about them with a guest." And they were—particularly Lester, the doorman.

"No offense, sir, but I don't talk about our guests," Lester told Campbell, afterward talking about little else other than the hotel's guests. He and the detective stood on the wide stoop just outside the Idanha's entry, a half dozen steps leading down to the street level. "Mister and Mrs. Grobermann were folks a person just doesn't forget," Lester recalled when asked about them. "They checked in the same day as that couple the police were looking for...the Brights. I took the luggage up for both parties... Never saw Mister and Mrs. Bright after that. But the Grobermanns..."

Lester chuckled softly.

"My goodness, they were a pair, those two. Mister Grobermann showed up at the bar the only night they were here and he was quite the entertainer. I was off duty, mind you, so you should speak with Mister Hershfield to get the full low-down. He was on the front desk that evening. But as I heard it, Mister Grobermann had everybody in stitches, imitating chimpanzees and so forth. Mister Hershfield got on the phone and passed the word when that little fellow started doing somersaults and what-have-you. A crowd showed up and Mrs. Grobermann bought a couple of rounds for the house while her husband was tumbling and telling jokes. Like I said, I wasn't here, but I remember the exact date. It was on November the nineteenth, nineteen hundred and nineteen."

"You say August Grobermann was a little fellow?" Campbell posed.

"Not just little, Mister Campbell. He was a runt. You know what I mean...a dwarf. Three feet tall or so."

"And Mrs. Grobermann?"

"Tall blonde and a beauty. Cold as a flagpole in winter, though. I shivered just looking at her."

The white-haired doorman smiled.

"The nineteenth of the month in the year nineteen-nineteen...the sort of thing that sticks in a man's mind, don't you think?"

"Do you remember anything else about them?" Campbell pressed him.

"Isn't that something? Nineteenth of the month in the year nineteen-nineteen."

"Really something...but perhaps—"

"I recall the date because my birthday is on the twentieth of November," Lester rambled. "I was sixty-two years old that day. Still had to work, though, birthday or not. I've shown up for work here at the Idanha every day for thirty-seven years. On time too. Never late."

It seemed Lester had nothing more to share and Campbell excused himself, before heading down the front steps of the hotel. He'd reached the street level when Lester called out.

"You know, Mister Campbell, the next day...the twentieth of November...is when the dwarf and his woman checked out. I remember because I brought their luggage down...put the bags in their car. Beautiful automobile. Never seen one like it before or since. It was a Cadillac touring car...Liberty Cadillac I believe they call them. His was green...the dwarf's...green Liberty Cadillac with a huge trunk. I remember the trunk because they checked out with more luggage than when they checked in. Went shopping while they were here in town, I guess."

Campbell reascended the steps. "Did you share that with the Boise police detective?"

"About the luggage? No, he never asked. Is it important?"

"It might be. You say Mister Hershfield was on duty when Grobermann was performing in the bar?"

"Did I say that?" Lester replied. He chuckled softly. "Here I am, claiming I don't gossip and then I go flapping my lips... but, yes, Mister Hershfield had the evening desk duty that night. Anything you want to know about what went on in the bar that evening, he can probably tell you."

Campbell grinned at the tall, slender doorman. "Thanks, Lester," he said.

Lester smiled, touching the brim of his cap. "My pleasure, sir...happy to help." He hesitated, then went on. "You know,

those goings-on happened around the same time Mister Lieutenant Governor Gerald Dredd went missing. Have you heard
about that?"

"I have."

"Just disappeared off the face of the earth. Peculiar thing.
Someone should look into it."

Campbell agreed, then trotted down the steps and walked
several blocks to the attorney general's offices at the Idaho
statehouse where he'd scheduled an interview with Bertram
Mole. It was a short meeting, the detective quickly sizing up
the attorney as a conniving little rodent but not a suspect in
Dredd's disappearance. Afterward he returned to the Idanha
and convinced one of the maids to let him into the room where
Felix Ombre and Gerta Frobe stayed as the Grobermanns of
Reno, Nevada.

"I shouldn't do this," she said, pocketing a silver dollar. They
stood in the corridor outside Room 4F.

"It'll be our secret," Campbell answered.

The maid gave him the key wrapped in a slip of paper with
her phone number. "Just this once," she said. She tilted a hip,
adding, "Will you need any help? I'm on my break. I'm Alice."

"Thanks but I'll be fine on my own, Alice," Campbell replied. He unlocked the door and stepped into the room.

Inside, he discovered that the only difference between Room
4F and his own 2C on the hotel's second level was the picture
on the wall. His was a desert landscape, the painting in Room
4F depicting a bend of the Boise River where tree branches
canopied over the banks. Otherwise, both spaces had a double
bed framed by two nightstands—their drawers empty save a
Gideon Bible in one of them. There was a single padded wing
chair in a corner and a small writing desk tucked against the
wall beneath the room's only window. He went to the bathroom
next and found it equally devoid of helpful evidence, the sink
and tub spotless, the wall-mounted medicine chest empty save
a complimentary sewing kit. Campbell returned to the main
room and meticulously examined every square inch of the floor,

afterward moving the bed off the ornate oriental area rug. He scrutinized the rug, top and bottom, then put everything back in place and left. That evening the detective had dinner at Morrison's with his sister and her roommate. Afterward they went for drinks in the lobby bar, and once the two women departed, Campbell approached the desk clerk. Hershfield was eager to tell what he knew, confirming that August Grobermann spent his only night in Boise entertaining a crowd in the bar with jokes, singing, and acrobatics.

"That dwarf was somethin' else," Hershfield reported. "He could juggle and play the harmonica at the same time. Did flips on the bar and handstands…all sorts o' whatnot."

"And the woman he was with?"

"The blonde? Quite a beauty but an icicle. Couple o' boys took a run at her, seein' as how her husband is a runt and all, but she wasn't havin' none of it."

"Was she there all evening?"

"She went to the privy at one point."

"What time was that?"

"Around ten, I suspect."

"Did you see her come back?"

"Well, it's like I told you," Hershfield said. "That midget was quite the entertainer and I had my eyes on him most of the time like everybody else."

"But did you see her come back?"

"Can't say that I did, although she left with him. Weird couple. She carried him like she was his mama."

"And what time was that?"

"Musta been midnight."

The next morning the detective and another silver dollar convinced Alice to unlock the door to Room 3D, where the Brights had stayed. She followed him in, uninvited, but left in a huff soon thereafter when Campbell showed more interest in the area rug than the available bed. Unlike the Grobermann's Room 4F, the detective found two discrepancies to distinguish the accommodation from his own: the painting on the wall depicted Mount Borah, and a dark, penny-sized spot marred the carpet's otherwise precise motif. He turned the rug over and lightly touched a corresponding stain on the underside.

"Blood," he murmured.

# 18

## They Were Coming Back

As his investigation proceeded, Robert Campbell discovered that Thaddeus, Wanda, Trixie, and Charlotte Cooler, along with Joshua Purdue of the vaunted Massachusetts Purdues, had all been guests of Idanha Hotel just prior to their debut appearances in Paradise. Iris produced an invoice that itemized three rooms billed to Dredd Enterprises in late March of 1919. "There were a lot of room service charges," she told her brother. The Coolers had registered as the Montegues of 225 Madison Avenue, New York City. "That's the home of J. Pierpont Morgan," Campbell chuckled. "Ballsy bunch, those Coolers."

After further digging, the detective unearthed a talkative Wanda Cooler. Rather than return to New York, she was still in Boise, plying her previous trade off Sixth and Main in what was known as Levy's Alley. She'd taken the name Daphne du Barry. "I have no idea what happened to Thaddeus," she told the detective after receiving five dollars and assurance that she was not a person of interest in his investigation. "Trixie headed back to New York...Charlotte too. Don't know if they made it."

After his ignominious ejection from the back door of Elysium, Joshua Purdue had made it to Boise, appeared briefly as Captain Starlight in a local theater production of *Robbery Under Arms*, then was last seen heading east in his roadster. Campbell found Gus, Nat, and Vic in jail, the former two on drunk and disorderly charges with Vic awaiting trial for assault. Unlike the other Coolers, the trio were cellblock regulars who worked between incarcerations as Boise bouncers or debt collectors. All three had verifiable alibis. "They're thugs, but not murderers," Campbell concluded for his sister. "They had nothing to do with Dredd's disappearance." Meanwhile, Felix "Le Lutin" Ombre and Frau Gerta were ghosts, although the detective was able to track their movements as far as Reno. "If Dredd is dead, I don't think they did it," he told Iris. "They had no motive. They're obviously professionals and he was a paycheck. Doing away with him wouldn't have been in their best interest."

"What about kidnapping?" she countered.

"There's been no ransom demand... No, Iris, I think your boss either ran off on his own or he's dead. You said he wouldn't leave his money behind, so..."

To interview Richard Bright, the third person at the November meeting in Dredd's office, Campbell took the Oregon Short Line to Portland, first slanting northwest to a layover in Huntington before going on to LaGrande and then west to his destination. With all the stops it took almost three days, giving Campbell ample time to appreciate the climb into the craggy Blue Mountains, the descent into Willow Creek Valley, and the subsequent reascension as the train entered the Cascades. In the Marine Corps he'd served in Cuba, China, the Philippines, and Mexico, but his American postings had been on the east coast, far from the landscapes that scrolled past his window as the train lumbered along the tracks. Out here, there were few signs of civilization: fences, an occasional ranch with horses roaming freely, the small cities of Ontario, Pendleton, and The Dalles. But, in general, the absence of people was startling. In the Corps, Campbell had slept within snoring distance of dozens of men for years, and after mustering out, took an apartment in Chicago where the only things towering overhead were apartment buildings. The utter majesty of the Oregon mountain ranges and the Columbia River Gorge astounded him, the forces responsible for such creations transforming his wonder into awe and then serenity.

*I could live here*, he thought.

In Portland, he found the Bright residence in a part of the city near recently chartered Reed College. It was a family neighborhood for the moderately affluent, the homes good-sized with generous front lawns. The Brights' abode—on SE Twenty-Eighth Avenue—was an impressive two-story house with charcoal shutters and a circular portico at the entry. Atop the portico, a small hemispheric balcony with an ornately forged balustrade was accessible from a window. Although the other homes in the neighborhood were well-kept, the grass of the Brights' home was several inches high and peppered with weeds. Overgrown shrubs encroached on the front walk and a single red Adirondack chair was on its side in the middle of the lawn, its partner on the front porch. A foreclosure notice was on the door and no one responded to the bell or Campbell's knock. He considered picking the lock, but with a neighbor across the street eyeing him while watering a lawn that didn't need watering, he decided to visit the bank that held the note. "They haven't made a mortgage payment since November," the chatty loan officer at Wells Fargo told him. "Neighbors say they've not seen signs of life for the better part of a year. They figured the Brights just took off for some reason. Can't say I'm surprised. Bit of a checkered past, that one. He was disbarred, you know."

"Could I get a look inside?" Campbell asked.

The garrulous loan officer abruptly sobered, leaning sideways to peer at a private office near the rear of the business. Inside the glass-walled space a severe fellow with thinning hair and a stern expression was hard at work distributing razor-sharp looks of disapproval among the various tellers and functionaries under his supervision. "My manager might not like it," the loan officer said, shifting in his chair until Campbell's head blocked his boss's view. Suddenly he brightened. "But you're thinking about buying the house, right?"

"Sure."

"Well, I guess there's no harm then." The loan officer retrieved a ring of keys from a desk drawer, extracted one, and handed it over with a wink. "Just between you and me, right?"

"Right," Campbell replied.

The detective returned to SE Twenty-Eighth Avenue. The

nosy neighbor was no longer watering his lawn, but the private eye had just exited his cab when the fellow spilled out his front door and half-ran to meet him. Although he wore no spectacles, eyeglass marks dented either side of the man's nose and a ring of feathery hair encircled a pate that was otherwise bald, save a single bushy patch growing out of his forehead like the stump of a rhinoceros horn. "Don Babbitt," the man introduced himself, squinting. After Campbell identified himself as a detective, Babbitt kept pace as they headed up the walk to the Brights' front door, lifting his chin when they were close enough to read the bank foreclosure notice.

"This place will be a bargain for someone," he said. "The yard's a bit of a mess right now, but Richard and Louise kept the place up. I'd bet the inside is perfect."

"When did you last see them?" Campbell asked.

"Haven't seen Richard in months," Babbitt replied. "And of course, we haven't seen Louise in years. Lovely woman, but always quiet even in the days before she went... I mean, before her illness."

Babbitt watched Campbell put the key in the lock, then moved to go in after the detective opened the door. "I've always wanted to get a look inside this place," he said. "The Brights didn't entertain."

Campbell stopped him with a hand on his chest.

"Sorry...official business."

Babbitt frowned. "I don't see what harm—"

"What did you say your name was?" the detective asked, pulling out his notepad. Babbitt paled slightly, his eyelids fluttering, and he stepped back, clearly discomfited by a promotion from innocent neighbor to bona fide suspect.

"I'll just leave you to it then," he said.

Babbitt hurried up the front walk, tossing a furtive glance over his shoulder that made him stumble off the curb. Campbell waited until the snoopy fellow had reached his own house, then stepped into the small entry of the Brights' home. He closed and locked the door, afterward allowing a few moments for his eyes to adjust to the unlit interior. The place was dark and cool and smelled of cleaning solutions. Just inside the front door was an umbrella stand with two wood-handled umbrellas. The entry opened into a spacious foyer, a set of steps to the second level on one side, an arched portal to the parlor on the other. A hallway to the kitchen paralleled the staircase, a side table with attached seat tucked against the wall at the base of the stairs. A candlestick-style telephone was atop the table. Campbell went to the phone and held the handset to his ear, tapping on the switch-hook. No operator answered. The phone was dead.

He next searched each room of the house, unveiling a consistent pattern of compulsive neatness. Pictures were hung straight, end tables uncluttered, the kitchen sink spotless, the dishes evenly aligned by diameter or height in the cupboards, canned goods similarly organized in the pantry. Upstairs, in the master suite, the bed was made, the bathroom fixtures gleaming. As expected for a couple away on a trip, the main bedroom closet yielded a dozen available hangers, the dresser drawers were half-empty, and there were no suitcases to be found. Campbell inspected the other second-floor bedrooms and then went to the study on the ground level. A large diploma from the Willamette University School of Law hung on the wall, its recipient identified as RICHARD CHARLES BRIGHT. The books on the shelves included a leather-bound set of Charles Dickens's complete works ordered by date of publication, and the desk drawers were unlocked with stationary, pens, pencils, erasers, a ruler, and a stapler among the various office supplies. Just off the top right edge of the ink blotter, next to a banker's lamp with a green glass shade, was a picture of Louise Bright in a small frame. On the opposite side, an empty coffee cup on a coaster proclaimed its user to be the WORLD'S BEST LAWYER. Closer inspection of the ink blotter revealed indentations made by a writing instrument on an overlying sheet of paper. Campbell ripped a blank page from his notepad, placed it over the indentations, and used a pencil from a cup on the desk to shade the depressions. Four names appeared, one of them confirming something the detective had suspected before leaving Boise:

COMPEYSON

SECOMPONY

McSPOONEY

PEYCOMSON

He underlined the last name, tucked the page into his note-pad, and then picked up a rolled-up blueprint lying just above the top edge of the ink blotter. He spread the drawing out on the desk, revealing a design for a sunroom addition to the house.

*They were making plans… They intended to return.*

He recalled Room 3D at the Idanha Hotel, the missing towel and sheets, the bloodspot on the rug.

"They never left Idaho," Campbell murmured.

The detective spent the night at the Imperial Hotel in downtown Portland. The next morning he visited the offices of Anderson, Olendorff, Hall, Seitz, and Sallee—Bright's former law firm. Sallee met with him.

"Richard has a fine legal mind and he's quite the personality," the amiable lawyer told Campbell from the chair behind his huge desk. "In the beginning clients loved him and he was well on his way to partnership until Louise fell ill." He recounted Mrs. Bright's gradual retreat into the American colonial cocoon on SE Twenty-Eighth Avenue. "Richard began to spend more time tending to Louise than at the office," Sallee recalled. "He skipped appointments and court appearances and wasn't prepared when he did show up. Eventually, we had no choice but to let him go." He rose and went to the window. His office overlooked the Willamette River with majestic Mt. Hood prosecuting the distant horizon. "We lost track of him for a few years…until that nasty business in Salem," the lawyer went on, his voice tinged with sadness. He faced the detective. "Richard offered a bribe to a fellow in the Department of Revenue… Asked us to represent him after he was indicted for it. We kept him out of jail, but he lost his license to practice law."

That afternoon, Campbell boarded the train back to Boise.

The trip to Portland had passed easily, the views elegiac, the monotonous rumble of the train as it rolled across the tracks causing him to frequently nod off. However, the return trek was endless. He drank too much coffee and too little whiskey, the miles falling away slowly. After three days of travel he arrived in Boise, and following a night's rest, borrowed Iris's car to resume his investigation. Thus far, the last person to have seen Dredd—a retired Warm Springs Avenue neighbor who spent his days surveilling cars and people who passed his house—reported that he'd sighted the missing man motoring east. Campbell headed that way, the city thinning into open range as he passed Penitentiary Road at the edge of the city. There were three ranches between the prison and Barber Park four miles to the east. One of the ranchers recalled seeing Dredd's Vauxhall motoring in the direction of Paradise.

"I seen Mister Gerald Dredd's swanky automobile head that way at least once a month fer years," he told Campbell. "Though not since November."

"Do you remember the exact date?"

The rancher laughed. "That was months ago and I'm eighty years old. You're lucky I remember it was November." He abruptly sobered. "I do recall when the article came out in the *Statesman*...about Dredd missin' and all. It was on December third, exactly two weeks to the day after I seen 'im drive up the road in that fancy car." He chuckled. "So I guess I do remember the date. Ain't senile yet, I guess. That would have made it... November twentieth, right? Anyway, when I read about the lieutenant governor missin' and all, I said to Phoebe...she's my wife...I said, 'Phoebe, it's been exactly two weeks since I saw Dredd drive that ritzy motorcar o' his up toward Paradise.'" The old rancher tapped the side of his head with a finger. "I remember that much. Still got some marbles in here."

Campbell politely listened to a few more stories, none in any way connected to the disappearance of Gerald Dredd. Eventually, he broke away in the middle of a description of the old man's uncle, a fellow with six fingers on one hand and four on

the other. He made it to the driver's seat of his car before the
rancher called out. "Another thing, Detective."

The old fellow approached, bending slightly to put his face
in the open window. His teeth were brown, his breath reeking
of chewing tobacco.

"I seen Dredd go up the road that day, but I never seen 'im
come back," he told Campbell. "No, sir, I never seen 'im since.
Hell, nobody has." He paused, clicking his tongue as he gazed
to the east where the landscape rumpled into jagged peaks. "So
I'm bettin' that whatever happened to 'im…it happened up in
them mountains."

Campbell thanked the rancher and returned to the Idanha
where he made a phone call to a former Marine Corps buddy
who was now a cop in Reno.

"What did you find out?" Campbell asked him.

"Not much, Bob. Your midget and his wife made it this
far, just as you thought, then sold the Caddie and bought train
tickets for Los Angeles. Thing is, there's no evidence they ever
boarded. They just vanished."

Campbell was to dine that evening with his sister and her
roommate, and with nothing to do until dinnertime, decided to
get a drink at a Levy's Alley speakeasy recommended by Lester,
the doorman. He left his room and stepped into the elevator.
On the way down, he thought about the old rancher. He agreed
with him. Whatever had happened to Gerald Dredd likely took
place in Paradise, making the small mountain hamlet the next
stop in his investigation. The elevator reached the main level,
opening into a small vestibule. He exited and veered around a
short wall to enter the lobby. Hershfield was at the front desk,
the reception area otherwise empty, save an old man asleep in
a padded leather chair. Across the lobby, the tearoom doors
were open. Inside, a young woman sat alone at a table near the
windows. Campbell had always believed his ex-wife, a glamor-
ous Chicago heiress, to be the most beautiful creature he'd ever
seen, but with his first glimpse of Bountiful Dollarhyde, the
detective knew he'd been wrong.

# 19

## THE ELEVENTH STICK

Bountiful heard the elevator bell and looked to the sound. A moment later Robert Campbell appeared. He wore a suit and tie, his clothes draping naturally over the lean, solid frame of an ex-Marine, his hat pulled just low enough on his forehead to keep rain out of his eyes the way a good hat should. He looked through the doorway of the tearoom as he traversed the lobby, then smiled and touched the brim of his brown fedora without breaking stride.

"Miss," he mouthed, the word silent.

Shortly thereafter, Geraldine Dredd Barkley joined Bountiful after meeting with Iris Campbell at Dredd Enterprises.

"Now that I'm eighteen Iris says no one can make me come back to Boise if I don't want to…and I *don't* want to," she told Bountiful. Iris had further revealed to the young heiress that Dredd Enterprises owned the former Peycomson residence. "Will and I can move in," Geraldine added. "If the council approves, of course. I know you can take the place back if you want."

"No one on the council will object," Bountiful reassured her, gently teasing, "After all, you've added one more to our population."

The Barkleys' courtship and secret nuptials had transformed Geraldine's once gloomy demeanor into a sunny one, while restoring Willie's sanity more expeditiously than might have been accomplished with old potions or new-fangled psychoanalysis. The former doughboy's hallucinations no longer visited him nor did he wander about at all hours of the night, calling out to the trees. Maude believed credit should go to the still at-large Thaddeus Cooler whose stage play had provided Willie with a traversable avenue for lucid thoughts. However, most folks in Paradise believed love had not just metaphorically, but literally, cured all. There were still a few in town skeptical of Geraldine. "The calf don't stray that far from the cow," they opined, but Bountiful saw in the young woman the same bliss she felt in the shadow of the majestic Sawtooth Mountains. Compared to the outside world, Paradise often seemed to fulfill its name—a place surrounded by beauty and suffused with the good will of genuine friends who stood by one another when trouble visited.

Although Geraldine had been added to the census, the loss of four Peycomsons now put the population of Paradise at 121, four below the incorporation threshold. It was a number made more ominous at a town council meeting the morning after Bountiful and Geraldine returned from Boise. The gathering included the Goodlows and the DeMilles, their hundreds of dollars in renovations giving them bigger dogs in the hunt than many in town.

"Meriwether lied," Bountiful reported. "The eminent domain lawsuit was never dismissed. The effort to take our homes is still alive." And Bertram Mole, she told the gathering, was as persistent as the creature who shared his surname. "There's a rumor that he's angling for an Interior Department job… Thinks acquisition of our land for the government will get it for him." Bountiful further revealed that the little attorney had tunneled far enough into the federal bureaucracy to get a census taker scheduled to begin in Paradise by early May. "That gives us about a month to get up to one hundred twenty-five people." A few moments of silence elapsed while the council digested what they'd been told. Then Maude spoke up.

"We could hire folks…like Dredd did."

"How would we pay them?" Oskar argued. "The city treasury can't cover it."

"The people in this room could," Maude said. "There's enough money among us to fund a few months."

"What about recounts?" Goldstrike reminded her. "Miss Bountiful thought we might need to keep our population up fer a year or more. Do we wanna grubstake four people that long?"

Maude pursed her lips, forming a thoughtful expression. "There's a way to get at least two with no cost. We'd only have to cover all four people for a few months."

"How many months ya talkin' about?"

Maude eyed Annie Goodlow and Sarah DeMille.

"Nine," she said.

Goldstrike promptly offered a motion for the two women to get themselves pregnant. It was seconded, but in the ensuing discussion, the DeMilles and Goodlows preferred to come on board absent an official vote.

"John and I were already trying," Annie confessed.

"Amon and I weren't exactly *not* trying," Sarah slyly added.

The members then considered hiring ringers to portray the remainder of needed residents, but the discussion hit a snag when Ed Riggins—there to cover the proceeding for the *Idaho World*—reminded the group that their proposal was fraud.

"Then don't go publishin' it, Ed," Goldstrike growled.

"Published or not, it's still a crime," Riggins replied.

The meeting adjourned without resolution. The Goodlows and DeMilles went home to presumably have another go at satisfying the motion to impregnate themselves. The rest—save Bountiful, Maude, and Goldstrike—headed for the Gold Rush Saloon. "Dredd's family has hired a private investigator," Bountiful told her grandmother and the former prospector after the others were gone. "He's from Chicago. I saw him when I was having tea at the Idanha. Lester...the doorman there...told me that he's Iris Campbell's brother and a former military police-man."

"This fella...he got the lookuva serious man?" Goldstrike asked. "Should we worry?"

Bountiful nodded. "I think we should. He had a way about him. He was...purposeful."

Maude reached out and touched her granddaughter's hand. "Are you blushing?"

"No."

"Yes, you are. You're blushing. Was he handsome, this detective?"

"Stop it, Grandma. I'm not blushing."

"We gotta get Lariat outta here, census be damned," Goldstrike broke in, saying what all three were thinking. They well knew what would happen to a Black teenager accused of killing one of Idaho's most prominent white citizens. Lariat would never see a courtroom, a tree and a rope dispensing the justice offered to defendants of African descent. "In the meantime…" the former Civil War minesweeper added. "I got me an idea to slow things down a mite."

ॐ

The next morning Maude and Goldstrike left Paradise and drove to Boise. They went to a hardware store where the old prospector purchased a dry cell battery and an alarm clock. They immediately headed back, and about five miles from home, Maude stopped the car at a widened bump-out bordered on the south by Mores Creek and on the north by the mountainside. A ROAD CLOSED sign affixed to an elongated sawhorse had been left there by the crew assigned to repair the pass following the November avalanche. Goldstrike hopped out and dragged the sign into the middle of the road, afterward riding the running board of the Model T as Maude drove on toward Paradise. About two hundred yards up the road, she stopped the car and watched from the driver's seat as Goldstrike stuffed the battery, the alarm clock, a coil of electrical wire, a blasting cap, and a drill into a knapsack. Last of all, he added the eleventh of the twelve sticks of dynamite obtained from Old Butch's nephew at the Belshazzar mine.

"I'll need about an hour," he told Maude. He crossed the road and ventured into the rocks, clambering over boulders and using irregular crevices and craggy shelves to climb higher. About sixty feet up the mountainside he reached a huge, rocky outcropping and slipped beneath it. He retrieved the hand drill from his bag and laboriously bored a hole into a natural seam, then removed the clear shield from the face of the clock and attached a wire to the little hand. He ran the wire to one pole of the battery and connected a second wire from the clock's big hand to the remaining pole. Last of all, he spliced in a blasting cap, carefully inserted it into the dynamite, and then shoved the explosive cylinder into the drill hole. With his makeshift bomb rigged to complete an electrical circuit and detonate when the clock's hands touched at noon, he set the timepiece for 11:30 and wound it. It immediately began to tick and Goldstrike scrambled down the side of the mountain. It was 11:45 by the time he reached Maude.

"We got fifteen minutes till she blows… Get goin'!" he shouted as he jumped into the Model T.

They raced up the road and drove into Paradise just as the big and little hands of the clock touched each other. A distant rumble followed, the ground beneath the citizens of Paradise shuddering almost imperceptibly as the outcropping broke free and slid down the mountain. Later that day a member of the repair crew was dispatched to retrieve the ROAD CLOSED sign. He returned empty-handed.

"There's been another avalanche. I couldn't get through," he reported to his supervisor. He described the pile of jagged rocks and irregular boulders on the road, the source of the rubble apparent: a high, deep wedge cut from the adjacent mountainside. "If I didn't know better, I'd say the rock face just exploded," he observed. "It's gonna take a while to open things up again."

❧

Driving his sister's car, Robert Campbell had reached the ROAD CLOSED sign before the explosion. As a Chicagoan, he was accustomed to work crews that left things lying around for years after repairs were completed and slowed only briefly before angling his car around the warning sign and going on. He was still a mile from Paradise when the concussive blast of the exploding dynamite was dampened by a deafening backfire from his sister's automobile. Four minutes later he was in town and had reached Nilsen's General Store, driving slowly as he passed. A crowd was gathered on the boardwalk fronting the establishment, some tracking his progress, others pointing at the road behind him. Among them were a man wearing armbands and an apron, a Chinese fellow with a long pigtail, an older woman with a substantial bosom, a grizzled character with half an ear and a long scar on one cheek, and the young woman he'd seen in the tearoom of the Idanha Hotel.

Campbell didn't stop, instead driving on until he reached the charred remains of Elysium. It was a crisp spring day, but radiant heat from the bright sun made it warmer and he removed his coat after climbing out of his car, at the same time glancing up the street. The grizzled fellow with the scarred cheek was headed his way. The detective smiled. "They'll send up their first flare with Goldstrike," Iris had predicted, and with the old prospector hurrying to reach him, Campbell tossed his coat onto the front seat, retrieved a flashlight from the glovebox, and then ambled up the front walk. At the base of the blackened porch stairs, he stopped and waited.

"This here's city property," Goldstrike growled upon reaching him. "Ya ain't allowed to rummage around in there. Who are you, anyway?" The detective handed Goldstrike a business card.

ROBERT CAMPBELL…PRIVATE INVESTIGATIONS

Goldstrike squinted at it, then warily eyed the detective. "What the hell're ya private investigatin' in Paradise? We ain't got nuthin' here."

"It's about Gerald Dredd. He disappeared. I've been asked to look into it. Do you know him?"

"Everybody knows 'im and wishes they didn't," Goldstrike said. "Talk to folks in Boise if'n ya wanna find out about Gerald Dredd. We ain't seem 'im in months." He held out the card for the detective to take back.

"Keep it, Goldstrike."

Goldstrike frowned. "How'd ya know my name?"

Campbell smiled. "Folks in Boise know about you. You're kind of famous."

"Famous! Whattaya mean famous? I ain't famous."

"Let's just say your reputation precedes you."

"What the hell's that s'posed to mean?"

"It's not an insult. I asked around in the valley about people up here. You were mentioned. That's all. I'm glad we ran into each other. I have a few questions…if you're agreeable, that is."

"Why wouldn't I be? I ain't got nuthin' to hide."

Campbell shifted his gaze to the dark opening where a front door had once stood. "First, I need to go inside and check things out. Do you want to come along…make sure I don't break any city rummaging laws?"

"Hell no!" Goldstrike exclaimed. "You shouldn't go in there, neither. A fella could fall through that goddamned floor."

"I'll be careful."

"Town ain't payin' for it if'n ya get hurt…or kilt."

"I understand."

Campbell cautiously climbed the porch stairs and went inside. After a winter covered in snow, the house smelled of rotting wood, the ash and snowmelt combining to produce a black slurry that formed clumps on the bottoms of his shoes. As he explored the ruins, using his flashlight to inspect the darker corners, it was apparent the blaze had started on the second floor of the home, near its center. The place had been outfitted with a few electric lights and outlets, one of the latter on the upper level black and misshapen, as if the heat of the fire had melted it. "Arson," Campbell murmured, agreeing with the assessment of the fire inspector he'd interviewed in Boise.

"Find anything?" Goldstrike asked after the detective rejoined him on the front walk.

"Probably nothing you didn't already know. Any thoughts about what caused the fire?"

"Thoughts! We got more'n thoughts… Them Coolers cleaned the place out and burned it down to cover their tracks.

With all yer goddamned investigatin' I'm surprised ya didn't already know that. Far as that goes, why ain't ya private investigatin' them Coolers? Seems like that might be a better use o' yer time."

Campbell nodded. "I did investigate them. They were paid to buy and then abandon this place. Probably by Gerald Dredd."

"Hell, my mule coulda figgered out that one!"

The detective didn't respond, instead heading for the side of the house with Goldstrike trailing. Halfway down the west elevation, they stopped in front of a door that slanted out from the sandstone foundation, providing access to a space below the house.

"Root cellar?" Campbell asked, lifting an eyebrow.

Goldstrike shook his head. "Horace Goodlow…the fella what built this place…stored wine down there. It's empty now."

Campbell pulled open the door and descended the staircase, the beam from his flashlight leading the way. Under the house was a ten-by-fifteen-foot space with a brick floor. Filled with empty wine racks and the dank smell of mildew, the cellar had been untouched by the fire. An inch-wide crack cut through the floor bricks for the full width of the room, but there were no bloodstains nor other signs of a struggle. He ascended the steps and then stepped out into the sunshine.

"You're related to Dredd's secretary, ain't ya?" Goldstrike asked, following the detective as he moved toward the back of the house.

"My sister."

"Ain't that a…whattaya call it?"

"Conflict of interest?"

"That's it…conflict o' interest. Ain't it a conflict o' interest fer you to be investigatin' yer sister's boss?"

"No."

"Ya sure?"

"I'm working for the life insurance company, not Dredd Enterprises."

They moved around the rear of the house, up the east elevation, and then returned to the front. "We might have to call us a council meetin' to figger out if we oughta be talkin' to you," Goldstrike said as they headed up the walk toward Campbell's car.

"If you like," Campbell replied. "You'll have time. I'm staying over for a day or two."

Goldstrike snorted. "You're gonna be here a helluva lot longer than a couple o' days. Avalanche this mornin' blocked the road between here and Boise."

Campbell shook his head. "I don't think so. I just came through. There was a ROAD CLOSED sign, but the pass was clear."

"Ya didn't feel it?"

"Feel what?"

Goldstrike shook his head, making no effort to hide his disdain. "City folks...all that goddamned noise in Chicago's turned ya deaf."

"How did you know I was from Chicago?"

A sly smile curled Goldstrike's lips. "I guess I ain't the only one with a *precedin' reputation*, Detective," he said. He went on to reveal that the shiver caused by the avalanche had been felt all over town, adding, "If ya'd lived in these mountains long as I have, ya'd feel the flutter of a bird's wing that's out o' place. Judgin' from the shake we got this mornin' I'd wager the pass is blocked five miles or so toward the valley. You probably just missed gettin' yerself buried...goddamned lucky if'n ya ask me."

Campbell shrugged. "Then I guess I'll be here for a while," he said.

The detective's calm acceptance of bad news impressed Goldstrike, recalling for him a composed officer he'd served under during the War Between the States. As steady at the front as he was at the rear, Goldstrike's commander had been killed at Rice's Station near the end of the conflict. *Ain't this a helluva thing?* he'd muttered before dying.

"You reg'lar army?" Goldstrike asked.

"Marine Corps...military police mostly. How'd you know?"

"Ya got the look… An officer, weren't ya?"

Campbell nodded. "You?"

"Private…Maine 11th. You drink whiskey?"

"Scotch."

"C'mon," Goldstrike said, motioning. "We'll go over to the Gold Rush and have us a few snorts…get the cut o' each other's jibs."

They rode together in Campbell's car to the saloon where the detective was pleasantly surprised to learn that Arnold Chang had a full case of Macallan single malt. The saloonkeeper opened a bottle and Mrs. Chang threw together some beans and ham while Goldstrike tried to get Campbell drunk. The old prospector could hold his liquor better than most but had never traded shots of scotch with a Scotsman, albeit American-born. Eventually, as afternoon stretched into evening and then night, it was Goldstrike, rather than the detective, who was inebriated enough to do most of the talking.

"Made and lost me the better part o' three fortunes since I come to this mountain," he bragged to Campbell. "Still, I been lucky. Most fellas, back in the day, beat a path home with less than they brung, but I managed to hang on to enough money to carry me through the time I got left." Goldstrike then waxed nostalgic about his former partner, Old Butch Cavanaugh. "Helluva a guy," he recalled. "Took me in and taught me everythin' I know. I left 'im fer a time. Got me some dynamite and figgered to blow holes in the rock, then waltz in and gather up nuggets like I was pickin' beans. 'Waste o' time,' Old Butch told me and he was right."

"You still have any dynamite?" Campbell asked.

"I had me some sticks, but they're in a tunnel I blasted up in them foothills. Been in there fer years…likely bled out by now." Goldstrike was suddenly wary. "Whattaya gettin' at, anyway?"

"Nothing."

"You ask too many goddamned questions, Campbell."

Goldstrike unceremoniously lurched to his feet and then staggered out the front door of the saloon without bidding his companion a good night. His shack on Mores Creek was southwest of the tavern, but the old prospector headed east up Goodlow Road and then north on Only Real Street to the Paradise School. It was ten p.m. when he reached it. He entered without knocking and waited in the foyer. Moments later he heard footsteps and Lariat appeared at the top of the stairs with a kerosene lantern in one hand.

"Goldstrike! What's wrong? Another fire?"

"Wake up yer grandma and Miss Bountiful, son!" Goldstrike shouted. "Then get yerself back under the covers."

"We're already up," Maude called out, stepping into the halo of soft light provided by Lariat's lantern. A moment later Bountiful joined her, tying the belt on her robe as she appraised the old man with a puzzled expression.

"What's going on, Goldstrike?" she asked.

"Get yerselves down here," Goldstrike insisted. "We gotta talk."

"You're drunk," Maude said, frowning.

"As a skunk… We still gotta talk."

They gathered in the kitchen. Bountiful worked on coffee while Maude and Lariat sat with Goldstrike at a round table in the nook, an overhead electrical light fixture competing with the moonbeams streaming through the bay windows.

"What the heck?" Goldstrike suddenly blurted. He leapt up, stumbled to a window, and peered out. After a moment, he turned around. "Thought I saw a light in yer carriage house," he slurred, wobbling a bit. "That detective's got me seein' things." He looked at Lariat, abruptly stiffening as if startled. "Whatta ya doin' here, youngster! I told ya to go to bed. We got grown-up talk to get at."

"I'm fifteen now," Lariat said. "I'm old enough to hear what you have to say."

Goldstrike considered the teenager for a moment, then re-claimed his chair. "I joined the Maine 11th at fifteen," he said. He continued to study Lariat, his eyelids slowly descending until it appeared he had fallen asleep. Maude pinched his arm and the old prospector jerked awake. "Ow... Goddammit, that hurt, Maude!" he yelped. Simultaneously, the coffee percolator released a long sigh of relief to signal the end of the brew cycle. Two cups of coffee later Goldstrike was still drunk but wide awake. "We gotta get you outta town, young man," he said to Lariat, waving a finger at him. He eyed Bountiful and Maude. "That goddamned Campbell is a bloodhound. There ain't no scent he won't pick up."

He took a swallow of coffee that mostly ended up on his shirt.

"He's a serious man, I'm tellin' ya. Drank me under the goddamned table. I knowed fellas like him when I was in the Maine 11th. He's what ya call... There's a word. Ya told me once, Lariat. Un-im-somethin'."

"Impeachable?"

Goldstrike grinned. "Yeah...that's it...'cept'n the opposite. He's *non*-impeachable." He scanned the faces at the table, his grin fading. "Mark my words... He's gonna figger out what happened in that there barn. And when he does, you can't be around, Lariat." He reached out and put a hand on the boy's shoulder. "Them bastards down in Boise'll string you up, sure as shootin'. They won't give a good goddamn that you was defendin' Miss Bountiful. Dredd's white and you're colored. They ain't gonna concern themselves no further than that."

"Stop it," Bountiful scolded the old man, angling a worried look at Lariat. "You're scaring him."

Goldstrike shook a finger at her.

"Well, Lariat *oughta* be scared, goddammit. Them bluenose sons o' bitches down in the valley *are* scary." He paused, then went on. "We gotta send 'im to college back east like ya planned, Miss Bountiful."

"Wait a minute," Lariat protested. "What are you talking about? What college?"

"Lariat, we've discussed this," Bountiful said.

"Yes, but I didn't think you were serious."

Bountiful reached out and took the boy's hand. "Even before…well, even before what happened, Grandma and I already knew you'd outgrown us. You know it too. Even if it were safe to remain in Paradise, it's past time for you to go."

"Don't I have anything to say about it?"

"You know I'm right."

Lariat studied the lacquered surface of the table as if the wavy pattern of the wood grain could divine his future. Finally, he looked up.

"Maybe," he said. "I'm still not going."

# 20

## The Suspect List Grows

Goldstrike spent the night on the sofa in the parlor of the Paradise School. He was the only one in the house who slept, waking up at mid-morning with a hangover. It was Saturday with no classes and the old man found Maude and Bountiful in the kitchen. A cup of coffee and some headache powder later, he sat at a round table with the women, watching Lariat through the nook window as the teenager twirled his trick rope near a pile of firewood neatly stacked against the stable. Goldstrike watched the boy jump in and out of a loop that spun close to the ground.

"How long's he been out there?"

"A long while, I suspect," Maude answered. "He was at it when we got up."

"He's scared," Bountiful observed. "He won't admit it, but he is." She rose from the table, warmed up their coffee cups, and then reclaimed her seat. Goldstrike didn't drink, instead studying the dark liquid, his face creased with worry.

"He ain't the only one scared," he said. He set his coffee cup on the table so firmly the two women were surprised the handle didn't break off. "It ain't gonna be like it was with Lily," the old prospector continued. "A hideaway here in town ain't gonna mean a good goddamn. We got get him outta Paradise." He paused, then exhaled hard through his nose, his frustration evident. "Hell, even that ain't gonna be enough. No matter where he goes they can haul 'im back to Boise to stand trial. That includes Washington, DC... What Lariat needs is an *alibi*." He nodded at the two women, adding, "We gotta give 'im one."

"Dredd's body is out there somewhere and whoever took

it is a witness…someone who knows what happened," Bountiful countered. "If this detective is as good as you think, he'll eventually find both the body and the witness. And there goes any alibi we manufacture." Goldstrike shrugged. The identity of the body snatcher was still a mystery with Willie Barkley no longer a suspect. "I was at Geraldine's apartment," he'd told Goldstrike when asked why his cot in their shack had been empty that night.

"I don't think we need to much trouble ourselves about witnesses," Goldstrike submitted. "The fella what made off with that body ain't gonna be eager to throw a hat in the ring, unless he has an alibi his *own* self." He paused, pursing his lips thoughtfully. "But I suspect ya ain't wrong, Miss Bountiful. If'n the body turns up, there's gonna be questions, witness or not. We don't know if Dredd told somebody down in Boise he was comin' up here that night…or if that somebody knew what he was plannin' to do or who he was gonna meet. Sure, it's been months and ya'd figger anybody what knows somethin' woulda spoke up by now, but…"

His voice trailed off and Goldstrike began to tap his fingers on the table as he considered their dilemma. Eventually, he looked up. "Here's what we're gonna do," he said. He pointed a finger at Bountiful. "If'n the body turns up, you're gonna tell that detective *exactly* what happened."

"Goldstrike, I don't see how—"

"Jes' stop flappin' yer gums and listen," Goldstrike groused. "You're gonna tell Mister Campbell what happened, but only up to a point. You're gonna tell 'im Dredd tried to have his way…was gonna strangle you and got hisself kilt fer it."

"Goldstrike, I'm not a good liar. I don't know if I—"

"Jes' *listen*, Miss Bountiful… Ya ain't gonna hafta lie all that much, 'cuz you're gonna tell 'im you wasn't the one what kilt Dredd. That ain't no lie. And ya didn't tell folks about it, 'cuz you was *protectin'* someone. And that ain't no lie neither, 'cuz ya *was* protectin' someone. But it ain't gonna be *Lariat* what got protected."

Goldstrike looked out the window where Lariat continued to twirl his rope near the carriage house.

"It's gonna be *me*," he went on. "I'll be the one what got protected. I'll confess...tell the goddamned detective my own self. That way you ain't lyin' and Lariat's in the clear." He nodded decisively, mouth drawing a straight line.

"Goldstrike, you can't—"

"Now don't go arguin', Miss Bountiful. It's settled. If the need arises, I'll be the only one confessin'. And I'll be the only one lyin'." He looked at Maude, adding, "That goes fer you too."

"What about the witness?" Bountiful posed.

"If'n he turns up, it's his word against mine," Goldstrike said. He winked, forming a crafty smile. "I got me a good poker face, don't I, Maude? I figger I can out-witness the fella what stole the body if'n it comes to that."

"He's not wrong, dear," the former madam agreed. "Goldstrike can bluff a buffalo out of its hide."

"But, Goldstrike, if you confess, won't they—?"

"Aw, don't worry, Miss Bountiful," the old prospector replied. "They ain't likely to hang me. They'd string up Lariat, fer sure, but the worst I'll get is prison...if'n they bother to take it to trial at all. Hell, everybody knows what Dredd was like. A jury will believe he came after ya, and they'll believe I wrung his goddamned neck fer it. Besides, I ain't afraid o' prison. Hell, I ain't afraid to get hung, neither. I lived me a decent life. Got less in front o' me than behind as it is."

He chuckled.

"Let the sons o' bitches hang me. I'll come back and haunt the livin' shit out of 'em."

❧

Robert Campbell spent his first night in Paradise kept awake by the unsettling sounds of tiny creatures scampering about in the dark of his Gold Rush Hotel room. After coffee and a plate of thick, blackened bacon and greasy potatoes at the Gold Rush, he asked Arnold Chang about other accommodations. The bar-keeper showed him what had been the best room in the hotel's salad days, a space with peeling wallpaper, a pile of folded cots to choose from, and as much grime and evidence of rodent roommates as the space Campbell wanted to vacate. "Not hotel dis place, no more," Chang apologized. "Close twenty year till dem Peycomson worker mens come." He bent to pick up a wrinkled copy of the *Idaho World* from the bare wooden floor, then handed it to Campbell, tapping on the top banner. "October t'irty, nineteen-nineteen… Worker mens leave 'round dat time. Since den, empty." Chang suggested the detective talk to Maude Dollarhyde about the Busty Rose. "Whore rooms in old days, but clean…no mice. Betta for city man like you."

Campbell thanked the saloonkeeper, then exited the Gold Rush and walked up Goodlow Road, noting the distinct line between fresh spring grass and the blackened crust left by the fire that destroyed the Coolers' once palatial home. The irregular border was less than fifty feet from the nearest wooden building in Paradise's modest business district. *The fire got close,* he thought. *This entire town could have gone up in smoke.* He passed the charred carcass that was once Elysium, turned onto Only Real Street, and made for the Paradise School. Once there, he climbed the porch steps and knocked on the door. Bountiful answered. Close up, the detective marveled, she was even more beautiful than he remembered, her sapphire eyes—level and unafraid—unsettling him.

"Mister Campbell," she said.

"You know my name?"

"We're a small town. News travels fast."

"I saw you at the Idanha Hotel…in the tearoom."

"I remember. You're here about a room?"

Campbell chuckled. "How'd that news beat me here?"

"It didn't. It was simply inevitable. I've seen the rooms at the old hotel. Come in. I'll get my grandmother."

Campbell removed his hat and stepped into the foyer. Less

than a minute later Bountiful returned with Maude, then excused herself.

"I didn't catch your name," the detective said as she gracefully moved down the hallway.

"I didn't throw it," she replied without slowing. Campbell watched her walk away until Maude's voice intruded.

"Best get those peepers back in your head, Mister Detective."

Campbell looked at her and was met by a razored aspect.

"Sorry," he said. "Forgot my manners for a moment. Your granddaughter...she's quite..."

"You're here about a room at the Busty Rose?"

Campbell smiled sheepishly. "I am."

Maude offered a brief description of the one-time house of ill repute's accommodations. In addition to the former madam's third-floor private suite—still leased by Dredd Enterprises—the wood-frame building on Paradise's main drag boasted ten themed bedrooms from its days as an operating cathouse. Among them were the Moulin Rouge, the Arabian Nights, the Hiawatha & Minnehaha, the Antony & Cleopatra, and the Buffalo Bill & Calamity Jane. The latter was a rustic space with exposed log purlins on the ceiling, a stuffed buffalo head mounted above the fireplace, a hitching post should the mood to be tied up arise, and the coup de' triomphe: a poster advertising BUFFALO BILL'S WILD WEST SHOW & CONGRESS OF ROUGH RIDERS OF THE WORLD. Obtained by Maude when she attended an 1895 performance of the famed frontiersman's traveling extravaganza in Boise, the poster bore Cody's signature.

"I think the Buffalo Bill will work for you," Maude said after they agreed on a dollar per day with two dollars down. She handed him a set of keys attached to a miniature bison fob carved from an actual horn. "One opens the front door. The other is for your room," she told him, afterward appraising the tall detective from head to toe. "Yeah...definitely the Buffalo Bill. It suits you. It's on the second floor, last room down the hall on the right. I'd escort you over there, but my hips are bothering me."

"I can find it, thank you," Campbell said.

Maude showed him to the door and the detective stepped onto the porch. He redonned his hat and then touched the brim.

"Good day, Mrs. Dollarhyde. It was a pleasure to meet you. Please tell your granddaughter that it was a pleasure to meet her as well."

He moved toward the front steps.

"It's Bountiful," Maude said.

Campbell turned back. "Ma'am?"

"My granddaughter… Her name is Bountiful."

Campbell nodded, then headed up the front walk. He was a bachelor after his brief marriage to a madcap heiress collapsed under the weight of his long absences in pursuit of insurance defrauders and her excessive interest in being debauched by other men. Campbell had since gone through a string of actresses, nightclub chanteuses, and career women, none of whom wanted to settle down with a $3600 per year gumshoe any more than he'd wanted to settle down with one of them. None, however, had unnerved him the way Bountiful Dollarhyde did and he found his mind veering away from the missing Gerald Dredd as he headed up the front walk. He recalled the efforts of The Fourth Mrs. Dredd to bed him, wondering if he could show similar discipline should Bountiful Dollarhyde make overtures. A moment later he dismissed the notion. *They'll be no recollections in a negligee from this girl… She's not the type.*

He reached Only Real Street at the end of the walk, but rather than go south to Goodlow Road and his room at the Busty Rose, the detective angled north toward the former Stiveley mansion. Along the way, he passed the one-time home of Ned and Irene Rimple—now owned by Amon and Sarah DeMille. On the front porch steps, a young Black man sat alongside a delicately pretty girl, their hands grazing. The one-time Feldstein

mansion was a little farther north and across the street. Two
small children—a boy and a girl—lay in the grass of the front
yard, pointing at the cottony clouds drifting high overhead.
They sat up as he passed, the boy soberly studying him, the
little girl shyly waving with curled fingers. He reached the home
where Richard Bright and his so-called family had resided as
the Peycomsons and assessed it from the end of the front walk.
The original owner, John Stiveley, had commissioned a Dutch
Colonial with two second-level rectangular gables and a central
square turret topped by an ornamental spire. The walls were
red brick, the foundation sandstone, and a huge porch spanned
the front elevation before wrapping around the west side of
the house. Supported by painted ionic columns fashioned from
meticulously milled Douglas fir, the porch's burnished copper
roof gleamed like a new penny.

Campbell walked to the west side of the house, scanning
the structure from foundation to eave as he moved toward the
rear of the property. There, he found a generous veranda with
a carriage house set back forty feet from the residence. He approached the one-time stable and peered through a window. It
was too dark inside to make out much of anything other than
a wall with tools and a pair of kerosene lanterns hanging on it.
Leaving further investigation of the carriage house for later, he
continued along the east side of the main residence, and upon
reaching the front, climbed the steps to the porch. He'd expected to find the place deserted, but when he peeked through
a picture window was surprised to see a furnished parlor with
a single electric lamp. It was turned on, illuminating a copy of
Collier's magazine on a side table. A vase with fresh meadow
flowers was on the fireplace mantel.

"Something I could help you with, sir?"

Campbell jerked, instinctively reaching for the .38 holstered
inside his coat as he turned to the voice. Willie Barkley stood on
the porch, just outside the front door. He wore his army blouse,
stitch marks where insignia had once been sewn. Campbell
pulled his hand from beneath his coat.

"You'll have to excuse me," he said. "I thought the place was abandoned."

"You're the detective."

Campbell nodded, handing Willie a business card. "And you are…?"

"Willie Barkley."

The former soldier tucked Campbell's card into a pocket without reading it. A moment later Geraldine Dredd Barkley stepped onto the porch and linked her arm in Willie's. Even without the photos Iris had shown him, Campbell would have recognized her as Dredd's daughter, the same full lips, the same almond-shaped eyes.

"What do you want?" she demanded.

"You're Miss Geraldine Dredd?"

She nodded.

"My name is Robert Campbell. I've been retained by Mutual of Omaha to look into your father's disappearance."

Geraldine frowned. "If this is about money, I don't care. Tell Mutual of Omaha to keep it."

"It's a million dollars…and, besides, you're not the beneficiary."

"Then I care even less."

"I've still got a few questions, if you don't mind, Miss Dredd," Campbell persisted.

"We don't know anything. Please just go."

"How long have you been living here?"

Geraldine sniffed petulantly. "We have every right to be here," she submitted, frowning. "Dredd Enterprises owns the house and my father owns Dredd Enterprises."

"In a way, that's why I'm here," Campbell countered. "Meriwether Peycomson and his wife used to own this house and now they're missing too. I'm trying to figure out if the disappearances are connected. Perhaps you've come across something the Peycomsons left behind—"

"The Peycomsons didn't know my father," Geraldine interrupted. "And they left nothing but furniture and kitchen items…dishes, pots and pans, that sort of thing. No personal items."

"Maybe I could get a look inside? The carriage house, as well, if you don't object."

"I do object. There's nothing of interest for you in this house. And the carriage house is empty."

"It wouldn't take long," Campbell persevered. "A quick look-around, a few questions. I'm just trying to find out what happened to your father. I would think you'd want to know."

"I don't *need* to know. I don't *care* what happened to him."

The young heiress nervously touched the neckline of her dress. She wore no ring, but the faint imprint of one was on her wedding finger. Campbell knew about Dredd's unhealthy infatuation with his daughter and Willie Barkley's shell shock. What Iris had told him about the real estate baron suggested he wouldn't embrace any son-in-law, much less a crazy one. Nevertheless, as the couple stood before him, arm in arm, it appeared he might have acquired both.

"Forgive me, Miss Dredd," he said. "I understand. My father and I didn't get along, either. But I really have just a few questions. Ten minutes at most…and we can leave the carriage house for later, all right?"

Geraldine looked up at Willie, tucking the hand with the ring imprint into the crease of his arm. The couple silently considered one another for a few moments. Then Willie soberly appraised Campbell. "A quick look-around and a few questions," he said. "But then you'll have to go."

They went inside, and after a brief search of the house turned up nothing of interest, Campbell was told that neither of the young people had seen Gerald Dredd since the night of the fire at the Cooler mansion. They denied knowledge of the Peycomsons' whereabouts and had never heard of Richard or Louise Bright. On the nights of November nineteenth and twentieth, Geraldine was in her apartment at the Busty Rose.

"And you, Private Barkley?" Campbell asked.

"How'd you know I was a private?"

The detective nodded at the stitchmarks on Willie's old uniform. "No stripes," he said.

The young couple looked at each other, Geraldine blushing.

"We were both at the Busty Rose," Willie finally admitted, quickly adding, "but it wasn't illegal. We were already married."

"Congratulations."

"Please keep that to yourself…our marriage," Geraldine said. "My family doesn't know."

Campbell reassured the couple that their secret was safe and rose to go. "Thank you for your time," he told them. He smiled at Geraldine, adding, "And forgive me for peeking in the window. I truly believed the place deserted. I didn't mean to upset anyone." Willie saw him to the door and Campbell descended the front porch steps, then headed up the walk. His interview of the secretive newlyweds had convinced him of two things. Until he knew more about Dredd's will, Geraldine and her husband were suspects. Moreover, despite her loose clothing, it was apparent that the young woman was pregnant.

The detective returned to the Gold Rush and gathered his things, afterward transferring them to the Buffalo Bill room before heading to Nilsen's where one of only two telephones in town were located, the other at the *Idaho World.*

"How much to use your phone?" he asked the storekeeper.

"First it was Peycomson and now it's you," Nilsen complained. "It was a nickel, but I gotta impose a wear-and-tear charge, doggonnit." They settled on seven cents with another three cents for privacy. Campbell handed over a dime, and after Nilsen withdrew to the boardwalk, the detective called Iris to explain why she wouldn't have her car for a while.

"That's all right," she said. "I hardly ever use it anyway."

"What do you know about Dredd's estate?" Campbell asked, shifting the subject. "What happens if he's dead?"

"Is he dead?"

"I think so but keep it to yourself for now. What about the estate?"

"Gerald's personal wealth is separate from Dredd Enterprises," Iris told him. "For his non-business assets, he's created trusts. There's a lot of money involved…more than enough for all his wives and children to live comfortably for the rest of their lives."

"What about the company holdings?"

"Gerald controls sixty-seven percent," Iris revealed. "Sixteen percent is owned by members of the board and the rest by a couple of private investors."

"What about the sixty-seven percent?" her brother asked. "How will it be distributed?"

"That's the interesting part," Iris answered. "Gerald had the will revised last summer. Geraldine gets thirty-four percent… more than half. I presume the remaining thirty-three percent is divvied up among the other heirs."

"You've seen the revised will?"

"No, but I overheard the discussion between he and Bertram Mole."

"So with the private investors' shares, Geraldine would have control of the company without any support from her family or the rest of the board?"

"Yes, if what I overheard ended up in the final will. As I told you, I haven't seen the revised document."

"Who are the private investors?"

"Angels…they're anonymous."

"Can you find out who they are?"

"I'll try."

"Does Geraldine know about any of this?"

"I don't know," Iris answered. "I've spoken with her about other things, but she's never brought up the will or the estate. Are you sure Gerald is dead?"

"Can you get a look at the will?"

"I'll work on it… So you're absolutely certain Gerald is dead?"

"Not absolutely, but probably," Campbell replied. He paused, then went on. "You sound upset, sis. I thought that's what you wanted."

For a moment or two the detective heard only the sound of his older sibling's breathing on the phone. Then Iris spoke. "I don't know what I want, Bobby," she said.

Campbell gave her a few seconds to elaborate, and when she didn't, he wrapped up the call. "I guess that's it then... I'll phone you again in a few days."

"Wait, Bobby... Before you hang up, there's something else you should know," his sister continued. "Last October, Gerald had a meeting with Bountiful Dollarhyde. Afterward he was very angry. He was in a terrible mood for days." Iris told her brother about the illegitimate children Friederich Dredd had allegedly scattered about the Pacific Northwest. "There's always been a rumor one of them might be colored," she finished up.

"Why wasn't this in the dossier?"

"When I prepared the files for you, I didn't think it was relevant," Iris explained. "I know Bountiful. She's a lady, not a killer."

"That's what some people said about Lizzie Borden."

"Not funny, Bobby."

After hanging up, Campbell made another call, this one collect. A secretary accepted the charges and connected him to Arthur Faiman, director of claims for Mutual of Omaha.

"Campbell," the insurance company executive practically shouted into the phone. "What have you found out? Is he alive or dead?"

"Dead," Campbell answered.

"So you found him? There's a body? It's certain?"

"I haven't found him yet," Campbell replied. "But he's dead."

"Still, there's no body," Faiman argued. "So how sure can you be?"

"One hundred percent."

"But there's no body!"

"One hundred percent, Arthur," Campbell repeated.

"Any evidence of foul play?"

"Not yet."

"So what are the chances he was murdered? We're not responsible to pay a benefit if he was murdered, you know."

"I know that."

"So whattayou think…seventy-thirty in favor of murder, eighty-twenty?"

Campbell hesitated, then answered.

"Right now, Arthur," he said. "I'd say one hundred percent."

# 21

## ROADBLOCKS

For most people in Paradise the avalanche Goldstrike engineered to subvert an investigation into Gerald Dredd's disappearance was nothing more than a fortuitous natural event. "That doggone landslide came at the right time. It oughta keep them census people outta here a good while," Oskar Nilsen observed. "But let's nobody forget. We're still four bodies short. We need four more people on the town roster soon as they clear that road and before one of them darned headcounters comes up here." He suggested they periodically check on the repair crew's progress and made a motion to that effect at the April 1920 meeting of the town council. The motion carried and Bountiful volunteered to conduct the inspection. She asked Lariat to come along. She needed time alone with him after receiving a letter from her former Howard University mentor.

> Dear Bountiful,
>
> How delighted I was to receive your missive. Mrs. Beale and I so miss your lovely smile and our many evenings of wine and conversation. To address the issue at hand, please allow me to offer a simple affirmative. Upon review of young Mr. Comfort's stellar academic record, and with your trusted recommendation in hand, I am happy to sponsor his matriculation into Howard University. Moreover, Mrs. Beale and I would welcome him into our home until such time that he is of age and ready to embark on his own life adventure.
>
> With warmest regards
> Joshua Beale, PhD

Bountiful was teaching Lariat how to drive, and for the first part of their trip to the site of the avalanche, he focused on the mountain road as they bounced along. Five miles outside Paradise they were met by pile of rocks and brush more than six feet high. Lariat braked the car to a stop and hopped out.

"Back in a minute," he said, afterward clambering up the mound of jagged stones and uprooted brush, occasionally slipping on a loose rock. He reached the top and scrambled across the surface of the obstruction. A few minutes later he returned.

"It's still blocked for at least fifty feet," he told Bountiful. "Goldstrike did a good job. It's gonna take a few more weeks to clear it."

They headed back to Paradise with the teenager behind the wheel, an argument mounting when Bountiful told him about the letter from Professor Beale.

"I'm not going," Lariat insisted.

"Yes, you are."

"I'm not."

"You are, Lariat. We've talked about this. It's not safe for you in Paradise."

"If it's so much *safer* in Washington, DC, why didn't *you* stay there?"

"It's not the same thing and you know it," Bountiful said. "Besides, this is not solely about what happened in the carriage house. You need more education than Grandma and I can provide. You have a chance to make something of yourself."

"I don't want to be anything more than I am. And I don't want to live anyplace other than Paradise."

"That's selfish, Lariat," Bountiful scolded him. "You have a gifted mind. It's something you should share with the world."

Lariat scowled. "The world doesn't want gifts from colored folks... Remember *Birth of a Nation?*"

Bountiful did. She'd taken Lariat to the New Boz Theater in Boise to see the movie-going public's first feature-length film. She'd looked forward to the innovations of groundbreaking director D.W. Griffith, but instead, they were ushered into the colored section of the theater and subjected to an homage to the Ku Klux Klan.

"You heard the white people cheer during the movie," Lariat recalled. "You saw the way they looked at us."

"I shouldn't have taken you to that horrible picture."

"I'm glad you did," Lariat said. "I could've gone my entire life without knowing how many white people hate me."

"You're being dramatic."

"Am I? I don't think so."

Lariat eased off the gas and allowed the car to glide to a stop along the side of the road. He turned off the engine, then twisted in his seat to look at her.

"Miss Bountiful, I don't want to leave," he said. "Please don't make me go."

"Lariat, there's a big world out there. Paradise is too small for you."

"I don't want a big world. I've got books. That's enough."

Bountiful shook her head. "Some things aren't in books, Lariat. Trust me on this. Some things you can't just read about. They must be experienced." She reached out and took his hand. "Not everything back east was good for me," she continued, "but a lot of it was very good. I met interesting people from all over the world, went to plays, viewed great art, listened to wonderful music, learned from brilliant teachers. Being away helped me understand who I am, so that when I came back, I knew what I wanted. You need to find out what you want...and where you want it to be. You can't know for sure if you never leave."

Lariat pulled his hand from her grasp and faced forward, staring through the insect spattered windshield of the Model T. He looked utterly forlorn.

"Look at me," Bountiful said, and after he did, she went on. "Grandma and I had the same argument. I didn't want to leave, either. I felt the same as you. I was happy in Paradise. But she knew I needed to go if I were to ever truly grow up...if I were to ever learn how to take care of myself."

Lariat considered what she'd told him, then responded. "Why aren't you married?" he asked.

Bountiful blinked with surprise, then laughed. "Where did *that* come from?"

"I just wondered. I'm sure you've been asked. You're so pretty and smart and nice. If I were your age, I'd want to marry you."

Bountiful smiled. "You think I'm too much the old lady for you?"

"You know what I mean."

Lariat again faced forward in the driver's seat, staring through the windshield at the distant peaks of the Sawtooths. *He'll be a handsome man*, Bountiful thought, his skin dark and flawless, his jawline distinct. He suddenly sighed, his brow furrowed.

"There's another reason I don't want to go," he confessed. "I'm in love...with Jeanette. She loves me too. We want to get married."

"Married!"

"Yes. We're in love."

"She's barely fourteen, Lariat. And you're just fifteen."

Lariat frowned petulantly. "So what? Lots of Mormon girls get married at her age...or even younger. Jeanette told me about it. Anyway, we're not that young. Remember Romeo and Juliet?"

"I do... I also remember how things ended for them."

Bountiful studied his face, recalling her time as a teacher in Washington, DC, schools. Her students had been Lariat's age, the girls dramatic, the boys clueless. Lariat was mature for his years, but the sparse spray of whiskers on his cheeks betrayed him. He would someday be a very good man, but for now he was still a boy.

"Have you discussed this with Jeanette's parents?" she asked.

Lariat shook his head. "Not yet...and I know what you're thinking...me being colored and all. It's against their religion. But Jeanette says they aren't so sure about their church anymore. She thinks they'll come around."

Bountiful narrowed an eye. "So you'll get married and live in Paradise... No more school, I take it, with a wife to support. How *will* you provide for Jeanette, anyway?"

Lariat grinned. "Easy. I'll work for the Paradise Electrical Cooperative. John...Mister Goodlow...said he'd hire me."

"Hire you as what?"

"An electrical engineer."

"You have to attend college to become an engineer."

"John says I already know almost everything a college would teach me. He promised to show me the rest."

Bountiful made a mental note to give John Goodlow a piece of her mind, then responded. "And what happens to Jeanette when you're dragged down to Boise and tried for murder? Never mind. I already know. She'll bake a cake with a hacksaw in it, right? Of course, you may not have enough time to saw through the bars before they hang you. How does Jeanette look in black?" Lariat didn't answer, instead exiting the car to give its crankstart a turn. The engine rumbled to life and he climbed back in.

"You don't understand," he said, putting the Model T in gear and then wrestling it off the rough shoulder and back onto the road. He pouted mightily for the rest of their trip. Once they were in town, he drove directly to the Paradise School, got out, and stomped off without closing the car door. Bountiful caught up with him in the foyer. His pout had faded into unease.

"Campbell's in there," he whispered, pointing his chin in the direction of the parlor. Bountiful cocked her head. In the next room, Maude was telling a story, her voice uncharacteristically thin and high-pitched, the words spilling out as if the former madam couldn't hold them back.

"Of course, things were different in those days. Men disappeared all the time. We didn't think much of it. Some gave up and went back to where they came from, but others just *vanished* and we never knew..." Maude abruptly stopped talking, breathing a sigh of relief when Bountiful and Lariat appeared in the parlor entry. "You're back!" she gushed. "How was your trip?" The parlor of the Paradise School boasted a set of tall windows with southern exposure on one end, another wide arched portal on the north opening into the home's dining room. Floor-to-ceiling bookcases surrounded a fireplace with an ornate, painted surround, its mantel holding several framed photographs. Two puffy sofas faced each other at the center of the room, perpendicularly framing the fireplace with a large coffee table between them. Maude was on one of the sofas with Robert Campbell on the other. He held a cup, and with Bountiful's appearance in the doorway, put it on the table before rising. Although not classically good-looking like Meriwether Peycomson, he had good hair and a crowbar handsomeness she found more than a bit unnerving.

"Miss Dollarhyde," he said with a slight bow.

"Detective," she replied, grateful her dark skin would mostly hide the faint rose she felt certain now shaded her cheeks.

"And you," Campbell added, eyeing Lariat, "are Mister Roscoe Comfort. I've seen you around."

"It's Lariat."

"Sorry...Lariat. I've heard about your rope tricks. Maybe you can show me a few?"

"Probably not. I'm pretty busy these days...with school and all. I should go now. I've got homework."

"Would you have time to answer a few questions?"

Lariat gave the floor a good going over before answering. "All right," he said.

Campbell sat and took up the notepad he'd used to log his interview of Maude. He opened it to a fresh page, scribbled Lariat's name at the top, and then eyed the teenager. "You know Mister Dredd?" he began.

"Everybody knows him."

"Do you remember the last time you saw him?"

"He came to the play on the night of the fire. I saw him in the audience."

"Was that the last time you saw him?"

"I don't where he is, if that's what you're asking."

A faint smile creased the detective's features. "It wasn't, but it's a start."

Campbell asked a few more questions, all surrounding November 20, 1919, the date Dredd was last seen. The detective was impressed by the young man's poise. Maude's answers had nervously veered into apocryphal tales of her notorious past, but Lariat gave succinct responses that were literally true, yet misleading. *They're both lying*, the detective mused, *but he's better at it*. Finally, he gave up and set the notepad aside.

"Thank you, Lariat," he said. "You should probably see to your schoolwork now. Perhaps we can talk again another time."

"I don't know why we would," Lariat answered.

After the young man escaped to the kitchen, Maude apologized. "He's in a mood, Mister Campbell."

"It's all right. I remember being Lariat's age. I didn't talk to cops, either."

"I should check on him," Maude added. She rose and headed for the kitchen. Halfway there, she stopped and turned. "Lariat doesn't know where Gerald is," she told the detective in a way that made him believe her. She went on to the kitchen and Campbell retrieved his cup from the coffee table. He sipped from it, then set the cup down and retrieved his notepad, keeping his eyes on Bountiful.

"How about you, Miss Dollarhyde?" the detective asked. "What can you tell me about Gerald Dredd?" His demeanor was penetrating and Bountiful looked away. *Coyote eyes*, she thought…*relentless, always on the hunt*. During her time in Washington, DC, she'd more than once been accosted by a white policeman intent on rattling her. She'd learned to keep her breathing steady and now focused on it, suppressing an inexplicable urge to tell Robert Campbell about Dredd and the carriage house.

"It's just as Lariat told you," she responded. "He was here on the night of the play. His daughter was in the cast."

Campbell scribbled a note on his pad, then looked up. "Did he stay to help fight the fire?"

Bountiful laughed humorlessly. "You obviously don't know much about Gerald."

"Gerald? So you're friends?"

"We know each other. I wouldn't call us friends."

"And you last saw him at the play?"

"No, I saw him in October. We met at his office in Boise. It was a couple of days after the fire."

"And the reason for the meeting?"

"Gerald…that is, Mister Dredd…wanted the government to condemn the properties in our town—"

"Hence, the penny mansions, right?" Campbell interrupted. "I remember the article. I saw it in the *Chicago Tribune*. I was tempted to apply."

"Do you want me to answer your question or not?" Bountiful snipped, fashioning the same look she offered students who spoke out of turn in her classroom.

"Sorry… Please continue."

"If you read the article, you know that Paradise needs a population of at least one hundred twenty-five to be incorporated," Bountiful went on. "Without incorporation, we're at risk to be acquired via eminent domain. Originally, it was to depend on the 1920 census, but Mister Dredd finagled the Idaho attorney general's office into filing a petition to make it happen sooner. I wanted him to quash the petition. That's why we met."

"And this was a scheduled meeting?"

"It wasn't."

"So you acted impulsively?"

"That's not the word I would use."

The detective took a few moments to reappraise her. His best friend in the Corps had been the grandson of slaves, but Bountiful Dollarhyde's skin was more café-au-lait than his friend's dark chocolate, her hair more loose than tightly woven, her nose more aquiline than Nubian. The piercing blue eyes confirmed her mixed heritage and the detective recalled what Iris had told him about Friederich Dredd's illegitimate children: *There's always been a rumor one of them might be colored.*

"So…your meeting with Mister Dredd," he pressed her. "How did it go? Did he agree to back off?"

"He did."

"And that was the last time you saw him?"

Bountiful aimed another schoolteacher's look at him. "You already asked that. Yes, we met at the very beginning of October."

"And you haven't seen him since?"

"We met in October, just as I told you…three times now."

Campbell allowed a few moments of silence, a Marine military policeman's tactic that had more than once provoked mere suspects to promote themselves to culprits. Bountiful was unaffected and he moved on.

"Mister Dredd was seen driving toward Paradise on November twentieth of last year… You didn't see him around that time?"

"I didn't see anyone drive into Paradise on November twentieth."

"You're awfully sure."

"We don't have a lot of traffic around here. Visitors get noticed."

"And since?"

Bountiful frowned. "For the fourth time, Detective, I saw Gerald Dredd in October. Unless you have something else to ask, perhaps you should go."

Campbell paused to write in his notepad, then looked up. "What can you tell me about Meriwether Peycomson?" he asked.

Bountiful blinked with surprise. "What can I tell you? Nothing, really."

"Do you know why he and his family left town?"

"His wife needed medical attention and Doctor June…our only doctor…has been away for months. Why are you asking *me*, anyway? You've been in town a while. You must already know why they left."

"I'm just verifying what I heard."

"They left a note on their front door. I suggest you go over there and read it for yourself."

"And you've not heard from Mister Peycomson since they left? No letters? No messages of any kind?"

"Why would he try to reach me?"

Campbell shrugged. "I've heard the two of you were close. I thought he might have contacted you, that's all."

"I'm not sure what you're implying," Bountiful said. "But I believe you've learned everything I know and I have papers to grade."

The detective closed his notepad and returned it to his pocket. "Forgive me, Miss Dollarhyde. I've obviously made a mistake. I didn't mean to offend you. I'm very sorry." He rose from the couch. "Would you thank your grandmother for the coffee…and her time?"

"I'll tell her."

Bountiful showed him to the door, but before the detective stepped onto the porch, he hesitated.

"Do know someone named Richard Bright?"

She shook her head. "No…should I?"

"You've never heard that name?"

"Never. Who is he?"

Campbell shrugged. "No one, really. Just a name that came up in my investigation."

# 22

## An Encore Performance

Campbell made for the Buffalo Bill room at the Busty Rose. There, he stretched out on the bed and stared at the log purlins on the ceiling, adding up the suspects in the case. The list was growing, but one thing seemed certain: the roster was likely confined to Paradise, Idaho. At dinnertime he visited the Gold Rush Saloon for a bowl of chili and a wedge of sourdough bread, washing it down with a beer. Afterward he returned to his room and read from a book Iris had loaned him. Written by muckraking journalist Upton Sinclair, it extolled socialism, something he found ironic. His big sister fancied herself a Bolshevik and yet aspired to reach the top of the capitalist pyramid at Dredd Enterprises. The book, a novel, was preachy and eventually sleep overtook him.

Around four o'clock in the morning, he shook himself awake, splashed water on his face, and quietly exited the rear door of the Busty Rose. All five of the penny mansions had carriage houses and he headed across open, uneven ground to the one behind the Paradise School. A coachman's door on the side was unlocked and he slipped in, then turned on his flashlight and scanned the space. A steep staircase, absent a railing and open to the ground below, ran up the wall to his immediate left. The rest of the main level was a standard barn layout with a dirt floor, four horse stalls, and a set of centrally placed stable doors facing the rear of the main house. The place was empty except for a few landscaping tools and an ancient surrey, its leather upholstery cracked, its canvas canopy home to an abandoned bird's nest.

Campbell climbed the narrow wooden steps to the top floor where he discovered a two-room stableman's apartment.

A window looked out to a meadow behind the building. The moon was at half-month, providing enough light to see an abandoned outhouse, lopsided with age. Behind it were the remains of a haystack that had decomposed into a huge compost pile. He went back downstairs and moved into the center bay, slowly turning in a circle while scanning the walls and ceiling, the light from his torch dimming as the battery grew weak. When he reached the wall with the staircase, he stopped. Its entire underside was closed off with a single door providing access to a closet beneath the steps. He went to it and looked inside. Although the span of the staircase was at least twenty feet, he discovered a closet merely five feet wide. Several old, cracked-leather bridles hung on hooks screwed into the wall opposite the door and a single kerosene lantern was suspended from the ceiling. Otherwise, the storage space was empty.

Campbell lit the kerosene lamp and doused his fading flashlight, holding the lantern in one hand as he continued his inspection. The barn's exterior structure comprised the back and right-side wall of the closet, the planks running horizontally. The downward slope of the overhead stairway limited the left-side wall to six feet in height. Its planks ran vertically.

"Curious," he murmured.

He used a knuckle to tap on the shortened wall, eliciting a hollow sound, then ran his fingers along its top, lightly pushing on each plank. There was no give and he methodically moved across and downward, pressing on each board every few inches or so. About a foot above floor level, a click sounded, and the entire wall rotated inward like a paddlewheel, the bottom half pivoting away from him to reveal a hidden compartment behind it.

The detective ducked under the bottom edge of the paddlewheel door and used the lantern to illuminate the space. Another set of stairs led downward into darkness and he cautiously descended them to reach a tiny vestibule ten feet below ground. A tunnel—lined with bricks and redolent of standing water—bore sharply right and he cautiously moved along it until coming upon an unpainted door, this one with side-mounted hinges and a doorknob. He doused the lantern's flame and retrieved his flashlight, then put an ear against the rough pine. There were no sounds from within. He tentatively turned the doorknob and pushed. The hinges squeaked.

"Who's there?" a voice called out from inside.

Campbell pulled his .38 from its shoulder holster, took a deep breath, and then stepped into the room, aiming both the gun and his flashlight at the voice. The weak halo of light revealed a small chamber with a narrow bed shoved against the wall opposite the door. A man was in it, head raised from his pillow, a patchwork quilt covering him. Old, with bushy eyebrows and a neck waddle, the fellow's white hair was thick, his Van Dyke goatee a bit overgrown. He had obviously been asleep—his hair disheveled, his eyes slitted against the beam of the flashlight.

"Don't shoot!" the fellow called out, putting both hands in the air.

Campbell reholstered his gun. "I'm not going to shoot… You can put your hands down."

The man in the bed lowered his arms, then threw the quilt aside and sat on the edge of the bed.

"You quite startled me, sir," he said.

"Sorry… Who are you?"

The fellow stood and squared his shoulders, then raked fingers through his hair to comb it into place and approached the detective with a hand extended. "Thaddeus Cooler, Esquire," he announced. "And you, good sir, I presume to be the eminent Detective Inspector Robert Campbell?" The actor shook Campbell's hand and then crossed to a small table where he struck a match. A moment later the room was aglow with light from an oil lamp. Cooler smiled warmly at the detective. "There," he said. "Much better, don't you think?"

After months hidden away, Thaddeus Cooler, Esquire, was delighted to once again have an audience and Campbell settled into a wood-and-canvas camp chair to listen as the actor dramatically accounted for his whereabouts since the fire. "I was a castaway…penniless, homeless, friendless," the thespian lamented, disclosing that the rest of the erstwhile Coolers had abandoned him, making their getaway in the family's only vehicle while he worked a bucket line on the night of the fire. "Once it was apparent the house was irretrievable and I the only remaining Cooler to shoulder the blame, it seemed prudent to go off-stage, as it were," he told the detective. Two days later Maude discovered him in the carriage house behind the Paradise School, huddled in one of the horse stalls, shivering and famished. "She was my salvation," Thaddeus asserted, reporting that the former madam had shown him the secret door beneath the staircase and the tunnel to the room where she'd once protected Lily Dollarhyde from Friederich Dredd. Afterward Maude took him up a second staircase to a panel in the kitchen pantry that allowed access to the main house. The actor had been warming both Maude's bed and her heart since the early rehearsals for *Our American Cousin*, and a bowl of soup, two whiskeys, and a confession later, she forgave him.

"I have been sequestered in these modest accommodations ever since," Thaddeus told Campbell. Cooler poured a collar of whiskey for each of them into a pair of glasses and sat on the edge of the bed, draping the quilt over his shoulders. Woolen socks warmed his feet against the damp chill of the tiny hideout and he sipped the whiskey to warm the rest of him. He talked without encouragement, admitting to occasional after-midnight trips up the staircase to the main house, where he raided the pantry off the kitchen or Maude's undercarriage in her second-floor bedroom. He further confirmed, after light prodding from the detective, that Gerald Dredd had paid him to buy and then abandon one of the penny mansions.

"But I had nothing to do with the fire," he insisted. "There was *never* a plan to burn the house down. Gerald wanted us to gut it in preparation for conversion to a modern hotel. We were supposed to remain in town until at least the New Year." He frowned, sniffing with disapproval. "No, my dear detective, it was all Trixie. *She* started the fire. She wanted out from the day we arrived. Native New Yorker, that one… thinks there's nowhere else in the world. She *ruined* my play, the little drunk! I should never have left her alone in the house that night. I should have insisted she join us at the theater."

Campbell had known his share of actors, too many of them inclined to offer up scenes from past scripts as present truth. But he believed the old ham. Thaddeus Maximillian Cooler was obviously a rascal but not the type to perpetrate violent crimes like arson…or murder.

"So you're an actor?" the detective posed.

"I am," Cooler proudly declared. "At one time on the Great White Way of Broadway, no less. Indeed, I daresay Mortimer Montegue was the go-to butler for New York casting directors from 1881 to 1889."

"Mortimer Montegue?"

"A stage name… One of many I've enjoyed both in front of the curtain and behind it over the years."

"Is your real name Thaddeus Cooler?"

"Dear me, no. I adopted that name as part of my current role here in Idaho," the actor revealed. He went on, dancing around his given name at birth without actually giving it. "I first toddled the boards, so to speak, as an infant in my mother's arms. She was an actress, as was my father. They were known as the Tent Show Barrymores. Vagabonds, the pair of them, bringing the greats…Shakespeare, Marlowe, Molière…to grateful audiences from Providence, Rhode Island to Dayton, Ohio."

"I saw the letter you wrote to the town council," Campbell interjected when it appeared the actor might explore his family tree rather than reveal anything he knew about the missing Gerald Dredd. "The address you claimed is J.P. Morgan's. You might have picked something less obviously fake."

"It was *not* fake," Cooler huffed. "I *did* live there!"

"You lived with J.P. Morgan?"

"Not exactly *with*," Cooler replied. "I was between parts, so to speak, and had become so proficient at playing butlers, I became one for a time. 'All the world's a stage,' don't you know?"

"You were J.P. Morgan's butler?"

"One of them… There were several. However, in my third year of employment I rose to first under-butler."

"And this was…'between parts,' as you put it?"

Cooler shrugged, adding a wistful expression. "When I say, 'between parts,' Detective, I confess it was a long time between. Fifteen years, actually. The theater is unkind to its aging masters."

"So what happened?" Campbell asked. "I would think J.P. Morgan's under-butler in Manhattan would be a better job than Gerald Dredd's charlatan in Idaho."

"Charlatan is a sour appellation, Detective."

"Sorry…please go on. You quit your job as a butler and…?"

"I did resign, that's true," Thaddeus concurred. "And you are correct. It was an enviable position; indeed, I would never have left Mister Morgan's service had he and I not suffered an unfortunate difference of opinion."

Campbell invited Cooler to elaborate with the lift of an eyebrow.

"Mister Morgan believed I had stolen a pocket watch," the actor explained. "I believed it deserved more attentive safe-keeping after a significant period of callous disregard by my employer. Had I been aware of its sentimental value, I would, of course, have returned it. However, the New York City constabulary were involved by that time, encouraging me to take my leave…hastily, I confess. I was forced to sojourn in secret with an associate in Newark, New Jersey, while considering alternative engagements. It was in that city's famed *Evening News* that I first learned of the penny mansions here in Paradise."

"So where does Gerald Dredd fit in?" Campbell asked. "How did the two of you connect?"

"Oh, I've known Gerald for years," Cooler replied. "I knew him from college days." When Campbell lifted another skeptical eyebrow, the actor quickly offered more details. "I didn't say we *went* to college together. Of course, we didn't. No, I knew Gerald when *he* was in college. Fordham University... It's in the Bronx, although he spent less time there than the Bowery. You've heard of the Bowery, haven't you?"

Campbell nodded.

"Ah, the Bowery," Cooler waxed. "Center of New York City entertainment in my day. I performed recitations there many times...all the popular haunts, don't you know...Windsor, People's, Tony Pastor's, Miner's. What a time it was! Why I—"

"So you met Dredd in New York?" Campbell broke in, before Cooler could give a talking tour of New York City Gilded Age cabarets.

Thaddeus chuckled. "Well done, Detective... You're quite right. Stay on script. Well done, indeed. You could have been a director." He paused to find his place, then continued. "I knew Gerald had returned to Idaho following his exit from Fordham and sent a telegram lauding my credentials as his biographer."

"His biographer?"

"When my stage career went into hiatus and prior to entering Mister Morgan's employ," Cooler explained, "I made a brief foray into the companionship trade."

He winked.

"Many actresses in those days made ends meet by making *their* ends meet with wealthy men's fronts. I handled referrals for a small troupe of consorts. Gerald was a regular. He had unusual appetites...whips, handcuffs...tastes likely foreign to proper society in Boise, Idaho. I sent him a telegram, which alluded to *his* salacious past escapades and *my* superb memory. Gerald prudently responded with an offer of employment."

"So you blackmailed him?"

Cooler winced. "Ugly word, that, Detective Campbell," he

said. "I persuaded him to make his position and mine coincide." He sighed. "I have since regretted our association. Nasty business Gerald had me part of...tricking the good folks of Paradise. I'd have declined had I met them beforehand...had I known these wonderful people as I do now."

Cooler explained how he'd recruited Wanda, Trixie, Charlotte, and Joshua Purdue of the vaunted Massachusetts Purdues from among his theater and companionship connections. "Wanda was a talented actress at one time," he revealed. "I fear demon rum forced her to pursue the slice-of-heaven-for-hire trade. Trixie is of that vocation as well, and although Charlotte has dabbled in the profession, she prefers to act on the stage rather than in the bedroom. Joshua is also an actor." Cooler suddenly fashioned the look of someone who has bitten into a piece of spoiled meat. "I'd never have involved poor Joshua had I known about Gustav and Victor and Nathaniel. Gerald turned over the rock they crawled out from under. Ruffians, all three of them. I was afraid they might actually murder dear Joshua. My young friend is... How do I put this delicately? A devotee of 'the love that dare not speak its name.' Such men are too often more adept at romance than roughhousing. It makes them targets for barbarians."

Thaddeus sipped at his whiskey, then smiled. "That is the entirety of it, Detective... Now you know everything."

"Do I?"

Cooler's smile faded. "I...am not quite sure what you mean."

"Do you know where Dredd is...or what happened to him?"

"Oh my goodness, dear boy, has something happened to Gerald?"

Thaddeus put a fist to his chest, his expression of surprise and anguish something that would have played well had Campbell been seated in the back row of a theater. From merely a few feet away, it didn't play at all, and under the steady, relentless gaze of the detective, the actor began to fidget, his eyes flitting about the small space.

"I...don't know what you expect me to say, Detective."

Campbell remained silent, staring at the former under-butler.

"I must say…sir, that your, uh…demeanor is most unsettling," Cooler stammered. "I dare say it is…accusatory! Indeed…accusatory!" The actor stood, the quilt dropping from his shoulders as he adopted a swordless *en garde* position. "For one who is innocent, such as I, an accusation is a slur hidden beneath a cloak of self-righteousness and I am insulted, sir! Yes… insulted!" Thaddeus next attempted to engage the detective in a battle of hardened expressions. He was truly a great actor, but his contrived indignance was no match for the steely gaze of a former Marine interrogator. He lasted all of ten seconds.

"Perhaps, if you were to tell me what you believe I know?"

"Perhaps you should tell me what you *do* know," Campbell replied.

Cooler's eyelids began to flutter and he waggled a finger toward the ceiling as if it might fortuitously snag an elusive memory.

"You know, it just occurred to me, Detective Campbell…I might have heard something. A rumor, don't you know…more so a deduction, I daresay."

"A deduction?"

"Yes, as with the great Holmes…a conclusion drawn from seemingly disparate facts. Yes…yes, I believe I might know something, after all. A place where one might look. It is just speculation, don't you know…an intuition, if you will, but yes, I do have a vague recollection that someone once mentioned an old mine in the foothills behind the Peycomsons' home. Yes, I'm quite sure now. There's a legend about an old mine."

"And you saw Dredd there?"

"Not so much *there*," Cooler struggled. "As not so much not…*not* there, if you will. As I said, I know of the mine only by reputation, of course, but in that context, I might have seen someone *like* Gerald heading in the direction of where one might logically find a mine if one were looking; indeed, it might well have been Gerald. It was merely a glance…indeed, a glimpse…a fleeting look from a distance, don't you know?

Nothing entirely certain…my eyes to some extent victimized by advanced years."

Campbell drained the rest of his whiskey and stood. "Get dressed, Mister Cooler," he said. "We're going on a little expedition."

"An expedition?"

The detective gave him a look that encouraged the old actor to immediately reach for his trousers. "You're taking me to that mine," Campbell said.

# 23

## A MUMMY, WORTHINGTON TREADWELL, AND THE HALLS OF MONTEZUMA

With the Spanish flu pandemic on the wane, eighty-year-old widower, Dr. Stanley June, had come home two days before Campbell discovered Thaddeus Cooler in the secret room beneath the Paradise School. Trekking in from the north on horseback with a pair of pack mules, he arrived with a fresh Mrs. June—the former Blanche Filbert—and a stepdaughter. The late husband of his new wife had succumbed to the virus. "I contracted it from him," the doctor revealed. "Blanche nursed me back to health, and since Mister Filbert left her piss-pot poor, I figured the least I could do was marry her." In the doctor's absence, not a single person in Paradise had contracted the dreaded illness, Wanda Cooler's prior claim notwithstanding. "You folks have been in literal Paradise," the bespectacled physician assured the town council. "It's a horrible disease... Lost twenty-five percent of my patients on the circuit." Added to Geraldine Dredd Barkley, the doctor and his new family bumped the population back up to 124, and on his first morning home, he confirmed that Annie Goodlow and Sarah DeMille had complied with the council motion to become pregnant. "Neither is due until December," he cautioned. "Good thing I came back with spares."

Dr. June had seen more than his share of death during his months away, and now that he was again semi-retired, looked forward to fly-fishing, home-cooking, and straightforward cases of poison oak, heartburn, and sniffles. Instead, on the morning of his second day back, he was roused from bed at six o'clock in the morning by a knock on the door. Oskar Nilsen and Robert Campbell were waiting on his porch.

"We found Gerald Dredd," Oskar told the doctor. "He's dead." Four other men stood at the end of Dr. June's front walk, and even without his glasses, the old physician recognized three of them: Goldstrike, Arnold Chang, and Ed Riggins. "Is that Thaddeus Cooler?" he asked, squinting at the fourth man. "What's that rascal doing back here?"

"No time to explain, Doc," Oskar replied. "Get dressed."

Dr. June disappeared into his house, returning with a coat thrown over his pajamas and boots on his feet, his leather house-call bag in one hand. "Let's go," he said and they headed out, marching across open ground north of the physician's property. As they hiked, the land described a steady upward slope until leveling out at a narrow logging trail about 500 feet above the town. From there, they headed east on the furrowed roadway until reaching a spur that angled north to an opening in the craggy rockface. It was the entrance to Goldstrike's abandoned mine, a tunnel the erstwhile miner had blasted into the mountainside almost fifty years earlier.

The search party approached the adit and entered, discovering a passage roughly seven feet high and seven feet wide. Campbell had replenished his flashlight with batteries and led the way. About forty-five feet in, his torch illuminated the back end of a car: a British D-Type Vauxhall. A figure was slumped in the driver's seat.

"Gerald Dredd," the detective told the doctor.

Dr. June approached and found the corpse to be mummified, skin dry and leathery, cheeks sunken. The head was twisted at an odd angle. He instinctively took the cadaver's pulse. "Dead," he confirmed. He cautiously palpated Dredd's neck, then added, "I can't do a proper examination in here. Let's move him outside."

Campbell opened the door and eased the body from the front seat, stumbling and nearly dropping the corpse as he moved toward the rear of the car. Thaddeus Cooler leapt forward and caught the body, afterward slinging the dead man over his shoulder and heading back up the tunnel, the rest following.

Goldstrike noted the detective's surprise at the old actor's display of strength. "Ya shoulda seen 'im tossin' boulders around when we was settin' them electrical poles," the old prospector remarked. "The sonuvabitch is strong as a goddamned bull."

Outside, the actor lowered the body to the ground and Dr. June resumed his examination, stripping off Dredd's clothes. "No gunshot wounds," the doctor told the group. "There's a cut on his leg, but it's superficial...not bad enough to kill him. Neck looks broken."

"Can you tell how long he's been dead?" Campbell asked.

Dr. June shook his head. The hike up to the mine had lent a bluish tint to the elderly doctor's lips and he moved to a nearby boulder and sat, faintly wheezing. "I'm no coroner, mind you, but it's likely been months, Mister Campbell," he said. "He'll have to be taken to Boise for a proper autopsy. In the meantime, we need to preserve the body. I suggest we put him back in the mine. He'll keep in there until we can transport him down to the valley." The doctor looked at Nilsen. "Oskar, go down the hill and get a couple of bedsheets from your store. We'll wrap him up like an Egyptian mummy and tuck him back into his car. And bring your truck up here to haul us back down or you'll likely have two dead men on your hands."

He glowered at Campbell.

"I'd have saddled my horse if I'd known we were gonna be out on army maneuvers," he griped. "Hell, we coulda backtracked to the west end of the damned logging road and driven here."

Nilsen set out. Meanwhile, Campbell spread Dredd's clothes out on the ground and knelt to go through them. The real estate baron had worn a good suit to his death—brown wool, pin-striped with wide lapels, a red silk pocket square.

"What're ya lookin' fer?" Goldstrike asked.

The detective didn't answer, his attention on a jagged rip in one trouser leg. It corresponded to the shallow cut Dr. June had identified on the victim's thigh.

"I don't see no funny business in this," Goldstrike added. "I suspect Dredd just got hisself lost. We had a helluva snowstorm around the time he went missin'. I don't know what things are like where you're from, Campbell, but up here a fella can get turned around in a snowstorm pretty goddamned fast. I knowed folks what thought north was south and east was west...froze to death lookin' fer shelter. I think that's what happened here."

"Maybe," Campbell responded, extracting a wallet from Dredd's inside coat pocket. It contained a driver's license, membership cards to various organizations including the Ku Klux Klan, some cash, and a photograph of Geraldine Dredd clad only in a slip. She appeared to have been about thirteen years old when the picture was taken. Campbell slid the photo into his coat, then put the wallet back in the dead man's pocket and began to search the trouser legs as if patting down a suspect. After a crinkling sound was elicited, he searched a pants pocket and found a small greeting card fronted by delicate violets. He opened it and read the message.

"Any of you know someone with the initials *HV*?" he asked, surveying the gathered faces. He was answered by a chorus of head shakes and resumed his search, running a finger inside the trouser cuffs. They were deep, the right one yielding lint, the left even more lint along with a button. It was fabric-covered, identifying its source as a woman's blouse.

"Find anything?" Goldstrike asked, edging closer.

"Not really," Campbell replied, the button hidden in the palm of his hand.

After Nilsen returned with his truck, they wrapped Dredd's body in bedsheets and then returned him to the Vauxhall. Campbell put the dead man's clothes and the greeting card into a paper sack. "Evidence...for the sheriff," he told the others. Then the men climbed into Nilsen's vehicle, Dr. June up front next to Oskar with the rest climbing onto the open truck bed. Driving carefully, the storekeeper negotiated the short spur from the mine to the east-west logging trail, then abandoned the road in favor of open ground to the south. "Logger's path takes us a mile west o' town afore it hits the main road," Goldstrike explained to the detective, shouting above the rumble of the engine. "We'd have to double back from there…take us a good twenty minutes, all told. We'll bounce around a mite goin' this way, but it'll be faster."

After covering about a quarter mile, they came upon the carriage house behind the Peycomson mansion. Campbell sat with his back against the cab, and as Nilsen drove his vehicle along the west side of the building, he surveyed the open ground they'd just traversed. Despite Goldstrike's contention that Dredd had sought shelter from the weather in the mine, the detective was convinced his sister's boss had met his end elsewhere—probably on the first day of the November snow-storm—the body and automobile afterward moved. *Tough place to reach in a blizzard*, he mused. *It had to be early in the storm…before the snow was too deep.* He touched his coat pocket and felt the out-line of the photo he'd found in Dredd's wallet—a too-young Geraldine in her slip. *Could it be that simple? An heiress in line to inherit majority control of Dredd Enterprises, an abusive father with a broken neck, a lover who'd killed in war and was proficient with a rope?* He'd nearly ruled out Geraldine and Willie, but it now seemed as if the usual suspects in such a case were suspects, after all.

Upon reaching Nilsen's General Store, Oskar parked his truck and most of the men headed over to the Gold Rush Sa-loon with Arnold Chang for a morning eye-opener.

"I need to make a phone call," Campbell told Nilsen. Oskar handed him the key for the mercantile's doorlock, collected a dime, and then joined the others. It was an hour later in Omaha and Arthur Faiman was already in his office.

"I found the body," Campbell told him. "He was inside an abandoned mine."

"Was it murder?"

The detective hesitated. As a military policeman, he'd been present at two hangings, rope marks evident after the nooses were removed. Dredd's neck had displayed the same circumfer-ential bruising. "No autopsy yet, Art," he said. "But the locals think he froze to death after getting lost in a snowstorm."

"Last time we spoke, you said he was murdered. You were one hundred percent sure. What changed?"

"The body's mummified, Art. We'll need an autopsy for an official determination."

"It would be helpful if it were murder, Campbell. It's a million-dollar benefit unless, of course, he was murdered. If that were the case, the company would be most relieved...indeed, *most* relieved. I daresay they'd be in a generous frame of mind."

"I'll call again when I know more."

"*Most* generous, I'd wager."

Campbell hung up on the insurance executive and next called Iris to apprise her of the morning's events. "I'll tell the family," she responded. "The wives will be delighted. I don't expect many tears from the kids, either. Any idea what happened?"

"Not entirely," her brother answered. "Tell me, did Dredd do business with anyone who has the initials *HV*?"

"No one comes to mind."

"Could it be an alias your boss used?"

Iris snorted. "I've never known anyone as desperate to put his name on things as Gerald Dredd. He would *never* use an alias." She paused. "What happened to him, Bobby?"

"Do you care?"

"Ours was a complicated relationship. I do and I don't."

Campbell waited for her to continue. When she didn't, he went on. "What about Dredd's will? Do you have it?"

"Not yet. One of his desk drawers is locked. It's probably in there, but I haven't found the key."

"Do you have a nail file?"

"I'm not going to break into it, Bobby."

"It's important, Iris."

"Keep your pants on. I'll find the key."

࿇

Following his resurrection from the tiny room below the Paradise School, Maude assigned Thaddeus Cooler the Moulin Rouge bedroom at the Busty Rose. It was a space with devilishly red walls, a red ceiling, a red carpet, and a headboard in the shape of a gigantic red heart. A continuous mural occupied two adjoining walls. The first half of the fresco depicted elegant Parisians in formal attire, sipping champagne from tables inside the famous Moulin Rouge cabaret, their attention on the second wall where leggy, bare-breasted female dancers in feathered head-dresses and can-cans formed a chorus line. Thaddeus was deliriously grateful for the change.

"Not to seem unappreciative, my dear Maude, but I had begun to feel like poor Fortunato," he told her after his first night on a soft mattress in the garishly decorated room.

"Who?"

"'The Cask of Amontillado'…Edgar Allen Poe? Fortunato was left to perish in a sealed catacomb. Walled in by the vengeful Montressor."

"Oh, Thaddeus…" Maude sighed. "You are so full of crap."

It was a sentiment shared by much of the town, even though the addition of the Junes, joined to the actor's encore performance, had put the population of Paradise at exactly 125.

"Back in the old days, we'd have strung up the sonuvabitch," Goldstrike opined, recalling the fire that destroyed Elysium. This garnered some support among the less forgiving in Paradise, although Maude believed her lover was truly contrite.

"'There's nothing in this world can make me joy… Bitter shame hath spoil'd the sweet world's taste,'" Thaddeus forlornly offered to anyone willing to listen.

"You see?" Maude submitted. "I'm pretty sure that means he's genuinely sorry."

"I didn't hear no goddamned 'I'm sorry' in the middle o' that bullshit," Goldstrike countered.

"You and I aren't getting any younger, Goldstrike," Maude reminded the recalcitrant prospector. "That goes for Oskar and Arnold and Ed and Doctor June too. We can't afford to hang Thaddeus until the census counter is done with us."

Maude had kept Cooler's entombment a secret from Bountiful, Lariat, and Goldstrike, but after the actor was discovered, she revealed to them what had happened on the night of Gerald Dredd's death. "Thaddeus was in my room when you knocked on the door," the former madam confessed, nodding at Bountiful and Lariat. "That's why I couldn't let you come in. After the three of us went to the kitchen, Thaddeus snuck down the stairs and listened from the dining room. When we left to retrieve Goldstrike, he went to the carriage house, took the body and the car, and then drove into the foothills. He planned to hide them in the forest until he saw the entrance to Goldstrike's mine."

Subsequently, Cooler had convinced Maude that the problem was solved. "Once it all blows over, I shall make a remorseful return to Paradise," he'd reassured her. "My addition to the census will put us nearer the target population, offsetting any residual ill will." The discovery of Dredd's body thwarted their plan and Maude now despaired that the secret she and Thaddeus shared with Bountiful, Lariat, and Goldstrike would also be unearthed. Cooler wasn't worried.

"It's true we've a dilemma, my dear…one that could put us all in a penitentiary," he conceded two weeks after Campbell disinterred him from the tiny cell below the Paradise School. Sitting together on the edge of the heart-shaped bed in the Moulin Rouge bedroom, he and Maude were again dressed after an hour romping under the covers. "However, a crime is not a crime, unless there are witnesses to corroborate it," the actor continued. "I have some expertise in such things. I played a lawyer…Worthington Treadwell…in *Justice is a Harsh Mistress*. We did three weeks at the Starling Theater in Bridgeport, Connecticut. Sold-out performances…indeed, several Broadway producers were so taken with my—"

"Thaddeus…"

Cooler chuckled. "Of course… Get to it. Forgive me, dear girl." He took a moment to step back into the character of Worthington Treadwell, then went on. "I submit, madam, that no crime has been committed unless there are witnesses to the act. Our friend, Goldstrike, has volunteered to play the role of murderer in our dramatization, but are there witnesses, other than he, to such a crime? There are not. Ipso facto, the crime does not legally exist."

"Ipso…?"

"Ipso facto," my dear. "By that very fact."

Maude frowned. "You really are full of crap, Thaddeus," she reiterated. "It won't be that simple. *We* knew a crime was committed. And you hid the body. I helped cover it up. We can be called as witnesses against each other."

"Not unless we testify to those effects in court. Yes, we knew Gerald had been killed, but were we obliged to report it? In *Justice is a Harsh Mistress*, Worthington Treadwell argues that failure to report a crime is not, in and of itself, a crime. He's a lawyer. I think he'd know."

"But hiding the body was a second crime. I know a bit about the law too. Thaddeus. By committing the second crime, we'd be material witnesses for the first one."

"Only with proof… And without our testimony against one another, there is no such proof. Moreover, there is a strategy to prevent such testimony."

Maude had returned Cooler's gold pocket to the old actor after he moved into the Moulin Rouge bedroom. Now, he retrieved it from a vest pocket and removed the fob ring.

"That didn't actually belong to Prince Albert, did it?" Maude said. "It wasn't a gift from Queen Victoria."

The old actor smiled. "Quite true, my dear… It is, however, a lie to which I confess without fear of societal rebuke." He slid off the bed and dropped to one knee. "Indeed, my transgression shall remain private, as shall all things between us because, my dearest, a husband and wife cannot be forced to testify against each other."

He slipped the fob ring onto her finger.

"Maude, my love, will you marry me?"

Maude caught her breath, her eyes suddenly watery. She held up her hand to look at the ring, the whisper of a smile on her face, her feet still dangling over the edge of the bed. Then her expression flattened and she blinked away her tears.

"How old are you, Thaddeus?"

"I am seventy-six years young."

"You don't look it."

"Ah, but that's the actor's secret. One is only as old as one *believes*."

"I'm seventy-nine," Maude said. "And I believe it."

"And yet it shall remain *our* secret when I am your husband."

The former madam stood and went to the window. The meadow abutting the rear of the Busty Rose extended from one end of town to the other, separating the tiny village from the northern foothills. The verdant expanse had mostly recovered from the fire and was blanketed in tall green sedge peppered with feathery rice-grass and spring blossoms: baby blue-eyes, white candytuft columbine, and sun-shaped blanket-flowers with orange centers and yellow tips.

"We're so goddamned old," she murmured.

Thaddeus rose from his knee and crossed the room. He stood behind the former madam and put his arms around her waist. "To paraphrase the Bard, my sweet, 'Age cannot wither thou, nor custom stale thy infinite variety.'"

Maude turned to face him.

"Okay," she said.

"Is that a 'Yes,' my dearest?"

Maude shrugged. "Sure… What the hell. It's a yes."

❧

The May meeting of the Paradise town council convened a week later. Maude and Thaddeus had yet to announce their upcoming nuptials and the main topic of discussion was the road to Boise. The work crew had efficiently cleared most of the obstruction, and blessed with good weather and a stern foreman, they were hard at work on the last of it.

"At the rate they're goin', they'll have the pass open afore long," Goldstrike reported.

"Bertram Mole'll probably have a man from the census up here right after," Oskar speculated.

"And Dredd's body will go to Boise for an autopsy," Maude added.

Once the meeting adjourned, Bountiful, Maude, and Goldstrike remained at the round conference table after the others had gone. Detective Robert Campbell was the only item on the agenda of their after-meeting. He'd made good use of his time in Paradise, interviewing everyone in town. Instinctively distrustful at first, people had warmed to him. "Nice fellow, that Campbell," folks commented. "Wouldn't be so bad if he stuck around." Goldstrike was less accommodating.

"He's a bulldog with a hat in its teeth," he suggested to Maude and Bountiful. "Findin' Dredd's body ain't never gonna be enough. He won't be satisfied till he figgers out who kilt 'im." The women agreed.

"We have to get Lariat out of town as soon as the road opens," Bountiful concluded.

When Lariat learned that exile to Howard University was imminent, he resurrected his opposition. "I'm not going," he told Bountiful. "Without me, the town doesn't make the census."

"Don't worry about us," Bountiful said. "Sarah and Annie are pregnant. Once they deliver, we'll be all right."

"Doc says they won't deliver until after we're counted."

"Don't worry."

"But—"

"Don't worry, Lariat… We'll be all right."

After dinner that evening, Bountiful threw on a shawl-neck sweater and a pair of high-waisted trousers, slid her hiking boots onto her feet, and went for a walk. June was fast approaching, but evenings in Paradise were still crisp with last winter, the chill in the air keeping her thoughts focused. Bountiful had told Lariat not to worry, but she'd done little else with Robert Campbell in town. They'd frequently crossed paths since the interview in the parlor of the Paradise School: at the mercantile, walking along the boardwalk, inside one of the Goodlow Road curio shops. Each time, they stopped and made small talk. Bountiful was distant but polite. The detective was circumspect—never mentioning Gerald Dredd—but his coyote eyes were ever-present.

Bountiful hiked west, then veered south on a horse trail until she reached Mores Creek. To the east, Goldstrike's shack sat near the water's edge more than one hundred yards away, but she headed in the opposite direction until coming to the clearing used as a sanctuary during the Elysium fire. The creek was wider there, its flow quieter. The road to Boise was above and to her right, slanting and curling on its way down to the valley, the rockfaces on either side forming a distant $V$-shaped wedge in the west that shone orange as sunset approached. The color of the wedge and the clearing reminded her of the fire that took Elysium—of Meriwether Peycomson and the momentary kiss they'd shared in the parlor of the Paradise School. It was a lapse of judgment that still haunted her.

*Why did he think it would be okay? Did I invite him to kiss me?*

After the fateful struggle with Dredd in the Peycomson carriage house Bountiful had told Maude about the kiss, prompting her grandmother to grimace and then shrug. "A strong chin doesn't make a strong man," she'd remarked and Bountiful now agreed. Meriwether Peycomson hadn't returned to help fight the fire after shuttling off the last of the evacuees to the clearing where she now stood. And he'd written the note that nearly got her killed in the carriage house. For all his charm and good looks, he had turned out to be nothing more than a coward and a scoundrel.

Bountiful heard whistling from behind—a melody—and turned to the sound. The whistling grew louder, replaced by a singing voice and the crunch of footsteps, the sounds in cadence as if the vocalist was marching. She recognized the song as the Marine Corps Hymn.

"From the halls of Montuh-zoo-ooh-ma..."

Robert Campbell cut off the song as he came around a slight bend and saw Bountiful in the clearing. For once, he did not wear a suit and tie, and instead, was clad in khakis, his white shirt open-collared and bit rumpled, the lack of scuff on his round-toed boots disclosing their recent purchase from Nilsen's General Store. Only his wide-brimmed fedora was familiar. He touched it in a salute.

"Good evening, Miss Dollarhyde. Looks like you caught me. I'm not much of a singer, as you now know."

Bountiful smiled. "I've heard worse."

"From a howling dog, I'll wager."

"Perhaps…but at least one that howls on key."

Campbell laughed, then removed his hat, rubbing the faint line it left on his forehead. "I've been taking walks in the evening…exploring."

"Looking for more bodies?"

"Do you have more?"

"One is enough, don't you think?"

Campbell nodded, smiling, then looked toward the orange V-wedge and took a deep breath. He held it as if to savor the aroma, then exhaled with a satisfied sigh. "This is my first trip to the American West," he said, again looking at her. "It's spectacular here…God's country."

"It is," Bountiful answered. "Sometimes, I forget."

"I can see how that might happen…if you live here," Campbell replied. "It's like that for me in Chicago. I'm used to noise. Here, it's so quiet I sometimes can't sleep." He cocked his head. "Are you heading back? May I join you?"

They walked together, going east until they reached the horse trail near Goldstrike's shack, and then north to the main road. The openness of the ruggedly beautiful, natural surroundings seemed to make them more open with one another than they'd been in the past, their conversation for the first time carrying easily and evolving naturally. Bountiful was surprised by how much they had in common. Both appreciated the bustle and clamor of cities like Washington, DC, and Chicago but treasured the reassuring comforts of insular institutions like Howard University and the Marine Corps. Each liked Dickens but preferred Twain, attended an occasional football game but were rabid fans of baseball, thought Harold Lloyd funnier than Charlie Chaplin, and picked scotch over bourbon. Upon reaching the Gold Rush Saloon, they stopped.

"Perhaps you've time for a drink?" Campbell asked.

Bountiful hesitated. When not picking at her for clues, the detective was an appealing man with a sense of humor and excellent manners. Unlike Meriwether Peycomson, he exuded strength of both body and character.

"Miss Dollarhyde?"

She studied his eyes. They were warm and steady and she might have accepted his invitation had they not they flickered to reveal the coyote behind them. She shook her head.

"Thank you, no. I have to get home."

"Perhaps, another time?"

"Perhaps."

Bountiful headed up the main road. Campbell watched until she'd turned onto Only Real Street and then went inside the Gold Rush where he had a single shot of Macallan before retiring to the Buffalo Bill room at the old Busty Rose.

# 24

## *HV* AND THE TWELFTH STICK

Robert Campbell had three theories to explain Gerald Dredd's death, two of them explanations that Arthur Faiman at Mutual of Omaha would like: Dredd had either been murdered or killed in the commission of his own crime. In both those scenarios the life insurance benefit to his widow would be voided. However, the detective had yet to settle on either hypothesis, the recipient of the card fronted by delicate violets and signed by *"HV"* still a mystery. Such a missive was typically sent to a woman. *But which one?* he asked himself when considering the most likely suspects: Geraldine Dredd Barkley and Bountiful Dollarhyde. He favored the possibility that Gerald Dredd had lured his daughter to the carriage house where he meant to have his way with her, instead getting himself roped and hung by Willie Barkley. It was a satisfying explanation—a villainous victim with sympathetic culprits a jury would be reluctant to convict. Seven weeks after cruising into Paradise, and not long after running into Bountiful on Mores Creek, the detective's preferred theory of the crime took a sharp right turn.

On the afternoon of May 21, 1920, the Chicago investigator went into Nilsen's General Store to call Iris, ten cents in hand. Oskar was in a chatty mood and added the surcharge of an open ear for him to fill with yet another account of the town's only theatrical production.

"In *Our American Cousin*…that was the name of our play…I was s'posed to be Sir Edward and it was an important part," Oskar regaled the detective. "Cooler thought right away I was perfect for it. And I was, too, doggonnit." He sighed. "But I had to give it up. Couldn't run a store and be in a play. Cooler

got Goldstrike to take my part, 'cuz between you and me, Detective, the old coot does pretty much nuthin' all day and was
available. But then he went and messed up his lines. Wrecked
everything. Cooler comes up to me afterward and says, 'Oskar,
why couldn't you have stuck it out? You woulda done it perfect,
I betcha.' Those were his exact words. God's honest truth...
Cooler's *exact* words."

"I thought Mister Cooler disappeared during the fire?"
Campbell pointed out.

Oskar frowned. "I can't be lollygaggin' around all day talkin'
to you," the storekeeper groused. "You wanna use my telephone or not?" He pocketed Campbell's dime and headed for
the boardwalk outside. "And don't be on it all day. I'm runnin' a
general store here, not a doggone telephone company."

After Nilsen was out of earshot, Campbell called his sister in
Boise. "Did you get a look at the will?" he asked.

"I did."

"Does it confirm the distribution of the company stock?"

"More or less. Geraldine gets thirty-four percent...just over
half her father's share of the company. Another sixteen percent
is evenly split among his other children, all in individual trusts."

"Geraldine's is in a trust, as well?"

"No, she's the only one with unrestricted control of her
inheritance."

"What about the remaining shares?"

His sister didn't answer.

"Iris?"

"I'm here," she said. "There was another change... Listen,
Bobby, don't get the wrong idea. I didn't know about this before I read the will, but..."

When she didn't finish, her brother issued a low whistle.
"The old bastard gave it to you," he said.

"Yeah...seventeen percent."

"So you and Geraldine, together, will control fifty-one percent of the company."

"For now," Iris replied. "Junior and Carl have already retained an attorney to challenge the will. All the wives too. I'll be spending the next ten years in probate court."

Campbell was puzzled by the new information. Dredd had spent much of his life chasing secretaries around his desk or bragging to his male friends about sexual conquests that were fictitious, imposed, or purchased. It implied an utter disrespect for women, and yet he'd left two of them in charge of his company.

"I know what you're thinking," Iris said. "But I'm not all that surprised. Once a person cuts through the posturing, Gerald was afraid of women. He was terrified of rejection. I think he craved acceptance from both Geraldine and me. He probably gave us the company because he thought we'd disapprove if he didn't."

"You're a regular Sigmund Freud, aren't you?"

"It doesn't take Sigmund Freud to figure out men like Gerald Dredd," Iris replied. "Any woman can do it."

After Campbell ended the call, he went next door to the Gold Rush Saloon, ordered a beer, and listened to Arnold Chang gossip. Tight-lipped when they first met, the saloonkeeper was as talkative as Oskar Nilsen once he let down his guard, and like the mercantile proprietor, he wanted to talk about *Our American Cousin*.

"Dey rehearse my place all day," he told Campbell. "Mista Coola order dem folks 'round. 'Go dere, sit here, speak loud… Project actors, project!'"

Arnold laughed, the sound like the bleating of a goat.

"He'n Goldstrike, argue all time. I t'ink Goldstrike head 'splode he don't calm down. Dat be ironical, you know? Goldstrike know all 'bout dyn'mite. Head 'splode, it be *ironical*. You get?"

Campbell nodded. The night they'd swapped whiskeys, Goldstrike had told him about his mine-sweeping days with the Maine 11th. The detective later learned about the obsolescent explosives left in the mine and Goldstrike's expedition to retrieve more from Old Butch's nephew.

"How much dynamite did Goldstrike get from the Balshaz-zar mine?" the detective asked.

"Not too much…twelve sticks, I t'ink."

Campbell had walked every square foot of town and knew the power line of the Paradise Electrical Cooperative had only ten posts.

"So he had two sticks left after the power line was finished?"

Arnold shrugged. "S'pose so."

The saloonkeeper then launched another story about the performance of *Our American Cousin,* recalling the scene where Sheriff Henry Wilcoxon, as Richard Coyle, sat in an empty space where a chair should have been. It prompted a fit of laughter that gave him a bloody nose, but after staunching the flow with a scrap torn from the corner of an old playbill retrieved from under the bar, Arnold went on to describe other characters in the play, paper plugging one nostril as he spoke.

"Could I get a look at that playbill?" Campbell interrupted after Chang cited one of the featured roles in the production. The old Chinese man handed it over and Campbell scrolled down the cast list, stopping at the fourth and fifth billings:

MISS FLORENCE TRENCHARD: BOUNTIFUL DOLLARHYDE
LT. HARRY VERNON: MERIWETHER PEYCOMSON

"May I keep this?" Campbell asked. Arnold nodded and the detective returned to the Buffalo Bill room. There, he opened a bottle of warm ginger ale and sat, reviewing the playbill as if concentration alone could provide an explanation that didn't point fingers directly at the only two suspects Idaho justice would likely treat harshly. He drained the bottle of ginger ale and flopped onto the bed, the unrelenting image of Bountiful's blue eyes competing with his detective's instincts. Campbell remained there for a long time, staring at the ceiling as sunset approached and shadows began to fill the corners of the room. Eventually, he dozed and then slept, waking just after midnight with his gumshoe's resolve back in place. Minutes later he had slipped out the back exit of the Busty Rose, heading into the darkness of the meadow behind it. The smell of rain was in the air as he approached the carriage house behind the Peycomson mansion. Without Geraldine's permission, he'd already surreptitiously searched the structure once, finding blood on the blade of the scythe and evidence that a pitchfork and a baling hook had been used as weapons. Campbell was certain Dredd had met his end there. And it had not been an accident—someone or a pair of someones had killed him and now, as unlikely as it seemed, he hoped a second search might exonerate Bountiful Dollarhyde and Lariat Comfort.

A raindrop struck his cheek as he reached his destination. It was followed by another, an accompanying gust of wind spraying the metal roof of the edifice with rain—scattershot sounds that made him flinch as if they came from gunfire. The stable doors were unlocked and he stepped inside, wrinkling his nose at the smell of pungent fertilizer. The place was pitch black and he turned on his flashlight, then began to walk the interior of the barn from the walls in, using his light to scan floor to ceiling as he worked his way around in ever-decreasing concentric circles. On one of the walls, he again noted four small holes, evenly spaced across eight inches, the splintered edges not yet grayed by age to match the surrounding wood. On his previous visit, he'd matched the holes to the tines of the pitchfork, confirming that someone had recently speared the wall with it. He took down the scythe from its hook, again noting the coffee-ground discoloration on the blade.

As with his previous search of the premises, he could see it all. She had expected to meet Peycomson. Instead, Gerald Dredd was here. There was a scuffle. Dredd forced her into the wall. The scythe dislodged. It fell, tore a hole in his trousers, cut his leg. She'd managed to grab the pitchfork and they'd faced off, circling and parrying. Eventually, he was able to rip the long-handled tool from her hands with the baling hook, launching it into the wall and leaving a tell-tale scratch on the hook. She was unarmed, then, and Dredd overpowered her.

*But someone else was here.*

Campbell shone the flashlight upward, illuminating the over-head crossbeam that ran from the center edge of the haymow to the far wall. Even from ten feet below he could see a few rope fibers stuck in the splintered surface.

*Willie or Lariat?*

He next moved to the middle of the center bay and began to rotate in place, reexamining the floor, walls, and ceiling with his flashlight. He stopped when the beam illuminated the source of the acrid smell permeating the interior of the carriage house: an open bag of grass fertilizer slumped against the wall with the hanging tools. He went to it and scanned the dirt floor around it, then lifted the bag and searched underneath. Last of all, he shone his flashlight into the open mouth of the sack. Inside was an orchid-colored envelope. He plucked it out, flap-side up, then turned it over to read the name printed on the face.

"Oh hell," he said aloud.

❧

The next day, May 22, 1920, the road between Paradise and Boise reopened. There was no celebration, the news arriving without fanfare when the repair crew turned up at the Gold Rush Saloon in the late afternoon to finish off their shift with beers. "That weren't no natural avalanche," the crew chief opined to Arnold Chang and a few others after knocking back half a bottle of ice-cold Hamms beer without pausing for a breath. "Looked to me like somebody intentionally blew the side of the mountain onto the road."

Word traveled fast, and within a couple of hours, everyone in Paradise knew the pass had been cleared and Dredd's body could now be moved down to the valley—possibly as soon as the next day. Early on the following morning, with dawn just beginning to paint the eastern horizon in violet and rose, Gold-strike arose in his shack on Mores Creek. He retrieved a canvas rucksack from a battered footlocker and packed it with a few blasting caps, wire, the push-handle detonator, and the last of his twelve sticks of dynamite. Afterward he set out, heading east along the creek.

Thirty years had passed since the Civil War veteran had first committed a crime on behalf of a Dollarhyde woman. Lily Dollarhyde and Goldstrike had both arrived in Idaho as teenagers and for nearly a quarter of a century the former minesweeper with the Maine 11th loved her as much as a man can love a woman. In the summer of 1890 he was enraged after learning what Friederich Dredd had done to Lily in the tiny hidden room below the Paradise School. "I'm gonna kill the sonuvabitch," he'd sworn, retrieving the Colt revolver taken off a dead Reb officer at Dabney's Mill near the end of the war. "Please don't, Goldstrike," Lily begged him. "They'll hang you." She made him promise, but after Lily died in childbirth nine months later, the grief-stricken prospector broke his vow, ambushing Friederich as he staggered home from a Boise saloon. The man who fathered Bountiful Dollarhyde ended up in the Pioneer Cemetery off Warm Springs Avenue, the Colt .44 Goldstrike used to kill him sent to the bottom of the Boise River. At the time, Bountiful's half-brother, Gerald, was twenty-two years old.

About one thousand feet up the stream the waterway bent to the southeast, but Goldstrike veered north, trekking into the foothills. It was wilderness out here, with only rabbits, deer, and a disinterested bear to view his progress as he gained elevation, cutting through pristine forest and thick duff to reach the east end of the logging road that ran to his old mine. He followed it west until coming to the wagon spur, then approached the dark mouth of the mine entrance. Just inside, an oil lamp hung on a spike driven into one of the support timbers. He took it down and lit it, afterward cautiously making his way along the tunnel. He still had aches on rainy days that traced their origins to the long-ago time when he'd blasted the rock, cleared it by hand, and shored up the walls and ceiling of the tunnel with railroad ties—a pair of verticals set every few feet, each buttressing an overhead cross-brace. It had been hard work, made worse by Old Butch's opinions. "You coulda panned enough gold to last a year or more if you weren't grubbin' around like a goddamned mole inside that mountain," he'd ridiculed his then-young partner. *He was right*, the former prospector mused as the license plate from the Vauxhall appeared in the glow of his lamp.

Goldstrike knelt and retrieved the dynamite, wire, and a blasting cap from his rucksack. Afterward he used the lamp to search for a decent fracture in the ceiling. He found one, jammed the stick of dynamite into it, and then inserted a blasting cap with attached wire. Next he retraced his steps, playing out the wire from a spool as he backed out of the tunnel. Once outside, he moved to a safe distance, rigged the detonator, twisted the handle to engage it, and pushed down. From inside the mine, a muffled explosion sounded and the entrance burped a cloud of dust and smoke. Goldstrike waited for a few minutes, then covered his nose and mouth with a bandanna and reentered the mine. Holding his oil lamp at arms-length, he moved along, the air thickening as he went deeper into the passage. He'd negotiated about thirty feet when confronted by a pile of timbers. Beyond them was an impenetrable wall of rock.

"So much fer yer goddamned autopsy, Detective Campbell," he muttered aloud.

৵

Around noon, twelve-year-old Oliver DeMille banged on the door of Goldstrike's shack. "Sheriff wants you down at the Gold Rush," he called out from the roughhewn covered porch. "They want to pick up the body."

"Tell 'em to go ahead," Goldstrike shouted through the door. "I don't give a good goddamn what they do with it."

"He wants you there."

"I don't give a shit what he wants! I ain't his goddamned show pony!"

"Aw c'mon, Goldstrike," Oliver pleaded.

Goldstrike climbed out of bed and let the boy in. A cup of coffee and a plate of beans with biscuits later he left the shack with Oliver and made for the saloon, arriving to find two vehicles parked on the street: a new Nash automobile, road dust speckling its otherwise unblemished paint, and a pickup with a makeshift cage in the truck bed large enough to hold four men. A logo on the door identified the truck as property of the Boise County Sheriff's Department.

Inside the bar and grill, Sheriff Henry Wilcoxon had commandeered one of the tables. He was a large man and his personality was large, as well, helping him keep the peace in Boise County without being unpeaceable. Big enough to overpower most men, he preferred coaxing rather than the Colt revolver on his belt, an approach that had made him one of the most popular sheriffs to ever hold office. Three others were with him, including Robert Campbell, a second fellow bearing the lugubrious aspect of a basset hound, and a small man with close-set eyes, a long nose, and pomaded hair combed so flat against his head it resembled a tattoo. Although it was midday and he was on duty, the big sheriff had already finished one beer and was a couple of gulps into a second.

"There's the feller we wanted to see," he called out when Goldstrike entered the saloon. He motioned him over, a grin on his face. "Now you already know Mister Campbell," he went on after the old prospector reached them. "And this here's John Locke, the coroner." He indicated the basset hound with a nod, then gestured at the third member of their party. "And that there's Mister Bertram Mole from the office o' the God-Almighty Attorney General of Idaho. He's of the opinion, Goldstrike, that we need your permission to enter the mine and remove Dredd's body."

"You have Fourth Amendment rights," Mole elaborated. The attorney's voice, like the rest of him, was thin and nasal. He didn't wear spectacles, but nevertheless held his head like a schoolmaster peering at an unprepared student over the top of pince-nez glasses. Added to his dismissive tone, it was clear that, despite his nod to the Constitution, he didn't give an actual damn about the old prospector's civil liberties. "Of course, if you refuse to allow access we'll just obtain a search warrant, so you might as well let us proceed," he added.

Goldstrike scowled. He couldn't have distinguished the Fourth Amendment to the U.S. Constitution from the Fourth Commandment of the Holy Bible but didn't like being told what to do. "If you boys are so goddamned worried about my rights," he growled, "maybe ya shoulda got yerselves one o' them search warrants afore ya come traipsin' up here to go trespassin'."

"Aw c'mon, Goldstrike," Sheriff Wilcoxon cajoled in an amiable drawl. "My missus is hostin' a card party tonight fer a bunch o' her hoity-toits. She's determined to have me there and I need to get Mister Gerald Dredd retrieved in time to be home by six."

Bertram Mole reaimed his headmaster's eyes at Goldstrike. "You've made me wait more than an hour already. So what, exactly, is your objection? Is there a reason we shouldn't be in your mine? Do you have something to hide?"

"No one is accusing you of anything, Goldstrike," Robert Campbell quietly interceded. "You own the mine, so Sheriff Wilcoxon needs your permission to retrieve the body… That's all."

"Then why didn't yer guv'ment man, over there, say as much to start with?" Goldstrike grumped. He glared at Mole, the two men lapsing into a brief staring contest that ended when the little attorney looked down and began to fiddle with the knot of his tie. Goldstrike nodded with satisfaction. "Go ahead and get the goddamned body, Henry. 'Bout time ya got it off my property, anyway. I oughta charge the county rent fer the time it spent in there already."

The five men exited the Gold Rush and piled into the sheriff's truck. Mole and the big lawman were in the cab with Goldstrike, Campbell, and Locke in the cage. "Sorry about the accommodations, boys," Wilcoxon joked to the men in the back. "But I won't lock the door so long as you fellers promise not to escape." He started the engine and they headed down the main road toward Boise. After a mile they reached the west turnoff to the same logging road Goldstrike had accessed earlier from a few miles to the east. It was a hairpin turn and the sheriff took it too fast. The truck leaned dangerously, the men in the rear shifting en masse to prevent a rollover. "Sorry, boys!" Wilcoxon shouted from the cab before speeding up again, the vehicle rocking side to side as they raced up the rutted logging trail. After a few minutes they reached the spur leading to Goldstrike's old mine. The sheriff turned onto it and parked just outside the entrance, the men then climbing out of the pickup and making for the dusty opening, save Mole who held back, first eyeing his immaculately polished shoes and then the retrieval party.

"I'll wait here," he said.

The rest went inside where Goldstrike tipped the teardrop shade of the oil lamp, flinching almost imperceptibly when he touched the smoky glass. He lit the wick and let the cover clatter back onto its base. "Let's go," he said, picking up the lamp by its handle.

Thin smoke still hung in the air as they moved along the tunnel. Locke, the coroner, began to cough. "I can't stay in here," he said, turning back. The rest kept going, Goldstrike leading the way with his nose and mouth covered by a bandanna, the sheriff and Campbell doing the same with handkerchiefs. When the fallen timbers and wall of broken rock emerged from the darkness, Goldstrike stopped and held up a hand.

"Cave-in," he said. "We'd best get outta here. Any moment now, this whole goddamned place could come down 'round our ears."

Campbell switched on his flashlight and used it to scan the ceiling and walls. "I think it's safe," he said. "Let's dig a little... see if we can break through."

"I got a spade in the truck," Wilcoxon said. "I'll retrieve it." He took the oil lamp from Goldstrike and headed out as Campbell trained the beam of his flashlight on the wall of fallen rocks.

"This reminds me of Cuba," the detective remarked. He

shone the flashlight on Goldstrike. The old prospector flinched, an arm flung upward to shield his eyes.

"Point that goddamned thing somewhere else!"

"Sorry," Campbell replied, shifting the aim of his light back to the cave-in. "I was just remembering Cuba...the Span-ish-American War...when I was in the Corps. He gestured at the wall of rock with his flashlight. "It was my first action as a young Marine. I'd been deployed there just a week when we came upon a railroad tunnel the rebels had blown up. It looked like a bigger version of this."

Goldstrike didn't respond and Campbell went on.

"I heard something about dynamite you might have left in here?"

"Yeah...fifty-year-old dynamite by now."

"Could it still explode?"

"I 'spect so. That's probably what happened."

"Didn't you also have dynamite left over after setting the poles for the power line?"

"Who the hell told ya that?"

"Mister Chang... He believed you got twelve sticks from the Balshazzar mine."

Goldstrike scowled. "Ya got somethin' to say, Campbell, then goddamned say it!"

The detective shrugged. "There are only ten posts for the power line, so I figured you had two sticks left. That's all I'm saying." Campbell trained the beam of his flashlight at the ceiling above Goldstrike, the dull reflection illuminating a tiny, perverse smile on the old man's face.

*He wants to tell me. He's proud of it.*

Before Goldstrike could respond, the sheriff returned with a flat-headed spade. Campbell took it and began to pry loose rocks from the cave-in. Goldstrike headed up the dark tunnel, guiding himself with a hand on the wall.

"Where ya goin'?" Wilcoxon called out.

"Gettin' some fresh air. It's too goddamned fusty in here fer me."

Campbell continued to work for a few minutes, his effort resulting in a lot of sweat but not much progress. Wilcoxon watched.

"It's caved in fer good, Detective," he said. "You're breakin' yer back fer nuthin'."

"What about mining equipment?" Campbell wondered. "Could we get some jackhammers in here?"

Wilcoxon shrugged. "I s'pose we could try that. Maybe bring in a tunnel-borin' machine too…though I doubt there'd be much o' Dredd left to autopsy by the time them power tools got done with 'im."

The detective worked on his own for a few minutes more before giving up. Then he and the sheriff went outside where Goldstrike, Mole, and the coroner, John Locke, silently waited, none looking as if they'd spoken a single word to each other because they hadn't. "It's caved-in permanent," the sheriff repeated for their benefit, afterward climbing into his pickup with Mole in the passenger seat and Campbell, Goldstrike, and Locke once again in the truck bed. "Hang on," the big lawman yelled through the open window. The engine shuddered to life and they were off, the truck swaying and shimmying as it barreled along the logging road with the three men in back clutching the bars of the cage. Campbell studied Goldstrike as they bounced along. He liked the irascible old prospector. He had an honorable way about him—never cheating at cards and paying for drinks when it was his turn. Once the whiskey loosened him up, he told a decent story, as well, one that usually rang of truth.

*But he's lying about the dynamite.*

Campbell was quite certain there *had* been twelve sticks, just as Arnold Chang remembered—ten used to excavate postholes for the PEC with one of the remaining two precipitating a rockslide that was engineered to prevent a census taker from reaching town, but at the same time, inadvertently sequestered a Chicago private investigator in Paradise. As for the twelfth stick, the detective knew an autopsy would never be performed on Gerald Dredd as soon as they encountered residual smoke in the mine entrance. When Goldstrike touched the hot glass of the oil lamp and flinched, Campbell's suspicion had been confirmed.

They reached Nilsen's General Store and the sheriff slanted his truck into a parking space next to Bertram Mole's Nash. "I shall inform the AG of our findings," the little attorney said after exiting the truck cab. "In the meantime, if the official census count is delayed by another mysterious rockslide, I have been authorized to launch a formal investigation." He aimed a look at Goldstrike. "Criminal charges could be filed. It's a felony to damage a state road. A person could go to jail...understand?" He stepped off the boardwalk, then climbed into his Nash sedan, started the motor, and immediately got into an argument with the gearshift of his new car, the transmission grinding as he tried to wrestle it into reverse. Eventually, the grating stopped, and after twisting in his seat to assay the road behind the vehicle, the little attorney hit the gas. Rather than back up, the car lurched forward, Mole's head whipsawing as his new automobile smashed into a sturdy hitching post in front of the saloon. The sound of the impact reverberated off the surrounding mountains, and seconds later, Oskar Nilsen bolted from his mercantile next door. Bountiful and Maude trailed him, the two women carrying cloth shopping bags. At the same time, Arnold Chang and a few early-bird drinkers emerged from the Gold Rush and Ed Riggins hurried toward the crash from the *Idaho World* building down the street, notepad and pencil in hand.

Inside the Nash, Mole remained motionless with both hands on the steering wheel, staring at the onlookers with round eyes.

"You all right, Bertram?" Sheriff Wilcoxon called out.

Mole blinked at the sheriff like a man who has failed to reach an outhouse in time.

"Bertram?"

Mole slowly peeled his hands off the steering wheel, exited the Nash, and then tentatively moved to the front of the car, cringing when he saw the damage to his new vehicle. The fenders were crumpled into the tires, preventing the wheels from rotating. Both headlamps were knocked off and lay in the dust of the street.

"I thought it was in reverse," he told the sheriff, his voice a whimper. "It's a new car…and I thought it was in reverse."

Wilcoxon shrugged. "Guess not," he said. Henry Wilcoxon didn't care for lawyers and was pleased whenever one of them suffered a comeuppance. But Mole seemed so forlorn and help-less, staring at the Nash's smashed front end, the soft-hearted lawman couldn't let him founder for more than a few seconds. "Hop back in, Bertram," he said, grinning. "We'll get ya goin'."

With Mole again behind the steering wheel, the sheriff tossed the headlamps into the rear seat. He and Campbell then worked together to pull the fenders off the tires, and once the Nash's wheels were freed up, Mole restarted the engine. This time, he was able to coax the gearshift into reverse and the vehicle backed onto Goodlow Road. More gear gnashing en-sued, but despite the little attorney's efforts, the car remained in reverse and Mole eventually gave up, the engine whining as he backed the Nash toward Boise and the valley below. Wilcoxon watched until the high-pitched wail of the car began to fade.

"He's gonna burn up his gearbox drivin' that thing in reverse all the way down the mountain," he observed, chuckling.

The crash onlookers had remained on the boardwalk, the entire town council among them, and the sheriff took advan-tage of the impromptu gathering to provide an update on the disposition of Gerald Dredd's remains. "So that there body's buried fer good," he finished up. "Ain't gonna be no autopsy." He surveyed the crowd. They remained silent, watching him like gallery spectators waiting for a judge to issue his verdict. Finally, Maude spoke up.

"So what happens now, Henry?" she asked. "Is it over? Is the case closed?"

Wilcoxon considered her question for a few moments, rub-bing his chin. Then, he nodded. "Far as I'm concerned it is, Maude," he said. He looked at Campbell, adding, "'Course I don't speak fer Mutual o' Omaha."

Every face turned to the detective.

"We still don't know how Mister Dredd ended up in the mine," Campbell observed. "Or how he died."

"And I s'pose you got some theories?" the sheriff grumbled, making clear, that once a case had been resolved by the chief law officer of Boise County, it damned well needed to stay resolved.

"I might have some ideas," Campbell said.

"Ya *might* or ya *do*?"

"I do. I have some theories. I suggest we have a meeting to discuss them." The detective looked over the crowd, fishing for a confession. No one nibbled the hook and he went on, eyeing Maude. "Perhaps at your home, Mrs. Dollarhyde? The sheriff and I, along with the rest of the town council... Young Mister Comfort too. Is that agreeable?"

Maude fashioned a pinched expression. "I guess... When?"

"Hell...let's do it tonight," Sheriff Wilcoxon interjected, the flicker of a smile betraying his delight at a chance to skip his wife's soirée in favor of a short meeting at the Paradise School followed by a longer one at the Gold Rush Saloon where whiskey and five card stud would be the only agenda items. "It probably shouldn't get postponed," he added in a more somber tone. "Official business like this and all. I'll give Doris a call and let 'er know. She'll understand." Wilcoxon grinned sheepishly. "Well, she may not understand, but she'll be all right. I'd probably just belch or fart or use the wrong pinky finger...embarrass her in front o' them snoots she's all hot and bothered to get in good with."

Campbell nodded. "Then tonight it is," he said. "Could you arrange for Mister Cooler and Miss Dredd to be there... Mister Barkley too?"

"Anyone else?" the sheriff asked.

"That should do it."

"You sure?"

"I'm sure."

# 25

## HYPOTHETICALLY

The meeting was scheduled to convene at seven-thirty, but when Campbell knocked on the door of the Paradise School at seven-twenty, he was the last to arrive. Lariat greeted him. "We're in the parlor," he said. Campbell followed him through the foyer and into the spacious room where he'd first interrogated Maude and Bountiful. Even though June was nearly upon them, a low flame flickered in the fireplace, spring nights in the mountains still warranting an occasional blaze. Maude and Thaddeus Cooler sat on one of two facing sofas, the actor evincing the confident smile and courtroom poise of Worthington Treadwell from *Justice is a Harsh Mistress*. Geraldine and Willie Barkley were on the opposing sofa, their hands clasped. Gold bands had replaced the faint rings of whitened skin on their wedding fingers. Next to them, Bountiful waited for the meeting to begin, her breathing even, her blue eyes unwavering.

Tucked against the far wall opposite the fireplace was a narrow game table with two upholstered wing chairs. A chess set was on the table with Lariat taking the seat behind the white pieces, Goldstrike playing the black. A game was in progress with white poised to claim checkmate in four moves. Lariat's eyes were on his pieces whereas Goldstrike glowered at the private investigator as if challenging him to a duel. Nearby, a pair of dining chairs had been pulled into the room for Oskar Nilsen and Arnold Chang. Ed Riggins was on his feet behind them, his ever-present pencil and pad in hand.

Sheriff Wilcoxon stood on one side of the fireplace, fanning himself against its heat with the greeting card Campbell had turned over as evidence. He nodded at the private investigator. "All right, everyone's here now," the lawman announced. "You've got the floor, Detective."

Campbell stationed himself on the end of the mantel opposite the sheriff. "First of all," he began, "I am not a policeman. I was contracted by Mutual of Omaha to investigate Mister Dredd's disappearance. The sheriff will decide if a crime has been committed. That said, I won't bother you with all the leads I pursued. I ended up with three theories for what happened. I've since ruled out the first of them." He looked at Geraldine. "Miss Dredd—"

"It's Mrs. Barkley."

"Mrs. Barkley... I beg your pardon. Anyway, at first, I believed you and your husband were involved in your father's death."

"Me? That's absurd! Why would I kill him?"

"Children have been known to do away with fathers...especially when an inheritance and money are involved."

"I've never cared about his money! You've no right to assume—"

The detective held up a hand. "Mrs. Barkley, it was just a theory and you're no longer a suspect...neither you nor Private Barkley. I'm just trying to walk everyone through my investigation as it unfolded."

Geraldine scowled. "Well, unfold it somewhere else," she said.

"Again, I apologize," Campbell replied. He glanced at Bountiful, for a moment unsettled by her flawless skin and full lips. Her expression remained flat, devoid of invitation, and he pulled his eyes away. "As I said...you and your husband are no longer suspects, Mrs. Barkley. So let's talk about theory number two. It's the story of an accident. A rancher outside Boise saw your father drive toward Paradise on November twentieth of last year. I believe that's the day he died. It was also the day a blizzard began up here. My second theory is that he never arrived. He got lost in the snowstorm, took a wrong turn, and ended up seeking shelter in the mine. The storm didn't let up for days and he froze to death."

"That ain't *yer* theory," Goldstrike blurted. "That one's *mine*, goddammit! I told ya as much the day we found the body!"

"You're right, Goldstrike. It's your theory. I just borrowed it."

"And it's the right one too… Don't see much point in lookin' further."

"Perhaps not," Campbell allowed. "But let's talk about my final hypothesis just the same. It's the theory of a crime rather than an accident, a crime in which Mister Dredd met his end in Meriwether Peycomson's carriage house."

"Peycomson!" Sheriff Wilcoxon exclaimed. "*He* killed Dredd?"

Campbell shook his head. "No…and his name was not Meriwether Peycomson. His real name was Richard Bright. I'm quite certain that Dredd hired him to buy one of the homes and then abandon it before the census count. The woman you knew as Evangeline Peycomson was actually his real wife and I believe neither of them left this area alive."

A collective gasp resounded, followed by the isolated crackle of the fire as silence took over the parlor. The detective studied Bountiful. She'd bowed her head at the news, but when she looked up, her eyes were dry.

"You're sure?" she asked.

"Yes," Campbell continued. "I believe they were murdered by an assassin known as Le Lutin. After leaving Paradise last November, the Brights checked into the Idanha Hotel in Boise and then disappeared. No one saw them leave and there's been no trace of them since."

"What about their son?" Bountiful asked. "What about Felix…and his nanny?"

"He wasn't their son. He wasn't a child at all. His name is Felix Ombre. He is the Le Lutin I spoke of. He's…a midget, I guess you'd call him. A little man. The nanny, Gerta Frobe, is his wife."

Goldstrike slammed his palm against the surface of the game table, causing a one of Lariat's rooks to vibrate out of position. "I knew somethin' wasn't right about that goddamned kid," he snarled. "Nobody seen 'im close up...the way they wouldn't let us get near 'im and all!" He shook his head, exhaling noisily. "I shoulda known, goddammit! Little bastard waddled like a goddamned duck! I knew a dwarf back in Maine who waddled like that. I shoulda known... Goddammit, I shoulda!"

"Where are they now...Felix and Frau Gerta?" Maude pressed Campbell.

The detective shook his head. "I don't know. I was able to track them as far as Reno. From there, it's anyone's guess."

"So *they* killed Dredd?" Oskar Nilsen piped up.

"They had no reason to kill him, Mister Nilsen," Campbell replied. "He was a paycheck. No, if my third theory is correct, someone else killed Mister Dredd." He paused, scanning the faces in the room as if one of them might reflect obvious guilt. None did and he went on. "As you all know, a note was discovered on the body. Would you read aloud the message inside that card, Sheriff?" The lawman stopped fanning himself with the greeting card and did. When he was finished, the Chicago investigator continued. "I believe that message was written by the man you knew as Meriwether Peycomson."

"So Peycomson...or Bright," Sheriff Wilcoxon interjected. "He's *HV*?"

"Yes," Campbell confirmed. "*HV* was Peycomson's character in *Our American Cousin*... Lieutenant Harry Vernon."

"He wrote the note, but he didn't kill Dredd?"

"That's right, Sheriff. If my theory is correct, Gerald Dredd paid him to write the note. He wanted to lure someone to the carriage house...someone he knew would refuse to meet him but would agree to see Peycomson."

"So the feller what got this note killed Dredd?"

"Not exactly. The person receiving the note met Dredd, but it wasn't a man."

Wilcoxon's eyes widened. "You think a *woman* killed 'im?"

Campbell shook his head. "It's not that simple. There was a struggle—"

"How the hell can ya know that?" Goldstrike interrupted. "You some sorta swami or somethin'? Seems to me you're jumpin' to an awful lot o' conclusions without much god-damned proof. I still say Dredd froze hisself to death."

"Perhaps, Campbell agreed. "But let me go on. You want evidence, but it's lack of evidence that often tells the tale." He looked at Geraldine, fashioning a contrite expression. "I've searched the stable behind your house, Mrs. Barkley…twice, in fact."

Geraldine bristled. "You had no right—"

"Actually, I did," Campbell interjected. "Forgive me for interrupting, but the property belongs to Dredd Enterprises and my sister, as acting CEO, gave me permission to search the premises." He waited for the young woman to mount another protest. When she didn't, he continued. "Some of the tools stored there were used in the renovation and it stands to reason workmen would have gone in and out to access them. However, I found no footprints in the dirt floor. Someone swept the place…with a tree bough from the looks of it. Why would the construction workers have done that? Why would anyone unless they were trying to hide something…like evidence of a struggle?"

"So you say Dredd paid Peycomson to get a woman alone in that stable. Then how'd he end up dead?" Wilcoxon posed. "And why did he want to meet her there to begin with?"

"Those are the right questions, Sheriff," Campbell replied. "Given Mister Dredd's history with women and the pains he took to deceive the woman he met in the carriage house, I think he intended to rape and perhaps kill her. He probably would have succeeded if not for someone else."

"Wait a goddamned minute!" the sheriff sputtered. "There's a *third* person?"

Campbell nodded. "A third person… Someone agile enough to climb into the hayloft from the outside, tightrope a six-inch-wide overhead beam without falling off, and lasso Mister Dredd. Our *third person* then jumped off the crossbeam, holding the free end of the rope. And that was it."

He snapped his fingers. "Broken neck."

Campbell studied Bountiful, then Lariat, then Bountiful again. Neither moved, the teenager ostensibly fascinated by his chess board, Bountiful resolutely focused on the photos lining the fireplace mantel, her lips pulled inward as if to stem a tide of damning words. The detective felt his heart sink and he fought off an urge to go to her, to take her hand—to tell her everything would be all right.

*She's caught…and we both know it.*

"So Dredd's body and the car were moved to the mine *after* he was dead," Sheriff Wilcoxon offered, interrupting the detective's thoughts. "And they…our two suspects…musta figgered that was it, until you went and found the body."

Campbell nodded. "That complicated things. An autopsy would have revealed hanging as the cause of death. So the autopsy had to be prevented—hence, the cave-in."

Wilcoxon nodded, then eyed Goldstrike. "Got anything to tell us?" he asked. The old prospector sat up straighter, glowering defiantly at the big sheriff. Then, his features relaxed and he leaned back in his chair, his eyes drifting over the pieces on the chess board. After a moment, he looked up at Lariat.

"How many moves till ya mate me, son?" he asked.

The teenager studied the board. "Four before you smacked the table and moved my rook…seven now."

Goldstrike nodded, then reached out and knocked over his king piece. "I concede," he said. He stood and faced the detective, wearing the face of a cornered wolverine. "I guess you're just too smart fer me, Campbell," he growled. "So I confess… I did it. I killed the sonuvabitch, toted his body up to my mine, and then blew the goddamned place up!"

"Goldstrike—" Bountiful began.

"I eventually figgered out how the Coolers and the Peycomsons was workin' fer Dredd," the old man continued. "I told Gerald that I'd keep my mouth shut if he paid me off. So it weren't no woman he was 'sposed to meet in the carriage house that night, Detective Campbell. It were me and there weren't no note 'bout it neither. I called Dredd on Oskar's telephone."

"When did you use my phone?" Nilsen protested. "You're s'posed to pay me a dime if you wanna make a phone call, doggonit!"

"I snuck in when you was down in yer cellar, samplin' whiskey."

"That ain't right, Goldstrike. The goin' rate is a dime. You owe me a dime!"

"Shut up, Oskar. I'm tryin' to confess here. Henry can arrest me fer usin' yer goddamned telephone after I'm done confessin'." He turned back to Campbell and went on. "Anyway, Dredd was 'sposed bring me money to keep quiet but tried to kill me instead. So I kilt *him*. Far as that fancy greetin' card goes, it don't matter who wrote it or who was s'posed to get it, 'cuz neither o' them folks killed Gerald Dredd. I did."

"Goldstrike, please—"

"Now, you stay outta this, Miss Bountiful," Goldstrike gently scolded her. "I did it and I'm confessin'."

"You acted alone?" Campbell pressed him.

"That's right."

"Walked the crossbeam and roped him?"

"Hell no. I roped 'im from the ground."

"Then threw the rope over the crossbeam and got Dredd to hold still long enough to hang him?"

Goldstrike sighed with frustration. "It weren't like that, goddammit. I broke his neck and *then* I hung 'im."

Campbell nodded thoughtfully. "He was already dead…but you hung him for a while, anyway? Why?"

"Make it look like suicide."

"Then why move the body? Suicide victims can't move themselves."

"Changed my mind. Fella my age is entitled to change it, if 'n he wants."

The detective scrutinized the old prospector. "You changed your mind, then cut him down and carried him out? Alone? That's quite a story. Dredd had to weigh at least two hundred fifty pounds."

Goldstrike formed a grim smile. "I'm stronger than I look," he said.

Bountiful stood. "All right, that's enough. Thank you, Goldstrike, but no more lies. The truth is—"

"I did it," Geraldine broke in. She rose from the sofa, her expression determined. "You're right, Mister Campbell. A woman went to the carriage house that night. It was me. I went there to meet Meriwether, but my father was waiting. He attacked me and I killed him." Stunned silence followed, save the pop and sizzle of the fire and the scratch of Ed Riggins's pencil as he scribbled in his notepad. Then Paradise, Idaho, was struck by the nation's second pandemic of the year, this one spreading confessionitis. Willie Barkley stood and put an arm around his wife.

"Geraldine is innocent," he said. "They're all innocent. I did it. I killed Mister Dredd. Then I moved the body and blew up the mine. I'm crazy, Mister Campbell. Everyone knows it. And—"

"Don't, Will," Geraldine murmured, putting a finger to her husband's lips. "I'm the only one they won't prosecute." She looked at the sheriff. "That's true, isn't it? If I say it was self-defense, they'll believe me, won't they?"

Wilcoxon shook his head. "That might be true if you was guilty, Miss Geraldine...which you ain't. Neither you nor Willie." He turned back to Campbell, but before he could speak, Maude succumbed to the new contagion.

"It was *me*," she exclaimed. "*I* did it. Gerald sniffed around after me for years and I guess he just couldn't...well, he just couldn't *resist* me any longer. I was the one in the carriage house and...and..." She looked at Cooler, blinking frantically. "And it was *Thaddeus* who hung him," she blurted, flinging an accusatory finger at the former actor. "*Thaddeus* and I did it." The faces in the room shifted to Thaddeus Cooler who was clearly shocked to have the production recast in mid-performance, his expression evenly split between contrived outrage and a kick to the groin.

"My dear sheriff—" he began, standing as if about to exit the stage. Maude stopped him, grabbing his hand.

"We hid the body together, didn't we, Thaddeus?" It was his cue in a play the actor hadn't rehearsed, and finding himself uncharacteristically short of words, terror flashed across his face, followed by manufactured indignation. He turned to Wilcoxon.

"My dear sheriff," he began again. "I had absolutely no involvement in this affair. Indeed, I must protest this miscarriage of…" His voice trailed off and he dropped his head, studying the floor as if lines from a play with a more favorable denouement were written there. Silent for several seconds he looked at Maude, his face sagging. "My sweet… Don't you remember? A wife cannot be forced to testify against her husband."

Watching her betrothed come undone for a few moments had put Maude back together. Her breathing was now steady, her features relaxed. She nodded. "I know, Thaddeus," the former madam said, her voice soft but determined. "But we aren't married. I'm not a wife… I'm a grandmother."

With his leading lady leading him into a prison cell Cooler's eyes flitted about the room, searching for a scene partner who wouldn't put him in the Idaho state penitentiary. Eventually, he gave up and gazed upward at the ceiling, murmuring softly.

"'It is more worthy to leap in ourselves…than tarry till they push us.'"

The old actor then shuddered almost imperceptibly, and as if the movement had molted the skin of one character from his body and replaced it with another's, he bowed gallantly and brought Maude's hand to his lips. "Do not despair, my dear," he said, afterward straightening to face the sheriff, no longer wearing the mask of a fugitive cornered by bloodhounds but the noble aspect of one about to face the executioner's axe with defiance rather than dread. "Indeed, it *was* I, good sir," he proclaimed with a dramatic sweep of an arm. "I dispatched the scoundrel and would do it again! What choice had I with dear Maude's life in the balance… What choice, indeed?"

Wilcoxon squinted dubiously. "You crawled onto the beam?"

"I did, my dear Constable Wilcoxon. An unlikely feat of legerdemain, I'll grant you, but legerdemain, nevertheless."

"And lassoed Dredd?"

"Neophyte's luck? An act of providence? Who knows how such wonders come to pass?"

The big lawman sighed wearily, looking around the room.

"Anybody in here actually innocent?" he asked. Greeted by a chorus of allocutions, he scowled and held up a hand. "All right, goddammit, that's enough confessin'." He crossed to the southern-facing windows and looked out. To the west, the sun had fallen behind the modest peaks of the Danskins, the red-orange glow of the evening sky making them look like the blunt teeth of a giant. "Detective Campbell…" the sheriff remarked, turning away from the window to face the private investigator. "You ever see this many people so goddamned anxious to get hung?"

Campbell shrugged. "I believe not," he said.

"I believe not, my own goddamned self," Wilcoxon agreed. He crossed back to his post near the fireplace, then continued, frowning ominously at the upturned faces. "All right, let's get somethin' straight… It's a crime to make a false police report. That includes fake confessions, so if anybody else is hankerin' to get a stretched neck, let me pledge right here and now that I won't argue with ya. I'll run yer false confessin' butt right up the scaffold steps, my own self!"

He next considered Campbell. "Now, you got yerself a theory about what happened up here, Detective."

"It's a hypothetical."

"Call it whatever ya want. I call it *conjecturin'*. I was at a police conference in Portland last year where they talked all about it…

how one man's conjecturin' ain't necessarily more true than another's."

"Depends on the evidence."

"Which yer theory…no offense, Detective…ain't got a whole hell of a lot *of*. Either the reg'lar kind or what them experts in Portland like to call *circumstantial*." He pulled off his Stetson, wiped sweat from his brow, and redonned the hat, afterward fanning himself with the greeting card as he continued. "Now, I got my own theory, and while I ain't got no physical evidence…the body bein' buried…I got me enough *circumstantial* evidence to choke a horse. And since this is my jurisdiction, and you bein' a private investigator and all ain't got no jurisdiction whatso-goddamned-ever, I'd like to throw out my theory. See if I'm as smart as a big shot Chicago detective. How's that sound?"

Campbell smiled. "You're right, Sheriff. This is your jurisdiction."

Wilcoxon faced the others. "So here's what I'm conjecturin', folks. I don't think anybody here knows what happened to Gerald Dredd. I think Mister Campbell has convinced y'all that foul play was in the mix, 'cuz he's from the sinful city o' Chicago where foul play is skitterin' about willy-nilly every night of the week and twice on Sundays. But this ain't Chicago. There ain't much foul play up here. Hell, I been sheriff fer ten years and I never drawed my weapon. Never saw nobody get murdered neither less'n it come from a bar fight or someone lookin' to take the fast route to *dee*-vorce. I think there's a much simpler explanation that doesn't need y'all confessin' fer each other like them misguided noble fellers in dime novels."

He dipped his head to indicate Geraldine.

"I think Mister Dredd drove up here that night to see *you*, Miss Geraldine. I know he hadn't seen ya in a good while and a father gets to missin' a daughter. I got growed daughters… three of 'em. One in Boise and one in Emmet, but Margie… she's my favorite…Margie, she married a feller what drug 'er up to Spokane. I miss 'er like hell, so I think I got a pretty good idea o' what it is to miss a daughter...and I think Dredd drives up here in that fancy automobile o' his 'cuz he misses *his* daughter.

"Now, snow had to be comin' down thicker'n wool on shearin' day by the time he's climbed outta the valley, but Dredd wasn't never the type to take no fer an answer...not even from Mother Nature. So he keeps goin' and gets into the pass with visibility about zero. Can't tell what's up and what's down, what's forward and what's back. And he comes up on the loggin' road west o' town and takes 'im a wrong turn...heads into the high mountains instead of goin' on to Paradise. After a while he realizes it's the wrong way, but it's too late...road's too damned narrow. He's got sheer rockface on one side and hellacious drop-off on the other. He can't turn around. So he drives on, hopin' the road'll loop back to the main. But it don't. It just keeps takin' 'im higher, until all of a sudden, he sees the openin' to Goldstrike's old mine and he figgers any shelter's better'n no shelter. So he drives into the mine and waits fer the storm to end. Problem is, it don't. Fer ten days, it don't, and by then, he's froze hisself to death."

The sheriff held up the card with the violet flowers on the front. "Now, I know what some o' y'all are thinkin'. What about this here note from *HV* and those marks on our victim's neck? Well, the note's pretty easy to sort out. While there ain't no proof of it, I won't dispute that Mister Dredd had '*HV*' write the damned thing so he could send it to someone else. But the fact remains that he had it with him when we found his body. So it don't make no damned difference who was *s'posed* to get it 'cuz that someone never *got* it. As fer them marks on his neck, I know a little about that sort o' thing and it ain't muchuva head-scratcher if ya apply the science of what a big city detective like Mister Campbell here calls fo-*ren*-sics."

The sheriff nodded knowingly.

"Forensics is a science where they study a dead feller to figger out what killed 'im and when it happened. I got a book about it and there's a page or two explainin' how a body gets all swolled up if it sits around after dyin' and don't get embalmed proper-like. I had a case over in Banks a while back where a feller died and didn't get found fer a couple o' weeks. He was swolled up like a puffer fish. Like to burst his skin wide open. So here's *my* theory. After Mister Dredd passed, he just swolled up a bit. He was wearin' a necktie, like always, and it cut into his skin…made a mark what looked like he'd been hung, even though he *hadn't been*. And then, he was in the mine undiscovered fer a few months and got hisself *dee*-siccated. That's what forensics calls it when a dead person gets un-swolled up and dries out. Anyway, he gets all dee-siccated over the winter and more time passes and he gets hisself mummified. But here's the thing… Mummifyin' a person don't get rid o' marks on the skin. Them Egyptian fellers what got mummified and then dug up after thousands o' years still had scars and tattoos and whatnot from stem to stern…and I figger mummifyin' didn't get rid o' the mark on Mister Dredd's neck made by his cravat."

He paused, offering Campbell the practiced look of one who had perjured his share of innocent but unworthy defendants into the penitentiary while never once forswearing a decent, yet entirely guilty, one-time offender into a conviction.

"That's it," he finished up. "That's how I see it. Dredd got lost and froze to death in Goldstrike's mine."

"And the cave-in?" Campbell posed.

"All right," Wilcoxon allowed. "Let's talk about the cave-in." He pointed a finger at the detective while directing his words at the others. "Now Mister Campbell over there would have you good people believe that the cave-in was intentional, but I'm conjecturin' that the dynamite Goldstrike left up there years back went off on its own. Probably got stirred up with all the folks what been traipsin' in and out o' late." He frowned at Campbell. "Unauthorized folks without no search warrant, I might add."

He next looked at Geraldine, his face apologetic. "Sorry to say this, Miss Geraldine, but yer daddy made hisself a good many enemies in this life and it's the God's-honest-truth that a lot o' folks wanted to see him meet his maker. Who knows? Maybe some of 'em are in this room. But that don't mean anybody done 'im in. The whole thing's a tragedy, I'll grant ya, and there's always people who like to compound a tragedy with chinwaggin' and finger-pointin'. But it won't change a damned thing. Fact is, yer daddy's dead and he ain't gonna be any less dead with a lot o' irresponsible conjecturin' and false confessin'. Especially, when it's plain as the nose on my face that this was an accident." The big sheriff resumed fanning himself with the greeting card, eyeing Campbell. "So whattaya think, Detective? What's yer take on this? Which theory ya like better…yers or mine?"

Before leaving the Buffalo Bill room at the Busty Rose, Campbell had tucked the orchid-colored envelope and the photo of Geraldine inside his coat, slipping the fabric-covered blouse button into a trouser pocket. He touched his chest, feeling the faint edges of the card and the photo. Bountiful watched, her features relaxed, her eyes probing. It was as if she could see through the cloth of his suit—visualizing the envelope with her name on it and the button ripped from her blouse during the fateful struggle with Gerald Dredd. Campbell slipped a hand into his trouser pocket. The button was still there. He pulled his hand free, leaving it inside.

"I guess your theory makes as much sense as anything, Sheriff," he said. "It's possible."

"*Possible?*" Wilcoxon sputtered, gesturing with the greeting card. "Ya think it's just *possible*? Seems to me yer version of things got itself an awful lot o' movin' parts, Detective. My version is simple and the simple explanation is usually the right one."

"Occam's razor," Campbell murmured.

"Occam's what?"

"Occam's razor, Sheriff. The simple explanation is probably the right one… Just like you said."

"He a forensics feller, that Occam?"

"Not exactly. He's just someone who would agree with you."

Wilcoxon grinned. "So me and Mister Occam out-vote ya, is that what you're sayin', Detective?"

Campbell hesitated before answering, again looking at Bountiful. Whatever had happened on that snowy November night in the carriage house was self-defense and he knew it. The sheriff knew it, too, and had swept Dredd's murder under a carpet where it belonged. And yet it seemed, as Bountiful calmly waited for his answer, that she wanted to replace Sheriff Wilcoxon's take on Occam's razor with the sharper edge of truth.

"Do you agree with Henry, Mister Campbell?" Maude interjected, her voice anxious and thin. "Was this an accident?"

Across the room, Lariat Comfort still sat at the game table, his eyes on the chess board and Goldstrike's fallen king piece. As a military policeman stationed at Parris Island, South Carolina, Campbell had once investigated a lynching. A Black soldier on a weekend pass in nearby Beaufort had been attacked and hung by a mob who believed he'd made too much eye contact with a white woman. No witnesses would testify. No arrests were made.

*Lariat will never see a courtroom*, the ex-MP thought.

During his seven weeks in Paradise the detective had developed a genuine affection for the people in the room. Goldstrike, Maude, Geraldine, Willie Barkley, and even Thaddeus Cooler, had all confessed to a crime not committed—putting each of their heads in a noose to protect Bountiful and Lariat. It was the sort of loyalty he'd not seen since his days as a Marine, the sort of out-of-family love he'd never truly known and was only just beginning to understand.

"I suppose Sheriff Wilcoxon could be right," Campbell said. "There are a lot of moving parts in my theory. It may well have been an accident."

"So the case is closed?" Maude pressed him.

Campbell didn't answer.

"Mister Campbell?" Maude persisted.

The detective looked down. The edge of the area rug stood

out against the polished oak floor, not a single wayward thread marring its pristine surface. *It all fits together*, he thought, lifting his gaze. Bountiful's sapphire eyes were on him.

"Sure," he said. "I guess we can say it's closed."

"So that's a yes?"

Campbell hesitated and then nodded. "It is, Mrs. Dollar-hyde…as far as Mutual of Omaha is concerned, anyway."

A second or two of silence followed. Then Oskar Nilsen spoke up.

"This was better'n that doggone play," he said, his observation prompting an explosion of laughter that went on for nearly a minute—some genuinely tickled, others profoundly relieved. Once it had subsided, Sheriff Wilcoxon clapped his hands.

"So that's it," he said. "We're done here and the night's still young. I'm goin' to the Gold Rush fer whiskey and poker. Who's comin'?"

The parlor quickly cleared. The card players, with Goldstrike and Thaddeus Cooler at the rear, went off to the Gold Rush Saloon while Lariat retreated to his attic room where *The Olde Curiosity Shoppe* awaited. Cooler couldn't resist the opportunity for a dramatic exit, quoting Puck from *A Midsummer Night's Dream*.

"'So good night unto you all. Give me your hands if we be friends and Robin shall restore amends.'"

"Who the hell is Robin?" Goldstrike asked as he and the old actor made for the front door.

Thaddeus chuckled. "Just one of the Bard's good fellows," he said. "A faery of the forest and like you, my dear Goldstrike, a very good fellow, indeed."

Before leaving, Sheriff Wilcoxon offered the card with the violet flowers to Campbell. "I guess this ain't evidence no more. You need it fer your report?" The detective shook his head and the sheriff took a poker from a stand next to the fireplace, stirred a few embers into flame, and then tossed the card into them. He looked at Riggins.

"Ed?"

The *Idaho World* editor hesitated, then opened his pad, ripped out the pages with the notes he'd jotted down during the meeting, and added them to the fire.

"So that's that," Wilcoxon said.

Geraldine and Willie were the last to go. The young woman's pregnancy had progressed, her breasts larger, her rounded belly now apparent. She followed Campbell's eyes and smiled.

"It's the maternity clothes," she said. "Sarah DeMille made them for me. They make it obvious."

"When are you due?"

"August."

"Congratulations," the detective said.

After the Barkleys were gone, Bountiful poured whiskey into each of two shot glasses. She handed one to the detective, still standing next to the fireplace mantel, and then reclaimed her seat on the sofa. Campbell sipped from his glass.

"I'm sorry about your friend…Bright," he said.

"Meriwether?" Bountiful replied. "I don't think we were truly friends…by the time he left, anyway. Still, I am sorry he's dead. He and his wife." She searched the detective's face. "You're quite sure? They were murdered?"

Campbell nodded.

Bountiful studied the dying fire. "Somehow, I'm not surprised. The last time I saw Meriwether, he was so…desperate. Almost as if he knew something terrible was about to happen." She looked at the detective. "There really was nothing between us, you know."

"I know," Campbell replied.

Outside the windows, the world had drifted from dusk to darkness and they sipped at their whiskeys until both glasses were empty. Bountiful rose and refilled them, then returned to the sofa.

"What do you really think…about that night?" she asked.

"Hypothetically?"

"If you prefer."

Campbell put his glass on the mantel, then took the poker

and used it to restoke embers back into flames. "Hypothetically," he began, "I think Dredd lured you to the carriage house with the note written by Bright. I think you went there to talk Peycomson, as you knew him, out of leaving town for good. You wanted to make sure Paradise would hit their target in the census. I also suspect you knew he might have other ideas."

Bountiful studied her glass of whiskey. "I wasn't worried about his 'other ideas.' He was a flirt but not a wolf. I knew I could manage him. But you're right. I wanted him to move back with his family...until we'd been counted." She looked at the detective. "That's all it was from my perspective."

"I believe you," Campbell said. He continued to poke at the embers, sharing with her Iris's suspicion that the young schoolteacher and Gerald Dredd had the same father. "At your October meeting," he continued, "I think you threatened to expose Dredd unless he backed off. He then plotted to kill you and probably would have succeeded had Lariat not intervened. Afterward the two of you went to Maude and Goldstrike for help, but by the time you returned Thaddeus had moved the body to the mine."

"Thaddeus," Bountiful echoed, chuckling softly. "You may not believe it, but when you found him, it was a surprise to me, as well. Grandma kept him a secret." She tipped her head. "Would you have discovered the body without him?"

Campbell shrugged. "Probably... He made it easy, though. The old ham was dying to talk after all those months without an audience." He continued to stoke the fire. "It's ironic, don't you think? Dredd died by hanging and his body was hidden by a bomb of sorts. He was literally hoisted on his own petard." He smiled at her. "Of course, it's all *conjecturin'* as Sheriff Wilcoxon would put it."

"Or lying."

"Let's just stick with 'hypothetical.'"

Bountiful swirled the whiskey in her glass, studying the movement of the amber liquid. "What now?" she asked.

Campbell reached inside his coat pocket and retrieved the photo of Geraldine Dredd in her slip.

"What's that?"

"Nothing, really."

He tossed the photo into the fire and watched it burn, then again reached into his pocket and produced the orchid-colored envelope. Bountiful caught her breath, touching her lips with the fingers of one hand.

"Forgive me if this seems forward, Miss Dollarhyde," Campbell went on, using the poker to turn the log, "but I believe you have the loveliest eyes I've ever seen."

A burst of new flames crackled and he tossed the envelope into them, watching until it had curled and blackened into ash. Afterward he returned the poker to its stand and joined her on the sofa.

"They're penetrating," he added.

He took the blouse button from his trouser pocket and pressed it into her palm. Bountiful stared at it, then at him.

"In fact, sometimes I get the feeling you can see right through me," the detective went on. "Hypothetically, of course."

Bountiful studied his face, for a moment puzzled, then intrigued—as if they'd simultaneously just met and yet always known one another. Then her fingers closed over the button and she slowly fashioned a smile, an eternally mysterious thing that made Robert Campbell instinctively draw nearer.

"You know, Mister Campbell," she said, leaning closer. "Hypothetically...I think maybe I'm starting to."

# EPILOGUE

The marriage of Maude Dollarhyde and Thaddeus Cooler never took place. Maude called it off. She broke the news to him in the Moulin Rouge bedroom of the Busty Rose. "When I was a girl the women who married became property," she told her soon-to-be ex-fiancé. "They owned nothing, they decided nothing, they inherited nothing. Everything belonged to their goddamned husbands." She scowled, then gathered herself and continued, speaking more evenly. "I understand why they married. Without a husband or family money, a woman struggles in this man's world. I struggled. I was a mill girl in Waltham, Massachusetts. If I'd stayed, married or not, I'd have become a mill woman and then a mill hag, my fingers covered in loom calluses all the way to the grave. I had no education...oh, I could read and write, add and subtract...but an education like Bountiful's? I'd have needed a fairy godmother to make that happen."

"Dear Maude, I understand the sorrows you've known," Thaddeus countered. "But you speak of times past. Women can own property now. They can receive a proper education, become doctors and lawyers. Why, you'll be able to vote in the November election! How about that? Your very first election!"

"One in which I'll vote for men who'll decide what's best for me," she said. "No, sweet Thaddeus, I won't marry you. I've been standing on my own for too long. If we married, I'd feel like my legs didn't belong to me anymore."

She removed the watch fob ring from her finger and handed it to him.

"Besides, you're not cut out for a place like Paradise. You've been on vacation, Thaddeus. I went on a vacation once...to Los Angeles, California. I visited for a week and thought I wanted to live there forever. Then I got back to Paradise and Bountiful and Lariat and my school and my friends...the people in this town I built a life with…and I knew, right away, that forever isn't more than a week unless you're home." She squeezed his hand. "You've had a few months of vacation, Thaddeus. Now, it's time for *you* to go home."

A few days later, on August 19, 1920, Maude and Bountiful drove Lariat and Thaddeus Cooler to the train station in Boise. Goldstrike and Jeanette DeMille came along. The actor was to accompany Lariat as far as Washington, DC, before traveling on to New England. Dredd Enterprises had offered a one-thousand-dollar reward for information leading to the discovery of their namesake, and after Robert Campbell claimed it, the detective had given half to Thaddeus for his role in the discovery of Gerald Dredd's body. "With this generous endowment, I shall open a school of acting in pastoral Vermont," Thaddeus told folks. "I shall shepherd thespians in the rough, much as I did here in Paradise."

Before Cooler and Lariat boarded the 9:15 to Laramie and parts east, Goldstrike took the young man aside to offer some advice.

"Don't get yerself too high and mighty in that there school, Lariat," he rasped.

"I won't, Goldstrike."

"Ya don't wanna forget the ones what got ya there."

"I know."

The former prospector grasped him by the shoulders and leaned forward until their foreheads touched. The boy's eyes were filled with tears. "Thanks for everything, Goldstrike," he whispered. "I'll miss you."

The old man didn't answer, his eyes locked on the young genius for a very long time. Finally, he released him and straightened. "There," he said. "I got me a right big deposit. It'll last till ya come back."

Maude and Bountiful were next, each giving Lariat a kiss on the cheek and a long tearful hug. Maude didn't let go until the teenager pulled away to say goodbye to Jeanette.

"I love you," Lariat told the young Mormon woman.

"I love *you*," she answered.

They embraced, their faces close together as they murmured the earnest and magical words young lovers whisper while still unaware that first love is rarely eternal. It took the wheeze of the train's brakes, followed by the sound of the whistle and the conductor's call to part them.

"All aboard for Twin Falls, Pocatello, Rock Springs, and LARE-uh-mie, Wyoming," he bellowed. "All aboard!"

Thaddeus gently pried Lariat away from Jeanette. "Our young prince must be off, dear girl. His future awaits!"

Lariat boarded the train, reappearing a few seconds later in the window of the nearest railcar, his hand pressed against the glass. Thaddeus followed, pausing on the carriage steps as the train shuddered and began to move along on the tracks.

"'Adieu, dear friends, adieu!'" he cried out in his final Idaho performance, removing his hat and waving it. "'Forever, and forever, farewell! If we do meet again, why, we shall smile. If not, why then, this parting was well made.'"

&

With the departure of Lariat Comfort and Thaddeus Cooler, the population of Paradise, Idaho shrank to 123, but the town would be vulnerable to the devices of Bertram Mole only briefly. Four days after the train carried the young genius and the old actor off to new lives, and more than three months after the date promised to Mole by the U.S. Bureau of Census, a pollster at last arrived in Paradise to make an official count. Early on the very same morning, with the sun yet to dispute the eastern horizon, Geraldine Dredd Barkley gave birth to a baby girl, Ann Bountiful. The infant weighed six pounds, three ounces and was the 124th resident of Paradise, Idaho. One minute later she was followed by the 125th, her six-pound, two-ounce twin brother, Anders William. The infants were born around four o'clock in the morning, and by noon, Goldstrike had already stopped by to get a good look at both, banking the first of what would become many deposits.

# Acknowledgments

My thanks to writers Leslie Gunnerson, Chris Dempsey, and Mike Christian for their valuable input as I wrote this book. I am grateful to Darryl Douphner for his friendship and shared experience as an LAFD firefighter and to Jennifer Bowen Neergaard and the readers of BookHive. Thanks to advance readers Michael Bourne, M. Allen Cunningham, Phillip Hurst, Barbara Quick, David R. Roth, and Shirley Reva Vernick. With this third novel in the Regal House canon, I remain forever in debt to the indomitable Jaynie Royal and senior editor Pam Van Dyk. As always, thanks and love to my wife, Pam, who prompted the idea for *The Penny Mansions* and tolerated the many hours I spent away from her while writing it.